Blood Thief of Whitten Hall

A Magic & Machinery Novel

Jon Messenger

This book is a work of fiction. Names, characters, places and incidents are the product of the author's imagination or are used fictitiously. Any resemblance to actual persons, living or dead, business establishments, events or locales is entirely coincidental.

No part of this book may be reproduced, scanned, or distributed in any printed or electronic form without permission. Please do not participate in or encourage piracy of copyrighted materials in violation of the author's rights. Purchase only authorized editions.

Blood Thief of Whitten Hall
Copyright ©2015 Jon Messenger
All rights reserved.
Printed in the United States of America
Second Edition: March 2019

www.CrimsonTreePublishing.com

Summary: In a world of science, magic is an abomination, but not the vile creation Royal Inquisitor Simon Whitlock once believed it to be. Accompanied by Luthor Strong, and Matilda Hawke, a werewolf, they return to the capital of Callifax, eager to convalesce after their last adventure.

ISBN: 978-1-63422-102-3 (paperback)
ISBN: 978-1-63422-103-0 (e-book)
Cover Design by: Amalia Chitulescu
Typography by: Courtney Knight
Editing by: Cynthia Shepp

Fiction / Science Fiction / Steampunk
Fiction / Science Fiction / Action & Adventure
Fiction / Magical Realism

CHAPTER One

SIMON WHITLOCK WALKED THROUGH THE NARROW bedroom to the armoire perched in the corner of the room. He pulled the doors aside, revealing a long row of similarly cut suits and blazers. For a moment, he stood idly by, perusing his options before settling on a tweed blazer. The air was still brisk despite it warming toward spring, and the blazer would ward off the morning chill.

Before buttoning the jacket, he pulled on the chain that disappeared into one of the front vest pockets. A silver pocket watch emerged. It spun lazily on its chain, reflecting the sunlight filtering through the townhouse window. Simon grasped the watch and opened its front, revealing the watch face on the right and a grainy picture of Veronica Dawn on the other. He paused, examining the picture of the dark-haired beauty before frowning as the time caught his eye. He quickly closed the watch and buttoned his jacket. Before closing the armoire, he pulled down a top hat from the high shelf.

The Royal Inquisitor walked briskly toward the townhouse's front door, pausing at its berth and running a hand through his coifed hair. A copious amount of grease held his mane in place. Finally, he ran his fingers across his thin moustache, ensuring he looked presentable before opening the front door.

Simon stepped onto the small landing at the top of the half-dozen stairs leading to the street below. He placed his top hat on his head, canting it slightly and allowing its brim to block the glare of the morning sun.

He waved his hand before his face as he descended the steps in an attempt to brush aside the palpable air of smoke. As he reached the street, an automobile rumbled slowly past, its exhaust belching a cloud of black smoke. Frowning, Simon paused momentarily, knowing his pace was only slightly slower than that of the automobile. He had no desire to follow too closely.

"Good morning, Inquisitor," a gentleman said politely as he walked past, tipping his hat in reverence to Simon.

"Morning," Simon replied, his spirits suddenly lifted. It was good to be recognized.

Simon turned with a renewed enthusiasm and glanced down the long row of similarly fronted townhouses. The endless row of red brick edifices was broken only by perfectly measured sets of identical stairwells leading to identical doorways. Only the bronzed numbers nailed over each doorway marked them as unique homes.

Beyond the townhouses, the angle of the street rose sharply as it built toward the hilltop that dominated the capital city of Callifax. Perched atop it, in plain view from anywhere within the city, was a sprawling castle. Its walls and towering parapets matched the majesty of the giant, red and gold banners flickering in the morning breeze.

Simon's eyes left the splendor of the castle only after he had walked a dozen feet. He paused before the stairwell to a neighboring townhouse before climbing the stairs. The Inquisitor paused only momentarily at the doorway, rapping politely with his knuckles before casually opening the door without awaiting a reply.

The interior of the home was well illuminated, with electric lights burning in a chandelier overhead.

"Luthor?" Simon said as he closed the door behind him.

"You're late," came the reply from the sitting room to his right.

Simon peered around the corner and found his dear friend and companion hidden beneath the morning's newspaper. Luthor Strong was sitting at a small, rounded table, the center of which was covered with a silver tray and a pot of steeping tea. The aroma was magnificent, and Simon quickly took his seat across from the apothecary.

Luthor didn't bother looking up as Simon sat across from him at the narrow table. The Inquisitor set his hat on the windowsill to his right as he placed a napkin in his lap.

"Good morning, Simon. I see my assassins have failed to kill you once more."

"Come off it, Luthor. You can't still be mad about that Haversham business. That was weeks ago."

Luthor folded the paper and dropped it unceremoniously onto the table. The diminutive man stared at his mentor with evident irritation, the muttonchops covering each cheek rising and falling as he ground his teeth in frustration.

"You abandoned me to my own devices with a demon. Yes, I'm still mad about Haversham."

"I came back," Simon retorted.

A creak of the wooden staircase interrupted the start of a familiar debate. Both men turned as Mattie walked down the staircase, still dressed in her pajamas with a bathrobe cinched across her waist. Her red hair was still damp from her bath and hung in ringlets over her shoulders.

"Morning, you two," she said as she walked into the sitting room. "Still arguing about Haversham, are you?"

"He used me as bait," Luthor complained. "Even you have to admit that's absurd behavior for a Royal Inquisitor."

"I have to admit no such thing," Mattie said matter-of-factly as she leaned forward and kissed Simon on the cheek. "Morning, Simon."

"Morning, Matilda. A pleasure as always."

She walked around the table and leaned forward, kissing Luthor passionately on the lips. The apothecary flushed scarlet and gently pulled away from the redhead.

"Mattie, that's not really appropriate etiquette in front of a guest."

She grasped his chin, turning his face toward her. "Then you're lucky I'm not a right and proper lady. Need I remind you that I'm an uncouth and uncivilized tundra werewolf? Nothing in that says I can't kiss the man courting me in front of an Inquisitor who, by the way, has seen far more disturbing things than two people being affectionate toward one another."

Luthor sighed as he leaned back into his chair. "It's not the public display of affection that concerns me, love. It's that Simon currently has a series of belittling thoughts flittering about in his mind."

Simon smirked softly, and Luthor gestured toward the Inquisitor.

"Now it appears he's settled upon one. Go ahead, Simon, let me hear it."

"I was just wondering if she worries about you straying from her affections or if her canine instincts have taken hold and she merely marked her territory."

Luthor frowned and shook his head. "See, this is precisely what I mean."

He turned sharply as Mattie stifled a laugh. "Actually, I thought it was rather clever."

"Don't encourage him!"

Mattie smiled and turned toward the kitchen. "Need anything from the kitchen while I'm up?" she asked.

"I don't believe so. Do you need me to fix you something to eat?"

Mattie shook her head as she walked toward the doorway. "No, but thank you. I know my way around a kitchen."

The two men waited until she left the room before turning their attention back to one another.

"You two have become quite cozy since our return," Simon remarked. "You surprise me, Luthor. I didn't think you would be scandalous enough to have a woman living with you."

The apothecary retrieved his newspaper and returned to his reading. "We have our separate bedrooms, if that's what concerns you. Of course, you're an Inquisitor who cavorts with werewolves, so I think you're hardly one to judge."

Without looking up, Luthor pointed toward the kettle in the middle of the table. "Tea?"

"Please," Simon replied as he turned over his cup and extended it. Luthor picked up the kettle and poured a perfectly steeped cup.

"Sugar?"

"Two lumps, if you please."

Simon raised his cup to his lips and sipped noisily. He closed his eyes and sighed blissfully. "I'm thrilled that even when you abhor me, you still don't lose your good manners."

Luthor set the kettle back down on the tray and returned to his paper. "My hatred for you and my civility are mutually exclusive."

The two men enjoyed their tea in silence while Mattie busied herself in the kitchen. Only the clinking of dishware being set upon a tray broke the quiet. The redhead returned shortly with toast and a bowl of porridge. A slab of butter melted merrily in the depths of the bowl as she sat in the third seat around the table.

"What brings you to our breakfast table this morning, Simon?" Mattie asked as she spread marmalade onto her toast.

Simon arched an eyebrow as he set his teacup gently onto its saucer. "I'm here every morning."

"I simply meant—"

"He knows what you meant," Luthor interrupted. "He's acting coy merely because today is of such importance."

Mattie smiled broadly. "Today's your recognition ceremony with the Inquisitors, isn't it?"

"It is," Simon replied, his smile equally as broad. "Apparently, they felt my work slaying a demon and two…"

The words froze on his lips, his mouth still pursed from the last word he spoke. The smile faded quickly from Mattie's face, replaced by a saddened expression.

"Forgive me, Mattie," Simon said, recovering as quickly as his embarrassed mind would allow. "I meant absolutely no disrespect."

Mattie shook her head and forced a smile. "No, it's I who should apologize. I agreed to let you bring the two werewolf remains to Callifax. It was the only way to convince the other Inquisitors that this particular magical threat had been eliminated. If you hadn't, the rest of my pack couldn't live in peace. Therefore, you owe me no apology. I shouldn't have dampened the mood."

Luthor coughed, breaking the palpable tension. "Will you see Ms. Dawn tonight as well?"

Simon nodded as he broke his gaze from the morose redhead. "Yes, I believe I shall, though there's no telling how late the Inquisitors' celebration may go."

"Will you… see her at work, perhaps?" the apothecary remarked, his disapproval evident.

Simon merely laughed at Luthor's discomfort. "More likely than not, since the hour will be late before I have time to visit with her."

Before Luthor could respond, Simon fetched his pocket watch. He leapt hastily to his feet before bowing apologetically to his hosts. "Speaking of the time, I will most certainly be late to my own sordid affair if I don't leave at once."

He bent over and took a final sip of his tea, sighing with satisfaction as he replaced the teacup. Simon leaned over and placed a kiss on Mattie's cheek.

"Do take care of Luthor today, Ms. Hawke. I would hate to see him cooped up once more in this dreadful townhouse."

"I'll do what I can," she replied.

Simon nodded toward his friend. "Luthor."

Luthor buried his face in the newspaper, though he read hardly a word from the page.

"I see you've returned to being a malcontent," Simon remarked.

Mattie sighed. "Luthor, please at least feign happiness for Simon's exciting day."

Luthor lowered the newspaper with a sickly smile on his face. "I hope you're painfully run over by an autobus on the way to the Grand Hall."

Simon laughed heartily and retrieved his top hat. "I could ask for no better sendoff. Shall we do this again tomorrow?"

"Of course," Luthor replied. "Do be a bit more punctual next time."

Simon nodded as he hurried toward the front door.

Chapter Two

Though their zeppelin had landed in Callifax nearly two weeks earlier, Simon still appreciated the nuances that made the capital city unique. The sun warming his face was his personal favorite, having suffered through the bitter cold in Haversham for far longer than his liking. Whereas the frozen tundra city had been a virtual ghost town, with few pedestrians braving the elements, Callifax teemed with life. The sidewalks were busy with pedestrians moving to and fro. The streets were crowded with automobiles and the much larger double-decker autobuses of the public transportation system. They left clouds of acrid black smoke in their wake, but Simon overlooked their smog in light of their technological marvel.

He raised his hand as a taxi passed. The black, open-sided automobile pulled to the curb beside where he stood, and he climbed aboard.

"Where shall I take you, sir?" the cab driver asked.

"The Grand Hall, if you please," Simon replied as he tried to get comfortable on the firm backseat.

The driver glanced over his shoulder, giving Simon a once over. "You're an Inquisitor, then?"

Simon nodded, though he merely wished the driver would continue onward. "I am."

"Here for the conference, are you?"

"I'm actually from Callifax, though I am attending the conference. Speaking of which, I'm in a spot of a hurry, if you don't mind."

"Of course, sir," the cab driver replied as he moved the tall gearshift into drive and pulled away from the curb. He raised his arm out of the side of the car, announcing to the vehicles behind him that he was merging.

Though Simon loved the intricacies of the technological age, being aboard a car made him uneasy. It jostled along the cobblestone streets, its firm wheels bouncing roughly on the uneven stonework. The open sides of the taxi let in the pungent fumes of petrol and exhaust, a scent that seemed to permeate his skin and clothing. He would smell foul by the time he arrived at the Grand Hall, but it was unavoidable. He would have been similarly tarnished had he walked, what with the fumes and smoke belching across the sidewalks as well.

Simon stared out the window, admiring the towering structures as they passed. The terrace of townhouses gave way to rows of storefronts, above which men and women glanced from the upstairs apartments.

As they reached the end of his road, the brick edifices of the buildings vanished and the paved sidewalks gave way to the lush greenery of a well-manicured lawn. A stone behemoth of a building rose from the center of the garden. An ornately carved wooden door was affixed in the middle of the gray stone building, flanked by rounded, stained-glass windows. At each of the four corners of the cathedral, pointed towers rose skyward, where crouched gargoyles topped them.

Simon drummed his fingers absently on the windowsill of the taxi as they passed the Callifax Abbey. He had been within the building a number of times, in the company of Veronica who, despite her predilections, clung firmly to her faith.

The interior of the building was every bit as opulent as its exterior appeared. Towering marble pillars held aloft vaulted ceilings. The golden altar near the front of the church was bathed in a myriad of colors, as sunlight filtered through an ornate pane of stained glass that dominated the far wall.

The taxi turned at an intersection, and the Abbey disappeared from Simon's view. The incline of the road rose slightly as they approached the bottom of the aptly, yet unimaginatively named Castle Hill. The taxi came to rest at the next intersection, yet their road didn't continue on.

Instead, a large, marble building rose before them.

The Grand Hall was built in the style of civilizations long since passed, a remembrance of a more enlightened era of thinkers and philosophers. The front of the building was pillared, with the tall, marble spires framing the large, wooden doors.

The taxi driver waited politely for a break in the ceaseless traffic before driving across the street and pulling to the curb. Simon fetched some silver coins from his jacket pocket and handed them to the man, knowing that his payment far exceeded the actual cost of the short trip.

"Thank you kindly, sir," the taxi driver said excitedly.

Simon climbed from the cab and watched as it pulled away before turning toward the Grand Hall. The marble building was recessed from the street, leaving a wide, stonework courtyard between the edge of the curb and the front of the building. A small row of trees flanked the sidewalk leading to the entrance. Young men and women sat in the shade, reading or talking amongst themselves.

Eyes fell upon Simon as he walked toward the front of the building, the young men and women looking up appreciatively at the dapper gentleman walking past. The morning had been filled with Inquisitors coming and going from the Grand Hall. The Inquisitors rarely had such meetings, in which members arrived from throughout the kingdom, but Simon's revelation of demons in their land had prompted the necessity for this particular gathering. As he neared the front doors, a shadow fell over him. He craned his neck upward as a zeppelin eclipsed the sun, passing high overhead on its way to the tall airship docks on the far side of the castle. Even the zeppelins came with increasing regularity, another necessity of the returning Inquisitors.

"Unless my eyes deceive me, I do believe that I'm in the presence of greatness," a man said from behind him.

Simon dropped his gaze and turned, coming face to face with a broad-shouldered man who stood a few inches taller than Simon did. The man wore no hat and his long hair was tied in a single braid that fell down his back. The man smiled broadly, an expression that seemed well at ease on his chiseled face.

"Indeeed, I am in the presence of a true hero of the crown," the man said. He turned toward a much younger man, barely out of boyhood, who stood beside him. "Peter, show some respect. You're standing before Royal Inquisitor Simon Whitlock, slayer of demons."

Simon smiled and laughed softly at the young man's awed expression. "Perhaps, Ambrose, you would be so kind as to carry a trumpet next time so as to better announce my presence?"

Inquisitor Ambrose Supperwood laughed before patting Simon firmly on the shoulder, nearly knocking him aside. "It's good to see that your fame has certainly not bewitched your sense of humility."

"Of course not," Simon remarked ironically. "I'm by far one of the most humble men you're likely to meet."

Inquisitor Supperwood turned toward his young charge. "Inquisitor Whitlock is an old friend of mine. We attended our schooling together a few years ago."

"We've been friends a long time," Simon corrected. "Neither of us are hardly old."

"Of course not. In fact, I believe we're still in our prime."

"Never felt better," Simon quickly agreed.

"Come on, then," Ambrose chided. "I don't believe this discussion of demons will advance far without the slayer himself."

Ambrose gestured toward the Grand Hall before them. Guards standing on either side of the doorway pulled the ten-foot doors apart as the two Inquisitors approached. Both guards bowed with a flourish at their presence, causing Simon some general discomfort.

"Are you feeling well, Simon?" Ambrose whispered as they entered the buildings entry hall.

"Of course," Simon replied dismissively. "I surmise there's just a small part of me that would rather forego today's festivities in lieu of another assignment."

Ambrose nudged Peter, who rubbed his arm where the larger man had struck him. "He has the bug, Peter. Give the man a sense of the glory that comes with being an Inquisitor and he yearns for more. Is that about right, Simon?"

Simon chuckled as he handed his top hat and jacket to a servant. "Nothing quite so abstruse, I'm afraid. It's not the fame for which I yearn—"

"Though you're generally not opposed, I should say," Ambrose interrupted.

"I certainly won't argue. No, it's less the fame and far more the freedom. There was a palpable excitement when Luthor and I discovered the real mystery behind the goings-on in Haversham. It makes my heart race at just the thought."

Ambrose shook his head. "Mr. Strong. Are you still traveling with the apothecary? When will you get a proper apprentice like Peter?"

Simon looked to the young and hopeful apprentice. "Never. No offense meant, Peter, but I simply prefer the company of someone closer to my own age. Besides which, Luthor proved invaluable in defeating Gideon Dosett."

Ambrose huffed. "An Inquisitor of your caliber, one trained by the Grand Inquisitor himself, should be teaching our future generations rather than dallying about with a medical professional. I apologize. This conversation is neither here nor there. What were we discussing before I rudely interrupted you?"

"I do believe that is the first time you've ever properly apologized for interrupting me. Perhaps you have changed. In any regard, I was discussing the thrill of the hunt. I should say you're more than familiar with that sensation."

Ambrose shook his head. "Alas, I'm not. I haven't received so thrilling an assignment in some time. In fact, my last assignment was investigating a demon bird harassing a logging expedition. It turned out to be merely a large bat to which someone had affixed a duck's bill. Can you imagine a more preposterous creature?"

"A forgery, then?" Simon asked as a valet directed them toward the large meeting hall.

"Most certainly, and poor taxidermy work at that. Even Peter saw right through the guise, though how the loggers hadn't is still beyond me. It was most certainly a waste of Inquisitor resources and time."

The meeting hall doors were open and the interior exceptionally crowded. The din of conversation rolled from the room, filling even the foyer with a general indistinguishable rumble of voices. Simon paused at the doorway and looked into the busy room beyond.

The meeting hall was a tiered affair, with rows of seats rising to either side of a central floor. The middle of the room was open, save for a raised dais near the far end of the chamber on which a pair of ornate chairs rested. Behind the chairs were two doors, closed at the moment, leading to hidden rooms beyond.

The middle of the room was as much of a divide between philosophies as was the central hall of parliament, in which either side of the room held the two opposing political ideations. In the Inquisitors' hall, however, the two sides worked toward a common goal, though the means to their end differed greatly.

To the left, the seats were filled with Inquisitors of Simon's and Ambrose's order, those who investigated reports of magical maladies with due diligence. Simon noticed many a familiar face amongst the Inquisitors and a few even offered friendly nods as he caught their eyes.

Simon's gaze drifted to the right side of the room, where the Order of Kinder Pel sat, talking amongst themselves. They looked no different than his own Inquisitors, though Simon knew there was darkness within the Pellites, one of fanaticism that would see magic destroyed by any means necessary, collateral damage be damned.

"They even appear as hulking brutes," Ambrose remarked as he too glanced toward the Pellites.

"Give them nary another thought," Simon said. "We should find seats. We're practically late as it is."

The two men wove through the rows of seats, Simon receiving a fair share of pats on the back and offered handshakes. There were seats available near the top of the tiered seats, the front-most seats having been reserved for those with more political clout than a mere second-year Inquisitor.

Simon and Ambrose sat and gave polite introductions to the men sitting on either side. They settled back in their chairs and glanced across the vast space between the two factions. A few Pellites glanced toward them as they talked in low tones.

The sheer number of Pellites filling the seats, which had nearly reached maximum capacity, took Simon aback. "I don't recall there ever being so many of them before."

Ambrose shook his head. "Their numbers have been growing steadily over the past year. The younger generation seems more astutely attuned to their brazen approach to investigations, finding our more practiced approach to be archaic and old-fashioned."

Simon laughed. "We're in our thirties, and yet somehow time has already passed us by, it seems."

"Still in our prime," Ambrose echoed from their earlier conversation.

Simon crossed his arms over his chest and frowned. "They're mere children, barely older than Peter, yet they're being sent on missions just the same as we are. It seems mildly blasphemous."

"I concur, yet we'll never be rid of the Pellites. Despite their brutish ways, their results speak for themselves. They have uncovered more hidden nests of monsters than we have, not in spite of their methods but because of them."

"They uncover these things through torture and inhumane practices. Thank you, but no. I'll remain true to our methods of inquiry."

"You're preaching to the preacher, Simon," Ambrose remarked.

The two doors in the back of the room opened, and everyone in the room quickly climbed to their feet. Through the doorways, two men entered. Dressed in heavy robes, the two elderly gentlemen walked onto the central floor before taking their seats on the raised dais.

The speaker of the house stepped forward and drove a tall staff onto the marble floor. The sound echoed through the silent chamber and, as one, the Inquisitors took their seats.

"This tenth meeting of the Inquisitors has come to order," the speaker announced.

As quickly as he arrived, the speaker retreated between the ornate chairs and walked briskly through the rear exit. For a moment, the room was cast in silence. The Grand Inquisitor and Grand Maester looked slowly around the room, examining those in attendance.

Slowly, the Grand Inquisitor stood. The elderly man, his hair white with age and his face deep set with wrinkles, looked around the room as he cleared his throat.

"There is a grave danger threatening the sovereignty of our great kingdom," he said, his strong voice belying his frail appearance. "We have known for years that the Rift posed a threat, that the magic seeping from its depths could upend our very way of life. Yet it seems we've underestimated the very nature of the Rift. As we struggled to contain incursions of magical creatures, a much greater threat was infiltrating our realm. I speak of demons!"

At the mention of the word, the room broke out in both angry and scared voices. Simon could easily understand the conflicting emotions carried by the crowd. He, too, had experienced both fear and anger when facing the demon in Haversham, nearly simultaneously.

The Grand Inquisitor raised his hand, and the room fell silent once more. The Grand Maester, leader of the Order of Kinder Pel, motioned toward the main entrance. A pair of guards wheeled a cart forward, prostate on which was a disturbingly familiar sight.

Gideon Dosett's body remained the inky blackness of his reverted demon self, rather than the slightly pale, fleshy tone Simon had known upon their first meeting. A single long, curled horn jutted from his forehead and curved around his ear. Where a second horn had once protruded, only a broken stump remained. Sightless red eyes stared at the hall's ceiling, no longer burning with their infernal fire but intimidating nonetheless.

Simon felt his gut churn at the sight of the demon's body. Though the Inquisitors in the room had all heard the story of its existence, only Simon, Luthor, and Mattie had faced the monster when it was alive. The memory of its raw power and the still-healing wounds it had given them all were still fresh in Simon's mind.

The presence of the demon's body caused a ripple of commotion through the meeting hall. Simon ignored the individual remarks, his eyes never leaving Gideon's body, as though he expected the demon to rise from its grave and seek revenge. Simon had known that they would be discussing the presence of demons in their kingdom but never had he expected the body to be presented before him.

The Grand Inquisitor raised his hand once more, and the room settled again. "We have brought forth the remains of the demon to end any discussion or skepticism of its validity. This should be proof enough that all is not well within our borders. The demon wore the guise of a human, worming his way into the confidence of even the regional governor before making his move toward the very throne of our city."

The Grand Maester, who looked at least a decade younger than the Grand Inquisitor, climbed from his chair as well. "For those who reside beyond Callifax, we ask that you seek out with all diligence any evidence of further demons within our borders. For those who are within the city, use every opportunity during your assignments to find proof that this demon was the exception within our lands, rather than the rule. It is up to you all to keep our kingdom secure from the occult menace from the south!"

Simon sat back in his chair and stared at the body. His eyes were not the only ones affixed to the corpse, but Simon quickly tuned out those around him. The meeting droned on, even as the conversation moved beyond the demon and its implications, but Simon barely acknowledged the further discussion. His thoughts drifted not only to Gideon Dosett and all that had transpired in Haversham, but to the tribe of werewolves that still existed beyond the frozen city's high walls. Simon had risked not only his career but his very life in concealing the truth from the rest of the Inquisitors, though he knew a secret that even Luthor did not. Technically, there was one other Inquisitor who knew of the werewolves' existence. It was only a matter of time until Simon would have to answer for his decisions regarding their continued existence.

Nearly an hour later, the speaker of the house returned and rapped his staff upon the floor once more, adjourning the meeting. Individual sects of Inquisitors would now segregate themselves into committee meetings to discuss further aspects of missions and policy, though Simon belonged to none of these.

Instead, he and Ambrose stood and prepared to make their way toward the exit. Simon glanced over once more toward the displayed corpse and shivered in disgust. His gaze drifted past the body to the Grand Inquisitor and Grand Maester, both of whom stood stoically before their ornate chairs. A bald Pellite stood beside the Grand Maester as they spoke in hushed tones. The Grand Maester's gaze drifted in Simon's direction, and Simon arched his eyebrow inquisitively. The bald Pellite nodded and began crossing the room's divide as he approached their tiered seats.

"Inquisitor Whitlock," the man said, gesturing for Simon to join him near the floor. "May I have a moment of your time, if you please?"

Simon glanced toward Ambrose, but the taller man merely shrugged. Together, they walked down an aisle that led to the floor, stopping before the Pellite.

"Thank you for meeting with me," the man said. "My name is Inquisitor Creary. Grand Maester Arrus is most impressed by your defeat of the demon and would like to discuss your adventures, or misadventures as they may have been, in a private meeting."

Simon glanced over Creary's shoulder and met the gaze of the stern Grand Maester. The Maester nodded slowly, acknowledging Simon.

"I'm most flattered by the invitation," Simon said, wracking his mind for an excuse not to meet with the Grand Maester. While he had nothing against the man, the thought of meeting with the leader of the Order of Kinder Pel was off-putting, considering how often Simon had spent railing against their very existence.

"If you would join me, the Grand Maester has time now, if that suits your schedule."

Before Simon could reply, another voice cut through the emptying chamber.

"Simon," the Grand Inquisitor bellowed. Simon looked up, relieved as the Grand Inquisitor gestured for Simon to join him. "We have much to discuss, you and I, if you would be so kind as to accompany me to my office."

"Of course, Your Eminence," Simon replied. He turned his attention back to Creary. "Forgive me, Inquisitor, but it appears I am needed elsewhere. Please apologize to the Grand Maester and let him know that I will most certainly meet with him at a more agreeable time."

Creary frowned and glanced over his shoulder, but the Grand Maester's expression revealed nothing. The Pellite turned back toward Simon without emotion, revealing neither disappointment nor relief at Simon's refusal.

"Forgive us, but we are needed by the Grand Inquisitor," Ambrose remarked, breaking the silence. "If you could kindly move aside. You're blocking the exit."

Creary turned his gaze toward the charismatic Inquisitor and frowned. The broad smile on Ambrose's face remained even as he dropped his voice low enough so that only Creary and Simon could hear his follow-on remarks.

"Now do run along and pull the wings from flies or whatever it is you Pellites do during your free time."

Creary's frown deepened with anger. "Be careful. Your tongue will get you in trouble one of these days."

Ambrose merely laughed. "My dear man. My tongue has quite some notoriety for causing trouble, especially with the fairer sex."

The Pellite turned abruptly and returned to the side of the Grand Maester.

Simon shook his head as he turned his attention back to Ambrose. "You're incorrigible, you realize? He wasn't being disrespectful, though I struggle to say the same about you."

"Any respect you perceived was a falsehood meant to deceive you. The Pellites are brutes, and none more so than the one with whom you were talking."

Simon glanced toward the bald man who now had his back to them. "Then who is this Inquisitor Creary?"

"He's the Grand Maester's confidant but also, more often than not, his enforcer."

Simon took in the man's broad shoulders and square jaw. Though he looked fit, he hardly seemed like a physical threat.

As though interpreting Simon's expression, Ambrose shook his head. "Do not underestimate the man. What he lacks in stature, he more than makes up for in brutality. The problem is that Creary is indicative of their entire Order, to include their more youthful recruits. They all lack class. That brute, especially, is a curmudgeon. In a sea of sophisticated rapiers, that man is a veritable battle axe."

Simon broke his gaze away from the Pellite and noted the Grand Inquisitor's rapid approach. "If that's the case, then I owe you both an apology and my thanks. Though, truth be told, I certainly didn't need your help when dealing with a strong arm from the Order of Kinder Pel."

"Of course not," Ambrose replied, his mood lightening considerably as he, too, hurried to finish their conversation before the Grand Inquisitor's arrival. "That being said, I enjoyed myself immensely at someone else's expense, which I categorize as the start to an exceptional party."

"Belittling Pellites is your idea of fun?"

"Naturally."

The Grand Inquisitor stopped in front of the two men, and they both bowed their heads respectfully. The Grand Inquisitor nodded in return, and the two men met his gaze.

"Join me, Simon," the Grand Inquisitor said. "There is much you and I have to discuss."

Simon nodded. He remembered being so excited about these festivities when the day began. Now it seemed he spent more time dreading his next encounter, and this meeting with the Grand Inquisitor was even more nerve wracking than a meeting with the Grand Maester would have been.

The Grand Inquisitor stepped away, heading toward the hall's main entrance. Simon turned quickly to Ambrose, knowing he had but a moment to spare.

"Will you still be here when I return?" Simon asked.

"If I were to judge the sour expression on your face, I would assume you meant to ask if I'd be here *if* you ever return. In either case, however, the answer is yes. I have yet to turn away from an opportunity for free liquor."

Simon nodded, though he lacked any mirth in his eyes. "Do be certain to keep control of your faculties between now and then. I may yet have need of your council."

Ambrose smiled warmly. "I make no promises."

CHAPTER Three

Simon followed the Grand Inquisitor out of the hall and into the foyer. Inquisitors moved aside as they passed, walking in silence. Beyond the entryway, a hallway led to offices near the rear of the structure.

The Grand Inquisitor's office seemed innocuous compared to the trappings of his attire. A simple wooden door, currently closed, marked its entrance into the wide but subdued interior.

They stopped at the doorway, and the Grand Inquisitor turned toward Simon. "Thank you kindly for the walk, Simon. Have a good rest of your day."

Simon arched his eyebrow in confusion. "Sir? Did you not have something to discuss?"

"Oh, I do, but nothing that won't keep until a later date and time. In truth, I saw the discomfort in your eyes when asked to visit the Grand Maester and figured I would save you from that horror."

Simon forced a smile at the thought. "You were right to do so, sir. For that I am eternally grateful."

The Grand Inquisitor patted Simon on the shoulder. "It wouldn't do to have my own apprentice courted by the Order of Kinder Pel, would it?"

"Former apprentice," Simon corrected.

"Former," the Grand Inquisitor agreed, smiling at his former pupil. "Even so, you're one of the brightest Inquisitors currently under employment. I can't very well have Arrus foolishly attempting to bribe you from my side."

Simon leaned forward and lowered his voice. "It would never work, sir. I simply couldn't bring myself to be, how did Inquisitor Supperwood so eloquently put it, 'a veritable battle axe in an ocean of refined sabers.' It was something to that affect, at any rate. He's far better spoken than I."

The Grand Inquisitor laughed heartily. "I can certainly discern the intent, even if you butchered an otherwise well-designed quote. Go home and enjoy your reprieve from work, Simon. We'll call upon you once more when we have an assignment."

The Grand Inquisitor began to turn, but Simon politely cleared his throat. The elder gentleman turned back toward him.

"Do you, per chance, happen to know how many Inquisitors are before me in the queue for assignments?"

A pair of Inquisitors walked past the two men, and they were forced to step out of the way. The passing Inquisitors nodded politely to the Grand Inquisitor. They waited for the men to pass before continuing their conversation.

"Are you so eager to be deployed? Was not a battle against vicious werewolves and a demon more than enough excitement for you? Are you building a resume on the backs of the mystical investigations?"

Simon chuckled but shook his head. "You know me well enough to know it's not the fame I seek. I'm merely not one to sit on my laurels for too long. I yearn for adventure and travel. It's a wanderlust that burns in my veins."

The Grand Inquisitor smiled. "For someone who claims not to be well spoken, you certainly do have a flair for the dramatic."

"I merely wish to know when I might expect another assignment."

The Grand Inquisitor stroked his smooth-shaven chin thoughtfully. "There are a number of Inquisitors still awaiting assignments, many of whom have been in Callifax for far too long, in my honest opinion. Perhaps a few weeks' time, maybe as long as a month."

Simon sighed. "A month is a long time, sir."

"Poppycock. A month is the right amount of time for an Inquisitor to unwind from his latest expedition, spend some time with that lovely lady friend of yours, and enjoy the sights of the city. You fought demons and werewolves, for God's sake. You deserve some time to yourself."

Simon furrowed his brow at the second mention of werewolves. He glanced over his shoulder to ensure no more Inquisitors could overhear their conversation.

"Have you, per chance, had the opportunity to read my report from Haversham, sir?"

The Grand Inquisitor frowned apologetically. "I regret to admit that I have not. These past two weeks have been a myriad of issues from the crown, one after another. I haven't yet found the time, though your report is in the top drawer of my desk even now. Is there something important you need to discuss from it?"

Simon bit his bottom lip but slowly shook his head. "As you said earlier, sir, it's nothing that can't wait until a later date and time. Please be sure to let me know the moment you do review my report."

It was the Grand Inquisitor's turn to furrow his brow inquisitively. "Is anything the matter, Simon? Did something occur of which I need to be made aware?"

Simon thought about his report, which was honest to a fault about his adventures in Haversham. It described Simon and Luthor's encounters with the werewolf tribe and, more precisely, how they allowed the werewolves to live following the destruction of Gideon Dosett. Even more damning was the admission that Matilda Hawke had returned to Callifax, a werewolf amongst the overly conservative residents of the capital city.

The myriad of thoughts fluttered about his mind, but he finally shook his head and smiled disarmingly. "No, sir, nothing that cannot wait. Have a good day, sir."

The Grand Inquisitor turned the handle to his door and opened it wide. "You as well, Simon. Give my best to both Mr. Strong and Ms. Dawn."

"I most certainly shall, sir."

Simon waited until the door closed behind the Grand Inquisitor before turning back toward the entry hall. A small group of Pellites huddled at the end, but they gave him barely a second glance as he passed.

The foyer itself was practically empty, though a fair number of voices escaped from the sitting room on the far side. Simon could see Ambrose leaning against the hearth, speaking with great enthusiasm to an older Inquisitor whom Simon didn't recognize.

Simon entered the room. Ambrose glanced toward him and raised his glass in salute, inviting him to join their conversation. As Simon walked toward the pair, Ambrose arched his eyebrow inquisitively.

Ambrose turned toward the other Inquisitor. "Forgive me, Bertrand, but I didn't expect that my counsel would be needed so hastily."

Bertrand laughed heartily before nodding to Simon. "A pleasure, Inquisitor Whitlock. Ambrose, we will speak again soon."

"Of course," Ambrose replied as Bertrand turned and walked away. Ambrose turned back toward Simon. "I see it was unwise of me to get so tall a tumbler of liquor. I honestly expected your meeting to go much longer."

"As usual, he was merely acting as a guardian angel, protecting me from the evils that are the Pellites. Our actual conversation was rather abrupt."

Ambrose shrugged. "Then do you have need of my counsel?"

Simon's gaze fell to the drink in Ambrose's hand. "What I need is a drink. Would you care to join me?"

Ambrose drained his glass of liquor, despite the hefty quantities, and set the empty tumbler on the top of the fireplace. "I thought you'd never ask."

Ambrose drank deeply of his stout, wiping away the foam from his lips with the napkin before him. His gaze never left Simon, who merely watched the people in the bar from across the table. Simon had barely touched his scotch, and most of the ice had already melted in his glass.

"If you don't drink that soon, I'll be forced to intervene before it grows far too diluted. I would drink it, you know, for the sake of the liquor."

Simon looked at his glass. With a smile, he lifted it to his lips and took a drink.

Ambrose leaned back in the bar's privacy booth. The curtains were not yet drawn, allowing a view of the moderately busy barroom beyond.

"Would you like to talk at all about what is on your mind, or shall we merely enjoy our liquor? By 'we,' I clearly mean 'me.'"

Simon impulsively took another drink from his scotch in spite of his friend's observation. The large swig of hard liquor burned slightly as it went down his throat and settled in his stomach. A warming sensation spread to his limbs.

He fiddled with the nearly empty tumbler as he glanced around the room once more. Simon found himself doing it more and more often, as though some unknown assailant was waiting patiently to strike when he was unsuspecting.

"You seem rather pensive," Ambrose remarked as he signaled the barmaid for another round of drinks. "You've actually seemed rather out of sorts since your return. Is anything the matter?"

Simon examined the faces of the disinterested bar patrons. "It's off-putting to know that there was a demon walking amongst us and no one was any the wiser. I, myself, held numerous conversations with the demon in human form and never had the slightest inkling that it was anything other than a smug businessman."

He leaned back in the booth and let his gaze drift across the room once more. "I'm not one to overlook details, as you well know, but that demon truly had the wool pulled over my eyes. It makes me feel…"

"Incompetent?" Ambrose offered.

Simon frowned. "I was going to say 'inadequate,' but thank you for your contribution."

Ambrose laughed, his mirth continuing even as the barmaid delivered their drinks. He flashed her a warm smile and winked as he handed her a silver coin. As she walked away, Ambrose composed himself, wiping a tear from the corner of his eye.

"You're neither incompetent nor inadequate, and you damn well know it," the charismatic man said. "You're one of the best Inquisitors in the field. I know it, you know it, and even the Grand Inquisitor knows it."

"Then what hope do we have if even I was duped by a magical monster?" Simon asked. "I just find myself perusing rooms, wondering if one of the faces on which my gaze nonchalantly passes is in fact another demon set to spread chaos within the kingdom."

Ambrose scanned the room, catching the passing eye of a half-drunk patron or two. "Certainly, Simon. Why that man over there, the one who is walking toward the water closet as though one of his legs was far shorter than the other, he most certainly could be one. Perhaps the man across the way whose head is nodding with a combination of exhaustion and intoxication, perhaps he is a demon as well."

"You mock me," Simon said flatly.

Ambrose turned his gaze back toward his friend. "I mock you because you deserve to be mocked. Your demon, this Gideon—"

"Dosett."

"Yes, this Gideon Dosett was in a position of power in Haversham. He was able to shape and influence the politics of the region, with the obvious help of his abyssal powers, of course." Ambrose spread his arms, gesturing wildly toward the assorted patrons. "The men and women you'll pass on a daily basis hold no influence and no affect to politics, literally, not at all."

"So you're saying I'm being paranoid?"

"You are being paranoid, but justly so. You fought and killed a demon. No one else can claim such a feat. As soon as word spreads to the corners of the kingdom, you'll be a celebrity. You'll have enough women throwing themselves at you that even I might get jealous."

"My God, that is an asinine number of women."

Ambrose laughed. "Exactly. You should be laughing and enjoying this time. Revel in their adoration; I know I do."

Simon shook his head. "You're incorrigible."

"You keep saying that, when what I think you mean to say is that I'm adorable." Ambrose looked down at his drink and arched an eyebrow in surprise. He didn't remember drinking most of his pint, and yet, it was nearly empty.

In contrast, Simon looked at his two-fingers of scotch, which was still mainly untouched.

"Another round?" Ambrose asked, reaching for his coin purse.

Simon glanced out the bay windows across the room and noticed long shadows stretching down the street in front of the bar. He fetched his pocket watch and glanced at the time. "Sadly, I must decline," he remarked. "I have a few errands left to run before I enjoy an evening date."

"So it begins," Ambrose chided.

"Nothing is beginning. My date is with Veronica."

Ambrose leaned back in the booth and picked up his pint of stout. He raised the glass in salute. "Give Ms. Dawn my regards. Perhaps we shall have to double date in the near future."

Simon furrowed his brow as he realized Ambrose had no intention of vacating the booth. "Are you not coming?"

Ambrose took a long draw from his beer before setting the empty glass on the table. He looked past Simon to where the barmaid stood near the bar. "No," he said, smiling knowingly. "I believe I'll have other plans this evening."

He motioned for the barmaid and pointed at his empty glass.

"Incorrigible," Simon repeated. "Enjoy yourself, but behave."

"That's unlikely."

Simon smiled as he wove his way through the bar toward the front door.

CHAPTER Four

"I HOPE YOU'RE HUNGRY," LUTHOR SAID AS HE WALKED into the dining room. He set a plate before Mattie before walking to the opposite end of the long table and setting down his own meal.

The electric lights were turned off in lieu of a series of candles lit in the middle of the table. The flickering light cast long shadows on the walls as Luthor moved around the room.

"This all smells delicious," Mattie remarked as she closed her eyes and savored the scents. "You've truly outdone yourself."

Luthor took his seat and smiled. "That's high praise from someone with such an exceptional sense of smell."

"It's the wolf in me. Fear not, I'll do my best to use restraint while eating, rather than simply devouring the meal."

"I do appreciate it," Luthor said, laughing softly. "It would be a shame to slave in the kitchen for nearly an hour only to have the meal decimated in mere minutes. Besides, tonight is hardly just about the meal. This is about enjoying one another's company."

Mattie smiled and brushed a loose strand of her red hair out of her face. "I'm certainly looking forward to it."

A loud knock sounded on the door, disrupting the otherwise touching moment. Luthor frowned, recognizing the knock almost immediately.

Without waiting for someone to answer the door, Simon hastily entered the foyer.

"Luthor?" the Inquisitor called.

Luthor lowered his head and covered his face with his hands.

"We're in here, Simon," Mattie answered when it was evident Luthor had no intention of responding.

"I was hoping if we didn't reply, he would merely go away," the apothecary said.

Mattie laughed as Simon appeared at the entryway to the dining room. "Have you ever known Simon to merely go away?"

"Sadly, no."

Simon paused, taking in the lit candles and carefully prepared meal. "Forgive me, but I'm not interrupting, am I?"

"Perpetually," Luthor replied. "I should have locked the front door."

"You most certainly should have. It was foolish not to; anyone could have simply barged in on your otherwise romantic evening."

"*Anyone* wouldn't," Luthor chided. "You're the only man in all Callifax who would enter someone else's home completely and totally uninvited."

Simon shook his head. "Nonsense, Luthor. I'm always invited. Your meal smells delicious, by the way."

Luthor gritted his teeth. "It does, and I would very much like to enjoy it undisturbed. What do you want, Simon?"

"I need to borrow a black tie, if you please."

Luthor finally turned toward the Inquisitor and frowned. "I most certainly don't please. Don't you have a black tie of your own?"

"Stained, sadly. Come, Luthor, I'm running late as it is. I'll merely need to borrow it for the night."

Luthor sighed as he twisted awkwardly in the dining room chair to better face his mentor. "The last time I lent you a tie 'for the night' as you so eloquently put it, you had it in your possession for nearly six weeks."

Simon shrugged. "Yet you did get it back, did you not?"

"Yes, after constant berating for more than a month."

"Yet you did get it back."

"Yes," Luthor replied, exasperated, "but only after I invaded your wardrobe of my own volition and took it back by force."

"You're arguing semantics. In the end, you did get it back."

Luthor turned back to his meal and the redhead sitting across the table from him, who wore an amused expression.

"Arguing with you is simply infuriating," Luthor grumbled.

"Then you should stop trying. As for the tie…?"

Simon left the question hanging, awaiting the apothecary's response. Luthor merely waved his hand over his shoulder in defeat.

"You already know where they're kept. By all means, help yourself."

Simon departed without another word, his heavy footfalls echoing as he rushed up the stairs. Luthor pinched the bridge of his nose to ward off the threatening headache. There were days he missed the simplicity of being bitten by werewolves over holding conversations with the Inquisitor.

Mattie pointed toward the upstairs, where Simon could be heard clumsily searching through Luthor's armoire. "Don't you ever worry that he might stumble upon any of your magical paraphernalia in his, what I have to assume to be thorough, searching through your belongings?"

Luthor felt more relaxed with the abrupt change of conversation. "There was a time when I foolishly kept incriminating belongings upstairs, but those days have long since passed."

Mattie glanced around the room as though expecting a secret wardrobe to suddenly appear. "If not upstairs, then where do you store everything? I've hardly searched the nooks and crannies of your home, but I've never seen anything."

Luthor picked up his glass of wine and took a small drink, enjoying the earthy notes. "I keep them in the basement."

"The townhouse has a basement?" Mattie asked, perplexed. "I've never seen a doorway or stairwell. How do you get to the basement?"

Luthor paused, his glass half raised to his lips for a second drink. He arched his eyebrow.

Mattie sighed. "Magic, of course. I should have guessed as much."

Luthor laughed. "Indeed, you should have."

Moments later, Simon rushed downstairs, haphazardly attempting to properly affix the long, black tie around his neck.

"Thank you kindly, Luthor."

"Think nothing of it," Luthor replied. "I'm sure thinking nothing of my generosity was your intent all along."

Simon didn't reply but instead rushed out the door, pulling it closed behind him with a loud crash. Luthor winced as the townhouse seemed to settle back into its general air of undisturbed calm.

They returned to their meals, passing casual conversation between one another as they ate. When the meal was finished, Luthor cleared the table and they retired to the living room.

Mattie sat on the heavily cushioned couch as Luthor crouched before the fireplace. He retrieved logs from a pile beside him and placed them in a small pile on the stone floor of the fireplace. Leaning away from the logs, he extended his hand and began drawing a rune in the air with his index finger. The air ignited in a trail behind the pattern, shifting and turning in response to his subtle gestures. Before long, a smoldering, red rune burned brilliantly in the air. It hung in place for a moment before collapsing onto the logs. A roaring fire suddenly flashed to life, filling the room with satisfying warmth.

"You are a very convenient man to have nearby," Mattie joked from her spot on the sofa.

"I aim to please," Luthor grunted as he pushed from his crouched position. He walked over and joined her on the couch.

Mattie gestured toward the fireplace. "Does the Cabal not mind you using your powers so blatantly? I would think they would place restrictions on their usage."

Luthor shrugged as he looked into her eyes. "I would hardly call starting a fire in the privacy of my own home a blatant use. That being said, the Cabal doesn't generally interfere in such frivolities."

Mattie nodded. "Speaking of the Cabal, have you spoken to them since your return?"

Luthor shook his head. "No, but that's hardly out of character. I rarely hear from them unless I'm required for a mission. Otherwise, I'm left to my own devices."

"Just like that?" she asked. "It seems rather dismissive that they contact you only when they have need of your abilities. I would think that the man who slew one of the five demons, against whom the entire Cabal was formed in the first place I might add, would be praised regularly."

Luthor shook his head dismissively. "The Cabal doesn't have the luxury of resting on its laurels, praising the victories already accomplished. They're busy searching for the next of the five demon lords. At least, I assume they are. It's all rather cryptic, to be honest."

Mattie arched an eyebrow and tilted her head to the side inquisitively. "You've never actually met them, have you?"

Luthor flushed. "Well, no, not exactly."

Mattie sat upright and furrowed her brow. "Have you ever seen any of the fellow members of the Cabal?"

"No, though I have spoken to them many times during our communications."

"Unbelievable. You work for a shadow organization so secretive that its own members are oblivious for whom they actually work."

Luthor frowned and crossed his arms over his chest. "You make it all sound rather devious."

"Forgive me, I meant no disrespect," she said hastily upon noting his displeasure. She placed her hand on his arm. "I merely find the whole process to be unnecessarily compartmentalized, if that makes sense."

Luthor placed his hand over hers. "It does make sense, from both your and their perspective. I understand how it must look to you, but you must also realize that they are a cabal of wizards, working and operating in lands that loathe their very existence. No matter how altruistic their purpose, exposure would lead to immediate execution for any of us discovered."

Mattie squeezed his arm gently. "This is truly dreadful after-dinner conversation. Wasn't this supposed to be a date?"

Luthor smiled. "Indeed it was… is. Perhaps you'd like to discuss something a bit more lively?"

"I have been curious about something," she replied. "How is it that we have been in Callifax for two long weeks and I have yet to meet this Veronica Dawn, of whom I've heard endless amounts from Simon?"

"Of all the topics of conversation we could enjoy during our date, you ask more questions about Simon?"

Mattie laughed. "It strikes me as odd that someone for whom Simon has such affinity has never come by, nor have we ever met the happy couple for dinner or other such outings. He's not ashamed of her, is he?"

"Ashamed of her?"

"Having never met her, nor even been invited to meet her, I have to wonder if she has some physical affliction."

"As in, does she have a hunched back or hooves for feet? Perhaps she's so hideous that she's kept chained in his attic? That when Simon says he's visiting her, he's actually going into his attic to feed her a bucket of fish heads?"

Mattie laughed heartily. "I meant merely that there is an expectation with a handsome man like Simon that the woman he courts would be equally as attractive."

Luthor slipped an arm around Mattie's shoulders and pulled her closer to him. She leaned her head over, resting it on his chest.

"To put your mind at ease, Veronica does not suffer a physical deformation. She's actually a very attractive woman."

Mattie placed her hand on his chest. "Yet, you don't seem to like her."

Luthor canted his head as he tried to formulate the best way to explain a complex situation. "It's not that I dislike her. The truth is that she's a very lovely woman, a bit coarse and undignified at times, but generally sweet and polite."

Mattie raised her head. "Then why did you this morning belittle him for planning an evening with her?"

"It's not Veronica personally with whom I have an issue. It's her occupation. It's very unbecoming of a lady."

Mattie arched an eyebrow. "Where, exactly, does she work?"

CHAPTER Five

A FEW STREET LAMPS WERE INTERMIXED ALONG THE street, casting pools of light onto the otherwise dark cobblestone. In a city of relative gloom at night, the glow from the exterior of the Ace of Spades illuminated the sky around it like a second sunrise. The brightly painted brick exterior was splashed with fluorescent lights too numerous to count.

A velvet rope cordoned off part of the sidewalk, keeping eager patrons pressed against the side of the building as they eagerly awaited their entry to the opulent interior.

Simon walked past the velvet rope and approached the building's front doors. A towering, suited man stood in front of the closed doors, large, wooden monstrosities with wrought iron handles. Beside each door, scantily clad women, adorned with feathers and headdresses, rested their hands on the door handles, ready to open for approved patrons.

The bouncer noted Simon's approach and smiled broadly toward the Inquisitor.

"It's been far too long since you last visited, Inquisitor," the man said, his speech broken by an unidentifiable accent.

"I do apologize. Work keeps me away," Simon remarked.

The bouncer nodded to the two women holding the door. In unison, they pulled the double doors apart. A flood of music and light poured from the building's interior. Laugher intermixed with the din of dozens of simultaneous conversations. Even from the exterior, the air was thick with cigar and cigarette smoke.

Simon pulled a silver coin from his pocket and palmed it in his hand. As he passed the bouncer, he shook the man's hand, discreetly transferring the tip. The bouncer nodded appreciatively before turning his attention back to the other disgruntled men and women behind the velvet cordon who clearly felt perturbed by Simon's avoidance of the lengthy line.

The Inquisitor entered the Ace of Spades and was immediately awash in the sights and sounds. The club entered onto a raised horseshoe that skirted the edge of the building, looking down on the sunken middle of the room and the stage on the far side. A bar and barstools lined the divide between the upper and lower floors, allowing for maximum visibility of the stage.

Most of the barstools had already been claimed, but Simon had no interest in sitting so far away. He walked down the carpeted steps and onto the sunken main floor.

The lights were mostly focused on the stage, where a burlesque dancer moved seductively, stripping away gloves and stockings in a painfully slow yet sensual display. Simon ignored the woman on stage as he turned and walked toward an empty table with a reserved placard. He pulled out one of the two chairs and sat, facing the stage at a slight angle.

The rest of the room was surprisingly dimly lit, with only the minimal lighting supplemented by individual candles stationed in the middle of the variety of tables. A number of couples huddled near the candles, leaning in close enough so that their conversation could only be heard by one another. A burlesque house was the perfect place for secret, and often inappropriate, rendezvous. It was hardly the place for a respected member of the Royal Inquisitors. Yet, of all the places he frequented in Callifax, the Ace of Spades was where he felt most at home.

A server approached him with a familiar smile. She wore thick makeup that left her face looking ghostly pale. A tight, striped corset cinched her waist and her billowing skirt ended just above her knees, revealing the stockings and garter beneath. There was a leather strap around her shoulders, holding a tray aloft before her.

"Welcome back, sir," she said. "Would you care for a smoke?"

She tilted the tray to reveal a row of cigars as well as a silver-plated cigarette case. Simon reached up and unlatched the cigarette case, pulling free a hand-rolled cigarette. The server retrieved a lighter from the tray and ignited it as Simon placed the cigarette to his lips. He drew a deep breath, feeling the soothing smoke roll into his lungs.

As he exhaled, he pulled a gold coin from his waistcoat. Simon placed it on her tray.

"This and a scotch," he said, "and keep them both coming."

The server smiled and gave a slight curtsey. "Yes, sir."

As she walked away, Simon let his gaze drift over the room. The room was filled with an odd assortment of patrons. There were the couples huddled together around the tables, but there were equally as many single men and even women sitting alone along the edges of the room. A man sat in the shadows in the far booth, directly across the room from Simon, watching the stage intently; his features were barely distinguishable in the dim light. In contrast to the man in the booth's obvious discretion, what was evidently a nobleman sat near the stage, his jacket etched with gold thread and a ridiculous hat perched upon his head. The Ace of Spades was a melting pot of patrons with a single true desire.

The server returned, setting a glass of scotch before him. To his great surprise and pleasure, she also set the remainder of the bottle in the middle of the table. Simon smiled at the woman. He had met her once before, during a previous visit, but he couldn't recall her name. With such exceptional service, however, he would make a better effort in the future.

Before he could thank her, the music abruptly changed. The fast-paced trumpets gave way to the slower rumble of trombones. The sound was earthy, as though it was rumbling through the very floorboards, up through Simon's legs, and freezing the air in his lungs.

He turned toward the stage and smiled broadly as the stage lights dimmed. Everyone blinked as their vision tried to adjust to only the light from the candles spread across the tables. Simon squinted his eyes virtually shut, leaving only a sliver open with which to watch the stage. He had seen this show before and knew better than to stare too closely.

As quickly as they had dimmed, the lights behind the stage flared to life. The audience rocked backward in their seats in surprise. As everyone settled, the thin silhouette of a woman appeared, her features indistinguishable as nothing more than a black, curvaceous shape.

The music began again, and the woman on stage began to dance. Her body was lithe and nimble, and she seemed to glide across the stage. As the music built, the lights at the front of the stage slowly began to glow as well.

The dark-haired beauty on stage wore a tight corset. Her black garter belt and underwear tightly hugged her narrow waist and wider hips. Long, silk gloves rose to above her elbows on each arm, and sheer stockings clung to each leg. Her dazzling smile and diamond necklace both glistened under the electric lights as she moved.

Simon watched her dance, entranced by her every move. To the catcalls of the audience, she slowly removed each of her gloves, tossing them behind her where they fell on the stage.

A crescendo of trumpets joined the rolling trombones and the dark-haired woman sat on the stage, flexibly lifting a leg upward until it rested beside her head. A flick of her fingers detached the clasps holding the garter to the stockings. In a fluid motion, she unrolled it, revealing the creamy smooth skin beneath. The other stocking was also removed before she rolled nimbly back to her feet.

The cheers from the crowd grew louder as she crouched and was handed a feathered fan from each side of the stage. The white feathers were a stark contrast to her dark lingerie, but she moved them handily, teasing the crowd with each movement.

This was what everyone in attendance had truly come for. This performer was the highlight of the Ace of Spades, and Simon was just as enthralled as everyone else in the audience.

The dancer brought the fans together, one facing upward and one down, until they covered most of her body. Shifting their grip so that both fans were held in one hand, her free hand disappeared as the music built. With a slight bend, she removed her garter, flashing it above the top of the upper fan for the audience to see.

Simon knew what happened next, and his heart began to race. With the fans still held in one hand, she slipped her free hand behind her once again. From his vantage point, Simon could hear the individual snaps of the latches being removed on her corset. Like the garter before it, the corset came free. She held it over her head as she brought the feathers closer to her body, concealing any exposed flesh and leaving everything, yet nothing, to the imagination.

The music grew to a maddening pace, quickly outstripping the fast-paced songs that had been playing when Simon had first entered the burlesque house. As the music grew to a deafening volume, the woman grasped a fan in each hand and threw her arms out wide. The front house lights went out and the music fell silent, leaving only the perfectly formed silhouette of the topless woman and the pair of feathered fans, held out to each side.

The audience erupted in applause, many climbing to their feet for a standing ovation. Simon stubbed his half-smoked cigarette in an ashtray and joined the applause.

The lights behind the stage turned off, casting the room in blinding darkness. Simon could hear the patter of bare feet hurrying across the stage as the dancer disappeared into the curtained wings.

As the house lights came back on, another dancer took the stage. Simon swigged the rest of his scotch and got to his feet. He followed the edge of the curved stage to an ornate door. The bouncer at the door held it open for Simon as he walked through.

The dressing rooms were a flurry of activity as women in various stages of undress rushed about, either putting on or taking off outfits for their upcoming performances. Most of the area was open, with rows of illuminated vanities lining the walls. Near the back, a few private rooms were established, though most of the doors were closed.

Simon smiled politely at the women he passed, but his attention was solely focused on one of the private rooms beyond. A bouncer, a man Simon didn't immediately recognize, stood before Veronica's private changing room.

The bouncer held up his hand as Simon approached. "Sorry, sir, but no one is allowed in the dressing rooms at this time."

Simon smiled knowingly at the man. "Trust me, Ms. Dawn will want to see me."

The bouncer shook his head. "I have strict orders not to let anyone in. No exceptions."

"You may want to let him in," a woman said from one of the nearby vanities.

Simon glanced over to the sea of tightly curled, blonde hair. The woman didn't look up as she applied a thick layer of brilliantly red lipstick.

"Gloria," Simon said. "How wonderful to see you again. I didn't think I would have the pleasure of your company until later tonight."

"You still will," Gloria replied. She finished with her lipstick, dabbing the excess on a napkin nearby. She turned her attention back to the bouncer. "Veronica wants to see him, trust me."

"I understand that, ma'am," the bouncer replied sternly, "but I have my orders. No one enters. No one."

"You can't later say that you weren't properly warned," Gloria replied as she turned her attention back to the mirror.

Simon sighed. "Please do move aside, or at the very least, knock on her door and ask if she will willingly see me. I can guarantee she will."

"Please return to the front room, sir," the bouncer said, unmoved by Simon's plea.

Simon placed his hands on his hips. "You're a damnably frustrating man. Just ask her."

"Sir, I won't tell you again."

Before Simon could reply, the dressing room door opened. The dark-haired beauty from the stage stood in the doorway. Her lithe frame was graced with a silk robe that hung only to her knees. The thin fabric clung to her curves as she leaned against the doorframe.

"It's perfectly all right, Marcus," Veronica said, placing her hand on the bouncer's shoulder. "Simon is an old friend."

The bouncer glanced at Simon before begrudgingly stepping aside. Simon nodded politely, swallowing his desire to smile smugly as he passed the brutish man.

The Inquisitor stepped through the doorway as Veronica retreated inside. He gently pushed the door closed on the small dressing room, allowing them a small iota of privacy.

The room was busy, with an assortment of barely concealing outfits hung on hooks along the wall. A small bench seat was pressed against one wall while a well-lit vanity sat against the other. The large mirror, framed in naked light bulbs, offered the faintest illusion that the room was in fact larger than it really was, but the illusion was fleeting. With Veronica standing in the center of the room, there was barely room for Simon to maneuver without pressing against her body, which he believed was entirely the point.

Veronica threw her arms around Simon's neck and drew him into a kiss. He could feel her smooth lips pressing against his as he slipped his hands around her waist.

They stood pressed together for an eternity before Veronica drew slowly away. She smiled and withdrew an arm from around his neck. With her free hand, she wiped away a smear of lipstick that had spread across Simon's lips during their embrace.

"I've missed you," she said. "Callifax is boring without you around."

Simon smiled. "Nothing about you is boring, my love."

Veronica smiled coyly. "Perhaps, but it's far more entertaining with you around. Anyway, boring is relative. You might think that what I do is exciting, but while I'm working, you're hunting werewolves and demons. It hardly seems fair."

Simon arched an eyebrow. "Would you prefer to be hunting magical monsters in the countryside?"

"Of course not." She laughed. "Can you imagine me carrying a gun and hunting beasts? I get squeamish merely seeing still-feathered chickens hanging by their necks in the marketplace. Cherish the thought of me on a hunting expedition."

"Oh, I most certainly do cherish that thought," Simon joked.

Veronica pulled her other arm from around Simon's neck and leaned back against the vanity's sole chair. The thin robe parted faintly in the front, leaving little to Simon's imagination.

"I do hunt, though the beast is much more cunning," she cooed. She reached forward with her hand and grasped Simon's belt. Her nimble fingers worked at its clasp.

Simon gently moved her hand aside. "Not here, darling. I do so hate mixing work and pleasure."

Veronica sighed and pulled her robe closed. "My prey is also clearly much more elusive."

Simon laughed as he stepped closer, wrapping his hands around her waist and kissing her on the neck. "I'm hardly playing hard to get. I'm merely waiting for more comfortable surroundings."

She placed her hands on his chest and joined his laugher. "What would the other Inquisitors think if they could see you now? The debonair man seducing a burlesque dancer hardly seems like proper Inquisitor behavior."

"You sound very much like Luthor, you know?" he asked, frowning. "There's a misconception that Inquisitors are upstanding citizens and above reproach merely because of the work we do. That simply isn't so. We're all fallible; we all have our vices, some more than others."

"Am I your vice, then?"

"One of many, my dear," Simon replied, "but certainly the most enjoyable."

"Speaking of Mr. Strong, did I read in your last letter that he has brought home a woman from your last assignment?"

Simon considered just how he would categorize Mattie and whether or not it was as simple as "bringing home a woman" considering all her other extenuating circumstances.

Eventually, he simply nodded. "He did; a lovely woman from Haversham."

"Excellent. It would be nice to visit you and Luthor while actually enjoying a woman's company. Perhaps we should invite them to join us for the movies. There's supposedly a fascinating film showing at the Majestic tomorrow night."

Simon smiled, knowing he could hardly deny Veronica once she had a thought firmly affixed in her mind.

"I make no promises, but I'll ask. Do be aware that Matilda is not quite… well, her upbringing lacks a level of civility we're used to seeing in the capital."

"Uncouth?" she chided. "Clearly, you have no idea what it's like to be in your company."

"You're hilarious," Simon replied flatly. "How much longer before you're finished for the evening?"

Veronica glanced at the clock hung above the changing room's doorway. "I have one more show in ten minutes and then I'll be finished. Will you stay and watch?"

"You couldn't pay me enough to miss your show."

Veronica smiled. "Fantastic. Now get out. I have to change and reapply makeup before I go on stage."

Simon arched an eyebrow. "I have to leave because you don't want to appear indecent in front of me, even after trying to ravage me moments ago?"

Veronica laughed and placed a hand on his chest while opening the door with the other. "Just get out."

She shoved him playfully on the chest, and he stumbled back into the hall. Veronica winked at him as she closed the changing room door.

Simon turned around with a broad smile cast upon his face. Directly behind him, the bouncer stood with his arms crossed over his massive chest. Gloria still sat at the vanity, shaking her head in mock indignation.

The Inquisitor cleared his throat politely as he quickly walked past both their disapproving stares and made his way back into the Ace of Spades' main hall.

CHAPTER Six

SIMON REMOVED HIS JACKET AND DRAPED IT OVER Veronica's shoulders as they walked. The night's air had turned colder. Between the humidity and gentle breeze blowing off the bay, the cold seemed to permeate their very clothing, chilling them both to their core.

Having recently returned from the frozen tundra, Simon shrugged off the cold as a mere irritant. He doubted he would have a true need for his jacket as anything more than a fashion piece until, perhaps, the next winter. Veronica, however, clearly lacked his natural warmth as she shivered during their brief walk to her home.

"You performed amazingly well tonight," he said as they walked between the pools of lamplight.

Veronica leaned into him, and he wrapped his arm over her shoulders. Her short dress fluttered in the breeze, and her stocking-covered legs were hardly protected against the chill.

"I'm glad you were able to watch me dance," she replied. "When I know you're in the audience, it feels like I'm dancing just for you."

"Me, the noble near the front, the oddly obsessive little man in the corner, and the dozens of other men and women filling every available seat."

Veronica poked him playfully in the ribs. "Only an Inquisitor peruses every face in the audience. Everyone else is there for their personal entertainment."

"It's both my blessing and my curse," he replied.

They stopped before a nondescript brick building. A doorman stood by the front door, illuminated by the light that spilled from the building's interior. He tipped his hat to Simon and Veronica as the couple turned and approached the apartment building's entryway.

"Good evening, Ms. Dawn," the doorman said. He tipped his hat toward Simon as well. "Inquisitor Whitlock."

Veronica pulled Simon's pocket watch from his vest and pressed the button at the top, swinging its silver covering open. She smiled momentarily at the sight of her own face staring up at her from the watch's left side. Her gaze drifted to the watch face as she looked at the time.

"It's hardly evening any longer, Mr. Jackson," Veronica replied. "I do believe it's already slipped into morning."

The doorman motioned toward the nearly moonless night above. "With this darkness, madam, it hardly seems right to call it morning."

Mr. Jackson pulled the doorway open, holding it as Simon and Veronica entered the lobby. Once they were firmly inside, the doorman stepped through himself, closing the door behind him.

He motioned toward the collapsible metal gate blocking a doorway near the front desk. "Will you be requiring the elevator this evening?"

Veronica looked up at Simon before shaking her head. "Thank you, but no. I believe we'll take the stairs."

"Very good, madam." The doorman tipped his hat once more before opening the front door again. "I wish you both a wonderful rest of your evening."

"Thank you, Mr. Jackson," she replied.

As the doorman retreated back into the dark cold of the night, Simon led Veronica to the stairwell. They climbed the broad stairs to the third floor before stopping on the landing. The long hallway led away from the landing in both directions. Without pause, Simon and Veronica walked along the plush carpet toward her apartment.

Stopping at the door, she opened her clutch, retrieving her keys from within. She slid her door key into the lock and turned it, but met no resistance. With a quick twist, she withdrew her key and dropped it back into her purse.

"Gloria must already be home," Veronica replied.

They opened the door and entered the small, two-bedroom apartment. The living room they entered was dominated by a leather couch, on which the blonde dancer sat enjoying an evening cup of tea. Her blonde curls were pulled back, held in place by a series of clips. She had foregone her revealing clothing for a long sleeping gown. She seemed very domesticated compared to the woman Simon had seen earlier in the night.

"I wasn't certain you would be home tonight," Gloria remarked as she blew on the top of her steaming cup of tea.

Veronica glanced up at Simon and smiled. "We took our time on the way home."

"Tea?" the blonde offered.

Veronica shook her head. "No, but thank you. I believe we'll be going to bed shortly."

"To bed, certainly," Gloria chided, "but not to sleep."

Simon blushed and was glad when Veronica led him toward one of the apartment's bedrooms.

"Goodnight, you two," Gloria called after them.

Veronica led him into the bedroom and quickly pushed the door closed. In a fluid motion, she brushed off both her and Simon's jackets, letting them fall forgotten to the floor. She glanced up at the Inquisitor and he reached forward, brushing a wayward strand of dark hair from her face. Sliding his hand around the nape of her neck, he pulled her to him.

Simon pushed the covers aside and swung his legs out of bed. He flinched as his bare feet struck the cold, wooden floor. After a moment of acclimation, he stood, naked in the chilled night air.

He walked to the window, pausing before the radiator heater and letting the warmth soak into his cold skin. After a satisfying moment of warmth, he leaned forward and retrieved his underwear and pants from the floor where they had been haphazardly tossed upon their arrival.

"Are you leaving so soon?" Veronica asked from her place in the bed, evidently disappointed that he had left her side.

Simon turned toward her. Her dark hair was splayed across her pillow. Her face was still flushed from exertion. Though the down comforter covered her body, he could imagine every curve of her naked skin beneath.

"Sadly, I must," Simon replied as he retrieved his undershirt and dress shirt from the floor as well. "I must get home and get at least some rest before I face the Inquisitors again tomorrow."

"You could rest here," she offered. "You don't always have to leave me so soon afterward."

Simon smiled wistfully. "We've spoken of this before. It won't do for an Inquisitor to be seen sullying the good name of an unmarried woman. It's indecent."

Veronica frowned. "You regularly visit a burlesque house and admitted to me that all Inquisitors suffer such vices. Why not just stay?"

Simon slipped his undershirt over his head. As he tucked it into his trousers, he walked to her bedside. "It's not the fact that we suffer from vices. Everyone knows that we're only human; it's that very quality that makes us so effective as Inquisitors. Yet the normal man has an expectation of a *perception* of decency as it pertains to their Inquisitors. They may know that we have our vices, they just don't want to see us appearing so, well, human."

"Everything about that sounds preposterous."

He sat down on the edge of the bed and ran his fingertips across her cheek. "I agree, darling, but I'm a servant to public perception."

She slipped away from his touch and rolled away, turning her back to him. "It makes me feel cheap, that you can't even stay the night, as though I were nothing more than your whore."

Simon paused, genuinely hurt at the insinuation. He leaned forward until his arms were draped over her covered waist. "You're a far better woman than any woman of court." He sighed as she refused to turn and meet his gaze. "I can stay, if you'd like."

She shook her head without turning around. "No, I think you should go."

Simon felt the jab of disappointment at her casual dismissal. "Will I see you tonight? I'll ask Luthor and Mattie if they would join us for a movie."

She turned quickly toward him with tears still shining in her eyes. "I'd like that. Perhaps another woman's opinion could talk some sense into you."

Simon thought about Mattie's brash outspokenness and smiled. "You have no idea how thrilled I am at the prospect of the two of you conspiring together."

"Do you think they would come to church with us this weekend?" she asked.

Simon frowned. His own predilection was to avoid the church services as well. It wasn't that he wasn't spiritual, but Simon had a hard time accepting faith in a spiritual being that performed obvious feats of magic in a time when his sole purpose was to eliminate the physical manifestations of that very same mystical energy. Furthermore, he doubted his mastery of debate would serve him well enough to convince Luthor, who had never truly spoken of religion one way or another, and Matilda, a savage werewolf raised without the convenience of the Callifax Abbey, to accompany them to church.

"I will ask," Simon said finally. "It's the best I can promise."

Veronica slipped an arm free of the blanket, revealing more of her body in the process than Simon was sure she intended. She reached up and touched his cheek. "I'll see you tonight for the movie. We can discuss it with them then, perhaps. I love you, Simon."

Simon leaned forward and kissed her sweetly upon the lips. "I love you as well. Until tonight."

Simon finished dressing and walked into the empty living room. The door to Gloria's room was closed, so he let himself out, locking the door behind him as he went.

He strode down the stairs, reaching the lobby in all haste. The doorman noted his approach from the other side of the glass door and pulled it open before he reached the entryway.

"Are you leaving us so soon?" the doorman asked.

Simon frowned and glowered at the well-meaning man. "Don't you start with me, too."

The doorman merely smiled innocently. "Have a good evening, Inquisitor."

"You, too," Simon replied as he walked into the dark night.

CHAPTER

Seven

THE GRAND INQUISITOR SAT AT HIS DESK. THE GRAND Hall was silent except for the muted footsteps of the few guards still pacing the complex. The Inquisitors were all asleep in their own beds or, as Simon had so recently been, enjoying the experiences of the capital's nightlife.

Though much of the Inquisitors' business was conducted during the day, the Grand Inquisitor found that the late hours of the night were the only time he could find peace and solitude. A stack of mission requests were stacked high on the edge of his desk awaiting his approval, matched by an equally large pile of folders of completed missions that still required his reading. Though the Inquisitors hired analysts to search for trends amongst the founded magical outbreaks, the Grand Inquisitor still insisted upon his personal review of every mission.

A single oil lamp sat upon the man's desk, illuminating the room with its flickering light. The Grand Inquisitor shifted in his chair and examined the wall beside him, where a series of grainy, black-and-white photographs had been framed and mounted upon the wall. The pictures were mostly faded from age, their once white paper yellowing and curling along the corners. Still, a much more youthful Grand Inquisitor stared back from many of the pictures. Though it had been only ten years since the founding of the Inquisitors, he felt greatly aged over the course of the past decade.

With a sigh, he shifted his gaze back to the two dominating piles of folders competing for his attention. He reached toward the finished reports but his hand hovered. Slowly, his hand drifted instead toward the cases still requiring an Inquisitor's assignment.

Pulling the topmost folder from the pile, he opened it before him. He quickly scanned the synopsis provided by the analyst who initially received the report. The file spoke of witchcraft in the marshlands to the north of the capital. No substantial evidence had been provided by the local council and, in the analyst's opinion, it was questionable whether anything substantial would be uncovered by an Inquisitor's intervention.

For a brief moment, the Grand Inquisitor considered rejecting the mission but at the last moment, he retrieved his pen and scribbled a name along the bottom of the report. An Inquisitor had now been assigned, for good or bad. He closed the folder and placed it onto a newly formed pile before sighing, realizing he was now finished with only one of dozens of reports awaiting his personal attention.

The Grand Inquisitor reached for the next folder on the stack but instead shifted his attention back to the completed mission reports. He retrieved the top folder and opened it, quickly reviewing the handwritten calligraphy of the Inquisitor who had been assigned. Like so many others, the report had been unfounded, with the reports of ghosts in the dense woodlands being nothing more than wind chimes and whistles hung from high branches by bandits in an attempt to protect their hideout and subsequent treasure. The Inquisitor had summarily decimated the bandit camp and retrieved much of the stolen coin, so the mission hadn't been a complete failure, though the local constabulary could have easily handled the case without Inquisitor intervention.

The Grand Inquisitor wrote a few minor remarks at the bottom of the report and closed the folder, placing it atop the one from moments before.

He nearly reached for a folder from the first pile, alternating back to those awaiting Inquisitor assignment, but the word "Haversham" stared at him from the top of the next completed mission folder. Curiously, the Grand Inquisitor drew Simon's report from the top of the pile and placed it before him.

As he opened the folder, Simon's small, tight handwriting was glaringly apparent. Like many of the things in his life, Simon's handwriting was reflective of a man who attempted to place as much as he could in as little space or time as possible. His handwriting was efficient and crisp, foregoing much of the floweriness that marked most of the handwriting of the age. The Grand Inquisitor smiled, knowing how many times he belabored the point to Simon during their tenure together as mentor and apprentice.

The Grand Inquisitor began reading the report with more attentiveness than he had offered the two previous ones. The slaying of a demon was worth his attention, not to mention the corpses of the two werewolves Simon returned as well.

As the Grand Inquisitor concluded the first page and began reading the second, his smile began to falter. His smile quickly became a flat effect on his face, which in turn deepened to a frown that was borderline disappointment and outright anger.

By the time he finished the last sentence of Simon's report, he slammed it closed. For a moment, he merely sat in silence. The Grand Inquisitor interlaced his fingers and rested them on the table as his face flushed with disappointment.

Taking a deep breath, he unlaced his fingers and slid a hand beneath his robe, retrieving a key kept upon a chain around his neck. He slipped the chain over his head and used it to unlock the drawer by his left elbow. The drawer slid open, revealing a small ensemble of seemingly innocuous items, to include a letter opener, a long quill, and what appeared to be a miniaturized snow globe. The Grand Inquisitor took Simon's report and dropped it into the drawer before closing and locking it quickly.

From the drawer to his right, he retrieved a sheet of parchment and placed it before him on the table. On the parchment, he wrote five simple words before folding the parchment neatly. He lifted the glass globe that covered the oil lantern and set it aside, exposing the flickering wick within. From the same desk drawer, the Grand Inquisitor took a stick of red wax, which he held to the flame. As it began to run, he removed it from the fire and pressed it against the seam of the note, sealing the parchment shut. Before the wax could cool, the Grand Inquisitor slipped a ring from his finger and pressed the signet ring into the pool of wax. As he withdrew the ring, the perfect form of the Inquisitor's seal was visible in the center.

Pushing back from his table, he carried the note across the room, opened the door, and stepped into the hallway.

"Messenger!" the Grand Inquisitor yelled into the hallway.

A few doors down, a door flung open and a young man rushed to his side. The young letter carrier, kept on retainer specifically for purposes such as these, stood at rapt attention at the man's side.

"I need this to be delivered to the residence of Inquisitor Whitlock at first light," the Grand Inquisitor said, his voice intentionally softened despite the gruff irritation he felt. "You know where he resides?"

"I do, sir," the messenger replied.

"Good. At first light, do not be late."

The messenger shook his head hastily. "No, sir."

The carrier took the letter and stuffed it into the inner pocket of his oversized jacket. The boy rushed back to his room to get some rest before he had to depart.

The Grand Inquisitor waited for the boy to close the door behind him before walking back into his office. He shook his head softly and frowned to no one in particular.

"Simon, you damnable fool. What have you done?"

A bothersome knock sounded at Simon's front door. He opened his eyes a crack. Though the dim light of dawn was barely creeping through his window, he didn't feel nearly rested enough to face the day as of yet. He closed his eyes again, hoping that whoever rapped at his door would soon leave him be.

Moments later, the knock sounded again, louder and more insistent than the time before.

Uncoordinatedly, Simon reached toward his pocket watch resting on the nightstand beside his bed. For a moment, he considered reaching past the watch toward the silver-plated revolver that lay beyond it, but he thought better of it. Tilting the watch toward him, he saw that it was barely past six in the morning. At most, he had been asleep for four hours.

With a groan, Simon slid his legs over the side of the bed and rested his face in his hands. His feet sought the slippers that sat somewhere along the side of his bed. Before he could locate the offending slippers, the incessant knock sounded once more.

"I'm coming," Simon grumbled, though he knew no one could hear him from his upstairs bedroom. "Be patient."

His toes touched the tops of the slippers, and he slid his feet into the warm shoes. Placing his hands on his knees, he pushed himself upright. A smoking jacket hung upon a hook on the back of his bedroom door. He retrieved the jacket, slipping it over his pajamas.

As he tied the belt around his waist, the persistent visitor knocked for a fourth time.

"I said I'm coming," Simon yelled, hoping that his visitor could hear his inflamed reply.

With a quiet string of profanity, Simon walked downstairs and into his foyer. A round window on the door was beveled, leaving the features of the knocker distorted. He could make out the person's youth only from his height and generally narrow build, but he could tell little else.

He unlocked the door and opened it to his visitor.

A young boy looked up excitedly. He quickly removed his hat, holding it to his chest.

"What is it, boy?" Simon asked coarsely.

"Pardon the interruption at such an early hour, sir," the boy began.

"I believe I would have used the term 'ungodly hour,' but do go on," Simon replied.

"Yes, sir," the boy continued, clearly familiar with gruff responses from his patrons.

Simon arched his eyebrow toward the boy as the young man merely stood in his presence. "What brings you to my door at such an ungodly hour?"

His question spurred the boy into action. He pulled his hat away from his chest and reached into an inside pocket of his jacket. From within, he pulled free a neatly folded letter. A red wax seal was emblazoned upon the front of the correspondence.

"I have a letter for you, sir," the boy replied.

Simon nearly asked the origin of the letter but immediately recognized the Inquisitor's seal. He frowned as he quickly took it. The boy stood patiently at the door, as though he had a further need to be in Simon's presence.

"Is there something more to deliver?" Simon asked.

The boy looked at him but shook his head. With a sigh, Simon realized why he was still standing by patiently. The Inquisitor looked to the interior table beside the doorway and noted a pair of copper coins. He took the coins and shoved them into the boy's outstretched hand.

"Be gone," Simon replied curtly.

The boy slung his hat back onto his head, leaving it dilapidated and crooked as he nodded to the Inquisitor. "Thank you kindly, sir."

The young messenger hurried down the townhouse stairs and ran down the street, back in the direction of the Grand Hall. Simon had no doubt he would report back to the Grand Inquisitor that his mission had been a success.

Simon closed the door and locked it behind him before breaking the seal on the letter. The wax cracked along its base, leaving the seal intact as Simon unfolded the letter.

With the parchment unfolded, he read the five simple words written across the middle of the page. The letter had no signature, but he had recognized the seal and knew the elder man's handwriting well enough.

The letter read simply:

I want to meet her.

Simon frowned and reread the letter, as though a secret continuation of the message would soon present itself. He knew more than well enough whom the Grand Inquisitor meant. Clearly, he had finally read Simon's report. However, those five deceptively simple words revealed nothing of the author's state of mind, whether he was calmly curious or infuriated.

I want to meet her.

Simon surmised that it was good the letter hadn't read, "Bring her to me at once." The second connotation was clearly angrier. Still, it wouldn't do to keep the Grand Inquisitor waiting for any amount of time.

Simon set the letter on the same table from which he had retrieved the copper coins before he hurried upstairs to bathe and hastily dress.

CHAPTER *Eight*

"**NO,**" **LUTHOR SAID ADAMANTLY AS HE PACED ACROSS** the sitting room floor.

"No?" Simon asked, arching an eyebrow inquisitively.

Luthor stopped and stared at his friend. "I won't drag Mattie before the Grand Inquisitor. Everything about that seems like an ill-advised idea."

Simon leaned back in the chair and crossed his legs. "I'm not entirely convinced refusing is really an option."

"There's always a choice."

Simon uncrossed his legs and leaned forward. "While you're technically correct, I'm fairly certain that refusing the Grand Inquisitor's invitation constitutes a poor life choice. It is, in fact, the type of life choice that significantly shortens one's life."

Luthor threw up his hands in disgust. "You should have never told him in the first place, sir. You had no right."

"It wasn't an issue of right and wrong, dear Luthor. It was an issue of responsibility. You yourself wanted this acceptance of Mattie and her ilk to progress. This is how it progresses."

Luthor finally stopped his pacing and took a seat across from Simon. "Maybe, but of all your acquaintances amongst the Inquisitors, was it absolutely necessary to tell the Grand Inquisitor?"

"Of all the Inquisitors, he's the most prone to support our cause."

"True, so long as he doesn't string us up by our necks first, or have us drawn and quartered. Perhaps he'd have us burned at the stake instead for heresy."

Simon shook his head. "If we were to ignore the Grand Inquisitor's invitation, what then?"

"I don't know," Luthor admitted. "We'd run, perhaps; take a zeppelin to the far reaches of the continent."

"Sail south, perhaps, into Khovus? I'm sure the Khovelian Knights would be beyond thrilled to have someone of your stature joining their ranks. Then again, I don't believe they'd be overtly keen to the idea of a werewolf in their midst. Certainly you'd be fine, so long as she never revealed her true nature."

"You're an insufferable bore, sir."

"Breathe deeply, Luthor. You're overreacting. You'll be prone to bouts of hysteria if you're not more careful."

Luthor narrowed his eyes dangerously but bit his tongue.

"I should have a say in this, shouldn't I?" Mattie asked from the doorway to the kitchen.

Both men turned toward the redhead, who merely folded her arms defiantly across her chest. "By all means, don't let me interrupt your heated discussion. Finish so that I might find out my fate, as it was decided by two men, neither of whom, I might add, have any claim to my life and subsequent well-being."

Luthor flushed with embarrassment but Simon merely arched his eyebrow, encouraging her to continue.

"Luthor," she said as she walked over and sat beside the apothecary, "I am truly touched by your genuine concern for my health. Simon, likewise, you are trying your best to fulfill the request made by both Luthor and me when we left Haversham. I can find no fault with either of your positions. However, this decision has to be mine alone and I would like to meet the Grand Inquisitor."

Simon's heart pounded in his chest as they entered the Grand Hall. The morning was quiet around the Inquisitors' offices. The great meeting had concluded a few days earlier, and many of the Inquisitors and Pellites had returned to their distal stations. A few remained, those awaiting assignments or recently returned, like Simon himself.

A valet took their hats and coats. Mattie drew her hands across her stomach as her thick jacket was taken. Her nervousness was palpable as she glanced periodically around the expansive entry hall. Her hands drifted upward and tugged on the tight collar of her dress.

"Quit tugging on it or the whole thing will tear," Luthor warned.

Mattie frowned. "I feel like a very weak man is trying to choke me to death, as though this whole day is going to result in my very slow demise. This dress, this interview, the entire thing is excessive. Why couldn't I have simply worn my normal clothes?"

Luthor touched her elbow and tried to look confident for her, though he was equally as nervous. "Your normal clothes make you look like a woman from the northern tribes."

"I am a woman from the northern tribes," she hissed.

"A fact that we wish to downplay as much as possible today, not just for your benefit but for your tribe. The Grand Inquisitor expects a savage, not a formal lady of court."

Simon could see the sheen of sweat along her exposed neckline as she pulled on her collar once more.

"Don't worry, Matilda," Simon said in an attempt to be reassuring. "There's nothing to fear."

The apothecary glared at Simon. "Have you taken leave of your senses?" Luthor asked, his voice a harsh whisper. "There are a hundred things of which she should be afraid right now, nearly all of which are your fault."

They fell silent as a few Inquisitors passed them. Those that walked to and fro nodded in deference to Simon, the demon slayer. Under normal circumstances, Simon might have felt a keen sense of pride at the respect shown, but for now all he felt was the same unbridled fear that was portrayed on both Luthor and Mattie's expressions.

Mattie forced her attention away from the ground and occupied her time examining the marble busts set into alcoves around the room. Each bore a plaque beneath the stone face, telling the story of the Inquisitor who had come and passed. She only halfheartedly read the inscriptions, though most of the causes of death were fairly mundane. One Inquisitor died of natural causes while examining a sudden and inexplicable illness in the marshlands. Another was thrown from his horse after returning from an assignment. None were slaughtered by hordes of magical beasts, as she would have expected. Only one that she found was slain by anything closely resembling a magical creature, and that was only because the man was crushed after a pixie spooked a wagon that, in the driver's haste to avoid the fairy, tipped onto the Inquisitor investigating the claim.

"Inquisitor Whitlock," a servant said as he approached the trio. "The Grand Inquisitor will see you now."

They exchanged glances before turning and following the servant, walking into the narrow hallway beyond the meeting chamber. The Grand Inquisitor's office appeared shortly thereafter, his seal emblazoned upon the wall beside the doorframe.

The door was closed, and the servant rapped gently. After a moment's hesitation, a quiet but stern voice from within replied, "Enter."

The servant opened the door and stepped aside. They received no fanfare or announcement of their arrival. Instead, they were quickly ushered into the chamber and the door hastily drawn behind them.

Pulling thick glasses from his nose and setting them on the table before him, the Grand Inquisitor looked up from a report. From his vantage point, Simon could clearly see his own handwriting, its small, compact letters exceptionally distinct amongst the more traditionally flowery prose of his peers.

The Grand Inquisitor offered no salutation to either Simon or Luthor, instead locking his gaze on Mattie. He pushed away from the table and stood. He walked around the table and approached the redheaded woman, who wore a brave façade, though her nervousness practically oozed from her pores.

"Is this her?" the Grand Inquisitor asked. His eyes never left Mattie, but his question was clearly directed at Simon.

Simon cleared his throat, knowing his future not just as an Inquisitor but as a living, breathing man hung in the balance.

"Yes, sir. May I present to you Miss Matilda Hawke."

The Grand Inquisitor harrumphed and walked slowly around Mattie. At first, she turned with him until he placed his hand sternly on her shoulder, keeping her in place. She bit her bottom lip as he finished his perusal and returned to stand before her.

"She doesn't look like much," the Grand Inquisitor remarked. "Are you sure she's this… werewolf?"

"*She* is standing right in front of you, sir," Mattie replied angrily, "and would greatly appreciate it if you could address her as though she were a cognizant woman rather than an inanimate object."

The Grand Inquisitor looked down on the brash redhead. "In Callifax, women know not to speak unless spoken to."

Mattie placed her hands on her hips. "Then I'm thrilled to not be from the capital. Where I'm from, women carry spears and stab insolent men in the throat for lesser offenses."

Simon swallowed hard and prayed to any deity that would listen that they weren't immediately executed. From his periphery, he could see Luthor tensing at her brash rebuttal. Simon added a second prayer that Luthor could hold his tongue through the rest of this interrogation, for that was truly what it had become.

The Grand Inquisitor walked back around his desk and sat once more.

"I would like to see the… other you," the Grand Inquisitor said, his tone leaving little interpretation that it was an order far more than it was a question. "I'd like to see the wolf."

Mattie glanced toward Luthor, who gritted his teeth but nodded. They had little option. She returned her gaze to the Grand Inquisitor.

"You understand that there are extenuating circumstances to my transformation, most glaringly of which is that I must be nude."

The Grand Inquisitor coughed politely. "Of course."

He turned his chair toward the far wall. Simon and Luthor turned away from Mattie as she stripped out of her clothing. They listened as her boots clicked on the wooden floor as she removed them. Her belt was dropped upon a pile of clothing, its buckle still ringing as it struck the hardwood. Following the belt, there was a dense silence in the room.

Simon fought the urge to glance over his shoulder, though he wasn't sure if it was more likely that he would see a naked Mattie, a werewolf, or nothing at all as she fled from the room. Instead, he kept his focus on the series of weathered photographs mounted on the wall.

The silence was broken by a guttural growl, one that portrayed a combination of pain and predatory glee. Something tore, like paper being shredded. The smell in the air was pungent, like a wet dog, Simon realized with a frown. He needn't turn around to know that her transformation was complete. He had seen her transform many times before and it was always disturbing to see the diminutive woman tearing at her flesh with sharpened fingernails, exposing the stark white fur beneath the bloody gashes in her skin.

Without warning, Mattie, now fully transformed, padded around the trio on all fours. She appeared far less like a werewolf and much more like a massive winter wolf, one far larger than Simon would have believed possible from the short redhead, had he not previously seen it with his own eyes.

The Grand Inquisitor sank further into his chair as her large maw turned toward him. Her eyes were nearly black as she stared at him, her nose rising and falling as she sniffed the edges of his heavy robe.

"Is… is this her?" the Grand Inquisitor stammered.

Simon smiled, for once feeling back in control of the situation. "Sir, once again, I would like to introduce Miss Matilda Hawke."

Mattie pulled her snout from the elder man, allowing him room to stand. The Grand Inquisitor stepped forward cautiously until his outstretched hand hovered inches away from Mattie's snout. She quickly turned her head and nuzzled his hand with her cheek. His hand sank into the thick, white fur.

"Remarkable," the Grand Inquisitor said. "It doesn't seem feral or aggressive at all."

"She, sir," Simon corrected. "Not it."

The Grand Inquisitor turned toward Simon. "Would it be okay if I touched her again?"

Simon shrugged. "That's hardly up to me, sir. You'd have to ask Ms. Hawke."

"You mean she can understand me, even in her more primitive state?"

"I can do far more than understand you," Mattie said. Though her voice was far more guttural and coarse, it was still unmistakably hers.

The Grand Inquisitor turned sharply back toward Mattie. "You can speak?"

"Did you expect that I turned into a mindless predator after the transformation?" she asked, her canine lips bending and twisting oddly as she pronounced each word.

"Forgive me, madam, but I actually did."

Mattie reared back, lifting her front paws from the ground and balancing on her back legs. She was able to look the Grand Inquisitor in the eyes, even as he stepped slowly away from her more imposing posture.

She placed her front paws on her hips in a mock of the position she took when defiantly speaking to the Grand Inquisitor earlier. The familiarity seemed to give the elder man pause, and he tilted his head inquisitively.

"Rest assured, sir, that I'm very much in control of my faculties," she explained. "My imposing visage is in no way an underpinning of a monster hidden within. It's merely, forgive the pun, another face that I wear."

"Truly remarkable," the Grand Inquisitor remarked. "Please, madam, I've seen enough. You may change back now."

Mattie walked over to her discarded pile of clothes on the floor and reached down, retrieving her blouse from the pile. She held it tightly between her paw and opposable thumb, feeling the fabric even through the thick pads on her palm.

"If it's all the same, gentlemen," Mattie said, "I would appreciate the courtesy of turning around once more. I'll be returning to human form as naked as a newborn babe."

Simon invited the men to his side. Again, they turned toward the far wall. The sound of her fur sloughing from her body was nauseating, and Simon hated the thought of the filth that was certainly piled upon the Grand Inquisitor's immaculately kept office. Within seconds, Mattie cleared her throat and the men turned toward her.

She was fully dressed once more, looking very similar to the way she had appeared upon her arrival, save for the new dampness to her hair. At her feet, a gelatin oozed across the ground, intermixed with faint clouts of white hair. As they watched, the sludge evaporated, filling the room with a musky mist before dissipating completely. The floor appeared slick with moisture but otherwise untarnished.

The Grand Inquisitor motioned toward the chairs on the near side of his desk. He walked around the table and sat in his own high-backed chair.

As they sat, he glanced toward Mattie. "You're not at all what I expected."

Mattie smiled reassuringly. "I've heard that many more times than you would believe."

"No, no, I'm quite certain I know exactly how many times you've heard that phrase recently," he replied, glancing toward Simon and Luthor.

"Forgive the intrusion, sir," Luthor said as the Grand Inquisitor made eye contact, "but I feel that we need to discuss what happens next. You've seen now that there's far more to Ms. Hawke than a mere title like 'werewolf' can truly do justice."

The apothecary glanced nervously toward Simon, as though he realized he had suddenly overstepped his bounds as a mere observer. Despite his awkward position, he cleared his throat and continued.

"I guess what I'm asking, sir, is… what are your intentions?"

The Grand Inquisitor sat back in his chair and stroked his chin thoughtfully. "I would refrain from providing an answer at this time."

Luthor began to speak but the Grand Inquisitor raised his hand, silencing him. "That's not to say that I've made a decision one way or another. You've provided me far more to consider than I would have thought possible when this day began."

Simon nodded. "Sir, we understand the conundrum in which we've placed you and, for that, we apologize."

"As well you should," the elder man quickly replied. "Mr. Strong and Ms. Hawke, please give us the room. There is some Inquisitor business that I must address with Inquisitor Whitlock."

Luthor glanced nervously toward the Inquisitor, but Simon nodded his approval. Hesitantly, Luthor and Mattie stood from their chairs. They walked to the door, opened it, and disappeared into the hallway. The door swung shut behind them and closed with a click of its lock.

Simon took a deep breath as he looked at his former mentor's somber expression. "Sir, I believe I can explain—"

"Have you taken a leave of your senses?" the Grand Inquisitor asked, striking the report with his open hand. Simon leapt at the sound. "You have brought a werewolf into the heart of our kingdom, within a stone's throw from the castle itself? Have you gone mad?"

"You've read my report, sir," Simon replied calmly. "You've seen Ms. Hawke with your own eyes. You know that things are a bit more complicated than we originally believed."

Simon leaned forward in his chair as he continued. "These are our citizens, not monsters ripped from the bosom of the Rift. They aren't here to overthrow our sovereignty. Quite the opposite—they're men and women loyal to the crown."

The Grand Inquisitor threw up his hands in disgust. "For someone so astute, you are absolutely blinded by this case. Bringing her here puts us all at risk. I don't merely mean your life and that of your apothecary companion. I don't even mean my own life, since I am now privy to your report. If word were to escape of what you've done, it would tarnish the very credibility of our organization. Our name and reputation would be worthless, if the people knew that we harbored monsters."

Simon bit his lip until he tasted coppery blood in his mouth. "What would you have done, were our roles reversed? Would you have slaughtered the tribesmen? I ask simply because I know I couldn't. I'm many things, sir, but I'm not an executioner."

The Grand Inquisitor leaned back in his chair and brushed the stray strands of hair from his face. "The three corpses that you brought with you from Haversham would say otherwise. You are very much an executioner, Simon. That's the very expectation of being an Inquisitor."

Simon shook his head. "On the contrary, sir, that's the very definition of being a Pellite. We're supposed to be better than they are."

The two men sat in silence, staring intently at one another in a quiet battle of wills. The Grand Inquisitor finally reached up and stroked his chin thoughtfully.

Taking Simon's report from Haversham, he closed it. He opened a drawer beside him and placed the report into it. With a key he retrieved from around his neck, he locked it tightly, ensuring it would be available for his eyes only.

"You've lost some perspective, Simon, perspective about what it is you were commissioned to do for the crown. You jeopardized everything we have worked for over the past decade, though your reasons are a mystery to me. Return to your homes and await my response. Whatever you do, Inquisitor, keep her close to your side at all times. You walk a fine line and play a very dangerous game with all your lives."

Simon frowned but nodded his consent. "In the interim, sir, we would ask the same discretion from you."

The Grand Inquisitor frowned as well. "You have some gall, but I shall grant your request."

Simon stood, understanding their meeting was at an end. "Thank you, sir. I look forward to your next missive."

He quickly exited the Grand Inquisitor's office, pulling the door shut behind him. Luthor sighed disappointedly when he noticed Simon's expression, though the Inquisitor revealed nothing of his private conversation. For a long moment, they merely stood in the hallway, absorbing all that had transpired.

"Everyone looks like a ghost has passed over their grave," Mattie said. "What happened after we left?"

"Let's just agree that it certainly could have gone worse and leave it at that," Simon finally said, breaking the sullen mood that had settled over the group.

The Inquisitor turned away from the pair and walked toward the building's entrance. Luthor shook his head and took Mattie's hand, leading her down the hall and past a small throng of conversing Pellites, as they followed Simon's departure.

CHAPTER *Nine*

"It wasn't being flippant earlier," Simon said as they rode in the back of the automobile. "It absolutely could have gone worse."

The clunky, black car rattled along the cobblestone street as the taxi driver drove them toward their respective townhouses.

"It could have also gone far better, sir," Luthor said morosely. "In what bizarre world did you believe that the Grand Inquisitor would be a champion for acceptance of a werewolf in Callifax?"

Simon chose not to reply, instead glancing out the window at the buildings that rolled slowly by.

"I'm not entirely certain what all this means for me," Mattie said nervously. "I know I wasn't taken from his chamber in shackles, but somehow, I doubt I'm truly a free woman any longer."

"You're not a prisoner," Simon replied without turning back toward them, "but it would be wise to stay close for the foreseeable future."

"So in essence I'm shackled to you by invisible manacles?" she asked, disgusted. "It's not a reassuring solution to our problem."

"Then what shall we do from here?" Luthor asked. "Will you take up residence on my couch to ensure we don't leave Callifax in the dead of night?"

Simon turned back toward them and sighed. "I don't have the answers you seek, either of you. I don't intend to suspend my life at the behest of the Grand Inquisitor, and neither should either of you."

"Are you proposing we just continue our lives as though none of this transpired, sir?" Luthor asked.

"To a degree, that's exactly what I mean," Simon said, suddenly more enthusiastic about the conversation at hand.

Luthor arched his eyebrow, knowing Simon's varying moods all too well. "I presume you have something planned?"

"Veronica has been begging to meet Mattie, and I believe tonight might be the best opportunity. There's a film showing at the Majestic, about which Veronica has heard nothing but rave reviews. Come out tonight and watch a moving picture with us."

Luthor glanced toward Mattie, who merely shrugged noncommittally. The apothecary wasn't sure Mattie had ever had the pleasure of watching a film, but the idea of leaving the townhouse tonight seemed mentally exhausting.

"Perhaps another night, sir. Tonight might be better spent recuperating from our ordeal."

Mattie placed her hand on his. "No. Though I'm loathed to admit it, Simon might very well be correct in this instance."

Simon furrowed his brow. "Why does everyone keep adding a caveat every time they admit that I'm correct? As often as I am correct, it's an exhausting habit."

Mattie smiled, though she wasn't entirely sure if Simon was speaking in jest or not. "We've spent very little time outside the four walls of the townhouse since our arrival and the few misadventures we've taken into the city, like today for instance, have not ended as I would have desired. A film, and meeting the mysterious Veronica Dawn, would be a welcomed distraction."

Luthor shrugged. "It appears we're accepting your invitation."

Simon smiled broadly. "Excellent. The film begins promptly at eight tonight."

The taxi rolled to a stop before their townhouses. The driver climbed quickly from his seat and opened the door so that the passengers could disembark. Simon set his top hat on his head as he climbed from the taxi, letting the brim of his hat block the warm sunlight. Luthor and Mattie followed suit. Reaching into his pocket, Simon retrieved a coin for the fare. The driver thanked them before climbing behind the wheel and sputtering away. The air was suddenly filled with noxious, black smoke as the automobile coughed soot from its tailpipe.

As the air cleared, Simon coughed softly. "I will have to meet Veronica before our date, so shall we simply meet at the Majestic at eight o'clock?"

Luthor nodded as he led Mattie toward their shared townhouse. "That sounds perfect, sir. We'll see you then."

The Majestic was a fairly nondescript building, nestled between taller apartment complexes. The two-story theater had a painted sign hanging from the upstairs balcony, announcing the name of the building. A smaller wooden sign hung below the Majestic's main sign, depicting the film that was currently showing. Blockish letters on the smaller sign read that tonight's film was "A Night on the Train," a film of which Luthor was completely unfamiliar. Truth be told, it had been ages since he had watched a moving picture. His enthusiasm was only slightly less than Mattie, who stood enraptured beside him.

"Do you see Simon?" Luthor asked, perusing the small throng of people milling about outside the theater.

Mattie craned her neck but quickly shook her head. "I don't, but we are early. Perhaps they have yet to arrive."

"Luthor. Mattie," Simon called from the midst of the crowd. He stepped out of the flow of pedestrian traffic with Veronica beside him. The brunette wore a far more formal dress than Luthor would have believed possible, considering her occupation. She smiled broadly at the apothecary, despite knowing his general feelings toward hers and Simon's relationship.

"Luthor, it's so good to see you again," Veronica said. "This must be the lovely Matilda, about whom I've heard so much." She leaned in close to Mattie and spoke just loudly enough for the two gentlemen to overhear. "You'd be absolutely amazed how often he speaks of you, as though you two share some devious secret."

Simon arched an eyebrow and smiled apologetically. "Nothing devious, I assure you, my love. Matilda simply has a practically animalistic personality."

Luthor frowned and glanced warningly toward his friend. In response, Simon merely smiled knowingly.

Mattie extended her hand to Veronica. "It's truly a pleasure to finally meet you, Veronica. Simon insists on referring to me by Matilda, but Mattie is just fine among friends."

Veronica shook her hand. "Then Mattie it shall be, since I'm assuming we'll become friends. It would do well to have another lady's touch around these brutish oafs."

Mattie glanced at the two gentlemen. "I do believe we will become friends, though I should warn you that 'lady' may be far too flattering a word for my capabilities."

"Has Luthor told you what it is I do for a profession?" Veronica asked bluntly.

Mattie nodded, though she glanced toward Luthor for assistance in what she assumed would quickly become an awkward situation.

"Then you're already well aware that being a true lady isn't exactly in my vocabulary either," Veronica finished, defusing the palpable nervousness.

Simon laughed, and the effect was intoxicating. The quartet continued laughing as Simon led them into the theater, handing their tickets to the doorman.

The interior of the Majestic was dimly lit. A number of electric lights were mounted to the wall, but their light failed to reach to the center of the expansive room. Most of the illumination was centered on the large, white screen hung from the back of the raised stage. The lights were covered in wooden clamshells, focusing all their light solely on the stage itself rather than blinding the audience members.

An usher met the group at the door and led them to their seats, which were situated near the middle of the theater. Simon turned as they entered their aisle, noting the narrow balcony high above. The rear doors to the interior balcony were open, revealing the night air and the external balcony beyond. A cool night's breeze filtered through the open doorways and cascaded down onto the audience below, cooling them in the otherwise warm theater.

Veronica sat and pulled Simon down beside her. Luthor sat beside the Inquisitor, with Mattie on the outside. They spoke little as other people entered the theater and found their seats. Before long, the theater was full of couples and individuals, all eager to watch the evening's affair. The din of conversation grew to a dull roar, so much so that Luthor had to lean close to Simon's ear just to be heard. After a few meager attempts, he simply quit trying to be heard and settled into his seat.

Simon pulled his pocket watch from his vest and checked the time. As the hands ticked around to eight o'clock, the house lights flickered on and off as a warning that the show would soon begin.

From the wings of the stage, a small band of assorted string and brass instruments emerged. They took their seats in a sunken pit just before the stage, practically disappearing from view. As the conversations fell silent around the room, the sound of tuning instruments filled the void.

In time, the instruments, too, were silenced and the house lights dimmed completely. Only a few lights along the side of the stage remained illuminated, revealing a dapperly dressed man as he emerged from behind the wing's curtains. The man withdrew a series of cards from his pocket, none of which were much larger than a telegram. He cleared his throat before he began reading. His booming voice easily filled the acoustically designed theater.

"Ladies and gentlemen," the announcer began, "welcome to the Majestic."

Polite applause rolled from the crowd.

"If you would please turn your attention to the screen before you, we will begin tonight's presentation."

From behind the group, the whir of a motor came to life. Simon glanced behind him as sepia light filtered through a narrow window in the back wall. He turned back around quickly as the image on the white canvas came into focus.

On the screen, a pair of heavily armored men stood stoically in the foreground, with a daunting castle looming in the distance behind them. The knights hoisted swords, pikes, and rifles as the narrator spoke again.

"For nearly ten generations, the Khovelian Knights have stood watch protectively over their kingdom. When it was threatened by the appearance of the Rift, the Khovelian Knights became a bastion of freedom, protecting not just their own kingdom but all the lands from the threat of magic. So long as the Knights have stood, our lands have been secured."

The silent image on the screen changed to a company of Knights standing around the slain body of a giant. The humanoid figure, even prone, appeared to be over fifteen feet tall.

"In ten generations, the Knights have never been defeated in battle. Even now, they patrol the edges of the Rift, slaying the abominations that seep from its demonic depths."

Simon leaned over toward Luthor. "I find the use of the word 'demonic' an interesting selection, don't you?"

"Ladies and gentlemen," the announcer continued, "please join me in showing our appreciation for the Khovelian Knights, our heroes and stalwart defenders of the freedoms we so richly enjoy."

The audience clapped politely again, though Simon could see some hesitation amongst the seated members. He wasn't at all surprised. Though the Khovelian Knights were very much aligned with the intents and purpose of the Inquisitors, the Kingdom of Khovus had hardly been an ally ten years earlier. The Rift had made strange bedfellows of the two kingdoms, though some of the elder population still remembered the tensions and sanctions levied against one another in their quiet, political war.

"Without further ado," the announcer said before quiet conversations could erupt throughout the room, "I present to you the acclaimed film, 'A Night on the Train.'"

The announcer stepped off stage, and the remaining stage lights dimmed. The projectionist held a bottle of brown fluid before the camera as the silent film began. As he rocked it back and forth, the liquid sloshed in the container. Its sepia projection, cast over the film's image of the interior of a rocking train, gave the audience the impression of movement on the screen.

As the film began, Veronica took Simon's hand in hers and squeezed it tightly. Though the moving picture had received rave reviews by critics and patrons alike, Simon absorbed little of what he watched that evening. He vaguely remembered a murder on a train, solved by a main character that resembled all but in title a Royal Inquisitor. Astute and perceptive, the man found clues where there were none and understood the nuances of the suspects on board the train. By the time the train arrived at its destination, the murder had been solved and the criminal brought to justice.

Simon sighed, wishing the solving of his cases was that simple.

As the silent film ended, the house lights came on and the audience shuffled toward the theater's rear doors. As they waited patiently in line for the throng of patrons to thin before making their own departure, Simon pulled his watch from his pocket. Pressing the button on its top, he opened the watch and checked the time. It read just before nine o'clock.

Looking up, Simon realized that there were only a few people remaining in the theater. Ushers waited patiently by the doors, eager to clean before retiring for the night.

The quartet stood and walked toward the building's exit. The night had turned colder while they were inside. Simon removed his coat and draped it over Veronica's shoulders. The brunette smiled sweetly toward the Inquisitor, and she pulled it tightly across her. Luthor, likewise, removed his jacket and offered it to Mattie, though they both knew it was unnecessary. Aside from living in a frozen tundra, Mattie's increased metabolism kept her warm despite the relative chill in the air.

"Forgive us, but we must head home," Luthor said as he stifled a yawn. "Mattie has made me promise to show her more of the city."

"This was truly an enjoyable evening," Veronica said. "We simply must do it again soon, though we should avoid attending another film. It was my fault, and I readily take blame, but it seems impersonal and doesn't offer us ladies a chance to get to know one another better. I hardly feel like I know the real you, Mattie."

"She's a bit beastly on the inside," Simon joked, which earned him a sharp elbow in the ribs from Mattie.

Veronica laughed. "Despite Simon's obvious lack of class, I'm so glad to see someone other than me putting him in his rightful place."

Simon rubbed his bruised side. "With a new bruise to add to my ever-growing repertoire, I believe that's our cue to say goodnight."

"Agreed," Luthor replied. "Veronica, it's always a pleasure."

"Always, Luthor."

Mattie took Veronica's hand. "We will certainly do this again. I can't help but feel you have a plethora of ammunition with which I could use against Simon the next time he decides to be rude."

Veronica squeezed her hand and offered a knowing wink. "More than you could ever know, but nothing I wouldn't feel too embarrassed to share."

Simon groaned and pulled Veronica away. "We simply must be off. Have a good evening."

"You as well, sir," Luthor replied.

Simon and Veronica turned as Luthor and Mattie signaled for a taxi. It was only a few blocks to the Ace of Spades and only a few more beyond that to Veronica's apartment, so they chose to walk rather than wait for another taxi to come by.

"Mattie seems very pleasant," Veronica remarked as they walked, hand in hand. "She and Luthor make a rather adorable couple, wouldn't you agree?"

Simon smiled. "An odd pairing, to be sure, but they seem to complement each other nicely."

Veronica smiled coyly. "An odd pairing? As odd as an Inquisitor courting a burlesque dancer?"

Simon glanced at his love and smiled mischievously, a look that clearly confused Veronica. "They are indeed far more odd a pairing than you could ever imagine. In due time, I look forward to explaining all their respective nuances."

In time, they arrived before Veronica's apartment. She paused at the door, even as the doorman held it open for her.

"Will you stay tonight?" she asked. "Just for this once?"

Simon smiled and brushed a strand of hair from out of her face.

"We'll see," he replied, a polite response, the answer to which Veronica already sadly knew.

CHAPTER Ten

BREAKING WHAT HAD EVOLVED INTO A MORNING ritual, Simon took his breakfast alone the next morning, choosing not to bother Luthor and Mattie. His dry toast and mediocre tea was hardly a good substitute for Luthor's more substantive morning meals, but the Inquisitor didn't feel prone to intrude. Instead, he glanced once more to the latest letter that had been delivered at an obscene hour. The Grand Inquisitor's seal was still evident, despite the severe crack that ran through its center from where Simon broke the wax globule.

He unfolded the letter, which very concisely demanded Simon's attendance at the Grand Hall that morning. Pulling his watch from his pocket, Simon glanced at the time. If he didn't hurry, he knew he would be late for his appointment, but he wasn't eager to repeat his previous day's reprimand. The retribution for not attending, however, would be far worse. With a sigh, he dropped his toast onto his plate and folded the napkin from his lap as he stood.

The sun was shining brilliantly as he emerged from his townhouse. A few automobiles rumbled along the road before him, infecting the air with their clouds of noxious fumes. His gaze shifted up the street and he frowned, noting the taxi parked on the curb. The taxi driver leaned patiently against the automobile's passenger door, glancing occasionally toward the watch in his hand.

Simon had no doubt the taxi had been sent to retrieve him. The leash he was normally allowed upon his return to Callifax was growing ever smaller, tightening like an invisible noose. The Grand Inquisitor clearly wanted to keep Simon close at hand until his misadventures in Haversham could be resolved.

The taxi driver looked toward the Inquisitor as Simon rounded the gate at the end of his sidewalk. Smiling, the taxi driver motioned toward his automobile. Simon didn't hurry toward the vehicle, though the chauffer held the rear door open for his easy entry.

"Good morning, sir," the taxi driver said, tipping his hat as Simon approached.

"It's not feeling like much of a good morning," Simon replied sourly as he climbed inside the shaded interior.

Without a reply, the taxi driver closed the door behind him before climbing into the driver's seat. The taxi started with a lurch and cough of the backfiring engine. With a rattle, the vehicle pulled away from the curb and merged into the sparse traffic.

The trip to the Grand Hall was blissfully short and devoid of any unwanted conversation. As they pulled to the curb before the pillared building, Simon didn't wait for the taxi driver to politely open his door. The Inquisitor stepped onto the sidewalk and hurried toward the entryway, leaving the confounded chauffer in his wake.

Guards opened the double doors and Simon hurried inside, the Grand Inquisitor's letter still clutched in his hand. The foyer was surprisingly empty, though he heard voices wafting from the sitting room.

"May I take your coat and hat, sir?" a servant asked as he emerged from a coatroom.

Simon removed his top hat and handed it to the man. The servant walked behind him and grasped the shoulders of Simon's coat as the Inquisitor slipped his arms free of the dense garment.

"Please let the Grand Inquisitor know that I have arrived," Simon said.

"Of course, sir," the servant replied. "I believe he's already expecting you."

"I should assume so."

The valet bowed before hurrying back to the coatroom. Simon barely gave the man a second glance as he walked into the sitting room.

The large room—filled with a series of couches, plush chairs, and a large fireplace that dominated the far wall—was mostly empty. A small group of Inquisitors sat on two sofas, facing one another, as they lost themselves in conversations of past investigations and other exploits.

Though his back was to Simon, a long, braided ponytail revealed that Ambrose was among the Inquisitors. Smiling, knowing that a friendly face would be much appreciated, Simon walked toward the group.

One of the Inquisitors noted his approach with a broad smile before motioning Simon to join them.

"Inquisitor Whitlock," the man said, though Simon couldn't quite recall his name. "To what do we owe this immense pleasure?"

Simon shrugged as he took an offered seat at the head of the couch closest to Ambrose. "If only I knew, though I doubt it's for anything good."

"Nonsense," Ambrose replied. "You're the golden child amongst the Inquisitors."

Simon laughed, recalling the berating he had received the day before. "I do believe this golden calf is quickly becoming a black sheep. My tongue has a tendency to get me into trouble."

Ambrose smiled and gestured toward the other Inquisitors. "From someone who is oft accused of letting his tongue talk him into unfortunate situations, let me welcome you to our prestigious group."

"We've all talked ourselves into trouble more often than we've talked our way out of it," one of the other Inquisitors remarked. "That's why they teach sword fighting and marksmanship during our training, but only offer the barest training in proper gentlemenship."

"Apparently, they assume we come from good breeding, rather than from the tenement houses like I did," Ambrose said.

"Or from the remote corners of the kingdom," another said.

"Or from overseas," replied the dark-skinned Inquisitor sitting beside Ambrose.

"Or from jail," Simon replied with a wistful smile.

"Do you know everyone?" Ambrose asked, gesturing to the other Inquisitors.

Simon glanced at the group. Though he recognized their faces, he struggled to recall their names.

"Inquisitor Merryweather you met briefly yesterday," Ambrose said, concluding that Simon would not be forthcoming with names.

Simon nodded to the older Inquisitor. His thinning hair had grayed slightly around his temples. "Bertrand, was it not?"

Bertrand smiled. "Indeed it was, Simon. It's a pleasure to meet you again."

"The fair skinned and dreadfully skinny Inquisitor seated beside Bertrand is Mister Connor Pettimore."

"A pleasure, sir," Connor replied with a nod of his head.

"And this dark-skinned savage to my right is Mister Thaddeus Poole, who has the unique distinction of being the only Inquisitor from the Marakath Kingdom."

Simon arched his eyebrows in surprise. The Marakath Kingdom resided on the westernmost continent. Few, if any, immigrants arrived from the distal continent.

"A foreign transplant, I presume?" Simon remarked.

Inquisitor Poole nodded, revealing the faint tattoos on the top of his dark, bald head. "My parents arrived in Callifax two years before the kingdom closed its borders. Few people realize that the privateers keeping foreign ships at bay also keep people from leaving the continent, as well. We've become naturalized as citizens of the crown by default."

"Can I offer you a drink, sir?" a waiter asked as he approached the group, interrupting the fascinating conversation that had been taking place.

"Scotch, please," Simon answered.

"One for me as well," Ambrose added, holding up his emptied glass.

"Very good, gentlemen."

The waiter departed, and Simon let his gaze drift back over the gathered men. From the corner of his vision, he noted the tanned folder resting against the armrest beside Ambrose.

Simon pointed toward the folder. "Have you received another assignment?"

Ambrose nodded. "Indeed. I only just arrived in Callifax, and they're already eager to see me gone. Apparently, my reputation continues to precede me."

The men laughed as the waiter returned with two tumblers of brown liquor.

"Where are they sending you?" Simon inquired.

Ambrose retrieved the folder and glanced at the printed words across its cover. "Burtons Grove."

Simon arched an eyebrow. "I'm not familiar with the name. Where is it located?"

The ponytailed Inquisitor flipped through the papers within the folder with a disinterested shrug. "It's a small town north of here, somewhere in the marsh." Ambrose looked up morosely. "Swamp and humidity aren't very agreeable with my disposition. Would you care to take this assignment for me?"

Simon laughed and held up his free hand. "No, but thank you. I nearly had frostbite from my last assignment. I'm not at all eager to delve into a swamp full of mosquitoes large enough to carry me away."

Ambrose sighed sadly. "I had forgotten the mosquitoes. Irrespective, the assignment itself sounds interesting. Apparently, there are reports of witchcraft."

Inquisitor Poole shook his head with a heavy laugh. "I've investigated four reports of witchcraft just this year. It seems to be the favorable allegation whenever there's the most mundane squabble between neighbors." His voice became suddenly nasally as he mocked his latest investigation. "My cow gave birth to a stillborn calf. It must be because my neighbor placed a hex upon the creature and certainly not because I live in abject squalor and hardly care for the nutritional needs of the beasts in my care."

"You sound awfully bitter," Ambrose teased.

The dark-skinned man huffed. "Not bitter, though jealous perhaps. I'm growing weary of investigating petty mockeries of true magic. I long for one assignment like Simon's, where I can face a real monster of the Rift."

Simon quickly shook his head. "You most certainly do not! Trust me; there was nothing fun about having a demon throw me the length of three tables."

The men laughed as they settled back into their seats. The valet from the foyer hurried into the room and approached Simon.

"It appears I'm being beckoned," he said, placing his half-finished scotch on the end table beside him. "Gentlemen, it has been a pleasure."

"Our good times are hardly at an end," Ambrose replied. "I can say with some certainty that we will still be in these very seats when you return."

Simon nodded toward his friend. "Then I guess I'll see you again shortly. If I don't return, assume my tongue got me into more trouble than I could successfully talk my way out of."

"If you don't return, we'll have a drink in your memory."

"Gentlemen," Simon said toward the remaining Inquisitors, "it has been a pleasure sharing your table today."

The valet stood by patiently, awaiting the conclusion of Simon's farewells. As the Inquisitor turned toward the younger man, the valet motioned toward the foyer and the hallway beyond.

"Inquisitor Whitlock, the Grand Inquisitor—"

"Yes, yes," Simon replied dismissively. "Just lead me to him."

The Grand Inquisitor's door opened with a faint creak, revealing the older man sitting behind his desk. Upon seeing Simon, he motioned for Simon to take the seat across the table.

Simon entered without pomp or circumstance and wordlessly took his seat.

The Grand Inquisitor glanced at the stack of reports before him and retrieved the topmost folder. Simon couldn't read the words printed across its surface, but one phrase was unmistakably written across the bottom: Royal Inquisitor Simon Whitlock.

"I'm sending you on another assignment," the Grand Inquisitor stated before Simon had a chance to question the folder.

Simon's heart fell. "Sir, I've only just returned from Haversham."

"You've returned under dubious circumstances, need I remind you? I've spent the night awake, pacing a hole through the carpet of my study, trying to decide what to do about you and your... new companion. The simple fact is that the evening has offered little insight. The only thing I have decided is that I won't have her in Callifax, sitting a stone's throw away from the king and court."

Simon frowned. "Are you intending that Miss Hawke should accompany me on this mission?"

"Miss Hawke and the apothecary," the Grand Inquisitor replied. "Everyone with knowledge of what you've done will accompany you on your assignment while I make any final decisions about your fate."

"If I may inquire, sir, what assignment have you given me?"

Simon felt utterly dejected, as though his mentor's dismissal was a knife being slowly twisted in his chest. Simon didn't hear notes of understanding in the elder man's voice, nor a sense that the Grand Inquisitor was growing accustomed to the idea of Mattie's presence as a person rather than just a monster. Perhaps, though Simon dreaded admitting it even to himself, Luthor was right. Telling the Grand Inquisitor what had transpired may have been foolish.

The Grand Inquisitor opened the folder and turned it toward Simon so that he could read the report. "There is an outpost far to the east of Callifax, called Whitten Hall. It is the primary supplier of iron ore to the capital but has recently ceased all shipments."

Simon frowned, knowing his mission had suddenly grown even more dismissive. "Sir, this is a problem for the Minister of Trade, not the Royal Inquisitors."

The elder man nodded and gently closed the folder. "Under normal circumstances, I would agree with you, but the ministry already sent tax collectors to Whitten Hall."

Simon leaned forward in his chair, feeling that the crux of this assignment would now be revealed. "What did they find?"

"Nothing," the Grand Inquisitor replied.

Simon felt the man's answer to be highly anticlimactic.

"Nothing," his mentor continued, "only because not a single tax collector actually arrived in Whitten Hall. Every one reported encountering supernatural occurrences on the train long before their actual arrival in the outpost."

"Supernatural?" Simon asked, genuinely intrigued.

"Men emerging from the smoke, attacking the passengers on board. It may be nothing, you must understand, but the Minister of Trade respectfully asked that the Inquisitors investigate these reports."

Simon took the folder and flipped quickly through the attached eyewitness accounts. Clipped to the back of the folder were three train tickets. The departure date was written boldly across each ticket. Simon frowned as he recognized the rapidly approaching departure. "When do we leave?"

"Immediately."

Simon looked up at the elder man, and his frown deepened. He had just returned and only recently reconnected with Veronica. Now, after settling back into his quiet, romantic life in Callifax, his world was about to be upended once more.

"Is there a problem, Inquisitor?" his mentor asked, though Simon knew it was a loaded question. There was only one proper answer.

"Of course not, sir," Simon replied with a sigh. "I couldn't be more excited about this assignment."

"Excellent. Then gather your companions. The armory and pantries here are, of course, at your disposal. Take what you need. As always, send word upon your arrival and report any of your findings. Perhaps this time, if you please, report with a bit more punctuality than you did in Haversham."

Simon nodded and stood. The Grand Inquisitor didn't offer his hand or wishes of good luck, nor did Simon expect any. He walked across the room and passed quickly out of the office.

Ambrose and the others were still in the sitting room, laughing heartily at stories of investigations gone awry. Simon pushed aside his sour demeanor and reclaimed his seat amongst the jovial men.

The charismatic Inquisitor noted the folder clutched tightly in Simon's hand. "You haven't already been reassigned to another case, have you?"

Simon nodded toward Ambrose. "Sadly, I have."

"You've only just returned," one of the other Inquisitors stated.

The dark-skinned Inquisitor smiled. "Heroics can't be confined to a life of quiet introspection, like he would find here in Callifax. Fortune favors the bold."

Simon forced a smile as smarmy insults raced through his mind. "If you are somehow managing a fortune doing this job, please tell me your secret."

The other Inquisitors laughed, knowing their pay was a mere pittance. As they had discussed earlier, they were Inquisitors because of dubious backgrounds that offered them little other recourse. There were only a few Inquisitors that came from a life of opulence and chose this occupation due to a sense of honor and duty.

"I knew they wouldn't keep you here long," Ambrose said. "Where have you been assigned?"

Simon glanced at the cover of the folder in his hands and read the town's name. "Whitten Hall, apparently."

Ambrose furrowed his brow. "Where is that, exactly?"

"I haven't the foggiest," Simon replied, shaking his head. "Though I do know that it's a train's ride away."

"A train's ride?" one of the Inquisitors asked. "You must truly be a black sheep if they're sending you somewhere even a zeppelin won't go."

Ambrose smiled apologetically toward Simon. "Even Burtons Grove has an airship dock."

Simon sighed, not at all surprised by this turn of events. A zeppelin would have been a far quicker mode of transportation, which means he had been assigned to Whitten Hall simply because it would take him from the capital city for a longer period of time. He truly was being dismissed.

"Have you told Luthor?" Ambrose asked.

"I've only just found out myself."

"Do you think he will take the news well, since I'm certain he's only just settling back into his normal life as well?"

Simon thought about having to tell both Luthor and Mattie and cringed. "No, I can most confidently state that he will not take the news well."

Ambrose stood and nodded toward Simon. "Well, I shouldn't take any more of your time, since I must prepare for my own departure, not to mention find a zeppelin pilot willing to fly somewhere as remote as Burtons Grove."

Simon stood as well, followed by the rest of the gathered Inquisitors. "Take care of yourself, Ambrose."

Ambrose glanced at the folder in his hands and shrugged. "I'm sure it will be nothing. We'll both be back here before you know it, and we'll share another bottle of scotch."

Simon shook the charismatic man's hand. "I look forward to it." He turned toward the other Inquisitors. "Gentlemen, do take care of yourselves."

"It's been a pleasure, Simon," the dark-skinned Inquisitor replied.

"Will you walk me out?" Ambrose asked, gesturing toward the door.

Simon nodded, and the two men took their leave of the sitting room. They were silent as the valet retrieved their coats and Simon's top hat. Together, they exited the building, stepping into the day's warm sunlight. The day had warmed considerably since his morning departure, and now Simon regretted having his coat.

"It's beautiful days like these that I'll miss once I leave Callifax," Ambrose remarked.

"Especially since you'll be spending the next few weeks in a putrid swamp."

Ambrose sighed. "Please don't remind me. I look forward to finishing this assignment, completing my report back here in the capital, and then returning south to my house. I can only imagine the state of disrepair into which it has fallen with me gone for so long."

"It's the salty air," Simon explained. "You should have never built so close to the ocean. It does terrible things to the stones and mortar."

"I forget your unrealistic fear of water," Ambrose chided.

"It's not unrealistic," Simon explained. "It's very human to be afraid of drowning."

"Most people just avoid such outcomes by learning to swim."

"A wasted effort if ever I've encountered one," Simon retorted. "It's far easier just to not find myself perched above a three-hundred-foot-deep body of unforgiving ocean."

Ambrose patted Simon firmly on the back. "I will miss our talks once I'm gone."

Simon turned toward Ambrose, his expression suddenly quite serious. "Be careful on your assignment. Don't approach it with your general sense of levity."

Ambrose smiled, though it was with understanding rather than mirth. "I will, though mark my words, this assignment will be nothing more than a neighborly dispute."

"Need I remind you that I believed the same of Haversham, and we all know how that turned out."

A taxi pulled to the curb, and Ambrose stepped toward it. "This would be my ride. We can share, if you feel so inclined."

A part of Simon wanted to accept Ambrose's offer, but a much larger part knew that the walk would do him some good and give him a chance to devise a way to tell both Luthor and Mattie the unfortunate news.

"Thank you for the offer, but no," Simon said with a wave of his hand. "Take care of yourself, Ambrose."

"You as well, Simon," the ponytailed man said as he climbed into the taxi. The driver closed the door behind him and pulled away from the curb, leaving Simon standing alone on the sidewalk.

CHAPTER *Eleven*

THOUGH LUTHOR PREPARED THE TEA WORDLESSLY, SImon could see the disdain evidenced by his demeanor. Mattie likewise was quiet, though her expression was far more steeped in confusion than frustration.

"It wasn't my idea, if that helps at all," Simon offered.

Luthor gently placed the porcelain lid to the teapot in place and carried the tray into the study. "It doesn't. I still don't understand how we've even received another assignment so quickly. Shouldn't we have been much lower in the queue? Shouldn't we have, at the very least, been offered some weeks or even months to recuperate before sending us on another investigation?"

Simon waited for the tea to be poured. He took a satisfying sip before placing his cup back onto its saucer. "Don't be trite; it's unbecoming. Besides, you already know the answer to that question."

"It's because of me, isn't it?" Mattie asked.

Simon nodded enthusiastically, oblivious to the disheartening effect it had on the redheaded woman. "Of course it's because of you, Matilda. The Grand Inquisitor needs time to process your very presence in Callifax."

"So the best way to process her presence is to not have her present,"

Luthor concluded.

"Precisely. I'm positively thrilled that we've all arrived at the same conclusion. It saves us endless hours of cyclic conversation about who's at fault and who's to blame."

Luthor frowned. "It's not cyclic, sir. The answer is you on both accounts."

Simon refused to be baited into the debate. He used his cup of tea as an excuse to not reply, as he took another sip of the scalding fluid. Upon realizing there would be no debate, Luthor resumed his seat at the oaken table.

A lighted lantern in the center of the table illuminated the square room. Bookshelves lined the walls on all sides, broken only by the sole doorway leading in and out of the room. The shelves were full of assorted tomes of knowledge, collected not only from Simon and Luthor's travels throughout the kingdom, but also from the apothecary's extensive studies prior to their business union. Entire shelves overflowed with tomes on herbal remedies and medicinal plants of the assorted regions.

Luthor motioned toward the folder that was still closed before the Inquisitor. "Please, sir, tell us what you know thus far."

Simon opened the folder. Despite the sheaf of papers stacked neatly within the tan folder, Luthor's eyes drifted to the train tickets affixed to the back cover.

"Would those be the tickets for our passage?" the apothecary asked curiously, since they were clearly not airship passes.

"Indeed they are," Simon replied. "Train tickets for the three of us. Our transport departs first thing tomorrow morning."

"A train?" Mattie asked surprised. "Why not by airship like to and from Haversham?"

"It's the region," Simon explained, recalling the heartache Ambrose felt when realizing he would have to convince a zeppelin pilot to fly to the remote swamps to the north. "Zeppelin routes are intermittent at best. Larger cities or those with important resources can often afford not just the cost of the docks themselves, but also the rather hefty payments necessary to assure inclusion on pre-established airship routes."

Mattie furrowed her brow. "I understand, but didn't you say that this outpost...?"

"Whitten Hall," Luthor said.

"Of course. Did you not tell us that Whitten Hall was a supplier of iron ore? Couldn't they afford the cost?"

"Indeed they could, a hundred times over," Simon agreed. "However, it's the physics of the situation that hinders airship movement. Raw iron ore—or even processed ore for that matter—is excessively heavy and moving tonnes worth of the raw material simply cannot be accomplished on a vessel that's expected to remain airborne. Load any majorly impressive amount of ore onto an airship and the cabin will be scraping the ground shortly after liftoff."

"Therefore," Mattie concluded, "the iron and thus the passengers are all moved by train?"

"Exactly."

Mattie smiled wistfully. "I've never been on a train."

Simon patted her hand affectionately. "Then you, my dear, are in for a treat."

Mattie turned her attention to Luthor. "How long will the trip take?"

Luthor stood and walked to one of the bookshelves, pulling a tall, leather-bound book from the shelf without hesitation. He carried the heavy tome back to the table and set it before him. Mattie slid her chair closer so as to watch. As Luthor lifted the lid, she could see the pages within were covered with assorted hand-drawn maps.

The apothecary flipped pages with practiced ease, finding the map he wanted with only the slightest hesitation. He ran his finger along the page until his nail settled on a star, underneath which was written "Callifax".

"Here we are at the capital," Luthor began. "Whitten Hall is annotated by this small circle, some distance away. I would expect by train for it to take upwards of four to five days. However, sir, this begs the more pertinent question—why is an Inquisitor traveling to Whitten Hall?"

Simon nodded and sorted through the topmost papers in the folder before him. "It seems that Whitten Hall has recently decided to cease all shipments of iron to the crown, a silent coup, if you will."

Luthor shrugged. "Which is tragic, to be sure, sir, but hardly a reason to assign so important an asset as an Inquisitor. This sounds like a task for the Minister of Trade. He should be sending tax collectors, rather than wasting our time."

"He has. It seems that every time a tax collector is sent to Whitten Hall, the train is attacked by monsters."

Luthor paused from his review of the rail map. He arched his eyebrow as he met Simon's knowing gaze. "You have my attention, sir."

Simon picked up a hastily written testimonial, though he already knew its content by heart. "It appears that creatures appear from a mist, originating from within the train itself. These abominations have scared away every tax collector long before the men reach the outpost."

Luthor frowned and returned to the map. "It's a hoax," he said matter-of-factly. "It's nothing more than a sloppy attempt to frighten away representatives of the crown."

"Agreed. It's been an effective ruse, though I would hardly consider it 'sloppy.'"

"Then we shall call it half-arsed or noncommittal," Luthor said as he removed his glasses and waved them around dismissively. "This case is solved before we even step foot on the train."

"Again, I'm prone to agree with you, Luthor. Sadly, our assumptions, no matter how well intended, are hardly taken as gospel by the crown. We have to investigate."

Luthor sighed. "I suppose I shall pack my things, then?"

Simon smiled. "Indeed, though try to pack your general optimism, if you could. It seems to be sorely lacking since the news of our new mission."

Luthor slid his glasses onto the bridge of his nose and returned his wistful stare to his companion. "Sir, my morose attitude is not due to the mission at hand, though I think the whole misadventure of eight wasted days on a train just to disprove a sloppy… forgive me, noncommittal hoax is a pathetic use of our time. No, my saddened demeanor is because there are no less than four libraries, sixteen alehouses, and five new apothecaries, all of which I intended to visit during our, what I presumed to be, lengthy stay in Callifax. While I have visited the libraries and apothecaries, my patronage in the alehouses is severely lacking."

"That is a dreadful business," Simon admitted. "Upon our return, I'll buy the first round. Out of curiosity, is your interest in apothecaries and alehouses in any way linked? You are known to brew some exceptional draughts, which put the intoxicating effects of alcohol to shame."

Mattie politely cleared her throat, garnering the attention of the two men. "What shall I pack for this trip? I know nothing of the area and, though I'm sure I loathe to admit it, I simply can't bring myself to pack another suffocating dress."

Simon laughed. "Whitten Hall is in the forest, full of men of wilderness persuasions and occupations. A dress would be sorely out of place in the environment."

"Thank the heavens," Mattie replied, exhaling audibly. "If I had to squeeze my body into another corset, I'm sure I'd scream. Except I couldn't, mind you, since the corsets in Callifax completely stop me from properly inhaling. I won't even bore you with the uncomfortable things these corsets do to my cleavage."

Luthor blushed. "Oh, I don't think we'd be bored at all by that conversation."

Simon laughed as he stood from his seat. "I shall leave you two alone as I go and pack as well."

"Give Veronica our best, should you see her," Luthor replied.

"Of course he's going to see her," Mattie chided.

"Just so long as he's not late for our departure tomorrow morning," the apothecary hastily added. "I don't suppose they'd keep the train just for an absent Inquisitor, now would they, sir?"

"I shan't be late," Simon replied. "Ten o'clock sharp on the west platform. I'll see you both there."

They walked the Inquisitor to the door before shaking hands and bidding each other good night. Simon retrieved his top hat from the coat rack near the front door before stepping into the cool evening air.

Much of the day had passed between his conversation with the Grand Inquisitor and the planning of their mission to Whitten Hall. Simon walked briskly toward his home next door and packed hastily. His clothing was hardly packed with any semblance of order or thought toward its later retrieval. Instead, he considered the multitude of ways in which he could tell Veronica that he was already leaving Callifax, sent away on another mission.

For someone so brilliant at solving puzzles and crimes, Simon was at a loss for ideas.

CHAPTER Twelve

SIMON WALKED THROUGH THE HAZE OF SMOKE THAT filled the air within the Ace of Spades. The house of ill repute wasn't quite as busy as it had been the night before, but most tables were still occupied. The Inquisitor took his familiar seat but waved away the waitress as she approached. He wasn't interested in either drink or cigarette tonight, his mind already awash with the bad news he had come to share with Veronica.

He drummed his fingers absently on the table as the house lights dimmed. The recessed lights around the stage's perimeter flared to life, filling the stage with a nearly blinding brilliance.

Simon smiled solemnly as Veronica took the stage. She wore a feathered bustier and matching undergarments, an outfit of which Simon was more than familiar. He doubted there was a single costume Veronica owned which he could not identify with little more than a passing glance. It wasn't just a result of his exceptional memory. Repetition bred familiarity, and he had most certainly been a repeat customer at the Ace of Spades.

As Veronica began her performance, Simon averted his gaze. Watching her act, as she removed articles of clothing, was a painful distraction from his actual purpose.

His gaze drifted over the room and settled on familiar faces. The shadowed man in the booth across the floor from Simon was in attendance again tonight, his features still mostly disguised despite the brilliance of the stage lights. Though the nobleman from the night before was curiously absent, another flamboyant and rowdy man of affluence had taken his place near the stage. The nobleman, if that was indeed what he was, called futilely toward Veronica to garner her attention, but Simon knew it was for naught. Despite the reputation of businesses like the Ace of Spades, the performers were professionals at heart. It was a burlesque house, not a brothel. In fact, his and Veronica's first encounter had ended poorly for him, as he had made the same incorrect assumption about her intents, as did the man near the stage.

Within minutes, the music faded into obscurity and Veronica's show ended. The stage lights faded to black while the house lights remained dimmed. The transition from stark light to relative darkness left orbs of blue dancing in Simon's vision.

Veronica quickly exited the stage under the cloak of darkness, followed by the rambunctious cheers of the audience, who were as equally blinded as Simon. As the Inquisitor blinked away the artifacts of the stage lights, he slid back from the table and walked toward the entrance beside the stage.

As the night before, the man guarding the doorway hastily stepped aside, allowing Simon to enter the backstage area. A new collection of women were quickly changing or applying copious amounts of makeup prior to their turn on stage. Simon recognized most but paid them no heed. He was focused solely on Veronica's private changing room near the back of the open area.

The door to her room was closed, though he didn't hesitate to knock. He could hear the sound of furniture and could imagine her turning her chair slightly from the vanity to peer toward the closed door. He knew her mannerisms as well as her stage clothing.

"Come in," Veronica replied, her voice muffled by the closed door.

Simon opened the door slightly and peered within, ensuring Veronica was decent. "Might I enter?"

"Simon!" she exclaimed. "Of course you may come in. I didn't think you'd be able to watch me perform tonight."

"Originally I thought I would be otherwise occupied, but it seems that all my plans are changing."

Her smile faltered as he entered. Though he had mentioned nothing of his mission, his expression told her all she needed to know.

"Are you leaving so soon?"

Simon nodded slowly as he pursed his lips with disappointment. "Sadly, I am. Luthor and I have received another assignment."

Veronica stood from the vanity and placed her hands on her hips. Though her stance decried defiance to his new mission, her expression was still softened with sadness and concern.

"You've only just returned. Isn't there someone else who could be going?"

"Dozens more, I would imagine," Simon replied, "many of whom would gladly leap at the opportunity."

"Yet they chose you?"

Simon rubbed the back of his neck nervously. "There are extenuating circumstances. As Luthor has repeatedly put it, I have been making poor life choices lately."

Veronica bit her lip, and any semblance of her stern consternation faded. The logical, emotionless man who had sat at Luthor's table faded with her sudden flood of emotion, and he quickly embraced her.

"Forgive me, my love. This was certainly not the way I planned our happy reunion."

Veronica wiped her eyes, smearing the thick mascara beneath her lids. "I waited for nearly two months while you were away in Haversham only to have you return and leave again so soon afterward. Will you be gone long?"

Simon sighed. "I most certainly hope not. The train ride is just over a week round trip. Our actual mission itself shouldn't be long."

Veronica broke abruptly from his embrace and turned toward the vanity. "My makeup has run," she muttered to herself. "I look a mess."

"Veronica? Please talk to me."

She turned slowly and sat on the edge of the table, her back pressed against the mirror. Her face was flushed from the inner turmoil and conflicting emotions.

"What am I to do, Simon? Shall I wait for you patiently? Shall I stand on the train platform day after day, hoping you arrive on the next train while secretly praying that you haven't encountered some terrible monster during your assignment?"

Simon stood without reply, staring at the disheveled yet still attractive brunette before him. Veronica stood once more and walked toward him before slipping her arms around his waist and laying her head on his chest.

"That's not me, Simon," she whispered, though her words carried clearly through the quiet changing room. "I'm not the doting lady in waiting who cares for house and home while her lover is away. You said it yourself; I work in a den of sin. For God's sake, I take my clothes off for money. I'm hardly better than the ladies of the night roaming the streets, searching for the sailors on shore leave with far too much alcohol in their bodies, too much coin in their purses, and far too little brains in their heads."

"You're far too pretty to be a prostitute and not nearly desperate enough."

He could feel her shoulders shake faintly with laughter. "You drive me to it."

"Would you prefer I left coin on your nightstand before I leave next time?"

She took a step back and stared at the taller man. Her expression was serious once more. "I would prefer you didn't leave at all, your and my reputation be damned."

"Very well," he said with a soft smile.

Her eyes widened in surprise. "You'll stay?"

"Under one condition—marry me."

Words failed Veronica as she sought a reply.

"I don't expect an answer now," Simon quickly added. "In fact, I would be quite put out if you didn't give this the amount of thought it so rightfully deserves. Think about my proposal and what I offer you, and I'll ask for your answer upon my return."

When Veronica still didn't speak, Simon cleared his throat uncomfortably. "When I said I didn't expect an answer, it was solely to my proposal. I would be quite fine if you were to say something, such as, 'Simon, you're a bloody fool,' or 'get out of my dressing room before I'm forced to throw a shoe.'"

Veronica smiled, though Simon could clearly see her mind still deep in thought. "Some days, I wonder how I ever fell in love with such an odd man as yourself."

"Alcohol would be my assumption," Simon joked.

She slipped her arms around his neck and pulled him to her. Her lips were velvety as they kissed deeply. As quickly as the kiss began, it ended abruptly as she placed a hand on his chest and forced him away.

"Go," she demanded. "You've already undone hours' worth of make-up during your brief visit. I have much more to do before my next performance."

"I'll see you when I return, I promise you that, and I'll expect an answer when I do."

The corners of her mouth rose in an imitation of a true smile. "You shall have it, but not until your return. Now get out of my dressing room before I'm forced to throw a shoe."

Simon laughed, but his laughter quickly faded as she playfully threw a heeled shoe in his direction. He slipped into the doorway and began pulling the door closed behind him. Before it closed completely, he slid his head back through the opening.

"Until I return, my love."

She replied by throwing the shoe's mate in his direction.

Simon carried a small suitcase with him as he climbed the three half steps to the station's main platform. The rest of his luggage had been sent ahead with a valet and had, presumably, already been loaded on the train.

Cresting the last step, he found himself walking alongside the engine of the train as it rested in the station. Polished brass glimmered in the trickling sunlight, a stark contrast to the oiled black of the smoke stack rising from its core like the maw of an angry dragon. Black smoke belched from the chimney, rising into the air before dissipating as it was caught by the blowing wind. A conductor stood beside the engine and nodded politely as Simon passed.

The cars behind the engine were all passenger cars. Their exteriors were richly stained red oak, banded together by more of the polished brass. Innumerable glass windows lined each passenger compartment, allowing Simon an unfettered view of those already on board. Though he sought Luthor and Matilda, he found his gaze continuously drawn to the opulence of the individual train cars by which he passed.

Those nearest the engine were dinner cars. Expansive tables were set at intervals throughout the cars' interiors. White tablecloths and spotless silverware rested on the tables. Those partaking in a late breakfast enjoyed steaming racks of braised meats and poached eggs that made Simon salivate, even without being able to smell the delicacies.

As he turned his attention back to the platform, the compressors beneath the train released a billowing cloud of white steam. The humid air, concealing everything beyond Simon's immediate reach, consumed the platform. He continued walking forward, unperturbed by his lack of vision, and nearly ran into Luthor, who emerged from the steam like a ghost of legend.

"Sir," Luthor said, as equally startled as the Inquisitor, "we were beginning to fear you wouldn't make it."

"Nonsense. I was here on time; you just couldn't see me through this insufferable steam."

Luthor smiled knowingly at the Inquisitor's lie. Mattie stepped to the apothecary's side and smiled broadly at Simon.

"We're glad you're here, nonetheless."

Simon glanced appreciatively at Matilda. Gone were the suffocating dresses she had been forced to wear during official court functions. A loose blouse that plunged at the neckline, revealing more of her figure than Simon was used to seeing, had replaced her high-collared shirts. She wore a leather jerkin and matching leather pants that seemed out of place in the kingdom's capital, but would probably be right at home in the wilderness into which they were traveling.

Though he had known her but a short time, Simon was constantly impressed by the different facets of the complicated female werewolf. She seemed completely different whether in the tribal furs of her people, the formal dresses of Callifax, or, as she was now, relaxed in a more masculine hunter's garb.

"All aboard!" the conductor yelled, his silhouette barely visible as the steam slowly cleared from the platform.

"Our personal effects?" Simon asked.

"Already loaded, sir," Luthor replied. "The only thing missing is us."

"Then by all means, please do lead the way."

Luthor led the trio toward one of the rearmost cars, a passenger car that rested just before the caboose. The car had been partitioned into individual cabins, in which the three could talk about their mission ahead in relative privacy.

A porter took Simon's small suitcase and showed the group to their room. Their other luggage was already stowed in racks above the two benches, which faced one another from either side of a broad table. Two separate high-backed and cushioned chairs sat on either side of the door, framed by electric floor lamps that illuminated the room.

Simon slipped the porter a pair of copper coins, hardly feeling generous after the young man barely carried his suitcase more than a dozen feet. With a frown he quickly tried to hide, the porter nodded and left the room.

"Pull the door closed, if you please," Simon said to Luthor.

The apothecary pulled and latched the sliding panel behind him, ensuring it would stay closed as they began their journey. As Mattie sat on one of the benches, Simon pulled the mission folder from his bag and tossed it haphazardly upon the table.

"Come, Luthor," he said as he sat across from the redhead. "We have much to discuss over the next few days."

As they began perusing the files within the folder, a whistle split the morning air and, with a lurch that rattled the trio in their seats, the train pulled away from the Callifax station.

CHAPTER Thirteen

THE TRAIN RATTLED ALONG THE TRACKS AS THE SCENery drifted lazily past. The plains beyond the city walls of Callifax quickly gave way to the forest that would parallel their journey the remainder of their way to Whitten Hall.

Simon stared out the window absently, and Luthor and Mattie discussed the mission ahead.

"Whitten Hall is an outpost," Luthor explained, "with a population of no more than one hundred and fifty, most of whom are indentured servants. Those numbers may be inflated, however, especially if there is a revolt in progress against the crown. I can't imagine all one hundred and fifty people have thrown their hats in behind this coup."

"One hundred and fifty is a small number," Mattie remarked. "Even Haversham had…"

She paused as she realized she had no idea the number of people that lived in her former home.

"It's a veritable metropolis by comparison," Luthor concluded, saving her the embarrassment of the ensuing silence.

Mattie laid her head on the apothecary's shoulder, pressing her body against his as she did so. "Why doesn't the governor stop this nonsense? Wouldn't he have a vested interest in stopping this revolution, since his station and funding come directly from the crown?"

Luthor breathed deeply as he tried to focus on the question at hand, rather than her close presence. "You have to remember that Whitten Hall is insignificant, or would be were it not for the veins of iron under its streets. The outpost has a chancellor of sorts, but the actual governor is located miles away."

Mattie huffed as she sat back. "You're letting a vocal minority control the financial future of the entire kingdom. It seems silly to me."

"Let me guess," Luthor said, suddenly amused by her fervor. "Were it your choice, you'd march an army into Whitten Hall and destroy the resistance with claw and fang?"

Mattie smiled at his obvious baiting. "I would and it would be effective. I'd have iron ore flowing again within a week."

"I would assume this is what you did in your tribe?"

"We did."

Luthor smirked. "Was it effective?"

Mattie crossed her arms as she leaned back in the booth. "Did you ever hear of a revolt within the tribes?"

"Only once, and that resulted in the death of Haversham's governor, one of its major business contributors, and half its arsenal of gubernatorial guards."

Mattie laughed. "Which, I might add, took less than a week to restore the balance of power in Haversham. Like I said, it's effective."

Luthor turned his attention to Simon, who still stared blankly out the window. "What of you, Simon? Where do you weigh in on the use of force to enact laws?"

The Inquisitor looked from the window and arched an eyebrow inquisitively. "Come again?"

"You've been so deep in thought since we left Callifax. What are you contemplating so deeply?"

Simon reached up and stroked his thin moustache. "I was considering the physics of how long I'd have to grow my moustache before I could properly sculpt it with wax. You know, with a proper curl on either end or perhaps even straight out like daggers that reached nearly to my ears."

Luthor frowned. "Do be serious, sir. We have a mission ahead of us that requires our utmost attention."

"You see, I would, Luthor, but it's incredibly boring. We have four days ahead of us on this train, during which there will be more than ample time to peruse the files and determine a strategy. For now, I'm far too interested in the lunch options in the dining cars."

"The Grand Inquisitor thought this mission important enough to assign us to it. The least we can do is take it seriously."

"On the contrary, the Grand Inquisitor assigned us to this mission because he didn't want a werewolf in the middle of Callifax and figured this would be the easiest means to an end. As such, I will take this mission exactly as seriously as he did and, at least for the time being, think with my stomach instead of my brain. Did you happen to see the lunch specials as you boarded the train earlier?"

Luthor didn't reply but instead fixed Simon with a disapproving stare.

"To be honest," Mattie said, interrupting their amusing repartee, "I'm feeling a bit puckish myself. Perhaps a break for lunch is in order."

"With the two of you around, I can't help but feel perpetually outnumbered," Luthor said, exasperatedly.

"If everyone around you is always wrong and you're the only one that's right, perhaps everyone else isn't the problem. Perhaps your real problem is perspective."

Luthor stood and offered his hand to Mattie. As Simon joined them, they made their way out of their private cabin.

The hallway leading through their passenger car was narrow and, as they passed another patron, they found themselves pressed tightly to the wall. The constant rocking of the train cars did little to help their predicament, and Simon braced himself with a hand on one wall and the other on the glass windows. He felt as though he were struggling to find his sea legs during a first trip aboard a ship, rather than rolling steadily along the railroad tracks.

Behind Simon, Luthor similarly stumbled with each step. Only Mattie seemed utterly unaffected by the motion of the train. Her exquisite balance kept each step perfectly in the middle of the hallway with no deviation as she made her way to the divider between rail cars.

As Simon opened the door at the end of their car, he was overwhelmed by the sudden gust of wind and roar of the train. The air itself was malodorous, filled with the pungent smoke from the engine.

A small catwalk spanned the space between the cars, with a narrow chain hung as railings. Simon grasped the chains firmly and groaned as they shifted more than he would have liked due to the slack in their hanging. With tentative steps, he led their way into the second passenger car.

Unlike their partitioned private rooms, the second passenger car was lined with long benches, which were half-filled with men and women, most of whom were dressed in workman's clothing. They looked to the suited men and the weathered redhead with a mixture of surprise and disdain.

The workers on their way to Whitten Hall intrigued Simon. Surely, they would have heard that Whitten Hall was in revolt against the crown and that work, if there was any to be had at all, would be scarce. Furthermore, it was doubtful those who controlled the iron mine would be so willing to accept strangers from the capital as a labor pool, since they would rightfully be on guard for soldiers of the crown. Still, during times of civil unrest and weakened economies, jobs were scarce. Perhaps Whitten Hall truly was the best option for men and women of their station.

The following two cars were sleeping cars. Like the passenger cars before them, Simon, Luthor and Mattie had designated private sleeping quarters, though a curtained partition was all that separated their stacked bunks from those nearby. The beds were shallow and were barely three feet in height. It allowed three beds to be stacked, one on top the other, but Simon loathed the time he would awake in the middle of the night and attempt to sit upright, only to strike his head on the ceiling directly above him.

Beyond the sleeping cars, they came to the first of the dining cars. A waiter met them at the door, though Simon didn't hear what the man had to say. He was far too involved in admiring the extravagant interior of the train car.

Though he had seen the well-dressed tables prior to boarding, his earlier impression didn't do justice to the actual interior. The dining car was slightly wider than the cars through which they had just passed, allowing for more space between dining tables. The walls and floor were the same rich red oak as had lined the exterior of the train cars. Above their heads, two chandeliers were affixed to the ceiling with straight poles, allowing for the glow of electric lights without the traditional sway of the glass chandelier. Instead, the room was bathed in a combination of quiet conversation and the faint jingle of glass and crystals in the chandeliers striking one another.

"A table for three, sir?" the waiter asked again, finally catching Simon's attention.

"Yes, please," he replied.

They were led to a table near the middle of the room, which suited Simon well. The Inquisitor took the seat against the wall, which offered him the best view of the entirety of the room.

Though Luthor waited for Mattie to sit, she remained standing and perused the room.

"Is something the matter?" the apothecary asked.

"I was just wondering if there was a water closet nearby," she replied.

The waiter gestured toward the far end of the car. "Just beyond those doors, madam."

Mattie smiled, knowing she hardly looked the part of a "madam" in her current attire. "Thank you. Gentlemen, if you'll excuse me for a moment."

Both men nodded. As Mattie walked toward the end of the dining car, Luthor sat down heavily across from the Inquisitor. Simon glanced at his friend as the waiter brought them a steeping pot of tea. Luthor clearly looked distressed, which had been readily apparent in his curt attitude since their departure.

"You've seemed unhappy ever since we left the station," Simon said, as he sipped his tea. "What's bothering you?"

Luthor gestured toward the train car. "This is what is bothering me, sir. We're already on assignment so soon after returning from the last. I'd only just removed the dust covers from all the furniture before we're off again."

"That's hardly my fault."

"It's entirely your fault," Luthor retorted. "You chose to tell the Grand Inquisitor about our misadventures in Haversham, and we were casually dismissed from the capital for it. That qualifies, in my book, as a poor life choice on your part. As a result, instead of enjoying the townhouse that I purchased and yet so rarely see, I'm with you, gallivanting across the countryside."

"Gallivanting?" Simon replied, aggravated. "That hardly seems like a worthwhile descriptive word for what we're doing."

The conversation halted temporarily as the waiter returned with a plate of assorted finger sandwiches.

Luthor glanced at the plate before him and selected the cucumber sandwich, knowing there was far less of a chance of ruining so simplistic a recipe. He took a bite before lifting his teacup and taking a sip. "All that

I'm saying is that I would appreciate a little predictability in my life."

"You should feel blessed," Simon said, leaning back in his chair and crossing his arms. "At least Mattie gets to accompany you on this trip."

Luthor nodded, setting his teacup down before him. "For that, I am most certainly grateful."

"This isn't easy for me either, you realize. I had to leave Veronica, the woman whom I intend to marry."

Simon looked up at Luthor, expecting a rise from the apothecary. Luthor furrowed his brow but remained silent.

"Do you have nothing to say in response?" Simon asked.

Luthor looked down, acknowledging the teacup resting on its saucer before him. "Would you feel better if you repeated your dramatic news as I took a sip of tea, so that I might choke on the fluid in surprise?"

Simon frowned. "It would be thoughtful of you if you did."

Luthor smiled disarmingly. "I may not always approve of your… future betrothed, and I might even categorize this in what is becoming a growing month of Simon's poor life choices, but believe it or not, I'm genuinely happy for you."

Simon took a bite of a fish sandwich before pursing his lips. His chewing became slow and deliberate before he swallowed painfully.

"Well, thank you," Simon replied. "It seems like an appropriate time. After all, I'm hardly getting any younger."

Luthor shook his head. "Sir, I'm not sure you were ever young. For, you see, young people enjoyed their youth by laughing and playing. You spent your ill-begotten youth pulling the wings from flies and pulling the entrails from frogs."

Simon arched his eyebrow in consternation. "Luthor, when I describe those events to you, I ensured it sounded very much like biology. When you describe them, somehow, they sound mildly sociopathic."

Luthor took another sip of his tea, concealing his smile behind the cup.

Simon glanced out the window, watching a copse of trees roll lazily past as the train chugged steadily along the tracks.

"What of you, Luthor?" Simon asked. "Are you considering marriage with Mattie?"

Caught unaware, warm tea rolled into the wrong pipe in his throat, causing him to choke. Simon laughed at his friend's discomfort. "There's the rise I was expecting."

Luthor coughed again, his face brilliant red from both choking and embarrassment. "Forgive me, sir, but you caught me a bit by surprise. No, we have no plans as of yet."

Simon arched an eyebrow. "That seems surprising, considering you're living together. You care for her, don't you?"

Luthor flushed deeper and he averted his gaze. "Very much so."

Simon suddenly sat forward and smiled mischievously. "My word, you haven't consummated your relationship, have you?"

"I hardly think that's any of your business," Luthor quickly retorted. "Regardless, we only live together due to her awkward position, being..." He glanced over his shoulder to ensure he wasn't overheard. "Due to her being what she is."

Simon laughed heartily. "You are full of surprises, my young apothecary."

"What has he done to surprise you today?" Mattie asked as she approached from the back of the dining car.

Both men quickly cleared their throats and stood politely, neither man meeting the other's gaze.

"Nothing, at all," Luthor replied. "He's merely chiding as usual. Did you find the powder room?"

Mattie walked around the table. Luthor pulled her chair away from the table, allowing her to sit. He gently pushed her chair in before both men sat.

"I did," she answered. "Thank you. Did you boys enjoy yourselves while I was away?"

"I certainly did," Simon replied with a wink.

Her eyes widened with pleasure at the sight of the sandwiches. She reached for one of the fish sandwiches, but Simon politely shook his head as a warning.

"Is it that bad?" she asked.

Simon frowned. "How they can have such opulent surroundings and yet still create such atrocious food is absolutely beyond me."

Mattie raised her hand, signaling for the waiter. The man quickly approached.

"Yes, madam?"

Mattie flashed the man a warm smile. "Do you serve any beef dishes?"

The waiter nodded. "Traditionally, our beef is reserved for dinner meals, but if the lady would like one now, it can be arranged."

"I would, very much."

"How would you like your steak prepared?"

Mattie shot a warning glance toward the two men before she replied. "Rare, if you please."

The waiter seemed momentarily taken aback but quickly recovered. "Very good, madam. I'll have it prepared at once." He turned his attention toward Simon and Luthor. "How are your meals, gentlemen?"

"It's as good as my mother used to make," Simon replied with a broad smile.

"Excellent, sir," the waiter said before departing.

Luthor glanced at the plate of tasteless, unseasoned food before him. "I thought you told me that your mother was a dreadful cook."

Simon sneered at the fish sandwich. "She was."

CHAPTER Fourteen

SIMON STRETCHED AND TRIED TO SIT UPRIGHT IN BED, but his forehead struck the shallow roof directly above him. For a moment, the grogginess of sleep clung to his mind and he felt disoriented. Slowly, he shifted his gaze to the narrow opening out of his stacked bunk bed and reality settled over him. He was suddenly acutely aware of the gentle rocking of the train as it clattered endlessly along the tracks.

Rolling onto his stomach, Simon slid from the bunk and dropped his feet to the carpeted floor below. As he had done for the past two nights, he had slept in his clothes rather than attempting to change into a gown. Despite the partition, the cramped sleeping car offered little privacy. It was as easy to sleep in his vest and pants as to bother changing into something more appropriate.

He slipped on his shoes before stumbling toward the vestibule that connected the sleeping car to the first of the passenger cars beyond. The cabin he shared with Luthor and Mattie was near the rear of the train, and he would have to pass through the rows of workers to reach their private car.

Despite this being the third day of their train ride, many of the workers looked none the worse for wear. Simon, however, felt utterly disheveled. His suit was wrinkled. His sleep had been constantly broken by the opening and closing of the car doors; each opening of the door introduced a roar of clacking train tracks and howling wind. His normally coifed hair was unkempt, despite his futile attempts at brushing.

Under normal circumstances, he cared deeply about what people thought of his appearance. He was a Royal Inquisitor, an honored member of the king's retinue. His appearance was a direct reflection of his professionalism.

Today, however, he felt his appearance justified the seriousness of their assignment. He was reminded of his and Luthor's misadventures with the "mummy" in the catacombs beneath Callifax, which, like nearly every other mission on which they'd been sent, had been nothing more than a hoax. Every Inquisitor had been aware that the report would result in nothing substantial, but Simon and Luthor had willingly investigated, as was their duty. This mission felt similarly useless. All reports pointed to a charlatan, keeping visitors to Whitten Hall at bay during a time of political upheaval.

Somehow, Simon doubted his current appearance would make much of a difference in regards to the conclusion of their investigation.

Entering their passenger car, Simon walked to the sliding door that opened to their private cabin. As he slid the door aside, he faced a pair of bright-eyed companions, both of whom stooped over the table as they perused the assorted mission files.

"Morning," Simon muttered, intentionally neglecting the addition of "good".

"Good morning, sir," Luthor replied, as he removed his glasses. "We're quite glad to see you awake."

"I'm not entirely convinced he is fully awake," Mattie whispered loudly enough to be heard by the Inquisitor.

"An astute observation, Miss Hawke." Simon spotted the teapot resting near the window. "Oh, tea! Glorious."

Luthor set his glasses on the table and retrieved both the teapot and a clean cup. He poured the dark liquid into the glass before dropping a pair of sugar cubes into the steaming tea. He handed the teacup to Simon before replacing his glasses on the end of his nose and reading quickly through the paper before him.

"Thank you kindly, Luthor," Simon said as he took a sip of the tea. His face screwed as the bitter fluid rushed over his tongue. "I see their culinary fouling isn't reserved solely to their sandwiches. Is there any milk, per chance, that could cut through the bitterness?"

"None, I'm afraid," the apothecary replied without looking up.

"Not at all surprising." Simon gestured over his shoulder toward the passenger car filled with miners and other manual laborers. "You know what I don't understand, if you would humor me?"

"Pray tell, sir."

"If Whitten Hall is in such an upheaval, why would there be so many workers aboard the train?"

Luthor shuffled aside some of the papers before him and retrieved a crumpled section of the newspaper. "How very coincidental you should ask, sir, for I made the same query earlier. It seems that Whitten Hall placed an advert in the paper, requesting miners and other assorted workers."

Simon took the paper and read through the column as he sipped his foul tea. "Yet, I see no mention of the political unrest."

"None, but I doubt very much it would matter. When the economy is suffering and jobs are scarce, the circumstances of employment matter less and less."

"It's true," Mattie added. "I was once forced to take a position as a servant's maid to provide income."

Luthor turned toward her in surprise. "Truthfully? I can't imagine that went well, considering you were no longer employed when we arrived in Haversham."

"No," Mattie replied, blushing. "My employer and I had a disagreement about what extracurricular activities were expected of a maid."

Simon smirked. "I can't imagine that ended well for him."

"Unfortunately, no. In my frustration, I might have bitten him."

"Hard enough to draw blood?" Luthor asked as he tried to stifle a laugh.

"Hard enough to remove a pair of fingers from the offending hand."

The two men shared a look and humored smile. "Then it's settled," Simon remarked. "No one shall touch Miss Hawke without her expressed consent."

"Indeed," Luthor concluded. "I'm far too attached to my hands."

"On the contrary," Mattie joked, "I wouldn't bite either of you *unless* I had your consent."

Both men blushed furiously, having been outwitted by the diminutive redhead.

"To the issue at hand," Simon hastily said. "Why would Whitten Hall request workers if it had ceased shipments of iron to the crown?"

"Forgive me, sir, but I have no answer," Luthor stammered as he tried to regain his composure. His eyes continued drifting to the still-smiling Mattie. "I know as much as you."

"Don't be absurd, Luthor. I know far more than you."

Before Luthor could reply, Simon glanced over his shoulder and scanned one of the handwritten witness accounts provided. "Have you found anything interesting?"

Luthor sighed, happy to be focused once more on the task at hand. "That depends solely on your definition of interesting, sir."

Mattie looked up and frowned. "Your definition of interesting hardly matters in this case. There's nothing remotely interesting about Whitten Hall."

Luthor smiled and sat on the bench. "Perhaps not the mining community itself, but there is quite a bit fascinating about the eyewitness reports, especially as they pertain to the attacks that took place on this very train."

Simon took another sip of tea before he recalled his displeasure with his first drink. "Yes, the attacks," he groaned as he set the tea down lest he make the same mistake again. "What have you discovered about the monsters that have attacked the train?"

"Quite a bit," Luthor replied, "and yet, surprisingly, next to nothing at all."

"Do explain."

"Well, sir, it appears that the attacks weren't against the train, as one would surmise, but instead took place within the train itself. Witnesses report seeing a thick mist filling the car moments before a monster appeared."

"Does the report give any inclination as to what manner of monster attacked the trains?" Simon asked.

Luthor turned the pages but shook his head. "It does not, only that the creatures emerged from a supernatural mist."

Simon frowned. "That hardly narrows down the genre of beast. How could they not know?"

"Normal men aren't like you and me, sir. A normal man doesn't stare into the face of the monster with abject curiosity. They merely turn and run."

Simon crossed his arms as he leaned against the wall behind him. "Then they're missing the best part."

Luthor reached up and pushed his glasses back up his nose. "Agreed, sir, but that's why you're an exceptional Inquisitor but a queer sort of human being."

"I take that as a compliment."

"As well it was intended, sir."

"So then the mystery continues," Mattie remarked.

"Indeed, but the mystery will have to wait until after breakfast," Simon offered.

"They've already stopped serving breakfast, sir. You slept through it."

"Then brunch and, failing that, lunch. I'm truly not a picky man."

Luthor shook his head. "No, sir, that you most certainly are not, though you are one that clearly thinks with his stomach."

"On the contrary, Luthor, I think with my mind, which, in turn, is fueled by a full stomach. Isn't the human body a magnificent invention?"

Luthor laughed despite himself and glanced at Mattie. "Shall we break for a meal?"

Mattie smiled sheepishly. "Blame it on my animalistic metabolism, but I could most certainly eat again."

"Then it's settled," Simon said. "To the dining car."

The Inquisitor led the trio back through the passenger cars. Their own sleep car beyond was nearly empty, save for a pair of inebriated gentlemen who still hadn't arisen from the previous night's festivities. Or, Simon realized with a sly grin, they had already begun the day's festivities a little early.

The second sleeping car was likewise nearly empty, though it was a narrower walk through which they had to traverse. Their passage was made more complicated by personal affects hanging from the sides of the beds, filling up the narrow walkway even further.

As they opened the door separating the sleep car from the dining car, they were nearly bowled over by a small group of men hastily retreating. Simon stood his ground even as the first of the men crashed unceremoniously into him. He grasped the man by the shoulder and thrust him against the nearest bunk beds. The other men halted behind him, though they glanced nervously over their shoulders.

"Have you forgotten your manners?" Simon asked angrily. "You nearly knocked over the lady."

"There's mist in the dining car," the man stammered, his eyes wide with fright. "It's like they said; something is coming!"

To his surprise, Simon let the man go. He and his compatriots hurried past the trio and escaped toward the rear of the train.

Simon and Luthor exchanged knowing glances as they turned toward the vestibule. Simon drew his pistol and pulled back the hammer, ensuring he was ready to fire when needed.

The dining car door had swung shut behind the men, but the narrow glass window gave them ample view of the room beyond. A white mist clung to the floor. It appeared to originate near the far end of the dining car, where it was thickest and had billowed upward, concealing the far wall completely. Its tendrils of smoke drifted across the dining car until they crashed silently against the door before Simon.

Simon pulled open the door and stepped aside as the mist wafted over the narrow catwalk and was quickly carried away by the strong cross breeze. With his pistol at the ready, he stepped into the room.

Despite the fleeing gentlemen they encountered earlier, the car was not empty, as he would have surmised. A few dinner guests appeared transfixed, either with fear or curiosity. They watched the mist ebb and flow from its point of origin, as though anticipating the inevitable emergence of the monster.

"You," Simon said, pointing toward the closest group of startled patrons, "come here. Hurry now, we haven't much time."

His calm words broke them from their stupor, and they rushed to his side. Luthor led them through the dining car door and to the relative safety of the sleeping car beyond.

"Madam?" Simon asked, gesturing toward a blonde woman. She stood unmoving even as the growing cloud of mist swallowed the table beside which she stood. "Madam, come to me."

As she turned toward him, a dark shadow emerged from the mist directly behind her. The creature looked nearly human, with the exception of its bloodless pale skin and elongated fingernails, which it used to point menacingly toward the woman. She screamed as her humanoid attacker stepped to her side and clutched her shoulders firmly in its grasp.

The creature tilted its head backward and opened its mouth, revealing a pair of spear-like fangs. The woman's eyes rolled backward as she edged toward a faint and her head lolled lazily to one side, exposing her uncovered neck.

The vampire, for that was most certainly what it was, quickly leaned forward, its fangs brushing the exposed skin just above her collarbone.

A gunshot rang out. The bullet whizzed past the woman's ear and struck the vampire in the forehead. The creature jerked backward, losing its grip on the woman as it did so. She collapsed where she stood, falling to the floor awkwardly with her legs splayed painfully beneath her.

The vampire vanished into the thick mist as it collapsed. The white smoke seemed to absorb it, leaving no trace exposed beyond its clinging tendrils.

"Open the doors and windows," Simon ordered. "We need to clear this mist from the room at once."

Mattie and Luthor hurried to either side of the room and unlatched the windows. A stiff breeze quickly filled the room. The mist spun and eddied at their feet as it was pulled from the dining car.

As the mist was drawn from the room, Simon approached the far side of the dining car with caution, his pistol still raised at the ready. The mist clung to his legs, cascading over his shoes even as it was drawn toward the open windows.

Slowly, the mist began to clear. Simon paused briefly at the side of the unconscious woman and placed his fingers gently on the side of her neck as he checked for a pulse. Her heartbeat was strong, but he felt the tackiness of blood as he withdrew his hand. Glancing at her prostrate form, he saw a pair of thin lines where the vampire's fangs had scratched through the topmost layer of skin.

As he turned his attention back toward the thick mist against the far wall, he was startled to see the soles of a pair of boots emerge from the white smoke. In nearly the same position as he had fallen after being shot, the vampire's corpse was revealed as the mist receded.

Simon felt his own heartbeat quicken at the sight. He assumed everything to be a trap, especially when dealing with the supernatural. Vampires, if his superstition studies were true, could transform into mist or polymorph into bats or wolves. A single gunshot, even one accurately placed between the monster's brows, surely wouldn't have been enough to bring it down.

"It looks dead," Luthor remarked as he approached.

"Appearances can be deceiving," Simon replied. Using the barrel of his pistol, he nudged the creature's foot. The foot fell limply to the side without resistance.

"I believe it more than simply looks dead. I believe this creature really is deceased."

As the last of the mist dissipated, they could see the large pool of blood that had spread underneath the vampire's shattered skull. The two men exchanged glances.

With a deep breath, Luthor approached the vampire. He knelt beside the creature's shoulder and reached for its neck.

"There's no pulse," Luthor remarked.

"Vampires shouldn't have pulses to begin with, should they?" Mattie asked from behind Simon.

"Did you have something special loaded into that pistol, pray tell?" Luthor asked. "Wooden bullets, holy water, or extract of garlic?"

Simon shook his head. "Nothing other than the normal lead bullets. Are vampires, by nature, allergic to lead?

"In my experience, most living creatures have a fatal allergy to lead," Mattie offered.

Luthor nodded. "True, though vampires are presumably immune to such simple attacks. By mythology, they were supposed to regenerate from simple wounds."

Simon joined Luthor and knelt down beside the vampire as well, running his fingers through the bright red blood. Pulling his hand back, he rubbed his fingers together, raised them to his nose, and smelled the pungent scent of blood.

"I'm assuming from mythological reports that they certainly didn't bleed this much."

Luthor shook his head. "The undead barely bled at all, having already been drained of all their blood when they were turned."

Simon reached up and pulled open the man's mouth. Reaching in, he ran his fingers along the canines.

"Do be careful," Luthor said. "I'm not saying I believe this to be a true vampire, but I would hate for you to become infected simply because of carelessness."

Simon snorted. "I think I'm safe. If I were to become infected with vampirism, I'm assuming you would kill me?"

"Without hesitation."

Simon grabbed a hold of the man's long fang and tugged, pulling it free from his mouth with minimal effort. He held the smooth, white tooth in front of his face so the apothecary could examine it.

"I don't think you need to worry about infections," Simon said. "It's a veneer. This man is no more a vampire than you or I."

Luthor took the tooth and held it up to the electric light. "It's an elaborate ruse, but for what purpose? How did he coalesce from the smoke?"

Simon looked at the corpse as Luthor took the veneer and stood, holding the false fang to the light filtering through the window. The corpse was well dressed, wearing a double-breasted suit jacket covering a vest underneath. Simon patted the exposed pockets but found nothing of interest. When he reached into the man's inner breast pocket, however, he smiled broadly. He pulled free a rectangular ticket, recently punched for the train ride.

"He didn't suddenly appear. He'd been on the train the whole time."

"Then how did he emerge from the mist?" Mattie asked. "It seemed fairly supernatural to me."

Luthor lowered the veneer and stepped over the expanding pool of blood. Near the back of the dining car, a table had been set nearly against the wall. Wisps of white mist still poured down the wall from a concealed origin. Reaching tentatively into the mist, Luthor felt the sharp edges of an alcove, inset into the wall just above head level. As his fingers probed further into the alcove, he came in contact with something that was bone-chillingly cold. He withdrew his hand with a start but quickly summoned the confidence to reach within the alcove once more.

The cold seemed to emanate from a concealed container, one clearly made of metal. As Luthor's hand found a handle, he withdrew the container. Mist trailed behind it, even as the metal bucket emerged from the alcove.

With a hasty wave of his hand, Luthor cleared away the clinging mist and smiled appreciatively.

"This isn't a case of supernatural at all, but rather science. Dry ice, to be exact. Mixed with water, it creates an impressive cloud of fog or smoke. Properly placed as it was near the upper corner of the dining car, it would flow down the wall, concealing the back portion of the train car while quickly crawling eerily across the floor. You're correct, sir. This is nothing more than a hoax."

"An elaborate one at that," Simon replied as he, too, stood from beside the corpse. "This is not a fly-by-night operation, but one that clearly consisted of significant preparation and planning."

All three of them were nearly thrown from their feet as the engineer applied the brakes on the train. Metal screeched as the wheels abruptly stopped their rotations. Sparks flew as metal ground against metal and the train slid to a stop.

"What in the devil?" Simon asked angrily.

His question was quickly answered by a loud commotion outdoors. They rushed to the window as a large portion of the train's population disembarked, their luggage in tow.

"There was a monster on board, I tell you," one man yelled, his voice being heard clearly above the din of nervous conversation.

"Come, Luthor, we need to put a stop to this nonsense at once."

They hurried off the train, stepping between the cars and emerging into the middle of the growing crowd of mortified patrons.

"Ladies and gentlemen, please calm yourself," Simon shouted, though his words were lost amidst the multitude of people talking simultaneously.

"No job is worth the risk of being attacked by a magical abomination," someone yelled.

"Ladies and gentlemen, if you'll simply listen to me," Simon tried again. "There is no threat. It was merely a hoax."

A few people nearby turned as Simon spoke, but most continued to ignore his warnings. Drawing his pistol, Simon fired into the air. The crowd grew suddenly quiet, and all eyes turned toward the Inquisitor.

Simon slowly lowered and holstered his pistol. He coughed politely as he ensured he had everyone's undivided attention.

"Forgive me for startling you all, but it seemed the only sensible way to get your attention. My name is Royal Inquisitor Simon Whitlock, on assignment to investigate the very rumors of attacks on the train to Whitten Hall. Clearly, I can confirm that attacks have occurred."

People turned to one another but Simon raised his hand, begging for continued silence and attention. "What is not confirmed, however, is that these attacks have anything to do with the supernatural. What I killed in the car behind me was no monster. It was merely a man, a charlatan, plying his crafts of deception and misdirection. More importantly, he's now dead, which means we can all board the train once more and be on our way."

"We appreciate everything you've done thus far, Inquisitor," a balding man stated as he emerged from the crowd, "but forgive us for not wanting to board the train once again. I would rather take my chances here, in the wilderness, than risk another attack of the same. I think I speak for a good portion of the ladies and gentlemen behind me."

Murmurs of assent spread through the crowd.

Simon shook his head and sighed. "I have neither the inclination nor the desire to explain all the reasons you're being foolish. If you don't wish to board this train again, then so be it. However, I have a mission that I would like to accomplish with all haste. Therefore, if it's all the same to you, those that are boarding, please do so now."

Luthor leaned over and whispered to Simon. "What of those that refuse to get back on the train?"

Simon arched an eyebrow. "To hell with them. I refuse to drag this mission out longer than absolutely necessary over general ignorance." He turned toward the confused conductor and smiled. "All aboard who are coming aboard."

Less than half the original patrons boarded the train before it pulled away from its impromptu stop. As Luthor watched those who refused to return to the train disappear into the distance behind them, Simon draped a tablecloth over the false vampire. The white linen quickly absorbed the deep red blood, leaving a halo around the corpse's broken head.

"Shall I do something about the woman?" Mattie asked as she knelt beside the still-unconscious blonde.

"Straighten her legs, perhaps, to assist with the circulation," Simon offered. "Otherwise, she'll come to eventually."

Luthor glanced toward the sheet covering the body and frowned. "For the work of a single man, it certainly had a devastating effect."

Simon nodded. "It had the desired effect, I would assume. The vast majority of patrons refuse to travel to Whitten Hall. Lesser government officials most assuredly wouldn't continue their trip. It's only through the bad luck of the bastard under the sheet that he chose to attack a train with an Inquisitor on board."

Mattie pulled the woman's legs from beneath her and straightened them, granting the unconscious woman some semblance of dignity. "Surely this wasn't the work of just the one man. The logistics alone seem far more than a person could manage on their own."

"You are correct in that regard, Miss Hawke. Someone put this man up to the task of impersonating a vampire, someone, I would presume, who lives in Whitten Hall. I very much look forward to having a stern conversation with that man upon our arrival."

CHAPTER Fifteen

"**H**AVE YOU SEEN THE OTHER CARS?" LUTHOR ASKED, as he returned from the loo."

Simon pushed aside the reports he'd been reading, his interest suddenly piqued by the unexpected attack by the false vampire. "I can't say that I have. There isn't another issue, I would hope."

"Not an issue in the traditional sense. Simply that the once filled train car is now a veritable ghost town. Those that are still on board seem hesitant to even make eye contact with one another. It's disconcerting."

Simon dismissed his concerns with a wave of his hand. "They're paranoid without reason. The culprit has already been proven to be nothing more than a simple man. A dead simple man, I might add."

Luthor took his seat beside Mattie. He glanced briefly at the paperwork before Simon but immediately looked away, having already become intimately familiar with its contents.

"What they ought to be doing, instead, is enjoying the scenery as it passes," the Inquisitor continued.

Luthor gazed out the window as the wooded countryside slid past the train. The forest was dense with untended undergrowth. To the side of the train, it fell away toward unseen ravines and crevices in the rock. The only visible breaks in the wood line occurred when the loose soil gave way to rocky gorges, filled to capacity with large rocks and a winding maze of footpaths.

Mattie followed his gaze out the window. "It doesn't look like a land on the cusp of a revolution, does it?"

Luthor shrugged. "I would hardly expect cannons and musketeers lining the edges of the train tracks."

"I would," the redhead replied. "Whitten Hall has ceased shipment of raw iron to the capital. If I were them, I would expect an army to appear on the next train."

Despite his blasé attitude, Luthor recognized the wisdom in her words. "Perhaps they know something we don't."

"That should frighten you," Simon added. "Any time we don't understand all aspects of the situation at hand—"

"We're caught unaware by a demon in our midst," Luthor concluded, though he doubted Simon would have finished his sentence in such a fashion.

"We don't think that another demon is truly a possibility here, do we?" Mattie asked, her fear evident.

Their encounter with Gideon Dosett in Haversham hadn't ended well for any of the trio, all of whom left with injuries that required nearly the entirety of the zeppelin journey to heal.

She discreetly turned her gaze to Luthor, who politely shook his head.

"I would very much doubt a return of a demon like we encountered before," the apothecary said, attempting to set her mind at ease.

"Can we be sure? We are dealing with an outpost that, for reasons we have yet been able to surmise, ceases iron shipments. This is a town that, from all accounts, was a loyal subject to the crown prior to this inexplicable change of heart."

Luthor nodded. "You're rightfully concerned that the denizens of Whitten Hall have been coerced, much like Dosett had done to the citizens of Haversham."

"And to me," she added.

"I can say with some confidence," he began, before sharing what he hoped was a knowing glance with her, "that another demon has not arrived so soon after we dispatched the first."

"Never discount a possibility until it has been definitively disproven," Simon said without looking up from the papers. "That adage is as true for demons as it is for epidemiological outbreaks."

The Inquisitor stacked the papers neatly and slipped them into the folder from which they came. Reaching to the edge of the table, he retrieved his top hat, placing it on his head at his traditional, slightly canted style.

"Regardless, our questions will soon be answered," he said, as the whistle blew from the train's engine and the passenger car lurched beneath them. "We'll soon arrive at the Whitten Hall station."

The engineer applied the brakes, and an ear-piercing screech of metal permeated the cabin. The trio flinched at the sound even as they clung to the edges of the benches for support. The train cars rocked, first forward as the brakes were applied and then backward as the engineer released the brakes and the train rolled smoothly into the station.

In contrast to the relative elegance of the Callifax train station, the Whitten Hall station was little more than a raised platform set upon the remains of a dusty wagon trail, long since degraded from disuse. A single ticket office sat upon the platform, its counter and glass partition both coated in dust. A printed sign in the window read, "Out to Lunch. Back in:" though the hands of the printed clock face beneath it were missing. Simon doubted they had been present in some time.

Though Simon hardly anticipated a fanfare upon his arrival, he was dismayed to see the platform nearly empty of people. A few dirty gentlemen stood idly by one end. They had the appearance and demeanor of foremen and would most certainly be welcoming the new laborers.

The only other person on the platform was a porter, holding a small sign that read, though Simon had to strain to see its small script and poor penmanship, "Royal Inquisitor Whitlock".

"There, sir and madam, is our welcoming entourage," Simon remarked flatly.

"It's a bit underwhelming, sir."

"Indeed it is. Come. Let's gather our things."

They stood from the bench and retrieved the small personal effects they wished to keep upon their person. Mattie carried nothing, though both men knew she was more than imposing without any additional armaments. Luthor collected his doctor's bag, filled as it was with vials and jars of assorted healing herbs and extracts. Simon gathered a single square, wooden box onto which had been affixed a leather handle.

They waited a few moments as they watched the laborers disembark.

As a group, they were collected by the waiting foremen and led to a set of covered, horse-drawn wagons.

When Simon was confident they were the last tenants on the train, he led them to the open door leading from their passenger car.

Though the porter knew nothing of the trio aside from the name scribbled upon his card, it took no effort to recognize the Inquisitor for what he was. The porter hurried to their side and nodded respectfully.

"Royal Inquisitor Whitlock, I presume?" the young man asked.

"I am. With me are Mister Luthor Strong, apothecary, and Miss Matilda Hawke, animal husbandry."

Mattie frowned at Simon's joke at her expense, though the porter was none the wiser.

"It is an honor to meet you, sir. Can I take your bags?"

The porter reached for the wooden box in Simon's hand, but the Inquisitor quickly pulled it from his grasp.

"My apologies," the porter quickly stammered.

"No offense taken," Simon remarked, "but all the bags currently in our possession will remain so. There are more than enough suitcases and such still within our cabin on the train. There is also a corpse underneath a draped sheet in the first dining car that I will need retrieved as well."

The porter blanched as he looked to the Inquisitor. "Sir?"

Simon arched an eyebrow. "A corpse, boy. I don't believe it is presumptuous of me to assume he was a resident of Whitten Hall before his untimely demise. Someone here should claim his body for a proper burial."

"How… how did he die, if I may, sir?"

Simon glanced at Mattie and smiled. "Lead poisoning. A fatal allergy, from what I'm told."

The porter nodded before turning to the train. He disappeared into the same doorway through which the three had recently disembarked. Luthor watched through the train's window as the porter appeared in their cabin and began fumbling with the heavy suitcases stored on racks above the benches.

"Do you always arrive to such little pomp and circumstance?" Mattie asked.

"Would you believe that even Haversham provided a far more impressive welcoming committee?" Simon answered.

A suited man appeared at the end of the train station and climbed the few stairs onto the raised platform. He wore boots on his feet that were covered in dust. Steel plates on the back of the boots clicked on the wooden platform with each step. He hurried to their side before stopping and removing his hat.

"Forgive my tardiness, gentlemen and lady," the man said.

A fine sheen of sweat stood out prominently from the man's brow, though Simon doubted they looked much better. The humidity in Whitten Hall was far higher than he had encountered elsewhere during his travels. The man's hair was cut close to his scalp, leaving skin visible through the thin, black hair. His eyebrows were heavy, leaving him with a stern visage that belied the pleasant smile he wore.

"My name is Tom Wriggleton. I was caught unaware that the train was arriving until I heard its whistle. I hurried as quickly as I could but, as you can plainly see, failed to meet you upon your arrival."

"Are you in the employment of the governor?" Simon asked.

Tom shook his head. "We are a small outpost, sir, hardly worthy of an appointed governor. There's one assigned for this region, but he so rarely makes an appearance in Whitten Hall. We have a locally elected chancellor who presides over the city council and makes decisions on behalf of the governor."

"Is your chancellor available?" Simon asked.

"I apologize, but he isn't, not today at least. Chancellor Whitten wanted to meet you in person upon your arrival, but business called him away at the last minute. He's expected back tonight and, I'm certain, would be thrilled to meet with you then."

"Chancellor Whitten, you said?" Luthor asked. "I presume it's not just a coincidence that he shares a name with the town itself?"

Tom smiled. "Not at all, Mr.…."

"Strong. Luthor Strong."

"Mister Strong," Tom continued. "It was Chancellor Whitten's family who first settled this region two generations past. His grandfather led the expedition that first entered this once inhospitable region of the continent and discovered the enormous veins of iron running just beneath the ground. Though we democratically elect our chancellors, a Whitten has held the position ever since the town was founded."

"Then what is your capacity in Whitten Hall?" Simon asked. "Are you a council member?"

Tom cleared his throat, the smile fading from his face. "Forgive me if I seem too forthcoming."

"There's hardly such a thing as 'too forthcoming' in the course of an investigation."

"You are, as I'm sure, aware of our tenuous current position."

"We are," the Inquisitor replied matter-of-factly, leaving Mister Wriggleton even more ill at ease.

"As one of the senior businessmen in town, I have been recruited as an advisor to the chancellor. With my help and the help of other members of town who have a vested interest in seeing an end to this circumstance in which we find ourselves, we hope to find an amicable resolution."

Simon arched his eyebrow. "The crown won't offer an amicable solution, not when their very livelihood and wealth are being held captive."

"To be honest, sir," Tom replied, "we had hoped you might be able to assist with that capacity."

"I think you misunderstand my purpose here," Simon said.

Tom fumbled with the brim of his hat as uncertain men are prone to do. "Perhaps this is something better discussed with the chancellor. In the meantime, I can show you to the rooms we have reserved for your stay in Whitten Hall, if you would prefer."

"In lieu of other options, please lead the way."

They walked down the few steps that led from the wooden platform to the dusty unpaved road that wound through the town. From the end of the train station, there was little of Whitten Hall left to the imagination.

The main thoroughfare ran parallel to the railroad tracks, with the storefronts and homes all facing the tracks. The single road was broken only by narrow alleyways between the buildings, through which Simon could see that the more elegant storefronts were merely facades, plastered upon the fronts of poorly constructed buildings for mere aesthetic value.

The forest clung to the backsides of the buildings, branches heavy with leaves hanging over the rooftops and draping like ivy down the sides of the structures.

Mister Wriggleton led the group across the dusty street. Hitching posts had been constructed in front of the majority of storefronts, though few horses were present in the town. Fewer still were the people of Whitten Hall. Simon noted a few faces peering at the Inquisitor and his companions as they mounted the porch on the front of a general store, but a second glance showed empty windows where once people had been watching. For a town of one hundred and fifty citizens, Whitten Hall felt very much like the train on which they had arrived—a veritable ghost town. It was hardly a bastion of rebellion, full of citizens refusing iron shipments to the crown.

Near the end of the short row of buildings was a combination of pub with an inn occupying the majority of the second floor. The door swung open with a creak of age and exposure to dust and humidity. The interior was quite a bit cooler, though the humidity still clung to the air like a blanket.

Tom didn't bother with introductions to the few men sitting haphazardly about the room. The bartender, a burly man with a long, handlebar moustache, paused briefly as he wiped the dingy bar with an equally dingy rag before going about his business.

Tom led the group up the stairs, which ended on a long, ill-lit hallway. Lanterns were mounted sporadically between closed doorways, but the meager light provided by the candles within hardly illuminated the hall.

Walking down it, their guide opened doors one after another.

"My apologies," he said, turning toward Mattie. "We were originally only expecting two of you; we had no idea that the Inquisitor had such an entrancing traveling companion. However, as you could easily surmise, we're not quite at our maximum occupancy. There are plenty of rooms available for your stay, though I will need to send someone up with fresh linens at once. Again, my apologies for the delay."

"There's no hurry," Mattie replied. "It will do me some good to stand and walk after such a long train ride."

Tom turned his attention back to Simon. "The chancellor is eager to meet with you upon his return and, I believe, will do his best to answer your questions. Until then, please make Whitten Hall your home. If you need anything at all, Gregory… forgive me, the bartender you passed as we entered, will be able to provide whatever you need. I do hope you enjoy your stay in our humble town."

Simon tapped his chin with his index finger as though deep in thought. "I do have one question before you depart."

Tom bit his lip nervously but nodded.

"How long is it until the next train departs for Callifax?"

Tom's nervous demeanor turned to relief. "The next train will be arrive in two days. I would presume that's the train on which you will be departing?"

"That is our intent," Simon replied. "I would hate to take up more of your time than absolutely necessary."

"Excellent, sir. Then I will leave you to your work and will come by later once the chancellor has returned. If there's anything you need, anything at all, don't hesitate to ask. If you can't find me here in town, my house is just outside the opposite end of the town proper. Good day, gentlemen and ma'am."

They watched Tom depart down the stairs before turning toward one another.

"You truly can't be done with this mission soon enough, can you, sir?" Luthor asked, irritated.

"There are a thousand things I'd rather be doing with my life than exploring the meager offerings of a backwater mining outpost. Four days to arrive, two days of waiting, and four days in return is more than enough time for the Grand Inquisitor to make a decision pertaining to our and Mattie's predicament. That is truly why we were sent here in the first place, was it not, to provide ample time to make a difficult decision?"

"There is more to Whitten Hall than meets the eye," Luthor responded.

"All of which a Royal Inquisitor, an apothecary, and a tribal woman from the frozen tundra are ill suited to investigate. This is, again, a task best suited for the Ministry of Trade, not the Inquisitors. Don't take yourself too seriously, Luthor, it's bad for the circulation."

Luthor sighed and turned away, choosing to enter his room rather than continue the conversation. Simon smiled broadly at Mattie before entering his room as well.

His luggage was still in transit from the train, having not yet arrived with the porter. Therefore, he had little to do other than examine the small confines of his hotel room.

A narrow bed sat in the middle of the left wall with a dresser pressed against the right. A large, stone fireplace dominated the wall across from the room's entrance and an inviting flame danced across a single piece of wood burning in its center. A candle rested upon the mantle without the benefit of a candleholder. Its red wax had run into a clump upon the surface, fusing it in place. Small fingers of wax crept over the lip of the mantle, running down toward the open maw of the fireplace beneath.

Simon sat his wooden box on the floor beside the bed and used the toe of his shoe to push it underneath the slightly raised bed frame. Satisfied, he turned from his room and walked back into the hallway.

Luthor and Mattie exited their rooms as well, clearly as equally thrilled over their accommodations as Simon. They shared equally disappointed expressions before Luthor motioned toward the stairwell.

"Shall we convene at the pub downstairs?"

"That is perhaps the best recommendation I've heard all day," Simon replied. "To the pub."

CHAPTER

E VEN FEWER PATRONS WERE SITTING IN THE PUB BY the time the group descended the stairs. The few that remained gave them curious stares as though strangers, especially ones of their caliber, were an oddity within Whitten Hall.

The bartender hadn't seemed to move since their arrival. He stood in the same place behind the bar, cleaning with the same dirty cloth.

They chose one of the numerous empty tables and sat. Simon glanced toward the bar but hesitated, unsure if it would even be prudent to order drinks from the surly bartender. To his surprise, a squat woman emerged from a room behind the bar and approached their table.

"Good afternoon, everyone," she said cheerfully as she reached their table. "Can I get you something to drink?"

Simon deferred to Mattie, allowing her to order.

"Whatever beer you have available," she said.

"We have an amber ale, locally brewed," the waitress replied. "I'm sure it's not nearly as impressive as the drinks available to you in the big city, but it does all right for our kind."

"It sounds perfect," Mattie said.

"And for the gentlemen?"

"A scotch for me, if you please," Simon immediately responded.

"Just a water, if it's all the same," Luthor added, drawing an odd glance from everyone at the table.

"Excellent. I'll be right back with your drinks."

The waitress walked away and Simon turned toward the apothecary. "Water seems like a poor choice, Luthor. So rarely do we have a chance to relax and enjoy ourselves while on a mission. You should be taking full advantage."

"We shouldn't be enjoying ourselves even now, sir."

Simon frowned. "Spoken like a true pessimist."

Luthor sighed. "All I mean, sir, is that we are on a mission and should be focused as such. You offer such a striking dichotomy."

"How so?" Simon replied, genuinely curious to hear the apothecary's answer.

"You have presented a truly disinterested persona ever since before we departed Callifax. Yet, upon meeting our representative at the train station, you resumed your truly Inquisitor-like demeanor and spoke with a genuine air of professionalism."

"It's simple, Luthor. I have hardly concealed the fact that I find our current assignment to be utter nonsense. However, when faced with a representative of the town, I'm not representing merely myself but the entirety of the Inquisitors. My professionalism is a reflection of my training and capabilities. I would be sorely put out if I presented something less than my full potential."

Luthor pointed enthusiastically. "That, sir, is exactly the level of interest I would like to see applied to this mission as a whole."

Simon furrowed his brow and stroked his chin thoughtfully before finally shaking his head. "Nonsense. This mission is absolute rubbish."

Before Luthor could offer so much as a discontented sigh, the waitress returned with their drinks. She set down three wooden flagons on the table before sliding them in front of the respective patrons. The trio glanced at their drinks before turning inquisitively toward the heavyset woman.

"Is this scotch?" Simon asked, as the identity of the fluid within the brown flagon was difficult to discern.

"Yes, sir. That is what you ordered, was it not?"

"Oh, no, madam, it most certainly was."

Simon lifted the flagon and examined the wooden vessel. Around the periphery of the mug, intricate pictures had been carved depicting a war between armies, the names of which no one was likely to recall.

"It's in a flagon?" Simon asked, though even Luthor struggled to discern Simon's intent with the posed question.

"Do you like it?" the barmaid asked. "I carved it myself."

"It's exquisite," Simon replied with a warm smile.

As the barmaid turned away, Simon's smile faded. Luthor waited until the woman was out of earshot before he turned toward his mentor.

"You were being facetious."

"Of course I was being facetious," Simon replied, exasperated. "First and foremost, scotch is served over ice in a tumbler. At most, I drink a finger or two at a time. This flagon is nearly full. The woman is clearly attempting to send me into immediate liver failure.

"Secondly, and far more importantly, *she served me scotch in a flagon*. Flagons are meant to be filled with mead and drunk by hairy men in skirts with horns upon their helms. What am I, a barbarian?"

"Are you quite finished?"

"Not even remotely, but I will cede the floor."

Mattie drank from her beer, licking her lips as she set her own flagon upon the table. "The beer is as I would expect, slightly flat and warm but with a good alcohol content that, somehow, makes you overlook its flaws."

"At least someone is remaining positive about this adventure," Luthor added.

"Misadventure," Simon corrected.

Luthor lifted his own glass to his lips. As he drank of the water, his expression froze on his face. He pulled the wooden mug from his lips and let the water dribble from his mouth and back into his cup.

"Whatever is the matter, Luthor?" Simon asked slyly. "Is the water not to your satisfaction? You seem, oh, what's the word, mildly pessimistic about your drink of choice."

Luthor cleared his throat and fought the urge to scrape the offensive taste from his tongue. He lowered his voice so as not to be overheard. "This water tastes faintly of urine."

Simon shrugged. "You're an apothecary. I'm sure there are some medicinal uses for urine."

Luthor flushed with frustration. "Certainly none that I can think of that require ingestion."

"It's amazing how quickly one's attitude can change when faced with the simple fact that our entire purpose in being here is utter bollocks."

Luthor shook his head in an attempt to clear away the early onset of nausea. "Our reasons for being here still aren't bollocks, sir, merely this drink." He cringed at the thought of bollocks being involved in the making of his drink.

The pub door opened, and a pair of heavily laden porters entered with their luggage in tow. The two men sighed as the door swung closed behind them.

"Inquisitor Whitlock, sir," the first porter said breathily. "Where would you like your bags?"

Simon stood, his flagon of scotch quickly and pleasantly forgotten. He approached the two men with a broad smile.

"Gentlemen, thank you kindly for your work." He recognized the porter who spoke as the same man he had encountered upon the train platform after their arrival. "Was the other business taken care of as well?"

The porter averted his eyes at the mention of the corpse. "Indeed it was, sir. The coroner claimed it and had it removed."

"Excellent. In that case, please deposit our luggage in our rooms upstairs."

The porters looked to the steep bank of stairs and audibly groaned.

As the men staggered under the weight of the bags, Luthor and Mattie stood from the table and joined Simon near the door. They watched as the men struggled increasingly with each step.

"I feel as though we should assist," Mattie offered. "It seems wrong that we merely watch."

"Nonsense, my dear," Simon replied. "I've never been one to tip lightly. They'll be well compensated for all their pains."

When the porters had disappeared from sight and their footsteps reverberated in the hallway above the pub, Simon placed enough coins on the table to pay for the drinks before the group retired to the upstairs.

Their doors were open as they reached the top of the stairs and suitcases were being deposited within. The two porters wiped a heavy sweat from their brows as they concluded their work. As they passed by the waiting trio, Simon handed them each a gold coin. They nodded appreciatively, though in hindsight, Simon realized the absurdity of the gesture. He had just offered a gold coin in compensation for their work. The very gold coin he just offered was the center of the controversy surrounding Whitten Hall. The iron had been mined from this very town, shipped to the capital, was paid for with the same coin with the king's face emblazoned upon it. The mere thought of it all made Simon's head hurt.

"It's still early afternoon," Luthor remarked as he stared at their still-open doors.

"I should hardly think unpacking will take until evening when the chancellor returns," Simon said, continuing Luthor's thought.

"Perhaps not for me," Mattie added. "Of the three of us, I clearly packed the lightest. I can't decide if that makes me a poor example of a lady or makes you poor examples of proper gentlemen."

"You a lady," both men replied.

The trio laughed heartily as they walked toward their respective rooms.

"I don't know about the two of you," Simon began, "but I have plenty to occupy my time until we are called upon. Shall we meet for dinner prior to our appointed meeting?"

Luthor glanced over his shoulder and groaned inwardly. "I don't assume we have many other options other than to eat at the tavern?"

"I would assume not."

The apothecary sighed. "Then I guess we shall meet for dinner. Until then, I will be consuming reagents until I'm sure I've properly destroyed any toxins within that abysmal glass of water."

"Until then," Mattie said as she stepped into her room.

Simon walked into his room, closing the door behind him. Dim light filtered through curtained windows, accentuating the meager light provided by the single log burning in the fireplace. For a moment, he considered lighting the candle as well, but it seemed a shame to further destroy the nub of the red candle as it clung to life on the mantle.

His suitcases were placed at the foot of the bed, but he ignored them. They were full of clothing and little else, most of which he would not require until the morning. Instead, he knelt beside his bed and reached underneath the low, wooden bed frame until his fingers closed around the wooden box he had concealed there.

He pulled the box free and placed it on the mattress. From his pocket, he withdrew a key and inserted it into a concealed lock. With a twist, he heard the satisfying fall of the tumblers.

Simon lifted the lid, revealing a collapsible crossbow, wooden stakes, blessed holy water, an assortment of silver bullets, and other objects within his Inquisitor's kit assembled specifically for slaying mystical creatures.

Despite Luthor's insinuations to the contrary, Simon always took his job seriously when it came to reports of the supernatural.

CHAPTER Seventeen

"THE CHANCELLOR WILL SEE YOU NOW," MISTER WRIGgleton said as he stood patiently in the hallway outside their hotel rooms.

The sun had set some time ago, and the flickering light from their respective fireplaces silhouetted Simon, Luthor, and Mattie.

"Chancellor Whitten is truly sorry for his late return," Tom continued with a disarming smile. "The political responsibilities for someone defying the crown is… well, as I'm sure you can assume, it's fairly astronomical."

Simon offered a weary smile in response. The hour was late and between the long train ride and the humidity within Whitten Hall, he felt drained. "Please lead the way, Mister Wriggleton. I don't believe either myself or either of my companions wish to keep the chancellor any longer than absolutely necessary tonight."

Tom nodded and stepped aside, allowing the trio access to the hallway. They walked down the stairs together, their guide in the front. The tavern below was far livelier than when they had arrived. Nearly all the tables were full with people laughing amongst themselves, their drinks all but untouched amidst the endless streams of conversation. Eyes turned inquisitively toward Simon and his friends as they reached the bottom of the stairs, but Tom seemed oblivious to the accumulated glances as he led them toward the front door.

Simon glanced to his right and acknowledged the pensive scowl from the bartender. Most of the townsfolk had seemed polite, despite their conflict with the crown and its representatives. Only the bartender seemed standoffish, which made Simon trust him far more than anyone else.

As they left the bar, the cool evening air struck them. The heat of the midday had faded, although the humidity remained. Simon could feel the beads of sweat soaking into the stiff collar of his dress shirt. The top hat, canted slightly atop his head, served little purpose in the dark night, save to capture the dampness that saturated his coifed hair.

Only a lonely pair of oil lanterns burned along the street. Despite the gloom, the outpost was alive with activity. The town that had appeared a ghost town upon their arrival was burgeoning with life. The storefronts had seemed desolate and isolated as the train had pulled into the station but, to Simon's surprise, remained open even at this late hour, allowing the businesses to flourish under the new patronage.

"There seem to be an abnormally large number of people in the town now," Luthor remarked, echoing Simon's thoughts.

Tom nodded as they walked toward the edge of Whitten Hall proper. "Chancellor Whitten travels with a large entourage. The town itself may be safe, but the surrounding countryside isn't by far. Bandits and highwaymen stalk the roads; if you travel off the major roads, as the chancellor does, then you have to fear the ravines and canyons that scar the land. You're just as likely to fall into a fissure as have your horse turn a hoof or throw a shoe."

"Wouldn't you be afraid of the crown retaliating while you're away?" Mattie asked. "It seems that you've taken nearly every able-bodied man out of the town to travel with the chancellor."

Tom glanced at Mattie as though he disapproved of her interjection into the conversation. Though he replied to her question, he directed his answer to Simon. "They take a risk by leaving the town mostly undefended as they travel but, to be honest, their presence in the town would hardly make a difference should royal soldiers arrive. We're poorly equipped to fight the crown face to face. The simple truth is that the chancellor has become a hero to the townsfolk. Even if Whitten Hall falls under crown jurisdiction once more, his safety is paramount to the town's independence."

Simon and Tom continued their conversation as they passed beyond the last of the dilapidated structures lining the town's sole thoroughfare. As the trail meandered into the dark woods beyond, Luthor fell in stride with Mattie, a few feet behind the two conversing men.

Even in the gloom, Luthor could see her visible scowl. It didn't take Simon's impressive detective skills to deduce the problem.

"It was a good question, and very apropos," Luthor offered as the group suddenly stopped.

Tom struck his steel knife against a shard of flint, causing sparks to illuminate the inky blackness of the road beneath the wood's dense canopy. After a few practiced strikes, the wick of a lantern hanging from a hook beside the road caught fire, pushing back the gloom.

Their guide lifted the lantern from its hook and bore it before him as they continued on their way.

After a few steps, Mattie huffed angrily. "That man is a right bastard, is what he is."

Luthor suppressed a chuckle, knowing his mirth would only fuel her fire. "It's not that he's a terrible man, quite possibly just the opposite. It's merely a different culture. In Haversham, you were encouraged to speak your mind. Your chieftain was even a female. In the rest of the kingdom, however, things aren't nearly as progressive."

"It's not being progressive to let a woman ask a question with the expectation you actually answer her. Not doing so makes you a right—"

"—bastard," Luthor finished. "You're right, of course. I can't rightfully defend a culture that doesn't let a woman speak her mind, especially when that woman is capable of removing a man's face with a single swipe."

Mattie smiled. "It does give me a sociological advantage, doesn't it?"

"I'll certainly be choosing my words carefully if I ever have to correct you."

She smiled and nudged him playfully with her elbow. "Damn right you will."

As they turned a corner on the winding road, they could see lantern lights filtering through the trees. A two-story manor house was set off the road a short distance, with a packed-dirt road leading to the columned entryway. Lanterns were hung from the house's exterior, both flanking the front doorway and lining the balconies on the second floor. It gave the building a haunted exterior, one that seemed ill lit and uninviting.

Tom turned onto the drive and led them toward the manor. Though the entryway itself was unmanned, Simon could see the shadows of rifled men standing guard on the balconies, perched in the shadows behind the hooded lanterns.

"This is the chancellor's home?" Simon asked as his eyes quickly scanned the building's exterior. Trees crowded the edges of the property but had been trimmed back from the house proper. Ivy crept up the side of the building, reaching nearly to the pinnacle of the tall brick chimney mounted to the home's left side.

"This is his family's home," Tom explained. "It's been here nearly as long as the mining community, built by the founding Whitten during the times of the iron rush. It's in a state of disrepair, having suffered lengthy vacancies as generations of Whitten's moved away to find their wealth beyond the trappings of managing an iron mine but, inevitably, one always returns. The current chancellor has only been back a few years and repairs have been slowed, what with the recent political designs."

Simon arched an eyebrow toward the man as they approached the lit doorway. "You've expressed quite some ingenuity in the number of ways you've managed to avoid saying that Whitten Hall is in revolt."

Tom frowned but quickly regained his composure. "One man's revolutionary is another man's criminal."

The door opened before him, forcing Simon to drop his voice to a whisper so as not to be heard by their host. "Too bad for Whitten Hall that those who see you as criminals have so many guns at their disposal."

The man who stepped from the manor's open door looked far younger than Simon would have expected. His skin was smooth, lacking the traditional lines of wear seen on those who spent so much of their time in the sun. The chancellor, for that was who Simon assumed him to be, was immaculately dressed, clearly attired specifically to impress his guests.

The chancellor marched confidently into the darkness of night to meet Simon as the Inquisitor approached.

"You must be Inquisitor Whitlock," the chancellor said, a broad smile spreading across his face. Even in the darkness, Simon could see the sincerity behind his obvious pleasure. "My name is Martelus Whitten, as I'm sure someone of your renown has already deduced."

"I would hardly call myself renowned, Chancellor, but I appreciate the sentiment."

The chancellor's smile lingered for a moment longer before he shook his head, as though awakening from a stupor. He stepped aside and gestured for Simon and the others to enter.

The interior of the house clearly lacked electricity. Candles burned in recessed sconces along the walls. An elaborate chandelier of candles, which dangled precariously overhead, brilliantly lighted the foyer. Despite Tom's admonition that the manor required upkeep, the interior was surprisingly well kept. The smell of wallpaper glue permeated the room, exuded from the recently refurbished walls. Plush, cushioned chairs adorning the sitting room to the right of the foyer, albeit antique, were well maintained and clean.

"Forgive me, sir," Tom said, breaking the still hush that had settled over the group, "but there is a mountain of paperwork that requires my attention."

The chancellor patted Tom firmly on the back before leading him to the door. "Of course, old friend. Get some rest tonight and I'll see you before we leave tomorrow morning."

Tom left, closing the door behind him. The chancellor turned back toward the trio. "Please, follow me. I wish I could offer you more comfortable surroundings, as I'm sure you're accustomed, but my home doubles as my office, unfortunately. We lack the trappings of affluence, in such a small mining community. We simply make do with what we have at our disposal."

Simon glanced toward Mattie. "You'd be surprised the austere living conditions in which an Inquisitor often finds himself, Chancellor."

The chancellor shook his head. "Please call me Martelus. We can dispense with the formalities, if it pleases you. I find titles often get in the way of two men truly expressing what's on their minds."

"Very well," Simon nodded as Martelus led them into a study.

Bookcases flanked a roaring fireplace, their shelves laden with assorted manuscripts and rolled maps. At quick glance, Simon saw an assorted collection of archaic and modern books on mining operations, intermixed without rhyme or reason with classical literature.

The study lacked a large, oaked desk as had seemed to become the norm amidst people of power. In lieu of the desk, two long couches sat perpendicular to the fireplace with a plush single chair at the head of the formation.

"Sit, please."

Simon and Luthor sat on the couch across from the chancellor while

Mattie quietly took the lone chair facing the fireplace.

"I would offer you a drink," Martelus began, "but I fear drinking so late would impede the rest of your investigation."

"You're a wise man," Simon replied, "though I'm not sure 'investigation' is quite the correct term. We were sent on quite a less auspicious task, one I might add that has already concluded."

Martelus arched an eyebrow. "Truly? On what mission were you sent, if I might inquire?"

Simon leaned forward, resting his elbows on his knees. "We were sent to investigate the matter of attacks occurring on the train."

The chancellor swallowed hard and looked away from the Inquisitor, clearly embarrassed.

"I see that you're intimately familiar with the issue at hand," Simon surmised.

Martelus turned back toward the group, a sad frown replacing the previously jovial smile. "I'm ashamed that I do."

Simon leaned back in the couch and nodded toward the chancellor. "Please do explain everything. I will fill in the blanks with what I know as well."

The chancellor cleared his throat. "We quite honestly meant no harm or even disrespect. You're more than familiar with our current situation and the strain between Whitten Hall and Callifax?"

Simon nodded his concurrence.

"Then you're also aware that it's only a matter of time until the crown sends its soldiers to reinstate the flow of iron to the capital. You're not the first royal representative to travel to Whitten Hall. We've had a plethora of tax collectors, constables, and even a handful of bounty hunters, all coming to either coerce or threaten our town, should we not comply with the crown's demands. To be honest, I feared you were yet another and it set me a bit on edge. A Royal Inquisitor is quite a bit more threatening than a simple tax collector."

Simon smiled at the compliment. "I can assure you that we're not here to take any political or legal action against your town. I merely want to know about the episodes on the train, if we could return to that issue."

"Of course," the chancellor replied, his smile slowly returning. He ran a nervous hand through his lush, brown hair. "With so many representatives from the crown arriving as quickly as the trains pulled into the station, I spent nearly as much time entertaining unwelcomed guests as

I did tending to my responsibilities as chancellor. To that end, one of the men in town, and forgive me but I cannot recall who, had the idea to stop visitors before they ever arrived."

"To that end, you staged vampire attacks on the train."

"I'm, again, ashamed to admit that we did. We meant no disrespect, as I mentioned before. In fact, no one was permanently harmed during our escapades. The 'vampire' attacks, if you will, were merely meant to scare away the passengers on board. You see, most royal representatives lack the intestinal fortitude once they perceive their lives are at risk, present company excluded, of course."

"Of course," Simon replied.

"Begging your pardon," Luthor interrupted, "but someone was harmed on this last train ride."

"Who was harmed?" the chancellor quickly asked.

"Your vampire," Simon replied flatly.

Martelus appeared crestfallen at the news. He lowered his eyes and shook his head sadly. "Wallace was a good boy; I knew his family well. Would it be a correct assumption that you had something to do with his untimely death?"

"You would be right in that assumption," Simon replied, though his words lacked any haughty underpinnings. "I regret that your man had to die, but staging vampire attacks on a train with an armed Inquisitor was a fatal mistake."

"I don't blame you, sir," Martelus replied. "Our staged attacks had worked so many times previously; I think we merely became overconfident that they would continue to keep the crown at bay."

Simon crossed his arms over his chest. "In that regard, your attacks most certainly did keep the tax collectors at bay. Despite your political… difficulties, my mission has nothing to do with your mine and your production, or lack thereof, of iron."

"I wondered as much. It seemed excessive to include a Royal Inquisitor in what is, at its core, a labor dispute."

Luthor cleared his throat. "Forgive my interruption, Chancellor, but would it be too forward of me to ask about your labor dispute?"

"Not at all, Mister… Strong, is it?"

"Indeed it is, sir. At its crux, why have you ceased iron shipments to the capital?"

Martelus smiled knowingly, as though he had answered a similar question hundreds of times previously. "You misunderstand our dilemma. We didn't cease shipping iron to Callifax. We ceased mining iron all together."

"I don't think I understand," the apothecary replied.

Martelus held out his hands, palms upward, as he continued. "You, like many who have come to Whitten Hall, assume that we're hoarding the iron ore that rightfully belongs to the crown. The simple truth is that we have no interest in the ore. What concerns us is a pay that more properly equates to the labor and dangers we assume working in the mines."

He raised his left hand as he continued. "On average, we mine nearly a quarter tonne of iron every day. Consider that every weapon in their arsenal, every vehicle on the road, every cannon guarding the king's parapets, is forged from the very iron and smelted steel that we provide, you can imagine our frustrations when our back-breaking labor is used to fill already fat coffers, every day that we are in operation."

He lowered his left and raised his right hand. "For our troubles, we're paid a mere pittance. The daily wages for the miners in Whitten Hall is barely five copper pieces. At the current exchange of one hundred copper coins per one gold coin, our nearly one hundred miners are paid five gold coins in total for a quarter tonne of iron they provide to the crown. Compound that for each day of the year, and you can see the incredible boon we provide the crown, but the utter lack of appropriate compensation."

"Then all of this is merely to increase your wages?" Simon asked.

The chancellor sighed but nodded. "It may seem trivial to someone used to the affluence of the capital city, but to those of us on the outskirts of the kingdom's benevolence, a few extra copper coins per day could make the difference between life and death, especially during the harsh winters when food is a premium and carries a premium's cost."

"I understand far more than you could imagine," Mattie said. To her surprise, the chancellor turned toward her and nodded appreciatively.

Simon glanced toward the entryway, as though seeing something beyond the thick wood of the closed door. "Our initial report stated that one hundred and fifty people lived in Whitten Hall."

Martelus smiled. "Yet you passed through our small town and noticed not nearly as many as that are still present?"

"You are a perceptive man," Simon replied.

"Not perceptive, but rather familiar with the questions asked by visitors. At the height of our mining operations, it's true that one hundred and fifty men, women, and children lived in Whitten Hall. When the decision was made to withhold iron shipments, however, we held a town hall meeting and offered those who did not support our plan a chance to leave town. Many did leave, though quite a few remained."

Simon uncrossed his arms. "Forgive my line of questioning. I didn't mean to impugn your motives."

"No offense was taken. As I explained before, we have no nefarious plans other than to contest the pittance earned for our skilled labor."

Simon glanced toward Luthor and Mattie but saw no further questions.

"This isn't the first time an element of the kingdom has chosen to stand against the crown," Martelus quickly added. "Were you here during the tradesmen uprising after the formation of the Rift?"

Simon frowned deeply and his eyes darkened.

"I see that you were," the chancellor continued, the fire dissipating in his voice. "Forgive me, I meant nothing by the comparison."

"It's I who should apologize," Simon replied. "Some wounds just seem fresher than others. I believe I understand your position well enough."

Content, he stood. Martelus quickly followed suit and extended his hand. As Simon shook, however, Luthor cleared his throat once more.

"You said that the mines are no longer in operation?" Luthor asked.

Martelus nodded slowly. "We have no reason to keep them open as we have no desire for the iron. The crown frowns upon requesting an increase in wages, but it's not treason. Stealing iron that belongs to the crown, however, is, and is far more an open invitation for an invasion by royal guardsmen."

"Would it be too much trouble, then, for us to see the mine?" the apothecary asked.

Simon glanced at him with a mixture of irritation and genuine curiosity, having known Luthor long enough to know that the apothecary rarely acted without good reason.

Martelus shrugged. "The hour is late, but I suppose I could take you. I warn you, though, there's little to see."

"Thank you, Chancellor," Luthor replied. "We'd be honored if you could grant us this request."

"Allow me to gather my things," Martelus said, "and we'll be on our way."

As the chancellor walked away, Simon arched his eyebrow toward the apothecary.

Chapter Eighteen

MARTELUS LED THEM FROM THE MANOR. AS SOON AS they emerged into the night air, they were flanked by guards carrying the same hooded lanterns that until recently hung on either side of the entryway.

At the end of the drive, they turned away from Whitten Hall and continued deeper into the darkness of the canopied woods. The chancellor spoke rarely, usually jovially, as they walked, but Simon heard little of the conversation, aside from his polite responses. He stole glances toward Luthor and sought an opportunity to speak in private.

The group approached a covered bridge spanning a wide but shallow river. As they stepped within, Simon dropped back a step until he was beside the apothecary.

"Would you care to explain why we're traipsing through the woods instead of enjoying a drink in the tavern?" the Inquisitor asked.

"Would you be referring to your flagon of scotch?" Luthor chided.

Simon frowned and glanced around, ensuring their low conversation wasn't overheard. "You know what I mean."

Luthor shook his head. "Something doesn't feel quite right about this scenario, sir."

"Do you have any empirical evidence or is this merely, as you stated, a feeling?"

Luthor frowned at the obvious derision. "No, I have no evidence. I have a habit of listening to my gut and right now it's telling me something's amiss."

"Mine's telling me I'm hungry," Simon teased.

"I'm serious, sir."

"As am I, Luthor."

"Don't you ever act simply on a feeling in your gut?"

"Basing my investigations on feelings that could just as easily be explained away as indigestion is absolute rubbish, Luthor. There's a reason the world of science is so universally accepted. We base our findings on fact and experimentation, not some sixth-sense nonsense."

"I don't have indigestion," Luthor muttered.

"You're jumping at shadows that just don't exist, Luthor. There's no conspiracy here to be uncovered."

Luthor turned sharply toward his traveling companion but continued walking across the wooden bridge. "You don't think his answers seemed a little too rehearsed?"

"They are rehearsed, since he's had to answer the same questions dozens of times for dozens of different people."

Luthor sighed. "He had an answer for every question, the perfect answer, I might add. That's a clear sign of someone who has fabricated a story."

"It's equally a sign of someone telling the truth, someone who's been forced to tell the same truth repeatedly."

"That's the same argument used for people who tell a lie so many times that they start to believe the lie as truth."

"Or it's merely the truth."

The clicking of soled shoes on the wooden beams filled the silence between them. The end of the covered bridge approached, and the gloom of the woods seemed far lighter than the inky blackness within the bridge.

Simon bit his lip as he considered his next words. "Since when did you become the skeptic and I the trusting mediator? I don't care for this new disposition."

Luthor smiled. "I'm not a skeptic, sir, but merely a cautious sort. Perhaps Mister Gideon Dosett set me on edge and made me far less trusting of politicians and businessmen. After all, Gideon was hardly a good man."

"He was a businessman," Simon replied, "and a fairly successful one at that. Honestly, even if he weren't a spawn of the Abyss, I still wouldn't have called him a good man."

They both laughed softly, drawing inquisitive stares from the chancellor and his guards. Simon merely shook his head, informing them that there was nothing of which to be concerned.

"What, pray tell, do you hope to find at the mine?" Simon asked as they emerged from the covered bridge.

Martelus glanced over his shoulder curiously, as though expecting the Inquisitor to rejoin him at the front of the group.

"I have trouble trusting a man who sits upon one of the richest iron veins in the kingdom, but expresses no interest in the wealth. I just want to be sure that the mine is, in fact, no longer in use."

"Then you will be satisfied?" Simon asked. "Afterward, you'll be comfortable returning with me to the tavern, drinking about two flagons more than what would be considered healthy, and enjoying the mundane scenery that Whitten Hall has to offer until our train arrives?"

"Consider it a deal, sir," Luthor replied.

Simon smiled and nodded before rejoining Martelus. As he matched the chancellor's stride, the man turned toward the Inquisitor.

"Is anything the matter?"

Simon shook his head. "My poor apothecary companion is still shaken after our last mission. He's being overly cautious, though I've pointed to your obvious sincerity. I'm sure all will be fine after we see the inoperable mine."

"Very good," Martelus replied, his broad smile returning. "As I mentioned earlier, we have nothing to hide. You'll see for yourself once we arrive in a few moments' time."

Throughout their walk, the branches of the trees to either side had interlaced above Simon's head, forming a tunnel multitudes darker than the night sky. Slowly, Simon noticed the moon peering through the thinning leaves. The bushes and undergrowth on either side of the road thinned, as did the trees that had previous crowded the packed dirt artery. Ahead, he could see that the trees transformed to severed stumps, which eventually gave way to open grass.

A warm glow radiated from a massive pit ahead. The light reflected off the sheer walls, revealing the layers of earthy strata. Martelus moved unerringly toward the lip of the quarry, pausing only as the road turned sharply and descended around the perimeter of the pit. The closer they approached, the louder the hum of machinery grew.

Simon paused at the edge of the carved fissure, staring downward to the rocky floor a hundred feet below. Generators rumbled, coughing black smoke into the air as they powered tall floodlights mounted around the perimeter of the quarry. Water pooled along half the stony floor, lying stagnant in a small pond that shimmered under the electric lights.

Luthor and Mattie joined him near the edge and admired the amalgamation of machinery sitting in various stages of disuse. Weeds grew along the sides of the train tracks, unkempt and wild. The tracks led into the obsidian mouth of a mineshaft. Mining carts were parked near the end of the line, which concluded near the center of the stone floor below, some rusted and others overturned, no longer along the tracks. A large crane and winch was affixed to the nearest wall, serving the obvious purpose of lifting the mined ore to the top of the pit for transportation.

As Martelus had alluded, everything in regards to the mine seemed to be in a state of disrepair from a lack of use. Little below gave Simon reason to believe that the remaining residents of Whitten Hall were, in fact, still mining the iron for their own venture.

Simon caught Luthor's eye, but the apothecary merely shook his head. Instead, the Inquisitor turned toward their host.

"Everything here appears copacetic," he said. "I don't believe any of my companions have any further questions or concerns."

"None, sir," Luthor replied begrudgingly.

"None for the moment," Mattie said, though her words were cradled in a tone of hesitation.

"Then please forgive my brusque departure, gentlemen and lady, but my work is never done and my bed calls to me even now."

Simon nodded. "Did I hear correctly that you will be departing again tomorrow morning?"

"Indeed you did. When you're starting even a peaceful protest against the crown, there are many other allies to court in the region. We can't change the king's mind without a unified front with the other outposts in the area. To that end, I travel and plead my case during each day and sleep woefully too few hours each night before repeating the process anew with each dawning morning."

"Sound dreadfully tiring," the Inquisitor remarked.

Martelus smiled. "I manage well enough, though I think everyone involved will be significantly happier once this business is behind us."

The chancellor motioned toward the road behind them. "You're more than welcome to accompany us as far as the manor if you feel so inclined."

"Thank you but no, Chancellor," Simon answered. "I believe my companions and I could use some time to merely walk and discuss amongst ourselves."

The chancellor nodded wearily and stifled a yawn. "Is your official business then concluded in Whitten Hall? Have you found all the satisfactory answers to the attacks on the trains?"

"Indeed, though I still feel terribly sorry for killing your man. Had I but known that it was all a ruse, perhaps things would have turned out quite differently."

"It was very much our fault," Martelus replied.

"If I may ask one last question?" Simon asked.

The chancellor paused nervously before nodding.

"When will the next passenger train be arriving in Whitten Hall? I don't wish to take any more of your time than necessary."

Martelus visibly sighed with relief at the simple question. "There are two trains that pass this way. The next one will arrive in two days' time, and the next two days after that."

Simon smiled. "Then in two days we will be forever out of your affairs."

"It was a pleasure hosting you and your friends. We can leave you a lantern to light your way but, if you'll excuse me, I'll have to take my leave."

"I completely understand," Simon said, offering his hand. Martelus shook, his hands cool to the touch after being exposed to the brisk night air. "Thank you for everything, Chancellor, and, believe it or not, I wish you all the best in your troublesome business ahead."

"You are indeed too kind, Inquisitor.

The chancellor and his guards provided Luthor a hooded lantern before turning and retreating down the dirt road. Their light bounced along the trunks of trees as they passed, but the forest quickly swallowed the dim light.

Once they were confident they were alone, Simon dropped the more formal pretenses.

"The chancellor isn't the only one exhausted," the Inquisitor said. "I may very well sleep until the train arrives."

Luthor frowned and crossed his arms defiantly across his chest. "Sir, I don't believe we're done discussing—"

"For tonight," Simon interrupted, "we most certainly are. The only thing we'll do tonight is walk back to the town proper and sleep—perhaps have a flagon of alcohol if we should be lucky enough to catch the barman at his post in the tavern. Beyond alcohol and sleep, I don't want to discuss this case any further until the morning."

If possible, Luthor's frown deepened. "This discussion isn't done."

"It is tonight."

"You're an insufferable bully at times, you know?"

"I do and I concur. Now, unless there's some other vitally important discussion that involves either alcohol or sleep, I say we set off back to the town. Agreed?"

Mattie and Luthor fell into step beside Simon as they walked back toward Whitten Hall.

Chapter Nineteen

SHORTLY BEFORE NOON, LUTHOR HEARD A FAINT knock at his door. He quickly pulled down the sleeves of his dress shirt and buttoned them firmly at the wrists. A kick of his shoed foot dispersed the salt poured upon the floor of the inn's room, and a carefully placed blanket appeared disheveled from a poor night's sleep while truthfully concealing his magical communions.

The apothecary opened the door far enough to peer through the space between it and the doorframe. To his surprise, he was met by a mop of unkempt red hair, only barely brushed or tamed. Mattie smiled at him and gestured toward the still mostly closed doorway.

"May I come in?" she asked.

"Is Simon with you?" Luthor asked as he opened the door slightly wider.

She glanced over her shoulder and peered down the short hallway. "No. I heard him awakening earlier and moving about. I'm sure he's a flagon or two into his daily drinking escapades by now."

Content, Luthor opened the door, allowing Mattie to enter his room. She eyed the blanket tossed haphazardly upon the floor and glanced toward the apothecary as he closed the door behind him.

"Closing the door while you have an impressionable woman alone in your room?" she teased. "Imagine the scandal."

Luthor blushed softly but quickly cleared his throat. "What can I do for you this morning?"

She used the toe of her boot to push aside the blanket, revealing the grains of salt spread across the floor. "Have you been… communicating with the Coven?"

Luthor glanced over his shoulder once more, though he was already sure he had closed the door firmly behind him. "I was."

"Do you truly think there's a chance another demon is present in Whitten Hall?"

Luthor could hear the genuine mixture of concern and fear in her voice, but he quickly shook his head. "Nothing that dangerous, I'm glad to report."

"Did the Coven have anything worthwhile to share?"

Luthor shook his head. "Sadly, no. They listened to my concerns, but they aren't in any position to scry into the goings-on in a place as remote as this. They can only tell me that there are no demonic presences in the immediate vicinity."

Mattie sat on the edge of his unmade bed, crossing her legs in a more masculine way than the dainty ankle crossing which Luthor was more familiar.

"Yet you do believe there's something amiss in the outpost?"

Luthor chose the solitary chair in the room, pulling it before the redhead before sitting. "I can't quite find anything specific, certainly nothing tangible that I can present to Simon."

"Yet you believe something's amiss?" she repeated.

Luthor nodded, unsure if more superfluous words were truly necessary.

"Thank God," Mattie exclaimed. "I was beginning to think that I was the only one."

Luthor sat forward excitedly. "You feel it as well?"

"Not feel, per se, but more *smell*. The whole town has an odd scent to it, like an underpinning of decay. It's not from any one location that I can surmise, but more a malodorous aroma that has permeated every corner of the town."

"Why didn't you mention this last night while I was being berated by Simon?"

Mattie furrowed her brow. "You two were quite thoroughly engaged in your debate. Besides, I hardly remember either of you even asking my opinion. I had become little more than a sideshow during your ongoing back and forth."

Luthor frowned, as much because he knew she was right as from his frustration at her lack of support the night before. "Your point is conceded. I'll ensure I don't make the same mistake again."

He gestured toward the closed door. "Would you come with me and plead our case again with Simon? Perhaps a unified front would convince him of the validity of our cause."

"He won't like it," Mattie replied, pushing a strand of offending hair from her face.

"I find myself garnering small amounts of pleasure from doing things that Simon doesn't like."

Mattie smiled as she stood. Together, they exited his room and took the stairs at the end of the hall to the tavern below.

True to form, Simon was sitting at a table, enjoying a drink as a plate of steaming food sat mostly forgotten before him. When he saw them approaching, the Inquisitor retrieved his pocket watch and checked the time.

"You've only just made it down during the morning hours," he remarked as Luthor and Mattie took seats across from him. "I quite nearly had to wish you a good afternoon."

"What can we say?" Luthor asked. "You kept us up to obscene hours of the night."

"*I* did?" Simon asked incredulously. "I seem to recall I wanted nothing more than to enjoy a good night's sleep and, perhaps, a drink or two."

"Which you seem to be thoroughly enjoying this morning."

Simon glanced at his watch again. "This afternoon," he corrected. "It's only just rolled past. Drinking in the afternoon is completely acceptable."

The Inquisitor glanced back and forth between his two companions when they didn't immediately reply. He could read their looks of consternation and forced an audible sigh.

"I presume you didn't join me this afternoon just for the delectable food and drinks in finely crafted flagons? Come on, then, out with it."

Luthor glanced briefly toward Mattie before returning his attention to Simon. "Have you informed the Inquisitors of your findings thus far?"

Simon set his drink on the table and shook his head. "I tried my best to be more responsible than I was in Haversham, but it appears a recent storm knocked down the telegraph lines between Whitten Hall and Callifax."

Luthor frowned. "I don't recall any serious storms in the region recently."

Simon reached for his fork but withdrew his hand in irritation. "Are we to begin this discussion anew?"

"Even you have to admit that it's a surprising coincidence that our one method by which we can contact the capital has been eliminated."

"It's not a coincidence," Simon replied. "It's an unfortunate situation, and I wouldn't be at all surprised if it was intentional."

Luthor smiled. "Then you admit that something is amiss in Whitten Hall."

"Yes, they are defying the crown. If the chancellor was tired of visitors, I can damn well assume he was bored to tears with the number of telegrams he received. Were I in his shoes, I would have personally climbed every telegraph pole between here and the capital and severed the lines."

Luthor turned pleadingly toward Mattie. Simon noticed the gesture and frowned considerably.

"Please don't tell me he's pulled you into this nonsense as well, Matilda. I expect better of you. You're the voice of reason to balance his irrationality."

Mattie shrugged. "I am sorry, Simon, but he's not wrong this time. There's something wrong with this town."

"Is this because you, too, have suffered gastrointestinal distress?"

Mattie furrowed her brow in confusion. Luthor shook his head as he explained.

"I merely told Simon I had a bad feeling in my gut."

She covered her mouth as she laughed.

"Don't encourage him," Luthor complained.

Simon interrupted. "Is it another gut feeling then, my dear?"

Mattie composed herself before shaking her head. "It's more the smell. Something smells wrong in the town. It's a scent I can't quite place, but it smells faintly of putrescence."

Simon pinched the bridge of his nose. "So when I complete my report for the Grand Inquisitor, I'll simply remark that we believe something to be amiss because one of my companions has a gut feeling that he promises is neither indigestion or hunger pangs, while the other believes the town smelled peculiar. I think this report will go over smashingly well."

"You mock us," Luthor replied angrily.

"You warrant mocking!" Simon replied, matching the apothecary's intensity. "You're both actively searching for conspiracies where no conspiracy exists. Can't you just enjoy the scenery and the poorly brewed alcohol for a few days before we board our train carriage home?"

He looked at both of their disapproving stares, neither of which wavered in the slightest as they glared at the Inquisitor.

Their intense moment was interrupted as the bartender delivered Simon another drink. He placed it on a folded napkin and didn't bother inquiring into Luthor or Mattie's drink requests before turning and walking away.

"I can't abide a situation such as this to pass without proper investigation," Luthor began. "You, of all people, should understand that."

Simon slid his new drink aside and lifted the folded cloth napkin. As he unfurled it, he read the scribbled script hastily written on its fabric.

"All we're asking is that you give this the serious consideration it deserves," Mattie added.

Simon set down the napkin and met their gazes. "You're absolutely correct. I'm an Inquisitor; the least I can do is inquire. It's my namesake, after all."

He discreetly pushed the napkin across the table. Luthor glanced around the nearly empty tavern, the population of Whitten Hall having reverted to its ghost town-like status, before he unfurled the cloth.

The words were muddied and smeared from the moisture of the drink that had so recently sat atop it. Still, the words were legible enough.

Chapter Twenty

THE TRIO RETIRED TO SIMON'S ROOM, WHERE THEY unfurled the napkin once more before placing it on the bed between them.

"Is it a threat?" Luthor asked, staring at the barely legible note.

"I read it more as a warning," Mattie replied. "I think the bartender meant it more as a warning that there is an as of yet unseen danger in Whitten Hall."

Luthor nodded. "As we've been saying all along."

"Let's not be presumptuous," Simon said. "Handwriting has no context. This wouldn't be the first time people have made incorrect assumptions after reading something."

"Then we go and ask him what he intended from the note," Luthor said, placing his hands on his hips.

Simon shook his head. "We can't."

"We most certainly can, sir. We go through your bedroom door, down the stairs, and into the tavern before—"

"That's not what I meant," Simon interrupted. "Gregory, our bartender accomplice, if that is what he is, operated very discreetly in giving us the note in the first place. You can be certain that he's being watched, or else he would have been far more forthcoming."

Luthor sat in the room's sole chair pensively, though his eyes never left the note.

"Besides, have you ever seen the tavern empty? Has there ever been an opportunity to contact Gregory without someone noticing? No, my dear Luthor, if we go storming downstairs like a herd of wildebeests, we're far more likely to condemn the bartender to a future most unfortunate."

Simon picked up the note from the bed. "If this is a warning at all, that is."

Luthor furrowed his brow in frustration. "How can you still cling to your belief that everything in this outpost is copacetic?"

"I don't, Luthor," Simon said morosely. He sat down heavily on the bed and sighed. "I just want to leave this mundane town and go home. I want to enjoy teatime with proper cups on proper saucers. I want to drink my scotch in a tumbler over ice, not out of a stained and foul-smelling wooden mug."

"I sense a 'however' in our future," Luthor said, turning knowingly toward Mattie.

"However," Simon began, "I can see the telltale signs as surely as you can. I find it odd that so many people accompany the chancellor on his daily journeys. I find it odd that a man planning even a peaceful revolt against the crown sleeps only a few hours a night, yet seems so clear of mind."

Simon stood and paced the room as he continued. "I find it odd that so many people left Whitten Hall, yet there was no mention in our mission report of refugees arriving in neighboring towns. I find it odd that the chancellor and his men travel some distance to neighboring towns each day, yet I have seen no sign of horses in Whitten Hall, despite the hitching posts along the street."

The Inquisitor stopped his pacing and turned toward his companions. "I find it odd that they went through so much trouble to give the appearance of disuse at the mine pit, yet only the cars removed from the tracks are in a state of disrepair. I, too, noticed that while weeds have grown unbidden around the rails, the rails themselves are free of overgrowth, as though they are still in use.

"Most of all, perhaps, I find it incredibly odd that for a town who has presumably closed their iron mine for the foreseeable future would continue to advertise open laborer positions and have train car after train car of willing applicants arrive. Speaking of which, have you seen any of the workers with whom we arrived? They were led away by the foreman and have not been seen in town since."

"Do you believe they could be taking the iron for their own devices?" Luthor asked.

"Potentially, though we won't know unless we examine for ourselves, will we?"

Mattie raised her hand politely, drawing Simon's attention despite his single-focused enthusiasm. "To play the devil's advocate, have we considered that they are merely performing general upkeep on the mine, under the assumption that at some point in the near future they will return to work in the very same tunnels?"

Simon arched an eyebrow and turned toward the apothecary, who merely shrugged noncommittally.

"It was the two of you who have drawn me into this investigation," Simon chided. "You lost your right to be the voice of reason, madam."

Mattie shrugged. "It's only that I've often found the simplest answer to be the correct one."

"Then are you insinuating we should not investigate the mine?"

Mattie smiled wickedly. "I'm insinuating nothing of the sort. It's been far too long since I've enjoyed any sort of adventure. This sounds perfectly thrilling."

Luthor stood from his chair. "Then I shall gather my things and we shall be off."

Simon shook his head and placed his hand on his friend's shoulder. "Not now. We'll wait for nightfall."

"Have you taken a leave of your senses?" the apothecary asked. "There is only a skeleton crew here in town now, with every other able body away from Whitten Hall. If ever there was a time to investigate the iron mine, now would be it."

Simon continued to shake his head as Luthor spoke. "On the contrary, now is the absolute worst time to go. Where do you suppose the rest of the town is during the daylight hours? If we presume that they are not, as they've alluded, visiting neighboring towns, wouldn't it be most likely that they are in the mine itself during the day and only return to the town during the hours of darkness?"

Luthor stroked his chin momentarily before pushing his glasses back up his nose. "You present a solid argument, sir."

"Of course I do. No, we'll wait until nightfall. It may be a bit more precarious to slip out unnoticed, but at least we'll be certain that the townsfolk are duly occupied within the town's limits. We should have free rein to investigate at our leisure, at least until sunup."

Mattie frowned, obviously disappointed. "What shall we do until then?"

"Act naturally," Simon advised. "We don't want to alert anyone to our goings on until our investigation is complete. Go enjoy the sights and sounds of Whitten Hall."

Luthor chuckled to himself. "That should take all of a half an hour at most."

Simon smiled. "I'll see you both back here in my room immediately after sunset."

The woods were far more ominous on their own than they had been when the companions were in the company of the chancellor. The hooded lantern gifted by Martelus was clutched tightly in Luthor's hand, its directed light pushing back, if not eliminating, the oppressive darkness surrounding them.

The hard-packed road was empty of other travelers, as it had been the night before when Wriggleton had guided them to the manor house. They had the road to themselves, though they walked close to the wood line, in case it became necessary to hide from other passersby.

As they rounded a bend, Simon could see the glowing lights of the manor house. He hastily motioned toward Luthor, who drew closed the screen on the front of the lantern. They were cast into darkness, and Simon was forced to blink repeatedly to wash away the dancing blue dots that lingered in his vision.

His eyes slowly adjusted until he could focus once more on the distant plantation home. The flickering lights from its outdoor lanterns provided enough illumination for the Inquisitor's eyes to quickly adjust to the gloom. He could see the edges of the trail ahead as well as the domineering trees to either side, their limbs intertwined across the trail overhead.

"Do you see any guards?" Luthor whispered quietly to Mattie.

Mattie wiped the sweat from her brow as she narrowed her eyes and focused on the home. In the darkness, her pupils reflected the dancing orange flames of the lanterns, yet seemed to glow with their own inner light. The manor home appeared to grow nearer in her vision, and the shadows that clung to the building's exterior faded away into shades of gray. She could see a pair of men pacing the upper balconies, watching only intermittently toward the road on which they traveled.

"There are at least two," she replied, "though I wouldn't be at all surprised if there were more concealed nearby."

"We could try to sneak by unnoticed," Luthor offered.

Simon shook his head, a motion noticeable even against the darkened tree line. "The risk is too great. We'll take to the woods until we're well past the chancellor's home."

The Inquisitor led them into the trees. They pushed past the initial undergrowth of thorny bushes and clinging branches. Beyond, the woods were far more hospitable and easier to travel.

The trio moved slowly, avoiding as best they could the fallen branches and dried leaves on the forest floor. Even so, each step brought an unnaturally loud crunch and an involuntary cringe from every member of the party.

After a few hundred paces, Simon broke from the group and moved back to the edge of the road. He crouched behind the thick bushes and peered across the road. No sign of the manor's lanterns could be seen, nor any sound of pursuit heard. He stood slowly and returned to the other two.

"We can make our way back to the road, if you're both ready."

Luthor nodded, but Mattie held up her hand pleadingly. "If it's all the same, gentlemen, I could use a rest. It seems my constitution is not at all suited for this humidity. I'm absolutely parched and could use a moment to myself."

Simon noted the sheen of sweat on her brow and nodded. He motioned a few feet ahead where the canopy seemed thinner and moonlight filtered through to the forest below.

"We can rest in the clearing just ahead. Can I offer you my arm?"

Mattie shook her head but smiled. "It's very gentlemanly of you, Simon, but I'm not yet an invalid. I can walk on my own."

The trio walked into the clearing and took seats against the thicker trees. Though the walk had not been overly taxing, even Simon admitted the humidity felt oppressive. He removed his top hat and wiped the accumulated sweat from his hairline.

"A good spy you will never make," Luthor chided. "Our discreet traipsing through the woods has left you vexed."

"Subterfuge was never my forte," Mattie admitted. "My one attempt at infiltrating civilized society ended in absolute failure when our good Inquisitor spotted me from across a crowded ballroom. I'm more of a hands-on sort of woman."

Simon smiled. "Admittedly, embarrassing though it is to admit, I have brought our fair maiden along to serve as our muscle."

"Which leaves you to be our brains and me to be?" Luthor asked.

"Our conscience," Simon explained. "Every good adventuring crew needs the one honest man to serve as its moral compass."

Luthor arched an eyebrow. "With you in our group, you may want to consider finding yet another honest man. You need two times the moral compass as most men."

"Do either of you have a drink?" Mattie asked.

Simon pushed aside his jacket and patted his pockets but could only produce a flask. Neither of his companions had to ask its contents.

"It seems none of us will make good spies," Simon admitted. "We planned our adventure without taking into consideration the basic necessities of life. Forgive us, Matilda."

Mattie waved her hand dismissively before leaning back against the cool bark of the tree.

As they rested in silence, the quiet was interrupted by a bird singing overhead. Simon tilted his head backward and peered into the branches. High above the trio, a bright yellow canary perched on a narrow branch, its vibrant feathers noticeable even at night. It opened its beak once more and sang into the night air. In the distance, another canary, hidden from their view, answered its cry.

"What sort of bird is that?" Mattie asked.

"A canary, I believe," Luthor answered as he stood slowly to get a better view.

"It is a canary," Simon confirmed as he watched the little yellow bird.

"I presume from both of your surprise that they're not indigenous to this area?" she asked.

"Not at all," the Inquisitor replied.

"They use them in mines to check for noxious fumes, though," Luthor explained. "It might have escaped."

The distant canary sang out, which was answered by their bird overhead.

"Both of them might have escaped," Luthor corrected.

Simon stood abruptly, startling the canary. The bird took to wing and disappeared amongst the trees.

"We must be off if we expect to be back in our beds before sunrise."

Luthor and Mattie nodded. The apothecary offered his hand and helped pull the redhead to her feet. With a sigh, they pushed through the woods until they had rejoined the road.

With a twist, Luthor removed the screen from the lantern and the nearby woods were filled with a brilliant light once more. They squinted against its glow until, once again, their eyes adjusted to the change.

Simon led them through the covered bridge and up the incline, which led to the lip of the mining pit. Even from a distance, he could hear the hum of the generators. The electric floodlights filled the quarry with a strong yellow glow, so much so that even upon their approach the pit glowed like a city at night.

Luthor doused their lantern, its light seemingly insignificant against the electric lights nearby.

Simon lowered himself to a crouch before finally placing his hands firmly on the ground and practically crawling to the lip of the pit. The other two, likewise, crawled forward until they could peer into the wide shaft before them.

Along the rocky floor, two men pushed heavily laden mine carts along the rail. Tarps were draped across the tops, blocking their contents from view.

The carts rattled along the rail, the sound of the metal wheels echoing along the rock walls until it reached the ears of the companions, perched at the crest of the quarry.

The two men paused at the mouth of the iron mine and lit lanterns on the front of the carts before continuing into the mine itself. The light from the lanterns reflected off the rocky walls of the entrance before quickly fading from view.

Simon slid back from the lip of the pit, followed quickly by his two companions. The Inquisitor sat in the grass and chewed on his bottom lip.

"I guess this proves that the mine hasn't been abandoned," Luthor said.

"Indeed, you're right," Simon replied, "though I doubt any of us believed it was."

"What do you suppose they were pushing into the mine?" Mattie asked.

"That's an excellent question, my dear," Simon answered. "I have every intention of finding out."

CHAPTER
Twenty-one

WITH THE QUARRY CLEARED OF THE WORKERS, THE trio cautiously made their way down the perimeter road. The trail descended steeply, hugging the edge of the pit as it circled toward the stony floor below.

The temperature dropped as they descended, as did the stifling humidity that had plagued Mattie since their arrival. Water seeped through small fissures in the rock, dribbling miniature waterfalls down the poorly worked strata of stone that they passed.

Within minutes, they had reached the mineshaft's coarse floor. The base of the pit seemed far wider from the bottom than it had appeared from above. The wooden crane that had stretched its arm barely to the lip of the quarry seemed enormous when viewed from below, its outstretched arm rising like a dagger toward the night sky above. The stagnant pool of water sat motionless to one side of the pit; the walls of the shaft blocked the wind, leaving the air still.

Mattie walked away from the two men and approached the edge of the pool. With the back of her hand, she wiped the sweat from her brow before dipping both hands into the cool water. As she raised it toward her lips, Simon quickly approached and knocked her hands aside. Water sloshed from between her fingers, painting the dry stone with its droplets.

"You had better have had a very good reason for doing that," Mattie threatened. "Neither of you thought to bring water along on our adventure and if I don't drink something soon, I'll most certainly faint from exhaustion."

Simon shrugged. "Drink at your own risk, but know that the pool is contaminated with cyanide."

Mattie looked to the small puddle of water still cupped in the palm of her hand. She tilted her hand, letting the water splash on the ground below, before quickly wiping her hand dry on the hem of her skirt.

"Who would put cyanide in the water?" she asked. "Is the chancellor and his kind really that devious?"

Simon shook his head. "It wasn't meant for you, or any of us, for that matter."

"Assume some of us have not been initiated into the ways of science, sir," Luthor remarked.

"In iron mining, cyanide is often used to dissolve the ore for easier extraction from the mine. Run off, like the pool at your feet, gathers nearby. Therefore, the poison wasn't meant for anyone in particular, though you would have been a most unfortunate victim had you drank from the pool's waters."

"You never cease to amaze me, sir."

Simon glanced toward the apothecary. "You're not the only one who does his research before an assignment."

Mattie stood from beside the pool and motioned toward the entrance to the mine proper.

The hooded lantern, which had seemed so unnecessary amidst the stunningly bright floodlights on the quarry floor, was still covered as they made their way into the mine. Simon was hesitant to uncover the lantern, knowing its light would illuminate the tunnels much as the workers' lanterns had. Upon entering the mine, however, he was forced to reconsider. The darkness beyond the reach of the floodlights' glow was impenetrable, as though dark tendrils actively sought and consumed the meager light from the real world beyond its borders. The further they dared enter, the more they were swallowed by its gloom until Simon could no longer see his hand when held before his face. Begrudgingly, he told Luthor to remove the cover from their lantern.

Simon squinted as the light filled the broad tunnel. Moisture on the walls reflected the illumination like gemstones. The Inquisitor glanced cautiously around the mineshaft, ensuring the trio was alone.

The tunnel continued forward a short distance before turning abruptly. The metal rail, which had begun in the base of the quarry, followed the curve of the mine and disappeared from view.

As Simon was examining the curving, worked-stone wall, ensuring neither of the workers they had seen previously was observing them, the light turned startlingly aside. Simon was left in darkness, as was the tunnel before him.

Irritated, Simon turned to see what had caught Luthor's attention. The apothecary and Mattie were examining a long, wooden table pressed neatly against the side of the wall. The wood itself had seen better days. What had clearly been years of exposure to the elements and the humidity of the mine had left the legs of the table partially rotted. Simon would not have trusted placing any significant weight upon the table, sure he was that it would collapse shortly thereafter.

Much to his surprise, there were items upon it. A series of small birdcages rested on the table's surface. Each was empty and the doors to the cages were left open, as though long abandoned.

Luthor pushed gently on the door to one of the cages, and it creaked ominously. The apothecary quickly withdrew his hand as the sound reverberated through the mine. Simon cringed and gently shook his head.

"Sorry, sir," Luthor whispered.

Simon glanced over his shoulder. "No worries, Luthor. What have you found?"

"I think we've solved the mystery of the non-indigenous forest canaries. I don't think they escaped. It looks like they were intentionally released."

"Odd," Simon replied, as he furrowed his brow. "Yet we know this mine hasn't been abandoned. Why release the creatures that warn of deadly fumes?"

Simon glanced past Luthor and noticed Mattie's pale pallor. She bit her lip as though fighting the urge to vomit. Luthor noticed the Inquisitor's concern and turned the lantern fully toward her.

"Mattie?" Luthor asked.

She shook her head and coughed softly. "Can't you smell that?"

Simon closed his eyes and sniffed the air, but could discern nothing other than the underlying pungent aroma of stagnant water and chemicals. "What is it that you smell?"

She swallowed slowly. "Forgive me. I forget that your senses aren't as sharp. There's a smell of… of rot and decay, similar to what I sensed in the outpost itself, only significantly stronger. Something has died in these tunnels, something most foul."

Simon needed no other provocation to draw his silver-plated revolver. He clutched the pistol in his hand as he turned deeper into the mine. Luthor set the lantern on the table, which creaked ominously under the lantern's weight. To everyone's relief, the table held. As Simon stared intently into the mine ahead, Luthor opened his doctor's bag and removed a narrow vial of clear liquid. As he uncorked the tube, the overwhelming scent of mint filled the air around them.

"Mint?" Mattie asked as she stepped closer.

"Mint oil," Luthor corrected. "Place a dab on your finger and run it into the insides of your nostrils. It will mask the other, more malodorous smells."

She pressed her finger to the top of the vial and turned it upward, letting the oil pool on her finger. As she turned the vial upright once more, she paused.

"Are you sure this is the best option? We might need my keener sense of smell."

Luthor shrugged. "You can either remain on the cusp of vomiting or you can happily accompany us, smelling nothing but the lovely scent of mint. It's your choice."

Mattie glanced at her finger before unceremoniously rubbing the insides of her nostrils. Even with the lantern turned away from her, Luthor could see her relief after the oil was in place.

Luthor retrieved the lantern and stepped beside Simon. "Anything, sir?"

Simon shook his head, though his eyes never left the turn of the tunnel. "I've neither seen nor heard anything that would have me believe they know we're here. Regardless, we'd best be on our guard."

The trio moved to the bend in the tunnel and paused. Simon's instinct was to cautiously observe around the bend before continuing, but he quickly realized the foolishness of that notion. The only way to observe around the corner would be to shine the lantern's light, which would immediately alert anyone around the bend to their presence. Gripping his pistol tighter, he opted to step around the corner in plain view. When no shouts of alarm were sounded, he sighed with relief.

Despite a few smaller tunnels branching from the main passage, they chose to follow the rail as it descended deeper into the mine. Their lantern was the only visible light, and its flickering flames gave the constant illusion of movement where none was to be found.

No one spoke as they walked. Their footfalls alone echoed far too loudly in the stone mineshaft. They cringed every time their booted feet struck a wayward stone, sending it skittering across the rocky ground. Yet, despite what they perceived as far too much noise, no one moved to hinder their advance.

Simon frowned as they continued walking. He was a poor judge of distance on the surface. Luthor had often chastised him during even routine hikes for misjudging the distance traveled. Underground, without the benefit of the stars or even trees to use as a judge, he was completely turned about. He would have presumed they had walked miles already. Each turn, he expected to find something of note, but turn after turn revealed nothing of interest. A mine car was abandoned in a larger chamber, pushed onto a conjoining rail and then forgotten, but it appeared far worse for wear than the ones being pushed by the workers.

Only his pocket watch gave Simon a sense of passing time. He glanced at it as often as he felt was sensible, though he was continuously surprised to see only minutes had passed after what felt like an hour. He was disoriented, and it didn't help that every wall and every ceiling appeared identically worked by identical tools.

His mind wandered as they made another turn. So distracted was he that his mind barely registered the oddity before him, even as his legs stopped moving of their own volition. Luthor and Mattie stopped as well, flanking him on either side. No one spoke, though no one had to.

The rail ended abruptly in the center of the chamber before them. Two mine carts in fine working order, clearly the same two which they had observed outside the mine, were resting against a wooden crossbeam at the end of the rail.

Beyond the rail's terminus, however, was what truly caught their attention. Before them, a tall, wooden door blocked the path ahead.

"Is there a lock?" Simon asked in a hushed tone.

"You'll have to give me a moment, sir," Luthor replied. "I'm an apothecary, not a thief. My experience with examining doors for locks is severely limited."

"Well, don't feel rushed on our account."

Luthor glanced over his shoulder disapprovingly before returning to his work. He pushed his glasses further up his nose as he peered into the narrow keyhole. The light danced behind him and his shadow repeatedly fell over the lock, blocking his view. The apothecary frowned as he leaned closer and looked through the keyhole.

As the apothecary worked, Simon glanced over his shoulder toward where the two mine carts had been swallowed by the darkness. A most cursory examination of the carts had revealed nothing telling, but had opened more questions than it had answered. The carts were free of the dust and debris normally associated with mining. A fabric of some sort had recently been pressed against the bottom of the mine cart, though they were both currently empty. Only thin, white fibers remained behind, clinging to the spots of rust at the bottom of the cart. With an exasperated sigh, the Inquisitor turned back toward the mysterious door.

Finally, after some consternation, Luthor leaned away from the door's lock and stood.

"So what do you have to say?" the Inquisitor asked.

Luthor brushed the accumulated dust from the knees of his pants. "It doesn't appear locked."

Simon frowned. "It isn't locked or it merely doesn't appear locked?"

"It's six or one half dozen, as far as I'm concerned," Luthor replied. "Once again, I'm an apothecary. If you want someone proficient in picking locks, perhaps you should stop hiring pharmacists and werewolves, and instead hire a slightly less trustworthy highwayman or cutpurse."

"You've had a foul disposition here of late, Luthor. It's unbecoming."

Luthor stepped out of the direct light and sneered. "You drive me to it, sir."

"Are you both quite done?" Mattie asked, again playing the role of mediator between the two longtime friends. She turned the lantern from one man to the other, ensuring the light shone brightly in their eyes. The two men took a moment as the artifact of the light cleared from their vision.

Luthor motioned toward the door, even as he blinked hard to clear his sight. "It doesn't appear locked. After you, sir."

The door was thick oak, most likely harvested from the very forest that grew around the mining pit. Simon ran his finger along the vertical wooden beams and felt the coarseness of the carved planks. Though the craftsmanship was lacking, the door was large and sturdy. It was anchored to the wall on oversized hinges, held in place by large bolts driven straight into the stone as though by some great force.

Simon closed his hand over the handle and glanced cautiously behind him. Both Luthor and Mattie nodded their readiness. With his free hand, the Inquisitor pulled back the hammer on his revolver.

To his surprise, the door wasn't locked. The handle turned easily, dislodging the mechanism holding the door closed. Simon pulled gently and found it opened smoothly on well-oiled hinges. Despite its apparent size and weight, Simon found little resistance as the door swung open.

The light from the hooded lantern flooded the chamber beyond the great door. Simon wasn't sure what he had expected beyond the out-of-place doorway in the middle of an iron mine, but the nondescript passageway seemed anticlimactic. The same worked stone as the rest of the mine continued in the hallway beyond.

Though slightly disappointed, Simon was also relieved. There was a part of him that thoroughly expected an ambush, that there would be a throng of workers beyond, armed with pickaxes and side arms awaiting anyone foolish enough to open the door.

The trio stepped through the doorway and continued down the hall. Unlike the passages before, this tunnel moved unwaveringly forward without any major bends. Though Simon continued to feel slightly disoriented from being underground in the deep, impenetrable darkness, he could still easily discern that the hallway was sloped gently downward. The further they moved along the passage, the further underground they went.

The grade of the tunnel increased as they moved deeper. The passage became narrower, no longer wide enough to accommodate one of the rail cars. The stonework seemed rougher, with far more edges than the stonework above. Though he had no basis for his assumption, Simon assumed this shaft had been dug in search of another vein of iron, though why anyone would place a door at the entrance to an exploratory shaft was beyond him.

Simon reached out experimentally and let his fingertips brush the stone beside him. With one arm outstretched and the other at his side, he still very nearly touched both walls simultaneously. Simon frowned to himself, though he didn't voice his concerns to the others. In such narrow confines, it would be difficult to maneuver during a fight. Should they encounter any of the workers, the Inquisitor would fight alone as Luthor and Mattie both struggled to squeeze into a place beside him.

The Inquisitor nearly stumbled as the ground suddenly leveled out once more. The passage widened and the quality of the stonework returned to its previous state. Before him, the hallway continued forward, though side passages were evenly spaced along the length of the hall for as far as the light from the lantern would reveal. The spacing of the side tunnels was far too uniform to have been caused by random events. Over each of the passageways, a curtain had been affixed to the rock entryway. The fabric draped over the side tunnels, blocking Simon's view of what lay beyond.

Simon glanced back at his counterparts, who merely shrugged before motioning toward the nearest passage. The Inquisitor nodded confidently, though he groaned internally at the thought of exposing what lay beyond the tarp. He didn't share the fear of the darkness like he did the fear of water, but Simon loathed the unknown. When you expected everything to be a trap, as Simon did, then every unknown was an obvious source of danger.

He stepped to the edge of the curtain and paused. Glancing over his shoulder, he could see Luthor's obvious concern. The apothecary wrung his hands together, clearly regretting his decision to leave his cane and concealed sword within at the inn. Mattie, by contrast, looked every bit the hunter Simon knew her to be. Her face was a mask of concentration as she alternated clenching and relaxing her fists. The sight of Mattie bolstered his confidence, knowing that she could become the deadly werewolf at the slightest provocation.

Simon pulled aside the curtain as Luthor shone the light into the room beyond. The Inquisitor's pistol hovered, unmoving in his hand as he arched an eyebrow in surprise.

"That's not what I expected," Luthor whispered.

"Curious, indeed," Simon replied as he stared into the bedroom.

A four-poster bed was pressed against the far wall, covered with a series of pillows and duvet. A nightstand was situated beside the bed, adorned with an oil lantern and a tattered but well-read book. A dresser had been placed against the wall nearest the entrance to the underground bedroom. Simon frowned as he realized the bedroom was finer furnished than the one in which he was currently residing back in Whitten Hall.

Without further word, Simon moved across the hallway to another of the curtains. Pulling it aside, he found a similarly adorned bedroom, with only the personal effects on the nightstand differentiating the two rooms from one another. An investigation behind a third curtain confirmed Simon's suspicions that the lower mine had been fully converted to barracks.

The trio gathered in the middle of the hall and huddled together so that they might speak in hushed tones.

"What do you make of it, sir?" Luthor asked.

"Someone is living here, though I can't for the life of me understand why."

Mattie furrowed her brow. "Could it be for protection?"

The two men looked toward her, encouraging her to continue.

"The chancellor said they weren't interested in the iron, merely equal wages. I would assume, however, that the workers of Whitten Hall are also not interested in the crown regaining possession of the mine before negotiations have concluded. Could they be living here in an attempt to keep royal soldiers from entering the mine without their knowledge?"

Simon stroked his chin. "It seems a bit excessive. Living in utter darkness as they are would take its toll not just on their physical bodies but their mental fortitude as well."

"There's more to this than meets the eye," Luthor remarked.

"Agreed," Simon replied. "We should continue our investigation." He retrieved the pocket watch from his breast pocket and frowned at the time. "We must do so with some sense of urgency. It's already past midnight, and I would hate to tempt fate by being here when the sun comes up."

They proceeded toward the far end of the hall. Their lantern light struck out nearly thirty feet ahead of them but exposed only further rows of the repetitive living quarters. After some time, their light finally played upon a change in the stone hallway. The passage narrowed slightly and curved away from the otherwise straight shaft.

As they advanced on the curve, Mattie stopped abruptly and doubled over as though in pain. Luthor rushed to her side to support her as her shoulders shook with dry heaves.

Simon didn't bother asking what had overcome Mattie. He could smell it as clearly as she, though he doubted it was such an assault to his senses as it was to hers. To Simon, the smell would always be associated with his time in Inquisitor training, in which he learned medical forensics while examining cadavers in the morgue.

It was the smell of death and decay, and the concentration was as strong as he had ever encountered.

"The mint oil," Mattie choked as she gestured toward Luthor. "How much more do you have with you?"

Luthor fumbled with the clasps of his doctor's bag and quickly withdrew the half-filled vial. Mattie uncorked the vial with little concern toward the stopper, which bounced merrily over the rocky ground. She poured the liquid into her hand and rubbed it furiously across her upper lip and into her nostrils.

Even in the orange glow of the lantern, the two men could see the color returning to her face.

Simon reached behind him, though his eyes never left the tunnel ahead. "Assuming Miss Hawke has not consumed the entirety of the mint oil, I believe it's wise to share it amongst the rest of us."

Luthor sloshed the minimal amount of fluid that still remained in the bottom of the vial and handed it to Simon. The Inquisitor took his share before returning it.

"The smell—" Mattie began.

"I smell it as well," Simon interrupted. "Unless I'm mistaken, it's coming from further ahead."

"I don't think we should go," she said, the nervousness evident in her voice.

Simon was forced to agree with her. The smell of death was overpowering, clouding his other senses with its palpable presence. Despite his better judgment, he shook his head.

"Your nose and Luthor's gut have brought us this far," Simon said, using humor to mask his own concerns. "Now it's time to find out why."

Simon proceeded along the tunnel and after the briefest of pauses, the other two followed suit. The tunnel curved gently to the left. The Inquisitor moved cautiously forward, in no true rush to discover what lay beyond the end of the curve.

As quickly as it had begun, the curve ended and the tunnel opened up into a broad chamber. As Luthor's lantern caught up to Simon, its light spilled into the beginning of the large room.

The light diffused far from the distal wall, casting only part of the room in its warm glow. The floor before them was clear of obstructions, but either side of the narrow trail was littered with debris. Broken pickaxe handles and warped metal heads were strewn about as though the chamber before them had been carved with some great effort.

Simon turned his gaze toward the leftmost wall, and he set his jaw against the sight. Bodies were piled unceremoniously against the wall, their limbs intertwined as they formed a pyramid of sorts. The Inquisitor performed a quick mental calculation and figured there were at least a hundred corpses lining the wall.

The stench was far stronger in the chamber, cutting through even the thick layer of mint oil he had smeared upon his nose. Behind him, he heard Mattie's most unladylike retching as the smell overwhelmed her.

"Lantern," Simon demanded, holding out his hand.

Luthor gave him the hooded lantern before moving to assist Mattie. Simon gave neither of them even a cursory glance as he advanced on the pile of bodies.

From a distance, they had appeared unusual. The oddity only grew more pronounced as he grew closer. The corpses were pale, as he would expect, but all of them appeared severely emaciated. The eyes, which were still open and staring accusingly at the Royal Inquisitor, were sunken and bruised. The cheeks were likewise sunken, as though the skin had been stretched across the jaw and cheekbones. Arms and legs, which had clearly once been strong and muscled, were thin and frail.

"What… what are they, sir?" Luthor stammered.

Simon looked across the pile. His gaze drifted quickly over the delicate female corpses and once sturdy men alike. Though he noticed the bodies of the children amidst the pile, he refused to spend any length of time further examining the atrocity.

The Inquisitor swallowed firmly, forcing down the lump of anger and disbelief that had lodged itself in his throat. "Despite what the chancellor told us, I no longer believe anyone ever left Whitten Hall. Everyone who ever disagreed with the new direction of the town is here."

Mattie wiped her mouth with the back of her hand as she approached the pile. "There are more here than just the few dozen who would have disagreed."

Luthor blanched as his mouth fell open. "The workers. My God, sir, these are all the workers they've been bringing on board."

Simon clenched his jaw tightly. "If I were to examine the pile further, I'd most certainly have noticed familiar faces of those who had joined us on the train ride. They didn't leave town, and they weren't put to work.

The chancellor and his men murdered everyone in town."

As the others stared at the pile of corpses in disbelief, Simon crouched before the pile. He reached forward and pressed closed the eyes of the nearest body. He knew the gesture meant little to the corpse and, truth be told, it was not even done with reverence to the deceased. The dead woman's eyes stared at him piercingly, making him feel dreadfully uncomfortable.

As he removed his hand, the woman's head lolled to one side. Simon paused and raised the lantern so that its light could better spill across the woman's face. Though discreet, there were noticeable paralleled puncture wounds on the woman's long neck.

CHAPTER Twenty-two

SIMON STEPPED BACK BRUSQUELY FROM THE CORPSE. He spun toward Luthor and Mattie, the lantern light flickering wildly as he turned.

"Sir?" Luthor asked, startled.

"Gather your things at once," Simon replied, his eyes darting around the room. "Things are not what they appear."

Simon turned the lantern from side to side in an attempt to push back the impenetrable darkness surrounding them. As the candlelight flickered within the hooded lantern, the shadows took on a life of their own, seeming to push against the meager illumination.

As Luthor pulled his doctor's bag closer to his chest, he backed away from the pile of emaciated bodies. Beside him, Mattie snarled. As the light played over her features, her eyes appeared glassy and yellowed as the first stages of her transformation overtook her.

Simon clenched his revolver in his hand as he scanned the room once more. He wasn't sure that he truly expected a sudden attack, but he couldn't escape the feeling that they were being watched. It was the same feeling that had haunted their steps ever since discovering the underground barracks. He recollected their steps, from the top of the mine pit to the entrance, through the heavy wooden door, and through the barracks. They had followed their intuition, but had their movements actually been prescribed? He wasn't so sure that he hadn't led his team directly into a trap.

As Simon painted the room with his lantern once more, a shadow detached itself from the darkness and wrapped its arms around Luthor, one hand grasping him firmly around the waist and another over his mouth. The apothecary tried to scream, but the sound was muffled. Before Simon could react, the figure pulled Luthor backward and they both disappeared once more into the darkness.

Mattie dropped her tunic to the floor as her upper body bristled and split as she transformed into the werewolf. Simon rushed forward, but a second figure stepped into his path.

The man before him wore the workman's clothes they had seen on the men pushing the rail carts into the mine, but little else resembled a man. The miner's skin was sallow and his cheeks sunken. The irises of his eyes smoldered inhumanly red in the candlelight. As the man opened his mouth, he revealed two elongated canines that Simon thoroughly doubted were veneers.

The Inquisitor pushed forward, knowing that Luthor's life was most certainly in grave danger. As he put his shoulder into the worker, instead of pushing through, he instead rebounded backward. He looked up, startled, as the miner grabbed him by his lapel and tossed him handily backward with a strength that belied his thin appearance.

Simon landed heavily amidst the pile of corpses. Dried elbows and knees dug into his back, sending a quick wave of pain up his spine. He cringed and arched his back as he rolled his head to the side. His pain was immediately forgotten as he stared into the dead eyes of the nearest cadaver. Simon quickly turned his head forward and kept his eyes locked on the miner, rather than once again catching the unseeing gaze of the bodies enveloping him.

The vampire hissed once more, revealing his dingy fangs. The miner looked wasted and hollow, as though it had been far too long since his last meal. Simon's hand instinctively fell to his throat, concealing his jugular from view. Undeterred, the vampire stepped toward him, kicking aside the litany of broken tools that littered his path.

Simon started to stand, but his hands struggled to find purchase amidst the husks on which he lay. As his hand closed over an unidentifiable body part, he realized for the first time that his revolver was no longer in his grasp. Panicked, he quickly glanced around the room. The hooded lantern, as he was well aware, had fallen from his grip when he was thrown and lay on the ground some feet away. Only a foot from the lantern, the silver revolver sparkled in the dim candlelight. Swearing softly to himself, he tried to stand once more as the vampire advanced on him.

The miner smiled maliciously as he neared and reached out a hand, each finger on which was stained with dirt and what Simon had to believe was blood. Reaching down, Simon's hand closed over what felt like wood. As he pulled the makeshift weapon free from the pile on which he lay, the Inquisitor realized it wasn't wood but bleached bone. Cringing, he held the broken femur before him, hoping it would be enough to deter the beast.

Before the weapon could be brought to bear, however, a howl pierced the air. The vampire was knocked aside in a flurry of teeth, claws, and fur. Simon could hear the vampire's flesh shred under Mattie's brutal assault.

Thankful for the reprieve, Simon pushed away from the bloodless corpses and regained his feet. He glanced briefly at the ensuing battle between vampire and werewolf and was relieved that one of the two magical monstrosities fought with him, rather than against him.

He rushed to the lantern, setting it upright even as he grasped the grip of his pistol. Though he was unsure if Mattie could handle the vampire alone, he was far more concerned with Luthor, who had yet to emerge from the darkness. Simon turned the lantern quickly, scanning the room. He could hear a scuffle in the darkness still beyond the range of his lantern and hurried toward the sound.

As he approached, an ethereal white pattern emerged in the darkness ahead. Its glow was faint, offering little illumination for the surroundings.

"Luthor!" Simon yelled, caution be damned.

A figure emerged at the edge of the lantern light, rushing toward the Inquisitor. Simon raised his pistol, ready to fire. His finger froze in the trigger well as he recognized the diminutive man rushing toward him.

"Luthor, thank God."

Luthor slammed into Simon, wrapping his arms around the Inquisitor's waist. Together, they tumbled to the floor, sending broken pick handles scattering in their wake. Only through great concentration did Simon keep the lantern aloft during his second graceless fall.

"What the devil—?" Simon began to complain.

His words were cut off as the ghostly white wisps in the air glowed with a blinding brilliance. With the extra light, Simon could see the startled second vampire, who merely stared transfixed as the object in the air reached its glowing pinnacle. Moments later, an explosion rocked the far end of the room, driving Simon back onto the ground even as he struggled to stand.

Slowly, he pushed Luthor off him and raised his head. The room was now partially lit, as wooden debris smoldered from the explosion. The vampire squirmed weakly on the floor as his shirt and pants burned merrily.

"What the bloody hell just happened?" Simon asked.

Luthor coughed and furrowed his brow. "My doctor's bag was in that explosion."

Simon glanced curiously at his companion. "What did you do?"

Luthor met his gaze and shrugged. "I made a bomb, though admittedly, I may have misjudged the correct portions of reagents in my mixture. The explosion would have ignited the rest of my vials, which caused the unnecessarily large explosion."

Simon glanced back toward the still-moving vampire. "Perhaps it wasn't large enough."

Coming to his senses, Simon glanced behind him. Both Mattie and her adversary had paused following the explosion. They stood like statues still locked in mortal combat for a brief moment before the vampire returned its gaze to the massive white werewolf. The miner raised his foot and kicked Mattie in the chest, sending her sprawling across the floor. She whimpered as she landed roughly but had the clarity of mind to raise her paws defensively as the vampire pounced on her prone form.

Simon scrambled to his feet and raised his pistol. Though he knew he had the skill to shoot the vampire, even as the two creatures struggled together, he doubted his bullet would do much to the fanged monster. Instead, he examined the ground nearby until his eyes alighted on a broken wooden handle. He lifted the heavy shaft and rushed toward Mattie.

The vampire had pressed her on her back and snapped its jaws toward her exposed neck. Only her incredible strength kept the vampire at bay, though it crept closer with every surge of strength.

Simon stepped behind the distracted creature and raised the makeshift wooden stake over his head. Grasping it with both hands, he drove the weapon downward. The splintered wood pierced the vampire's back, just to the left of its spine. The sharpened stake tore through the thin skin and shattered the ribs beneath. It passed unhindered through the creature's heart before striking the monster's sternum, where it finally came to rest.

The vampire's struggling immediately ceased. A last gasp of surprise escaped the creature's lips before it slumped limply over Mattie's paws.

With little effort, Mattie was able to roll to her side, casting the remains of the vampire onto the ground.

Luthor breathed heavily as he reached the Inquisitor and werewolf. "It looks like a stake to the heart is still effective."

Simon turned toward Luthor and raised his pistol. The apothecary's eyes widened in surprise, and he raised his hands defensively before him. With his free hand, Simon pushed Luthor aside as he took aim at the burned vampire, who limped weakly toward the tunnel leading back to the barracks.

"Bullets won't stop a vampire," Luthor warned.

"I agree," Simon replied, "except I'm not trying to kill it."

Simon squeezed the trigger. The bullet struck the vampire in the back of his knee as he limped away. Even from a distance, the group heard the shatter of bone. The vampire howled in pain, a sound that reverberated through the wide chamber, before he fell to the ground.

"An excellent shot, sir," Luthor remarked. The apothecary pulled his spectacles from his face and wiped the soot from the lenses. As he placed them back on his face, he turned toward his mentor. "Shall we question our captive?"

Simon raised the pistol and pointed it toward Luthor. The apothecary froze, his eyes darting from side to side.

"Is there another behind me?" he asked.

Simon remained unflinching, the end of his pistol pointing directly at Luthor's forehead.

"Simon?" Mattie asked. She was half covered with the clothing she'd retrieved, having since transformed back to her human form. "What are you doing?"

"Show me your neck," Simon demanded.

Luthor furrowed his brow. "My neck?" Realization dawned on his face as he stared at the Inquisitor. "You can't be serious."

Simon pulled back the hammer on his pistol. The cylinder on the revolver rotated, slotting a fresh round into the chamber.

Luthor swallowed hard, as he realized that nothing about Simon's demeanor seemed to find humor in the situation.

"Show me your neck," Simon repeated. "I won't ask you again."

Luthor angrily grasped his collar and pulled it aside. He turned his head first left, and then right, showing his unmarred skin. Satisfied, Simon released the hammer on the pistol and lowered the weapon.

"Forgive me, Luthor, but I had to be certain."

Luthor released his collar in a huff. "You could have taken me at my word."

Simon holstered his pistol as he searched the ground at his feet. "You've known me for over a year now. When have you ever known me to take someone merely at their word?"

Luthor crossed his arms across his chest. "Had I been bitten, even if I hadn't turned, you genuinely would have shot me, wouldn't you?"

Simon glanced up from his search momentarily. "Without hesitation. I'm very glad to know I didn't need to."

Mattie cleared her throat. "Excuse me, gentlemen, but our captive seems to be escaping."

They followed her gaze across the room. Simon turned the lantern so the light fell directly on the vampire, since neither he nor Luthor were blessed with Mattie's low light vision. The vampire had, indeed, crawled some feet from where he had originally fallen. His shattered leg didn't bleed as would have a normal man, yet the disturbed debris clearly showed the path he had taken.

The Inquisitor glanced back down at his feet and located yet another wooden shaft from a pickaxe. He retrieved the weapon before advancing on the prostrate vampire.

The monster heard Simon's approach and rolled onto his back. He hissed, again revealing the elongated canines.

"Do your worst, Inquisitor," the vampire said angrily. "I will tell you nothing."

Simon stopped beside the prone abomination. "You misunderstand. This isn't an interrogation."

The vampire closed its mouth and furrowed its brow in confusion. "Then what—?"

Simon dropped to a knee and slammed the wooden stake into the vampire's chest. The monster was caught unaware, so much so that it didn't offer so much as a scream of surprise. Its mouth fell open for a moment as it stared at the pickaxe handle before its body went limp. The vampire's head rolled backward, striking the cavern floor.

Luthor and Mattie shared an unbelieving expression as well.

"You killed him," Luthor said. "He could have provided insight as to what they were doing in Whitten Hall."

Simon stood, leaving the stake in place. As he turned toward his companions, they saw his stern expression. "I know the mythology of vampires, perhaps not as well as Luthor, admittedly, but well enough. Not a one amongst us could confidently state that a single scratch from a vampire's fangs wouldn't infect us with their disease. Interrogating a creature such as this could only end badly for everyone involved."

"Where did they come from?" Luthor asked sullenly.

Simon glanced toward the far end of the room, which they had yet to explore. "Our answers lie ahead. Of that, I feel certain."

He glanced at the body at his feet. "First, however, we must hide these bodies. If others arrive, they can't know that we've been here."

Luthor looked toward the scorch marks across the wide room.

"Burn marks are unusual but explainable," Simon said. "Corpses, especially those with wooden stakes driven through their heart, leave no possible alternative explanation."

"Where shall we hide them?" Mattie asked.

Simon glanced hesitantly toward the pile of corpses. He hated that he couldn't think of a better alternative.

When the vampire bodies were successfully concealed beneath the remains of former townsfolk, Simon hefted the hooded lantern and faced the unexplored far end of the chamber. Despite knowing its ineffectiveness against vampires, Simon drew his revolver once more. Its weight offered him comfort.

They moved forward, the light from the lantern pushing back the darkness ahead of them. Near the end of the chamber, the tunnel narrowed considerably, as though returning to the exploratory tunnel that they had walked through following the barracks.

Immediately after entering the tunnel, the chiseled rock of the walls transformed to exquisitely carved white limestone. Simon paused and placed his hand on the wall. It was roughly worked, with the tool marks still marring its surface. Despite the coarse work, the images were far smoother than would have been possible using the tools they had discovered in the previous room. As he withdrew his hand, Simon noticed a thick layer of dust.

He gazed down the tunnel to where his light diffused. The smooth walls gave way to etched walls and ceiling. Simon walked forward cautiously, despite not seeing any side passages that would have held ambushers. The carvings on the wall caught his eye, and he paused to examine them further. Humanoid figures stood in stoic poses against a backdrop of landscapes unfamiliar to Simon. Mountain ranges that didn't exist anywhere in their kingdom stood like dragon's teeth behind monstrous champions in the foreground. Simon touched the face of the carved hero, exploring the expressive snout on the bipedal creature. He didn't have a name for the abomination in the image, though it appeared demonic in nature.

He stepped away from the wall and examined the curved ceiling above him, towering like a cathedral's roof. The sculptured walls and vaulted ceiling seemed so out of place compared to the rest of the mine. Everything appeared alien, to include the whiteness of the walls compared to the dull gray of the previous mine shafts.

Beyond the carvings of demonic creatures, the images gave way to hieroglyphics. Simon knelt and examined the writing, despite it being written in a dialect with which he was unfamiliar. Though he knew not what was written, the words repeated along the wall. The same four pictographs repeated over and over again along the wall, reaching as high as the vaulted ceiling far above.

"What is this place?" Luthor whispered.

Simon shook his head. "I don't know, but this passage seems older than Whitten Hall, possibly even predating the mine itself. It's... fascinating."

Luthor didn't seem to share Simon's enthusiasm.

Glancing away from the wall, Simon noticed a glow piercing the inky blackness ahead. He lowered the hood on the lantern, casting them in darkness. To his surprise, the gloom wasn't impenetrable. He could see light leaking from around a doorframe far ahead. He uncovered the light, and the clarity of the doorframe's edge disappeared once more.

They pushed forward until they stood before a white stone door. Archaic braziers, clearly having not been lit in hundreds of years or more, sat on either side of the door. Despite its apparent age, the metal was surprisingly clear of rust. Simon realized that little of the oppressive humidity reached this far into the mineshaft, leaving the old metal unscathed by the passing years.

Much like the walls before, the door was carved from top to bottom with intricate carvings and the same repetitive hieroglyphics.

A ring had been affixed to the stone door as a handle. Without querying his friends, Simon grasped the door ring and pulled it toward him. The door slid open quietly, despite its enormous weight. Light poured through the opening, blinding the trio.

Simon raised a hand to his eyes to block out the multitude of torches hung around the wall. The smell was both smoky and pungent, causing Simon to cough slightly as the thick smoke in the air burned his lungs.

At the sound of his cough, a rustle of movement was heard from within the room.

Simon squinted against the light. As his eyes adjusted to the brilliant glow, he could see a figure seated atop a stone throne in the middle of the room.

The ancient man raised his head toward his newest visitors.

"Have you also come to take my blood, to join the ranks of the new den?"

CHAPTER Twenty-three

TORCHES BURNED IN SCONCES ALONG THE WALLS, IL-
luminating the square room. The walls were a similar white limestone to the hallway through which the trio had just passed. They
had been carved with the same repeating series of symbols, though the
careful carving that appeared in the hallway was lost, as though the carvings became more frantic the more times they were produced.

Against the far wall, a dais had been carved from the floor, on the
top of which sat a stone throne. The throne's surface appeared to have
once been flawless, but it had recently been marred by chisel marks, cre-
ating holes along the sides of the rock seat.

Atop the throne sat an archaic man. His shoulders were hunched
from exhaustion and, though he watched Simon as the Inquisitor entered, the man's head slumped toward his chest. His pale white skin had
the consistency of leather but the color of fresh snow. His pale scalp bled
seamlessly into his wispy, ivory hair. Large patches of hair were missing, and the man's skull was scarred with bald sections. Nails, which had
grown too long from poor maintenance, protruded from his fingertips as
he grasped his stone throne.

Simon paused at the sight of the figure. Most jarring was not the
man's appearance but the dichotomy of the man's ancient appearance

intermixed with the modern technology protruding from his skin. His wrists and ankles were bound in tight leather straps. Heavy chains dangled from each of the manacles, affixed to the chair. From his arms, needles pierced his thin flesh and tubes, stained red but currently dry of fluid, ran from the syringes and led to rubber-corked glass jars beside the throne. Simon leaned to the side for a better view of the jars and, not at all to his surprise, they were partially filled with a vibrant red blood.

"You're not one of his minions, are you?" the ancient man asked. His voice was barely raised above a whisper, though the sound carried well through the empty room.

He raised his hand to brush the strands of hair from his face, but the chains reached the limits of their range less than a foot from his lowered head. With a sigh, the man lowered his arm once more.

With great effort, the archaic figure raised his chin from his chest and rested the back of his head against the back of the stone throne.

"Speak or be gone," he said. "I have no time for visitors. No, no, that's not correct. I have nothing but time, but what I lack is interest in visitors."

"What are you?" Simon asked. He wished he had the foresight to collect another wooden stake from the previous room.

The ancient man laughed, though the sound was more equivalent to an asthmatic wheeze. As he opened his mouth, the elongated fangs were evident.

"He's a vampire," Luthor said, disgustingly.

"Not *a* vampire," the archaic monster corrected, leaning forward with great effort. "I am *the* vampire, the originator, the pure!"

"Kill him and let us be gone," the apothecary whispered.

"I can hear you, little man. I went for nearly a millennium without so much as a whisper, caressed only by the sound of my own voice. I grew so accustomed to the silence that I could hear water droplets sliding between the cracks in the stone. I could veritably hear my hair growing. I pulled it out in droves just to further appreciate the silence. Yet you whisper as though you can't be heard. Your whispers are like someone screaming in my ears."

"He's gone wonky, sir," Luthor said, no longer bothering to be quiet. "Finish him like we did the others. We should be gone from the mine sooner rather than later."

Simon heard his friend's plea but chose instead to step closer to the beast. "You said 'his' minions. Of whom do you speak?"

The elder vampire wrenched his arms upward until the chains were taut. The leather straps bit into his wrists, but he seemed oblivious to the pain. "Free me from this prison and I'll answer your questions."

"Answer my questions and I'll decide whether or not to end your life," Simon retorted.

The vampire lowered its arms and laughed heartily. "Were I in my prime, I would have dispatched you without so much as a thought, moved quicker than the human eye could track, or flown through the air until I appeared as little more than mist. I would have—"

His diatribe was interrupted as he was overcome with a bout of harsh coughing.

"He won't talk, nor would I expect him to," Luthor said. He glanced nervously into the blackened tunnel behind them. "Hurry and finish this."

"Who is 'he'?" Simon reiterated.

The vampire wiped spittle from his lips and grimaced. "Free me, mortal."

Simon took a threatening step forward. "I'll sooner free you from this world than release you from this prison. Tell me what I want to know."

The vampire shook his head in defeat. "This world is a prison, human."

"He's talking in riddles," Mattie said. She grasped her wrist and pulled downward, stripping the skin from her hand. Beneath, the claw and fur of the werewolf was revealed. "I'll end this if you won't."

Simon grasped her arm as she tried to pass. The vampire sucked air between his teeth in surprise.

"A monster walks beside you, but you leave this one strapped to the throne."

Mattie caught Simon's gaze and stared at him sternly. "We don't have time for this, Simon."

"We can't kill him," Simon replied. "The two we've already slain have put us at great personal risk. Something tells me this one's death will be significantly more noticeable, and recognized far sooner. If we kill him, we will never leave Whitten Hall alive."

"So we just leave a vampire alive, sir?" Luthor asked incredulously. "There has to be a better option."

"Perhaps there is, Luthor, but not one that I can conceive on such short notice. Come, both of you, we're leaving at once. Let the vampire rot in his cell."

The trio turned away reluctantly, glancing over their shoulders at the imprisoned ancient monster. Simon stepped through the doorway and grasped the edge of the heavy stone door. As he started to push it closed, the vampire's whisper reached his ears.

"Martelus Whitten," it said. "Now I've told you what you wanted to hear. When we meet again, I expect you to remember this favor."

Simon paused for the briefest moment as he absorbed the newest information. Finally, he pushed the door shut behind him and rejoined the others.

Their ascent out of the mine was uneventful, though they remained on edge throughout their walk. Simon placed an expended lantern from the barracks atop the scorched rock in the large chamber, hoping to conceal the true origins of the explosion that nearly claimed their lives. He doubted the vampires would be fooled for long, or truthfully at all, but it made him feel better for putting forth the effort.

It was still dark as they reached the floor of the quarry. Simon pulled the watch from his vest pocket and checked the time. He nodded appreciatively as he realized it was still a few hours before dawn.

The vampire's parting words, albeit not as surprising as he imagined, still haunted Simon. The chancellor had presented himself well, convincing Simon and his entourage that there was merely a labor dispute ongoing in Whitten Hall. All the while Martelus hid the truth that he and so many of his fellow townsfolk were vampires and murderers, having slaughtered over a hundred people to feed their insatiable thirst for blood.

As they climbed the perimeter trail that led to the lip of the pit, Simon's mind was already awhirl with possibilities. Martelus and all that had been turned would have to be destroyed, of that he was certain. Unfortunately, they numbered forty or more, while Simon had only a group of three. Even the element of surprise wouldn't be on their side much longer, ending as soon as the chancellor realized that two of his minions had been staked through the heart.

The trio reached the trail that led back into the woods, without sharing so much as a word of surprise between them. Simon glanced over his shoulder, catching the weary expression on his two companions' faces. He nodded his understanding and led them into the woods. He no longer felt comfortable traveling the road, even when they were far removed from the chancellor's manor house.

After walking for a while, Simon could feel the sweat beading on his brow. The humidity that they had so refreshingly avoided while in the mine had returned with a vengeance, draining their remaining energy.

"Can we stop for a moment?" Mattie asked. Of the three, she was the most affected by the weather.

"The river should be just ahead," Simon replied. "It would be good for all of us to stop and drink our fill."

The underbrush wasn't as thick deeper within the woods. They moved with little impediment, following the faint glow from the hooded lantern. Simon glanced within at the light and noticed that the candle was nearly extinguished. The wax had run into an amorphous clump at the bottom of the lantern. A weak flame consumed what little wick remained, but even that repeatedly threatened to go out.

To his relief, Simon heard the trickle of the stream ahead. He pulled the hood of the lantern down, concealing most of the light that spilled from it. The lantern was useful but grew more unnecessary the closer they got to the stream. The canopy of leaves was nearly nonexistent, allowing moonlight to filter down onto the exhausted group.

Simon covered the lantern completely as he knelt before the stream. Mattie took her place beside him and lapped handfuls of water into her mouth. When the Inquisitor was satiated, he assumed Luthor's cautious watch of their surroundings as the apothecary took his turn by the water's edge.

Eventually, they had all drank their fill. With his belly full, Simon lifted the hood of the lantern once more. He frowned as they remained in darkness. Glancing into the lantern's interior, he saw that the small flame had succumbed and their light was fully extinguished.

"We have no light," Luthor stated. "I'll be hard to traverse the wilderness without a light."

"I couldn't agree more, Luthor, which is exactly why we're not going to. We're going to sleep here in the woods tonight."

"Sir?"

Simon sat on the forest floor, resting his back against a tree. "We'd be lost without our light, which means we'd be just as likely to stumble upon a group of vampires returning to their daytime homes amidst the mines as we are to find our way back to the inn. Even were we to find our way back, we'd be sleeping tonight amidst a den of vipers, the analogy working just fine considering their shared love of elongated fangs."

Mattie slumped to the ground as well. "Aren't they just as likely to find us here as they are in town?"

"If they were actively looking for us, then I would say yes. They've already proven to have far superior night vision. However, they aren't yet looking for us. More than likely, they won't discover their deceased brethren until the sun has already risen. That gives us, at best, a day's head start before they begin their pursuit. We'll get a few hours' sleep here in the woods and then make our way back to town, gather our belongings, and move expeditiously back toward Callifax."

Luthor drove his fist into the open palm of his other hand. "I can't believe we were duped twice now by those we were supposed to trust."

Simon patted the ground beside him, encouraging the apothecary to sit. "That's not at all true, Luthor. Your instincts put you at odds with the chancellor upon our very first meeting. Matilda's keen sense of smell identified the pallor of death that hung over the town immediately. It was only I who was in too big of a hurry, and far too stubborn, that I held out a glimmer of hope that this assignment might be above keel. I should have seen through the chancellor's lies sooner. He never let his people leave of their own volition. He killed them… *ate* them, if you will. Moreover, he invited new workers, who arrived weekly, to serve as more of their food."

Luthor accepted the offer to sit. He removed his bowler cap and wiped the accumulated sweat from its brim. "So that's it for us, then, sir? We'll collect our things and leave Whitten Hall behind us?"

Simon nodded. "Until we can notify the Inquisitors of what we discovered here, then yes, that's all there is. We have only one other responsibility: to collect Gregory, our bartender accomplice. He warned us something was amiss, even if we ignored the warning and dove headlong into the vampires' home."

"Just him?" Mattie asked as though she were taken aback. "There are at least two dozen people in the town during the day, meaning that they couldn't possibly be vampires. We should be taking as many as possible with us as we leave."

"Were it at all possible, my dear, I most certainly would. However, we'll be moving quickly once we leave, to put as much distance between us and our pursuers. A large group will slow us down. Moreover, I can't guarantee the innocence of the rest of the town. It's far more than likely that a good portion of them are in collusion with the vampires. No, in this instance, we'll take just the one who will be our advocate before the Grand Inquisitor, confirming what we've witnessed. After that, we can return with an army that rivals the vampires."

Luthor fidgeted with the brim of his hat. "We're going to look conspicuous when we suddenly leave town with our luggage in tow. If there are conspirators within the town during the day, they'll be doing their best to stop us."

"On the contrary, Luthor, we'll be doing exactly what they want. The day we arrived, we met with the chancellor. He said the next train would be arriving in two days. That was last night. We'll sleep tonight in the woods, which means that the train will be arriving in Whitten Hall some time tomorrow. They wanted us gone, and we will be more than happy to oblige. We should be miles away before the vampires are able to begin their pursuit and by then, it'll be far too late."

Mattie frowned and placed her arms over her knees. The Inquisitor glanced toward her and arched an eyebrow inquisitively.

"What's bothering you, Matilda?"

Mattie shook her head. "We're working so hard to convince the Grand Inquisitor that I'm not a threat, quite unsuccessfully thus far, might I add. He needs to know that those of us infected aren't a danger to the crown. Instead, the very next mission on which we are sent, we encounter another group of infected citizens of the kingdom and, quite naturally, they're slaughtering civilians. They're a threat. What possible chance is there of convincing the Grand Inquisitor, once he comes to the natural conclusion that exceptions can't be made for those infected, that we should be allowed to live?"

Simon nodded understandingly. "It's a difficult path, to be sure, but a bridge we'll have to cross when we come to it. For now, we can't allow ourselves to be distracted."

He gestured toward the uninvitingly hard forest floor. "Get some rest, both of you. Dawn will be here sooner than we think, and we have a full day ahead of us."

CHAPTER Twenty-four

BEFORE THE SUN AROSE THE FOLLOWING MORNING, Simon was awake. He removed his jacket from where it had draped over him like a blanket during the cooler, if not still humid, night. He roughly brushed the clinging grasses and fallen pine needles from the jacket before shaking it, dislodging the dirt and moss accumulated from the forest floor.

Though Luthor snored softly from his place beside a pine tree, Mattie was already awake. Her hair was damp, as though she had bathed that morning, leaving her blouse and leather jerkin damp from the water dripping from her hair.

"Morning," Simon said, stifling a yawn.

"Good morning," she replied as she gathered the meager belongings they had taken with them on their adventure the night before. "How did you sleep?"

"I slept like absolute rubbish, but thank you for asking just the same. There's something about sleeping with a rock repeatedly jabbing you between your shoulder blades, all the while having the fear of being taken in the night by blood-sucking vampires, that results in a night of ill-begotten sleep. How did you sleep, Matilda?"

Mattie glanced up from her work and shrugged. "Fine," she replied simply, her answer a strong counterpoint to Simon's rambling.

Simon walked across their narrow clearing and kicked the sole of Luthor's outstretched foot. The apothecary awoke with a start, tilting his bowler cap from in front of his eyes so quickly that it toppled completely from his head. Though his eyes settled on the Inquisitor, Simon was sure that Luthor didn't actually see him.

Luthor reached up with the back of his hand and rubbed his eyes furiously. From the inside pocket of his suit, he withdrew his wire-framed glasses and placed them on his face.

"The sun is rising, Luthor, and so should we," Simon said.

Luthor muttered something unintelligible before glancing toward the quickly brightening sky. The sun was beginning to crest over the tops of the nearby trees. Simon followed Luthor's gaze and enjoyed the sudden warmth of the brilliant sun. He often took for granted the glow of the dawn, though that was likely to change when faced with denizens of the night. Suddenly, the morning sun seemed like the most glorious thing he had ever seen.

Luthor stood and retrieved his hat. Though on his feet, he still looked sadly disjointed and uncoordinated. Mattie glanced at the two men before shaking her head slowly. They had no mirror with which to appraise their current disposition. Neither man could appreciate the clinging pine needles in their hair, or the tussle of their normally perfectly coifed locks, or even the heavy wrinkles present on their attire. She walked to Luthor's side and affectionately removed a blade of grass from the apothecary's muttonchops.

"Go down to the river and wash up, both of you," she said, motioning over her shoulder. "If your plan is to be incognito, you certainly won't succeed looking as you do."

Simon and Luthor exchanged curious glances, looking over one another and seeing their disheveled appearances. With a noncommittal shrug, Simon led them from the clearing and down to the stream.

They knelt beside the water and splashed handfuls of water across their faces in an attempt to wash away the sweat and grime from the night before.

Luthor reached down and filled the cup of his hands with water before taking a long drink. With a satisfied sigh, he sat back on the river's bank.

"Do you think they found the bodies?" he asked.

Simon ran his wet fingers through his hair, taming the unruly mound. "I should sincerely doubt it. If they had, I doubt anywhere in the woods would have been safe."

"Then there's hope for an unopposed escape?"

Simon wiped his mouth on his sleeve before sitting beside his companion. "One can only hope, though we can hardly become complacent. At least some of the people in town are colluding with the vampires, of that I'm sure."

Luthor furrowed his brow and stroked his chin thoughtfully. "Something has been bothering me since last night."

Simon smiled. "Just one thing?"

Luthor returned the smile, though he still seemed disturbed. "If the chancellor's intent was to lure more workers to Whitten Hall to feed, why go through the ruse of the fake vampire on the train? All that accomplished was to scare away over half their potential food source."

Simon nodded as he picked up a flat stone. With a quick throw, he sent it skipping across the water. "I thought about that as well and believe I understand why."

"Pray tell."

"You are correct that over half the passengers disembarked and never came back aboard following the attack, but consider for a moment the sorts of people that fled the train. The government officials who had been sent previously who, according to our initial report, were deterred from reaching Whitten Hall by the very faux vampire that we killed. Had those men gone missing, the crown mostly likely would have assembled soldiers to inquire as to their disappearance. The staged attack on the train removed the more spineless of the government employees long before they could become a threat."

"Quite right, sir, quite right. That would be why the chancellor was so hasty to ensure we boarded the next train, isn't it? With us gone without incident, their malicious plan could continue unabated. What of the other workers who left, though?"

Simon stroked his chin. "I would dare say that those who disembarked, never to return, were not nearly as desperate as those who remained aboard. The type of man who would remain on the train despite the sorcerous attacks would likely be the type of man without a family or a future, whose only chance lie in an advert requesting manual laborers to Whitten Hall."

Luthor rested his elbows on his knees and watched the sunrise reflect off the gently moving stream. "In essence, they thereby eliminated everyone whose disappearance would cause alarm and inquiry. Devilishly brilliant, they are."

"And most deadly," Simon replied. "I couldn't count the number of dead within the mines, but assuming four trains have run before our arrival and using our train as an estimated average, there are potentially one hundred and fifty bodies discarded in the mine."

Luthor blanched and shook his head. "It feels wrong of us to leave without proper redress."

Simon patted the apothecary on the back. "Their crimes will be addressed, of that you can be certain."

"Are you two quite done primping yourselves?" Mattie asked as she emerged from the woods.

"Nearly there, though it takes some time to emulate perfection," Simon chided.

The two men stood and stretched muscles that had grown stiff from sleeping upon the ground. Simon ran his hand across his cheeks and felt the accumulated stubble. He wished he could shave, if for no other reason than to maintain appearances. Luthor often carried such nonsense as straight razors in his doctor's bag, but the bag had been destroyed, Simon realized wistfully.

Mattie handed the two men their hats, which had been left at camp as they cleaned themselves. Simon placed his upon his head, concealing the still uncooperative hair thereunder.

They turned toward the covered bridge that spanned the stream, which was visible from where they stood by the water. The bridge wasn't long when viewed in the sunlight. It had seemed far longer when they had crossed it in the dead of night the previous two nights. With the sun arisen, it appeared as an ill-painted and ill-maintained wooden bridge. As they stepped into its cooler interior, sunlight filtered through cracks in the boards, leaving the path before them striped with its light.

For a moment during their walk, Simon considered taking them back into the woods to avoid the chancellor's manor house, but decided against it. He doubted any humans lived in the house during the day, since most of the chancellor's security forces were most likely vampires like himself. Besides, Simon had already crafted a cover story about the trio enjoying a morning stroll. It would be far more curious for them to be discovered traipsing through the woods as opposed to casually strolling along the road.

The outpost of Whitten Hall came into view as they rounded a corner. As it had been when they first arrived, the town was a veritable ghost town. A few men walked primarily between buildings before disappearing into their cooler interiors. No one seemed at all interested in Simon and his companions' comings and goings.

Luthor stepped beside Simon and pulled his hat down further over his eyes to block the now-glaring sun. "You don't suppose the vampire in the chair would reveal that we were there, do you?"

Simon paused at the edge of town and stared pensively toward the distance. "It had crossed my mind, but I don't believe so. Everything the vampire said made it seem like he was at odds with Chancellor Whitten. I could be wrong, of course, but I don't believe he would turn us in."

Luthor nodded contently before they walked into town.

The inn was one of the first buildings they reached after entering the town proper. Reaching the inn without being recognized should have been the simplest thing to accomplish.

Simon's luck never held up that well.

"Inquisitor Whitlock!" Tom Wriggleton yelled as he approached from the train station. He jogged the rest of the distance and arrived somewhat out of breath. "I thought I recognized you, though to be honest, I'm surprised to see you all out so early."

Simon smiled humorlessly. "With this being our last day in Whitten Hall, it only seemed right to take a stroll and stretch our legs before we are forced to sit for four days on our train ride home."

Tom nodded, though he bit his lip inquisitively. "Begging your pardon for mentioning it, sir, but you all look awfully tired."

Simon sighed, eager to be done with the conversation already. "We're not much of morning people."

Tom frowned as he stared into Simon's impassive gaze. Gingerly, the man reached out and plucked a pine needle from Simon's shoulder.

Simon glanced at the offending flora and arched an eyebrow defiantly. "It was a very difficult walk over lots of rough terrain. Now if you'll excuse us, Mister Wriggleton, I believe we must pack before our train arrives."

"Of course," Tom replied flatly.

As they turned away, Simon noted a few other Whitten Hall residents emerging from nearby buildings. Unperturbed, he led his group into the inn.

The tavern portion was half-filled with patrons enjoying assorted drinks. Though the room still looked fairly empty, it was far busier than it had been over the past few days, especially during the hours of sunlight. Simon nodded politely at the assorted stares they received as they passed through the room. Luthor and Mattie pressed closer to his side, keeping out of the reach of the tables as they passed.

"They know," Luthor muttered through pursed lips.

"I know," Simon replied, though his polite smile never faltered. "Get your things as quickly as you can and meet me in the hall."

Luthor and Mattie nodded, though they imitated Simon's smile and gracious nods of recognition as best they could. They hurried upstairs, even as they heard the front door open behind them.

Simon hurried into his room, locking the door behind him. Pulling his suitcase from the closet, he stuffed clothes unceremoniously into the bag. He had to press down firmly to hold it closed as he latched the leather straps into place. From beneath the bed, he pulled the more appropriate Inquisitor's kit. He quickly opened the wooden box, revealing the assortment of instruments designed to slay mystical creatures.

Without hesitation, Simon removed a small pile of sharpened wooden stakes and slipped them into his jacket pocket. The smooth handles protruded from his jacket, but he was certain that discretion was no longer necessary. Likewise, he removed a series of extra bullets. He frowned at the selection, realizing that aside from his regular rounds, there were few options other than silver. He bit his lip thoughtfully as he tried to remember if vampires disliked silver. They had been so effective against the demon in Haversham, though completely ineffectual against the werewolves who, by mythology, should have been susceptible. Shrugging, he reloaded his revolver with silver bullets.

A gentle rapping at his door caught his attention. He quickly closed his Inquisitor's kit and stuffed it under one arm, even as he lifted his suitcase in the other. Simon pulled open the door, revealing a nervous Luthor and Mattie.

He stepped out of his room and joined the others in the hall.

"What are we going to do, sir?" Luthor asked in a low whisper so as not to be overheard. "They know. Whether they found the bodies or the ancient vampire told them, they know."

"Calm yourself, Luthor," Simon replied. "I know that they know. I know that you know that they know. They very possible know that I know that you… to hell with it. Everyone knows."

Mattie frowned. "Don't be so hasty to disregard him, Simon. It's still three hours until the train arrives. We can't very well go stand on the platform and hope that Wriggleton and his goons simply leave us be for that time."

"We can lock ourselves in our rooms," Luthor offered.

Simon glanced back and forth between the apothecary and werewolf. He smiled devilishly, an expression that Luthor knew all too well translated into trouble.

"Sir?" Luthor asked.

"I think we shall go downstairs and enjoy a drink. Then, with our accomplice bartender in tow, we shall go wait at the train platform."

"Forget about Gregory," Luthor pleaded. "We can come back for him when we have numbers on our side."

Simon shook his head. "He took a risk to warn us. We shall take a risk with saving his life."

Mattie leaned against the wall calmly and picked at the dirt under her fingernails. "It doesn't solve the problem of the townsfolk. They won't leave us alone once we've reached the platform."

Simon arched his eyebrow toward Mattie. "We're sorely out of options. If we stay here, they'll certainly knock down the doors to get to us. If we go outside, they'll come after us. If we flee into the woods, they'll pursue only until nightfall, until the true hunters awaken. No, our best option is to take our chances in the open, where we can't get backed into a corner but are still within distance of the train when it arrives. Besides, my dear, I'm not concerned. After all, they're only human. We've handled far worse."

"I hate when you're like this, sir," Luthor interrupted.

"Like what, Luthor?"

"Brash and overconfident. Somehow, you walk away practically injury free while I wind up visiting a chiropractor upon our return to Callifax, just to reset the number of misaligned bones throughout my body."

Simon turned toward the stairs as he continued the conversation. "Nonsense. Need I remind you that I was quite manhandled by Gideon Dosett no more than a month ago?"

"Need I remind you that you left me to my own devices with the very same man and let me take a good thrashing before you made your dramatic, if not late, entrance?"

They reached the stairs and began descending. "You're never going to let that go, are you?"

"Not so long as we both live and possibly even after one of us has passed… preferably you."

As they reached the tavern, they realized it was busier now than it had been when they had first entered. The mirth shared between the men faded away as Simon led the trio to empty seats at the bar. The bartender gave them all stern looks before approaching.

"What do you want?" Gregory asked, his voice rumbling from his broad chest.

"Scotch," Simon answered, "though preferably in a glass if that's even an option here."

Gregory glanced at the other two, who merely shook their heads.

"People are watching us," Luthor muttered.

Simon kept his gaze directly forward but nodded slightly. "They're doing more than that."

He could feel the stifling presence of the other bar patrons pressing in around them. From his periphery, he couldn't see that anyone had moved, but the mood of the tavern had clearly shifted away from their favor.

"We should leave," Mattie said, her voice carrying from the other side of Luthor. "This isn't a very defensible location, at least not against so many."

Gregory sat a tumbler of scotch in front of Simon. The Inquisitor sighed contently as he grasped the ice and liquor filled glass. "See, now was this truly so difficult?"

As the bartender began to turn away, Simon reached out and grasped the large man's wrist. He didn't bother concealing his actions, nor did he lower his voice when he spoke. Gregory tried to pull his arm away, but Simon's grip was like steel.

"You took a chance with your warning," Simon said to the larger man. "We're leaving Whitten Hall aboard the next train. Come with us. We can keep you safe."

Gregory furrowed his brow in confusion before looking up. His gaze fell past Simon's shoulder, even as the Inquisitor heard someone approaching.

"Gregory didn't write the note," Tom said as he took the seat beside Simon. "I did."

Tom placed a napkin on the bar between them. It carried the same warning as the one they had seen previously in identical handwriting.

"And it wasn't a warning," Tom continued. "It was a threat."

Simon released the bartender's arm and slid his hands toward him. "Well, this is certainly awkward."

Simon lashed out with his open hand, catching Tom in the middle of his chest. Caught by surprise, Tom tumbled from the barstool and crashed to the floor below.

The nearby townsfolk leapt to their feet, holding assorted makeshift weaponry in their hands. Knives, clubs, and even mining picks were visible as they were drawn from bags or concealed beside table legs.

Simon threw back his jacket and reached for his revolver. As his fingers closed over the weapon, something heavy struck him solidly across the back of the head. Simon's head exploded in pain, and lights danced before his vision. He stumbled forward unsteadily, the revolver slipping from his grasp even as it slid free from its holster. He barely heard the clatter of the silver weapon striking the ground. Darkness was consuming the dancing lights in his vision until his view of the bar was nothing more than pinpricks of light at the end of long, dark tunnels. Though it seemed like it was happening miles away, he could sense blood trickling through his hair and down the back of his neck.

Simon's eyes fell closed as he pitched forward. He was unconscious long before he struck the ground.

CHAPTER
Twenty-Five

SIMON'S HEAD LOLLED TO THE SIDE AS THEY CARRIED him into the windowless upstairs room. Luthor stole a glance at his mentor, but the Inquisitor's eyes didn't so much as flutter. The apothecary wanted to ensure Simon wasn't too badly injured, aside from the visible welts and bruises, but he could do little with his hands bound behind him and a dirty rag stuffed into his mouth.

Mattie stumbled along beside him, driven forward by the same coarse hands that shoved Luthor every time he slowed his pace. A small trickle of blood stained the leg of her pants from where she had fallen on the stairs, but she seemed otherwise unharmed. Despite being similarly bound, they had granted Mattie the decency of not placing a soiled rag in her mouth. She carried her head high, even when being pushed unceremoniously.

"Here," Tom Wriggleton said as the group stopped before an unmarked door. Gone was the man's pleasant demeanor, replaced instead by a stoic, if not angry, visage. Tom had refused to answer any of Luthor's questions, even as he barked orders at the other townsfolk. "Put them in the closet."

Someone opened the door and Gregory walked into the narrow broom closet, carrying Simon in his arms. The Inquisitor offered no resistance or even a grunt of anguish as the bartender dropped him heavily onto the floor. Luthor and Mattie were likewise driven into the inner enclosure. Firm hands on their shoulders pushed them both to the floor. One of the guards gruffly brushed his hand across Luthor's face, intentionally knocking the man's glasses from his nose. They fell to the floor and skidded across the hardwood.

With Simon's unconscious form in the middle of the narrow broom closet, neither Luthor nor Mattie had room to fully extend their legs. Instead, they sat with their knees pressed nearly to their chest as they looked up at their captives.

"What should we do with them?" Gregory asked, his voice filled with bile.

"Keep them here," Tom replied, his answer no less venomous. "When the chancellor awakes, he can decide their fate. Keep guards posted outside the door. The three of them are crafty. I don't want any of them escaping before the sun sets."

Without another word, they slammed the door shut, casting the trio into near darkness. Footsteps could be heard outside the room as a few guards shifted into position.

Luthor spat out the rag, which had only been stuffed into his mouth rather than tied in place. Extending his tongue, he scraped it across his upper teeth in an attempt to wipe free the awful taste that now filled his mouth. He spat onto the wood floor in disgust.

"Are you all right?" Mattie asked. She shifted closer to Luthor to see him in the dim light.

Luthor arched his eyebrows as he realized there was light to be seen from within the close confines of their room. The slats that formed the outer wall were warped from exposure to the elements. He could feel the humid breeze seeping from between the boards and could see rays of sunlight filtering through, albeit blurrily without his wire-framed glasses.

"I'm fine," Luthor replied, "though I'm far more concerned about Simon's well-being."

Though he was still shrouded in darkness, they could see the Inquisitor's swollen cheek. Though Gregory's makeshift club had been more than enough to render Simon unconscious, the other townsfolk had gleefully joined in assaulting his prostrate form.

Luthor felt the sweat drip down his back, though he doubted it was solely from the humidity in the stifling room. He pulled against the bindings on his wrists, but the rope held firmly.

As he strained, the sound of a train's whistle split the air. The ear-piercing howl blasted for nearly a minute before falling silent.

"The train is arriving," Mattie said matter-of-factly. "We need to ensure we're on board when it departs."

"I couldn't agree more, but I don't think our captors would be so accommodating."

Mattie glanced toward the narrow beams of light between the loose boards. "How long do you suppose it will remain at the station?"

Luthor shrugged. He squinted toward the beams as well, but the view was blurry without his spectacles. "I suppose as long as it takes to unload their passengers and baggage. I don't think they were in the station longer than a half hour at most when we arrived, and I feel that we would have had more passengers, seeing as how Simon handily shot and killed the false vampire on board."

Mattie frowned. "That doesn't leave us much time to escape, overpower our guards, and board the train."

"Not to mention the need to defend the train from what will most certainly be invaders, who will more than likely assault the engineer first and foremost, thereby disabling the train. I don't know that it's possible."

"It is possible, if we act now. We need to check on Simon, and we need to escape." Mattie glanced first toward the door before letting her gaze fall to Simon, ensuring the Inquisitor was still asleep. "Do that *thing* that you do and set us free."

"That *thing* that I do?"

"Now is not the time for you to feign ignorance. Magic us free."

Luthor glanced nervously toward his mentor and shook his head. "I can't take that chance, not with Simon in the room and guards posted just outside."

"Damn them and damn you, too, Luthor, if you won't save yourself," Mattie replied angrily. "Who cares if Simon discovers your secret, if it's being used to save us all. If Simon can't see the benefit of having a wizard in his entourage, then he's a blasted fool as well."

"What if I were to use my magic? Then what shall we do afterward? Shall we kill everyone in the town on our way to freedom?"

"Yes, if it be necessary," Mattie replied, exasperated. "They certainly didn't harbor any reservations about killing us."

"They didn't kill us."

Mattie frowned deeper. "You sounded an awful lot like Simon, just now, arguing semantics as though this were a science experiment for which the outcome is somehow a mystery. They're vampires, Luthor. There's only one outcome, and I certainly don't have to wait until nightfall to find out what it is."

Mattie huffed and pulled on the ropes tied around her wrists. With a violent tear, the rope snapped neatly in half. She brought her hands before her, showing the white werewolf fur coating her arms and ending in padded and clawed hands.

"You may have reservations, Luthor, but I most certainly do not. If they think they know the monsters in their town, they're about to be thoroughly surprised."

She crouched beside Simon as the fur sloughed from her arms, revealing the pink flesh beneath. She touched his cheek gingerly, probing the swollen skin and searching for broken bones beneath. Her hand traced toward the back of his skull until she felt the matted blood from where Gregory had struck the Inquisitor. Though she desperately wished him awake, she didn't envy the headache that would accompany his waking.

Satisfied that there was no permanent damage done, Mattie stood. With a discontented sigh, Luthor began tracing a hex onto the floor behind him, one that would easily free him from the ropes.

As Mattie stepped toward the door, the floor beneath her feet creaked loudly from her weight. Luthor froze as he glanced nervously toward the door, though Mattie didn't slow her stride at all.

They could hear the guards shuffling outside as they talked in hushed whispers. The handle groaned as it turned and the door was flung open.

Luthor squinted against the invasion of light. There were more guards beyond the door than what he had originally presumed, all of whom were armed.

Mattie lunged toward the nearest guard, bearing him to the ground. She growled gutturally as the transformation began to overtake her. Driving her elbow into the prone townsperson's face, she scratched at her chest with her free hand, drawing bloody streaks across her skin. Her eyes locked on a guard against the far wall, and she coiled her legs underneath her to lunge.

Before she could leap, however, the butt of a rifle was driven into the side of her head. Mattie rolled to the side, turning a painful strike into a mere glancing blow. She could feel the blood seeping from her temple, and her thoughts grew cloudy as she tried to concentrate on her attackers.

Within the room, Luthor stole a glance once again toward Simon before beginning his rune anew. Though it wouldn't take long to create the spell, he knew the battle beyond the broom closet would be over in a matter of seconds, for good or for bad.

Mattie rose to meet one of the guards, who approached her wielding an axe handle like a club. She caught his wrist as he swung at her and drove her fist painfully into his gut. The guard doubled over in pain, allowing her to drive her knee into his face. Though she had yet to transform, her strength was still impressively greater than a normal human, regardless of the form she took.

Mattie cringed as she was struck from behind. The club landed across her shoulder blades, driving the wind from her lungs. She swung blindly behind her as she stumbled away, but her efforts were met with another strike, this time across her outstretched arm. Before she could recover, the butt of a rifle was driven into her stomach. As she bent forward, the club was brought down across her back once more.

The fight left her even as she collapsed onto the hardwood floor. Though not unconscious, her body burned with agony, a pain that radiated down her spine and settled firmly in her lower back.

Rough hands grasped her beneath her armpits and lifted her upper body from the floor. With her legs trailing behind her, they dragged her back into the broom closet.

Luthor paused once more, his rune nearly completed. One of the guards knelt before him and scowled.

"You want to try to escape, too?" the man growled.

Luthor quickly shook his head. "No, I'm quite fine where I am."

The guard smiled humorlessly. As the man stood, he drove his heel down onto Luthor's discarded glasses. The lenses shattered as the frames bent.

Luthor groaned inwardly. "That was entirely unnecessary."

They ignored the apothecary as they bound Mattie once more. Her hands were tied behind her again, as were her feet. A cord was run between her bound limbs and pulled tightly until her hands and feet nearly touched one another. In her wounded state, she moaned loudly, but her struggles were weak.

Without another word of warning, the guards stood and exited the room, slamming the door shut behind them.

Luthor slid to Mattie's side. He traced the rune behind him, and the ropes untangled of their own volition. They fell to the ground behind him as he brought his arms to Mattie's side.

"Hold on, Mattie," he whispered. "I'll have you untied in a moment."

"Leave me be," she said hoarsely. She turned her face toward him, her disdain evident. "You're a coward, Luthor Strong. You have every opportunity to be a hero the likes of which this kingdom has never seen, and instead, you cower for fear of being discovered."

She turned her head away from him, though her final words carried easily through the room. "Leave me bound. I'd rather take my chances with the vampires than be beholden to further conversation with you."

Stunned, Luthor stopped, his hands hovering above the bound redhead. Her words stung far worse than anything he had experienced before. While his physical injuries would heal in time, he had no spell to repair his emotional wounds.

Slowly, he slid back to his place against the far wall. He absently drew a rune in the air, and the shattered glass of his lenses fused together once more. The metal frames of his spectacles bent into the general facsimile of an oval and the lenses rolled as though sentient back into their place. Luthor picked up the glasses and placed them back on his nose before wrapping his arms protectively around his knees.

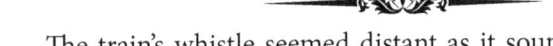

The train's whistle seemed distant as it sounded a second time. A hiss of steam followed as the train began moving away from the Whitten Hall platform. Luthor hung his head even as he imagined the mine's foreman welcoming the new employees, though Luthor knew he was truthfully welcoming them to a hasty demise.

The train had left as quickly as it had come, on its way back to Callifax. It would be eight days until it returned, though Luthor knew that eight days was far too long to survive in such an inhospitable land. Mattie had been correct that their fates were sealed. Unfortunately, with both Mattie and Simon injured, it would have been impossible for Luthor to escape while carrying them both in tow. He would have been captured almost immediately. Likewise, escaping alone while leaving the Inquisitor and werewolf to their fates was never an option. His chance came with Mattie and he hesitated, choosing to protect his secret rather than protect his friends. Perhaps she had been correct. Perhaps he had spent so long protecting the fact that he was a wizard, infected by magic in a land where magic was an abomination, that he had grown weak. Indecision had stolen his power and hesitation his pride. Luthor hung his head in shame as he wallowed in his self-pity.

The lines of sunlight on the ground lengthened as the sun began to set. They crept toward Luthor accusingly, as though each inch crept forward was another reminder of their impending doom.

Mattie had still offered not a single word of solace to Luthor since her recapture, nor had Simon awoken from his earlier beating. Though Mattie had ensured him that Simon was not seriously injured, Luthor was beginning to have his doubts. He considered casting a spell to heal Simon, but he didn't see the point. Simon's tactical wisdom was unsurpassed, but there was little chance of escape from their current confines, at least not in time to escape the vampires once they'd fully awoken.

He sighed as he glanced toward the redhead. "I'm sorry, Mattie. I should have trusted you and followed your lead."

She didn't offer a reply and kept her back to him.

"The sun's setting," he added. "Chancellor Whitten and his ilk will be here soon afterward."

He felt foolish for merely stating the obvious, but he was struggling to find a conversation piece that seemed worthy of his obvious betrayal of her trust. As he anticipated, she offered no reply, not so much as a shrug of her shoulders to acknowledge that he had even spoken.

The light beyond the far wall slowly faded into oblivion, casting the broom closet into inky darkness. Simon didn't stir to wakefulness, nor did Mattie offer much in the way of conversation. The silence in the room only added to the air of anticipation.

Shortly after the sun set, a myriad of footsteps were heard in the hallway beyond the closet door. Luthor set his jaw as he quickly sketched a rune down the length of the unwound rope. As quickly as it had fallen away, the rope wound around his wrists, albeit significantly looser than it had been when originally tied. He knew he could slip free from the knots if needed, though he had no idea where he would go once free.

The door opened, spilling light into their room. Luthor fought the instinct to raise his hands to his eyes, to block the glaring electric light. Instead, he sat in the room, trying not to look too defiant as Chancellor Whitten stepped inside.

Even before he spoke, Luthor could tell the chancellor's demeanor was significantly different than the cordial man they had met earlier in their visit. Gone was the faint hunch in his shoulders. Likewise, the soft expression of his face was hardened with a combination of power and confidence. As he noticed Luthor's intensive stare, Martelus smiled, exposing the elongated vampiric fangs.

"Mister Strong," the chancellor said as he knelt beside the seated apothecary. "It's good to see you again, though, if I were to be completely honest, I would have hoped you would have been aboard the train and long gone from Whitten Hall by now."

"It's never too late for us to leave," Luthor offered.

"On the contrary, I believe we're well past that point now, don't you?"

Martelus glanced toward Simon's unconscious form and shook his head wistfully. "That's such a shame, you know? I had truly hoped that Royal Inquisitor Whitlock would be awake by the time I arrived. My men are eager to please me, as I'm sure you can imagine. They get overzealous sometimes. I'll certainly have to reprimand them later."

Luthor spat on the ground, his spittle striking the edge of the chancellor's polished shoe. "They're eager to please you because they're fools. They think you'll turn them into one of you, a vampire."

Martelus arched an eyebrow as he glanced back to the apothecary. Luthor mistook his expression for one of surprise as he continued.

"We know what you are and what you've done here. You're going to suffer for killing all those people."

The chancellor smiled, exposing his long canines in a more threatening manner. "I've already suffered far more than you could imagine, and I'm sure one day I'll be brought to bear for the crimes I've committed. That time, however, isn't now, and you are most certainly not the one who will judge me."

Martelus pulled a handkerchief from his breast pocket and wiped the spittle from his shoe. "You and your friends had your chance to leave Whitten Hall well enough alone, yet you chose to pry. Sadly, those poor decisions are the exact reason none of you will leave here alive."

Luthor looked quickly to Mattie, but the redhead hadn't moved. He wasn't sure if she was feigning sleep or still harboring her resentment toward him, but in either instance, Luthor decided not to address her until well after Martelus had departed.

The chancellor stood and turned toward his entourage. "Bring the Inquisitor with us. I believe he'll make an exceptional meal for the Original. Let his blood be a source for more of the tribe."

A vampire behind him gestured toward Luthor. "What of the other two, sir?"

Martelus glanced over his shoulder and smiled maliciously. "Leave them both. We'll dine on them ourselves."

Vampires stepped into the room and grasped the limp Inquisitor. Luthor kicked toward them, but he received a vicious backhand to his cheek for his efforts. Within seconds, the vampires had pulled Simon away and the door slammed shut on them once more.

The vampires carried Simon between them. The disease in their blood carried them far quicker than a normal human could move and within moments, they arrived at the perimeter of the mining quarry. Led by Martelus, they stepped over the edge of the cliff and fluttered effortlessly to the rocky pit floor.

Simon was dropped awkwardly into a mining cart. The vampires didn't bother with a tarp to conceal his frame as they pushed him into the consuming darkness of the mineshaft.

Through twists and turns, the chancellor led his night tribe unerringly deeper into the mine. Eventually, the cart struck the barrier built at the end of the laid tracks. Beyond the cart, the door into the underground barracks was thrown wide. At the late hour, the barracks were once again empty, aside from the vampires who now entered their halls, dragging the sluggish Inquisitor between them.

Simon felt his feet bumping along the stone floor as awareness crept back into the edges of his mind. His first thought was one of pain and anguish. His mind reeled from sparks of agony radiating from the back of his head and from his battered face.

He tried to force his eyes open, but only one responded. His left eye slid open slightly. For the briefest of moments, he feared he had gone blind during his assault. As panic threatened to overwhelm his thoughts, he forced the emotion into the background and focused his other senses.

His dress shoes rattled on the slightly uneven stone floor. The humidity was lessened but still omnipresent. Voices echoed off nearby walls as his kidnappers talked amongst themselves.

He knew he was in the mines. It wasn't blindness that had overcome him, but rather an impenetrable darkness. Simon tried to regain his composure, but firm hands held his arms out to each side as he was dragged along. The vampires had him captive, of that he was sure. They had little need to use lights within the mines. Though he wasn't nearly as keen on mythology as Luthor, he was certain seeing in the darkness was one of their supernatural abilities.

"He's coming to," one of the vampires said to an unseen leader, though Simon had little doubt who they addressed.

"It matters not," Martelus replied, confirming Simon's suspicions. "He's far too weak for it to make any difference now."

As they entered a new chamber, the sound of the echoes changed drastically. Sound seemed far more muffled, as though the walls were much more distal than they had been shortly before. His mind remembered the chamber of discarded debris and the corpses of those unfortunate souls who had come before.

In the distance, the darkness was penetrated by flickering torchlight. As they approached, Simon was able to drape his head backward and see the ornately carved walls of the ancient chamber in which they had met the elder vampire.

Panic finally did settle into Simon's chest. He had no doubt of their intent as they approached the tall, limestone doors that separated the square room beyond from the rest of the mine. The Inquisitor struggled against his captors, but to no avail. His limbs still lacked the energy to fight against the vampires, though even at the peak of his might, he doubted he could singlehandedly break free from a pair of vampire assailants.

Martelus pushed open the double doors. Simon squinted against the series of torches lining the walls of the chamber beyond. The acrid scent of confined smoke filled his nostrils, forcing a choking cough from deep in his bruised chest. Ribs that were either bruised or broken screamed in protest to the sudden coughing, only adding to Simon's great discomfort.

On the raised dais, the archaic vampire sat chained to his stone throne. Tubes ran from his arms to jars that were no longer filled. Though the rubber tubing was stained red from previous blood flow, nothing drained from the needles pressed into the veins of his arms.

"Why have you come again, blood thief?" the ancient vampire asked with an exasperated whisper. "I have nothing left to offer."

Martelus smiled, though he clearly disliked the wizened creature on the throne. "You misunderstand. It's not something that I want from you but rather what I offer."

The chancellor stepped aside, revealing Simon dangling from between the two vampire guards. Simon's chest still faced the ceiling as his shoe's heels were pulled along the stone floor. His head, however, listed backward so that he viewed the world upside down. His awkward position, however, also exposed his neck to the elder vampire.

The ancient man licked his dry lips lustfully as he spied Simon's exposed neck. The Inquisitor struggled to cover his throat, but he barely had the strength to lift his head, much less dissuade the hungry monster.

"Bring… bring him to me," the ancient vampire stammered. "Bring him to me, please."

"He's yours to dine upon," Martelus explained, "but do not forget our agreement. We will return for your blood once it flows again."

The Original closed his eyes even as he waved dismissively toward the chancellor. "Can you not hear that, blood thief? Can you not hear the strength of his heart? Can you not smell the sweet aroma of his fear saturating the air?"

The ancient vampire opened his eyes and glared with disdain toward Martelus. "Of course you cannot. You're a charlatan, a mockery of the true vampires of old. Your senses are dulled by your delusion of power. You feed because you're hungry, but you cannot take a moment to savor the meal before you."

The chancellor glanced in frustration toward his men. "Yes, yes, old man. At the end of the night, we shall return—"

"For my blood," the ancient vampire interrupted. "Yes, I'm well aware of what you desire, blood thief. I would deny you your prize if I could."

Martelus gestured toward his men, who dragged Simon to the base of the dais. The elder vampire raised his hand, signaling for the nubile vampires to pause before their assent.

"A moment, if you will," the white-haired vampire demanded. "A meal should be savored, you savages." He breathed deeply once more before gesturing for them to approach.

Simon felt the fear pounding through his veins, which, he was certain, only heightened the vampire's desire for his blood. The Inquisitor tried to calm himself, to control the raging emotions and eclectically pounding heartbeat, but it was for naught; he was consumed with the horror of being fed upon by the abomination before him.

In hindsight, he wished only that he had listened to Luthor and destroyed the vampire when they had the chance. He had feared premature discovery by Martelus and his night tribe but clearly, their best efforts had not deceived the vampires for very long.

The vampire guards climbed the pair of stairs to the foot of the throne. With little effort, they lifted Simon from his feet and draped him across the Original's lap. The ancient vampire licked his lips in anticipation.

Martelus shook his head and gestured for the guards to follow. "I have no desire to see him feed; it disgusts me to watch."

The guards quickly retreated as the weathered creature closed its boney hands around Simon. Despite its frailty, it mustered the strength to pull Simon toward its awaiting maw.

Simon yearned to break from the vampire's grasp, but his efforts were feeble. The beating he had taken left him without the strength or ability to resist, even as he saw the elder vampire open its mouth wider, revealing the pointed fangs within.

Martelus glanced over his shoulder as he and his men reached the door, just as the Original closed its mouth over Simon's neck.

CHAPTER Twenty-six

LUTHOR SAT ON HIS HANDS, THE ROPE STILL LOOSELY tied around his wrists. They had taken Simon minutes earlier, whisking him away to the wizened vampire trapped within the mine. Despite Simon's multitude of skills, escaping a den of vampires was hardly amongst his forte. The apothecary saw no feasible way that Simon alone, weakened as he was, could be free of the vampires without being drained of his blood or worse, turned. The thought of a Royal Inquisitor vampire was terrifying. He needed help and the only people available to save him were the two people trapped within the broom closet, one of whom still hadn't turned to face Luthor since her recapture.

He glanced around the room, at least as much as was visible in the dim light filtering through the back slats and under the doorway. Mattie was still facedown on the floor, her hands and feet tied awkwardly behind her. Luthor had seen livestock similarly bound and doubted she was any more comfortable than the pigs had appeared to be. At first, he had assumed she remained in her predicament to spite Luthor, out of anger for his apparent unwillingness to use his magic to save them. Now, he wondered if she could escape at all. Even her lycanthropic powers might be limited by her ability to gain leverage.

"Can you break free of your rope bindings?" Luthor asked.

Mattie shifted in the darkness, the first sign of life she'd shown since Simon was taken. He saw her struggle against the knots, all of which held firm. "Simon is dead, if not now, then soon."

Luthor frowned, despite her words echoing his own concerns. "I don't believe that, and neither do you."

"You're wrong," she replied bluntly. "You saw his state when they carried him away. He wasn't conscious, though I doubted he would have offered much resistance even if he had been in full control of his faculties. They took him to that monster in the mine. It'll kill him when they arrive."

Luthor sighed in the darkness and leaned heavily against the wall behind him. "Believe what you will, but I don't believe he's dead yet."

Mattie turned her face toward him, though he couldn't see her expression in the gloom. "What difference does it make, Luthor? Alive or dead seems to be of little consequence. If Simon, by some not-so-small miracle is still alive, what good does it do us? Will he march into a city of vampires and their human cohorts in an attempt to save us? By chance, if he did survive thus far, he would certainly know that returning to Whitten Hall is suicide."

"You don't know him as I do."

"Perhaps, or perhaps he doesn't know you as well as he thinks he does."

Luthor furrowed his brow and pursed his lips. "What's that supposed to mean, exactly?"

Mattie rolled over onto her side, though it clearly took a great effort. "You've lied to him about your magic. If he knew the real you, the man with the runes carved into his skin, would he still be so accepting of your friendship?"

She didn't offer him a chance to reply before continuing to berate him. "How do you think he would respond if he knew you had a chance to save him, but you didn't because you placed your own safety higher than his life?"

They sat in silence, despite the palpable tension in the narrow room. Luthor wanted to reply, to defend his actions in some way, but he couldn't find the proper words. Despite the sting of her accusations, he knew she wasn't entirely wrong. He couldn't be certain that using his magic would have been the difference between confinement or escape from Whitten Hall; she had a much higher expectation of his magical abilities than he did. Yet the fact that he couldn't predict the outcome only further eroded his resolve.

"I'm not a terrible person, despite what you might believe," Luthor said softly.

Mattie sighed in the darkness. "I've never, until this moment, thought of you as anything but a selfless man. Yet you betrayed our trust, both Simon's and mine. How can you suddenly ask forgiveness?"

Luthor shook his head. "I'm not going to ask for forgiveness. I'm going to earn it, the way I should have earlier. I've spent so long hiding what I am from Simon, thinking that at some point I would find the right moment to reveal the truth, that even when that moment is staring me in the face, I refuse to act. We're going to save Simon and, by my word, I won't let you die here."

"I don't think that's your decision to make," Mattie retorted. "A tribe of vampires sits just beyond that door. What can two people do against that?"

"Two people?" Luthor asked. "Not much, to be sure. Luckily for the both of us, neither of us are right and proper people, are we?"

"So now you intend to use your magic?"

"Desperate times, desperate measures, and whatnot."

Luthor stood, and the ropes fell harmlessly from him. He traced a familiar rune into the air above Mattie, and her ropes began to unwind. In the silvery light of the glowing rune, he could see the red burns on her wrists and ankles from where the ropes had been pulled painfully tight. His heart ached for her pain, but she seemed to ignore her personal discomfort as she stood.

She rubbed her wrist distractedly as she stood nearly nose to nose with Luthor. "You've set me free, so be it. How can I be sure that this isn't further proof that you will only use your magic to be self-serving?"

"You can't," Luthor replied, "at least not until we find and rescue Simon. I'll use every spell at my disposal to ensure his and your safety; I give you my word as a Strong and a gentleman."

"How, pray tell, will we accomplish that?"

Luthor smiled. "We show these vampires that they aren't the only abomination in Whitten Hall, and a far cry from the most dangerous."

He kicked outward, striking the wall with the toe of his shoe. The sound reverberated through the small room.

The vampire guard beyond the door paused as a dull thud sounded from within the broom closet. He held a finger to his lips, requesting silence from the other vampire, who leaned calmly against the far wall. The three humans who had been positioned further down the hallway stood cautiously as the vampire nearest the door tilted his head to listen.

The noise sounded again, as though someone were breaking through the wooden walls of the closet.

"They're escaping," the vampire said as he drew a pistol from his waistband.

He grasped the door and threw it wide, ready to pursue their escaping prisoners.

Brilliant red light flashed from within the room, and the vampire paused in midstride. His mind reeled at what he had just seen, an angry red symbol hovering in the air before his chest. It was only when the vampire behind him howled in agony that the one at the door realized something was amiss. He glanced downward and noticed the gaping hole in his chest. The flesh, bone, and organs had all vaporized, and the edges of the wound glowed red like smoldering coals. Black ichor dripped from the wound, despite its cauterization.

The vampire pitched forward, permanently deceased. The vampire behind him clutched the smoldering stump where his right arm had once hung. Luthor stepped aside at the sight of the vampire, and a massive, fur-covered beast charged from the room.

Mattie drove the vampire into the wall, breaking bones with her sheer size. As the vampire tried to escape, she clamped her maw over his head and shook him violently from side to side until she heard the satisfying snap of his neck.

The humans at the end of the hall raised their weapons, but a shimmering wall appeared between them and the escaping prisoners. At the pull of the trigger, lead bullets ricocheted harmlessly from Luthor's protective barrier.

As quickly as it had appeared, the wall evaporated. The werewolf hurtled herself down the length of the hall while the men reloaded their flintlock rifles. She bounded into their midst, using her considerable bulk to manhandle the human guards. Luthor approached cautiously, carrying her discarded attire, as Mattie flung one of the men into the hallway wall. The man crumpled to the floor, and Luthor doubted quite seriously that he would rise again.

With the guards dispatched, Mattie stood on her hind legs and shook her long, white mane. "Others would have heard the gunshots and the scuffle. More vampires will be here soon."

"Quite right you are, which is why we won't be."

Luthor took her by her wrist, despite the fact that she towered over him in this form and outweighed him by several stone. They hurried down the hall and entered the bedroom he had been occupying during their stay. Luthor slammed the door shut behind him and locked it. As an added precaution, he placed a chair under the door handle. Though he doubted it would keep a vampire at bay for long, he only needed a momentary delay.

They hurried to the far window and pulled it open. The cool night's breeze entered the bedroom, a comforting wind compared to the stifling heat of their makeshift prison cell.

"Forgive me, my dear, but you'll have to be in human form once more for us to escape through so narrow a window."

Despite her limited canine facial expressions, Luthor could clearly see her disapproval. She gestured with her great white paws for him to turn about. As he turned his back to her, she shed the werewolf skin, revealing the naked human beneath.

She dressed quickly as they heard the first footsteps hurrying up the stairwell from the tavern below. Luthor offered Mattie his hand as she slipped through the open window, but she brushed it aside. Grasping the windowsill with her fingertips, Mattie hung as far as possible before releasing her grip. She fell gracefully to the ground, landing in a practiced crouch.

Luthor followed suit, slipping his legs out the window and resting his stomach on the window ledge. He wasn't afraid of heights, exactly, but he preferred viewing them from the safety of a zeppelin cabin, rather than experiencing them firsthand as he dropped from a second-story window.

The door shook as someone attempted to enter the room. The handle jiggled from side to side, though the lock remained firmly in place. Luthor lowered himself further out the window until his arms rested on the windowsill and only his head remained visible. The door splintered open as a vampire drove his fist through the wood. Its hand searched erratically for the locking mechanism.

As the vampire's hand closed over the handle, Luthor lowered himself out of the window and dropped to the ground below. He landed in a heap, crashing through a bush. Hands closed over him, and he struggled momentarily before recognizing Mattie's face. Relaxing, he accepted her assistance as he stood.

Above them, the bedroom door creaked open and booted feet hurried toward the window. Luthor and Mattie scrambled away from the inn and ran toward the woods as the first of the vampires peered out the open window. Hissing angrily, they dropped gracefully to the ground and hurried in pursuit.

CHAPTER

Twenty-seven

THE ANCIENT VAMPIRE WITHDREW ITS MOUTH FROM Simon's neck and threw back its head with a heavy sigh. Simon slid from his weakened grasp and fell awkwardly to the limestone pedestal at the vampire's feet. For a long moment, Simon lay there unmoving before finally beginning to stir.

The Inquisitor coughed and reached up meekly toward his neck, feeling the thick saliva coating his throat. As his eyes fluttered open, he moved with a sense of urgency, his fingers frantically searching for puncture wounds across his flesh.

"You won't find any," the vampire said softly.

Simon glanced inquisitively upward at the frail vampire.

"Bite marks," the ancient man continued. "Holes in your neck. You won't find any. I didn't bite you."

Despite the vampire's reassurances, Simon continued a furtive search across his skin.

"Stop that nonsense at once," the vampire demanded, though his words fell on deaf ears. He coughed hoarsely and wiped spittle from his lips. "Despite my longing to feed and the near point of starvation at which these savages keep me, I want you alive."

Simon slowly lowered his hand, using it instead to push himself up from his prone position. Cautiously, Simon glanced over his shoulder toward the closed stone doors that served as the only entrance and exit from the room. The room was empty, his other captors having departed with the chancellor.

He looked back to the elder monster and arched an eyebrow inquisitively. "You want me alive for what purpose?"

The vampire leaned forward, his bones audibly creaking from the effort. "You, young human, are my path to freedom from this infernal prison."

"Why me?" Simon asked, furrowing his brow nervously. "Why spare my life when you've clearly taken so many others?"

The vampire sagged in his chair, his shoulders slumping forward. "There's strength in you, a different sort of power than what I see amidst the chancellor and his ilk. There is honor and strength unbridled."

Simon shifted his weight and slid his feet from the dais, resting them on the step. Despite his bone weariness, he forced himself onto his knees and finally to an unsteady standing position. He felt naked without a weapon with which to defend himself. His pistol was gone. The Inquisitor kit had been left with the rest of his packed belongings, he assumed in his room at the inn. Even the stone chamber in which they found themselves lacked the wooden beams and discarded axe handles of the coarse stone room beyond the doorway. He was unarmed, in the presence of a truly ancient evil.

"If you think I'll set you free, you're sadly mistaken. I destroy magic within the kingdom, not release it upon its citizens."

The vampire reached toward Simon, but the chains on his wrists caught on the throne. The chains snapped taut, forcing his arms backward. The vampire looked at his prison and sighed disconcertingly.

The vampire sat back on its stone throne, resting one arm comfortably on the chair's armrest. Its hand settled perfectly into a well-worn groove in the stone, where it had been polished smooth from years of wear. Its other hand stroked its chin as it observed the wary Inquisitor.

"You speak of destroying magic in all its forms, yet you travel in close confines with that which you purport to hate."

Simon narrowed his eyes as he took another cautious step down the stairs. "My companion is different from you. There's goodness in her. She's a victim of circumstance, not a monster borne of evil."

The vampire wheezed in a faint semblance of a laugh. "You know this of me? You know that I'm evil incarnate?"

Simon shook his head. "I don't need to know of you. I see your offspring and the evil they've committed. Tell me that you, yourself, haven't partaken of the meals they've offered."

The vampire leaned forward slowly. "I have fed. To tell you otherwise would be to tell a lie neither of us would believe. Yet you know nothing of me. You know nothing of my time spent in this abysmal stone prison, its walls serving as a far better cage than any metal bars ever could. You know nothing of the torture I've endured, staring at the same walls, with the same burning torches, with my same writing carved into the walls from a time where my sanity had wandered far from my body."

Simon leaned against the nearest wall for support but glowered at the vampire. "I can't give you what you want. There's enough of a vampire problem in Whitten Hall without releasing yet another."

"I am nothing like them!" the vampire hissed. "Calling them vampires is blasphemy. They are insignificant specks, their life not even measured as a grain of sand in the great hourglass of existence. I was alive when your kingdom was but a conglomeration of tribes, slaughtering, raping, and pillaging one another for the glory and the pleasure. You were child playthings when I was already ancient!"

His exuberance resulted in another coughing fit. As the vampire settled once more, it pushed loose strands of wispy, white hair from his face.

"You say you're not evil then?"

The vampire glanced toward Simon, his skin stretched taut across his skull. "I could not deceive you and say that I have not committed evil deeds, but the deeds do not define the man."

"The deeds are the man, not the words," Simon countered. He was engaging in dialogue with the vampire despite his predilection, knowing he had little else he could do until he was certain the path beyond the stone doors were clear of vampire vermin. "Convince me you're not evil. Convince me that the patron of the night tribe against which I fight isn't evil incarnate. Tell me your tale of how you came to be in this prison."

"Do you know of the Rift?" the vampire whispered, closing his eyes as though recalling fonder times long past. "Whitten spoke of it, a vestibule between our worlds." He drew a deep breath from between his clenched teeth. "Long ago… long, long ago, yes, I was from the far side of the Rift."

"The Rift only came about a decade ago. How is it that you've been here so long?"

The vampire opened his eyes slowly and fixed his scarlet pupils on the Inquisitor. "Many lifetimes ago in my world, the one of magic as you refer to it, I was a man of position and power. I had a small army at my command and vassals who bowed so low that they kissed the ground in my presence. I was a creature of the night, and their respect for me was only equaled by their fear.

"For years, I satisfied my bloodlust by feeding on the flesh of our enemies. No one missed the highwaymen who vanished in the night. Invading armies were splintered as their scouts were found emaciated, drained of their blood. Because of my gift, our kingdom lived in peace."

Simon glanced around the room, longing for a weapon.

"Do I bore you already with my tale?" the vampire asked.

The Inquisitor looked back to the thin creature. "You're hardly providing a convincing argument of why I shouldn't kill you. It sounds like you were every bit the monster I believe you to be."

The vampire sighed heavily. "I was, to be sure. Please forgive me, but you must hear the horrid tale of my youth to fully appreciate why I deserve my freedom now."

Simon gestured for the vampire to continue, knowing he had little other choice at the moment.

The vampire clenched its hands into fists. His fingers moved begrudgingly, having spent far too long grasping the arms of the throne. "The Barony was a utopia for those under my protection, but our enemies grew wary of our borders. Bandits refused to traverse our forests. Neighboring fiefdoms forewent invading our lands for easier conquest elsewhere. And I? I grew hungry."

Simon stepped cautiously forward until he was certain the strength had adequately returned to his legs. Intrigued, he sat on the bottommost step of the dais, knowingly out of reach of both the hands and feet of the bound monster.

"You fed on your people."

"Not the healthy or strong; never those who contributed to the well-being of the lands," the vampire said, as though his words justified his actions. "I fed on the ill and the elderly, on those disabled, those who were more a burden on their families than a boon. In the blindness of my youth, I thought they should be appreciative of the service I provided."

"They turned on you, didn't they?" Simon asked matter-of-factly.

The vampire's gaze grew distant and unfocused as he recalled a time nearly forgotten. Eventually, he shook his head and returned his focus to Simon. "Forgive me. Without regular sustenance, my mind has a tendency to wander."

The vampire wheezed as he continued. "They came to my keep with torches and pitchforks. They stood at the far side of the portcullis and demanded my blood."

"Is that when you fled; how you found your way to our world?"

The vampire paused and appeared perplexed. He furrowed his brow sadly. Were it not for the state of undeath in which it found itself, Simon was sure the vampire would have shed a morose tear. "Flee? No, my boy, I slaughtered them to a man. My anger fueled my bloodlust and I descended on them, even as my army marched through the gates. They were peasants and laborers, ill-equipped to face my wrath. Before I could recognize the error of my wrath, their blood flowed like rivers through the streets. I opened their arteries and filled my moat to capacity."

Simon swallowed slowly, aghast at the monster's admonition. There was no glee upon the vampire's face as he recalled the wholesale slaughter of his subjects, as though only remorse remained. The Inquisitor took a deep breath and focused on the vampire. Despite the Inquisitor's outrage at the admitted atrocities, there was also a burgeoning sense of sympathy for the creature, as though his years trapped in this realm had served as a sort of penance. Simon yearned to hear the end of the story.

"Then how is it you came to be in our lands?"

The vampire lowered its hand back to the worn armrest and smiled at Simon. "You men of science never cease to amaze me. Your curiosity is stronger than your stomach. I speak of the genocide of my people and all you want is for me to finish my story. You're all mind and no heart; so very different from my own lands."

"Your story," Simon insisted. "I must know how it ends."

"A vampire must eat," the creature on the throne said. For a moment, Simon thought he was referring to feeding on him, until the vampire quickly continued. "I had sustained my life by feeding on the infirmed and the convalescing. Yet in my fit of rage, I had killed them all, not just the weakened but also every living man, woman, and child residing in my barony. Without them, I had no source of sustenance and I grew hungry once again."

The vampire reached up and rubbed his eyes. "I found food where I could, in the veins of the very soldiers who had helped me slaughter my servants. When they discovered my treachery, they, too, fled. I was finally truly alone, the lord of an empty, lifeless land. All had abandoned me, save for my closest vizier, a witch who had the ability to scry the worlds.

"It was he who told me of your world. He had foreseen it, he told me. There was a bleed between our worlds, a small, unstable portal. It led here, to your world, though it was a time so long ago that you have barely recorded it in your books of history."

"It was a feeding ground for you," Simon said as he spat on the ground in disgust.

"Judge me as you like, but I saw in your world a feast of flesh the likes of which you could not imagine. I didn't see the men and women of your land as anything more than food. In my land, there are others of my kind, but here, amongst your ancestors, I knew I would be a dark god."

"Then how is it you wound up a prisoner in a dark cavern?"

The vampire glanced around the room, where his unkempt fingernails had carved into the limestone over the centuries of captivity. "The portal was unstable, flickering at its periphery even as we arrived. One moment, it showed the surface world, full of life. Yet when I stepped into the bleed, the portal shifted to here, depositing me in a natural cavern far beneath the earth. No entrance. No exit. No hope of escape. Only silence and with it, introspection and reflection."

Simon toyed absently with a discarded sliver of limestone. "Would you have me believe that you discovered the error of your ways during your time in captivity, that you became a changed man?"

The vampire chuckled softly. "Young human, I don't believe you understand how great a time passed while I was imprisoned, nor how strongly the silence of a stone cell weighs upon your mind. I don't know how to convince you of the sincerity of my words, but hundreds of years alone made me realize the error of my more youthful indiscretions. I want my freedom, but not to return to the sins of my youth, but rather to atone for them."

Simon shook his head, still unsure of the creature's sincerity. Luthor had once called Simon a bleeding heart for so willingly accepting people at their word, though in Luthor's defense, he had been referring to a damsel in distress and not an ancient evil from beyond the Rift. There was a part of the Inquisitor that wanted to believe the vampire could change, but a much stronger part of him knew that few people, if ever, really changed their hearts.

Changing the subject, Simon recalled the narrow exploratory tunnel carved off the main mine, which led toward the room in which they now found themselves. "The miners found you when they were searching for another vein of iron, didn't they? They blasted directly into your chamber."

The vampire sighed, knowing his words were falling on deaf ears. "I could barely lift my head at their presence. They fetched the chancellor, who saw in me a potential for power and glory, the likes of which he could never attain as merely a servant of another king. He saw in me opportunity, and I saw in him my own evil mirrored in someone else's eyes. He fed me enough to regain my strength but immediately siphoned the new blood from my veins, using it to create his own abominable vampire army. Had I not spared your life, you would have become the latest in a long line of victims to his growing lust for conquest."

Simon pushed away from the step and brushed the dust from his wrinkled suit.

"Set me free," the vampire urged. "Unbind my limbs and let me take my revenge on the chancellor. I want to atone for the sins of my past and putting an end to the vampire horde I helped create is the first step to that realization."

"I appreciate you sparing my life—"

"Release me!" the vampire interrupted, begging as he already sensed Simon's hesitation.

Simon turned away from the vampire and walked toward the stone doors that led from the chamber. He had no weapons and would soon be walking into a den of vampires unarmed, but he saw few other options. Remaining in the presence of the elder vampire wasn't feasible, since Martelus' men would eventually return, expecting to collect their blood sacrifice. His only hope was that it was now daytime, and the vampires were slumbering in their alcoves. Simon paused and stroked his chin, wondering if the vampires even slept at all. His escape would be short-lived indeed if the vampires were awake as he passed through their barracks.

"Have you no honor, no integrity? Even you, who Whitten warned was one of the best of your kind, lacks the honor to set me free even after I've spared your life. If you and Whitten's kind are representative of your world of science, then you deserve to burn when the demon lords come to claim this land."

Simon turned sharply toward the archaic creature. "What did you say?"

"I hope you burn," the vampire spat, though even his attempt at disgust seemed abnormally feeble.

Simon shook his head, no longer feeling disgust toward the vampire before him. "No, about the demons."

"The demon lords will cross through the Rift and enslave your world," it replied.

"Exactly how many demons are there?"

The vampire seemed taken aback by the sudden shift in conversation. "Five of them," it stammered. "What difference does it make? It will take but one of them to destroy you and your kind."

Simon smiled to himself. "No, it'll probably take at least two by my count."

Before the vampire could respond, Simon placed his hands on his hips. "What do you know of the demon lords?"

The vampire grasped the arms of his chair nervously as he spoke. "It has been ages since I left the land, so it's possible those ruling have changed, but there were always five demon lords who ruled over our realm. Each possessed a special power, which gave them sway over the minds and souls of those under their rule. Their power was unbridled and unsurpassed, even by one as strong as me."

Simon heard him speak but fixated on the mention of controlling men's minds, as he had experienced so recently upon his unfortunate encounters with Gideon Dosett. "You seem to have no love lost for these demon lords."

The vampire frowned. "If I was a savage in my youth, they would have been spiteful gods, tormenting and destroying those beneath them on little more than a whim. Perhaps my imprisonment has granted a different perspective to their brutality."

The Inquisitor stood in the center of the room and stared intently at the vampire. "Assuming the demon lords have already arrived, how can we stop them?"

"You couldn't, at least, not alone. You would need powerful allies with even more powerful abilities."

"Like yourself?" Simon asked.

"Myself and others, like your traveling companions," the vampire replied.

"If the demon lords are here, not just in our kingdom but throughout our realm, would you fight for us if freed? Would you be an ally against a greater evil?"

The vampire nodded slowly and attempted a smile that only drew the taut skin further across its skull. "Yes, if it will prove my good intent. I will stand with your kingdom against the demons."

Simon stroked his chin thoughtfully, feeling the now two-day-old stubble that covered his usually clean-shaven face. Mattie had proven herself an incredibly capable and trustworthy ally, not just in Haversham but since. It was possible, though even Simon felt hesitant to admit it, that the ancient vampire could be another unusual companion against a growing evil at their borders. The threat of magic was growing. If Gideon Dosett was but the first of five demon lords, he would need powerful friends, indeed.

"I'll set you free from this prison, though not now," Simon finally said after a lengthy pause.

The vampire sighed disconcertingly.

"You're right, I owe you my life," the Inquisitor continued. "I don't know if your words were true or hollow, but I've been accused of being far too forgiving in the past, offering second chances to those who don't deserve our benevolence. I see potential in you, vampire. When next I return to you, I promise that I shall take you from this prison once and for all."

The vampire nodded hesitantly. "I look forward to your return." It pointed to the doorway behind Simon. "You should hurry before the sun rises and the vampires return to their berths."

Simon nodded toward the vampire before turning toward the stone doors once more. He pulled them open but paused at the doorway, glancing back once more to the weary vampire who, for the first time, raised his head proudly with a sense of hope. Despite the bindings on its wrist, the vampire raised his hand appreciatively. Simon nodded once more and hurried into the large chamber beyond, letting the door swing shut behind him.

He collected a torch from the wall and held it aloft as he entered the debris-strewn room beyond the vampire's carved prison. He stepped gingerly through the discarded waste, the whole while keeping his eyes averted from the pile of bloodless human remains he knew to be piled against the far wall.

As he neared the center of the chamber and could finally see the narrow path leading upward toward the vampires' barracks, he stooped and collected a pair of wooden stakes from the debris.

Reaching the far side of the room, he rushed up the passage, knowing that whether the vampires had returned to the mines or not, his fate was already sealed.

CHAPTER Twenty-eight

LUTHOR AND MATTIE SPED THROUGH THE DARK FORest, their every step dogged by vampires. The monsters moved with incredible speed, but the dense underbrush of the nearby woods allowed the two companions to stay ahead of their pursuers.

The apothecary grunted as Mattie released a low-hanging branch, which snapped backward, striking Luthor in the face. He could hear her breathless apology but he ignored it, knowing they both ran with reckless abandon and little attention to courtesies toward one another.

Luthor wasn't entirely sure the direction they were running. At first, he had wanted to run out of town in the opposite direction of the mines, knowing that path would lead, after some time, back to civilization and the other Inquisitors. However, the quick pursuit of the vampires had undermined his plans, forcing him and Mattie to flee toward the chancellor's manor house and, eventually, the mine itself.

"Use your magic and force them back," Mattie said, gasping for air. She was in far better shape than Luthor, who labored to keep up with her long strides. Were it not for Luthor being in tow, he was certain she would have already transformed into a werewolf and fled on all fours.

"I… I can't… concentrate on drawing a rune," Luthor replied through hitched breaths. "We'd have to stop first."

He glanced over his shoulder but couldn't see any of their captors. Despite their view being free of pursuers, they could hear the vampires crashing through the underbrush all around them as they sought the pair. Stopping was equivalent to committing suicide, for it wouldn't be long until one or more of the vampires stumbled upon them which, in turn, would alert the others.

His legs were starting to cramp from exertion. This scenario had been his fear when they were still bound in the closet. Freeing himself from their bindings had been easy and could have been accomplished at any time, yet he had no idea what to do once they were free. It was a four-day train ride from Whitten Hall to Callifax. If he recalled the map of the area correctly, it would be at least a half-day's hike to the nearest outpost in the region, though there would be no guarantee that the next location would be any safer, nor was he sure he could maintain so grueling a pace for the time required.

He wasn't a planner. He researched their missions and provided historical and mythological context for their assignments, but it was Simon and his brash overconfidence that provided the true way ahead. The realization that his inaction might have been the cause of Simon's death struck him doubly hard.

"I can't keep running like this," Luthor stammered. "They're undead... they'll never tire. Right now, I think they're just toying with us until we're too tired to fight."

"I think you're right," she replied as she scanned the dark forest around them. "At this rate, I don't think it will be much longer, either. We have to be ready."

Ahead, Mattie slowed her pace. She reached up and tore her leather jerkin free, dropping it into the grass. Luthor leapt over the discarded garment even as she slipped her tunic over her head. Luthor saw the smooth curve of her exposed back as her pace slowed to a quick jog. His already pounding heart raced a little quicker, despite knowing that this was merely the first stage of her transformation.

"They are getting close," she said over her shoulder. "We'll have to stop to defend ourselves soon, whether we want to or not."

"I'd rather stand and fight..." Luthor began before pausing to catch his breath once more. "...than continue this inane chase."

The underbrush cleared ahead, providing a small clearing through which the moonlight filtered. Mattie stopped in the middle of the clearing, tearing at her flesh as she turned. Her skin dropped in sheets to the carpet of grass at her feet. Luthor's stomach dropped at the sight, certain that he would never grow accustomed to seeing such a bizarre transformation.

She tore aside her leather pants, ruining the clothing as her fur-covered legs erupted from behind her peach-colored flesh. The werewolf stood before him moments later in her full majesty.

Luthor dropped his hands to his knees as he stopped beside her, gasping for breath. He ran a sweaty hand over his upper arm, activating a rune concealed beneath his sleeve. His protective shell shimmered around him briefly before fading to complete transparency.

"They're coming quickly," Mattie said, sniffing the air. "Prepare yourself."

The first vampire crashed through a bush beside Luthor, slamming its claws into his chest. The protective shell flashed, delivering an electrical current through the monster and sending it flopping limply to the ground. The impact sent the apothecary tumbling. He saw the moon briefly before his view changed to the soft grass and soil. He quickly regained his senses and stood, even as a second creature erupted from the underbrush.

It reached toward Mattie, but her heightened senses were far quicker. She slid effortlessly out of its clawed grip before swiping with claws of her own. Her elongated nails tore the skin of the vampire's chest, though the wound refused to seep blood. Injured but undeterred, the vampire merely took a step backward before hissing, exposing its fangs. Mattie snarled in response, her canines far longer than the vampire's.

Cold hands closed over Luthor's shoulders as a new adversary emerged. The protective shell sparked once more, but most of its magic was spent. Luthor could sense the vampire's obvious discomfort as pulses of electricity rolled through its arms, but it merely tightened its grip in response, digging its nails painfully into the soft skin of his upper arms.

Luthor cringed as his spell faded. The pain was intense, as though the vampire was interested only in shattering his shoulders before feasting on his blood. Clarity of thought was fleeting, even as he tried to concentrate on activating another rune, either one drawn in the air or one of the remaining ones tattooed on his body. With the vampire's grip intensifying on his shoulders, his arms lacked the strength to do either.

His vision blurred from the pain. He could see Mattie dueling the vampire before her. In the hazy periphery of his vision, he could see the electrocuted vampire stirring, the electricity stunning but failing to kill that which was already dead.

The vampire behind him said nothing at all, though he could feel its warm breath and smell the scent of decay as it opened its mouth. Luthor closed his eyes, despite the fact that he could see nothing of his captor. He would rather not be fully aware of the moment of his demise.

Instead of fangs piercing his neck, the vampire lurched forward, slamming his weight into Luthor's back. They both stumbled forward, the vampire's grip releasing from his shoulders. The apothecary could feel blood seeping from the fingernail wounds on his arms, and the cold numbness spread through his upper limbs as circulation returned.

He turned slowly, still painfully aware that he lacked the feeling in his arms to cast another rune. To his surprise, the vampire had collapsed to his knees. The sharpened tip of a stake protruded from his chest, toward which he stared in utter disbelief. The vampire released a hiss of anguish as it pitched forward into the grass.

Simon stepped nimbly over the fallen form, driving a second stake into the spine of the electrocuted vampire. It arched its back in horror even as the Inquisitor withdrew the weapon and drove it downward again, this time with far more accuracy as the wooden handle pierced the creature's heart.

Luthor stared at his mentor in awe, amazed that the man was still alive, much less that he had come to their rescue. For a moment, he considered the irony, that they had escaped their vampire captors with the intent of finding and freeing Simon but instead found themselves in his debt.

"I don't—" Luthor began before Simon silenced him with a wave of his hand.

The Inquisitor stepped past Luthor and entered the clearing, pausing beside Mattie. The vampire at her feet was shredded, its flesh flayed from its bones. Despite its inability to properly be killed by normal means, the creature was in obvious debilitating pain.

The vampire noticed the Inquisitor, a look of surprise evident even upon its vampiric features. "We thought you were dead."

"She thought you were dead," Luthor corrected. "I never doubted your seeming immortality for a moment, sir."

Simon shrugged. "There was a brief moment where I was sure I was dead as well. I've never been so glad to disappoint everyone, myself included." He glanced down at the squirming vampire, admiring the wounds even as they slowly regenerated. "Finish this one, if you please, Miss Hawke."

Mattie clasped her large paws on either side of the vampire's head, using her opposable thumbs to hold his head firmly in place. With a sharp upward jerk, the vampire's neck snapped. Its eyes fluttered for a second before its body went limp. Mattie placed her foot on its chest and yanked upward, tearing the head from the body. She tossed it aside, not bothering to even admire her superhuman strength.

Luthor paled at Mattie's brutality, but he shifted his attention to the Inquisitor instead. "Forgive my asking, sir, but how is it that you aren't dead? When last we heard, you were being taken before the elder vampire."

"And so I was," Simon replied, "though clearly, he didn't bite me."

"Why not, if I may be so bold as to ask?"

"I had something he needed."

Luthor furrowed his brow. "Your blood, sir?"

Simon shook his head. "My freedom, the one thing he could offer under the auspice that I would, in turn, offer him his."

"You didn't, though, did you?" Mattie asked. "You didn't actually release the vampire."

"I promised him I would free him from his prison when the time was right and I intend to uphold that promise, though the full story will have to wait for a more optimal time. These three weren't the only vampires out tonight, searching for the two of you. I eluded at least two more who will certainly have heard the scuttlebutt."

Luthor cringed at the thought of running further, but he gestured toward the far side of the clearing. "Lead the way, sir. You seem to have a fair better idea of where we should go from here."

Mattie retrieved her clothing but remained in the form of a werewolf. She held her shredded pants aloft and slowly shook her white mane. Discarding the ruined leather pants, she claimed only her tunic, jerkin, and boots.

Simon set off at once, leading them further into the gloomy woods and further away from Whitten Hall. They paused often, listening intently for the sound of pursuit. With all the activity within the forest, the insects and other animals had all fallen silent. Every crash of underbrush or snap of a twig was a sign of pursuit rather than a random woodland creature.

A few times, they heard vampires pursuing them, though they always seemed far off from their current position. After a moment's hesitation, Simon led them onward.

Eventually, the sound of pursuit was replaced by the gentle lapping of the stream. They came across the narrow river before long, its dark waters reflecting the moonlight as the canopy of leaves parted overhead. Simon glanced downstream to the covered bridge, but instead led the companions the opposite direction. A few hundred feet up river, he paused before a dilapidated tree, which dangled awkwardly over the water. Its roots had pulled partially from the ground, lifting like a basket toward the night sky.

"We'll spend the night here until dawn," Simon explained.

Luthor looked at the leaning tree and arched an eyebrow inquisitively. "We'll stay where, exactly, sir?"

Simon walked to the water's edge and crouched, pointing toward the mound of dirt before him. Luthor followed until he noticed a natural cavern of soil, created by the cage of tree roots. The space beneath the tree would be tight for three people and maneuvering would be difficult, but it would be impossible to spot unless the vampires knew of its location.

"How did you find this?" Mattie asked, even as she realized her large bulk as a werewolf would never fit within its close confines.

"I was following the river as I tried to avoid detection. I stumbled upon it entirely by accident, but I tried my best to remember its location for future use."

A distal curse alerted them that their pursuers were gone, but hardly forgotten.

"Hurry inside, both of you," Simon ordered.

Mattie glanced at the dark chasm and then to her few remaining articles of clothing. She looked pleadingly toward Simon, who frowned his disapproval.

"I have nothing but respect for you, Matilda, but in this instance, your modesty be damned. Change out of that outrageous shape this instant and get inside before you get us all killed."

With a frustrated sigh, the white fur melted from her body, revealing the nubile flesh beneath. Luthor and Simon turned aside as Mattie fumbled with only a tunic and jerkin with which to cover her exposed body.

She eventually slipped the jerkin over her naked chest and tied the tunic as well as possible around her waist, hoping the thin fabric left something to the imagination.

Luthor climbed into the hole with little provocation, followed closely by Mattie. The space was far smaller than Luthor had led himself to believe, and the sense of claustrophobia settled over him immediately. As Mattie joined him, he knew that there would be no escaping their bodies being pressed together. He was glad for the darkness as Mattie draped her bare legs over his as they struggled for space within their hiding spot.

Simon increased the level of discomfort tenfold as he pressed into the root system. The shadow of the tree fell over them all, concealing them from view.

Simon leaned toward them, though the action was unnecessary in such close quarters. "We'll stay here until dawn. Do your best to get some sleep between now and then."

Luthor could barely see the river beyond the exit of their newest prison. On both sides of the river, vampires would be searching for them until the first rays of sunrise crested the trees nearby. Moreover, he would be spending the next few hours pressed tightly into the root system of a dying tree. Despite Simon's warning, the apothecary seriously doubted sleep would come tonight.

Luthor awoke the next morning with incredible pain radiating from his neck to his coccyx. He tried to stretch, but found himself still confined beneath the overhanging roots. Simon stirred near the entrance, but he didn't awaken enough to leave the protective cover. Mattie, who normally awoke far earlier than Luthor, had her head pressed against the soil between the thick roots, her red hair flattened on one side from where she slept.

The apothecary cleared his throat as politely as possible, but to no avail. The others slept soundly, the events from the night before clearly draining them both. Luthor wiggled free an arm from where it had been trapped against his side and gently shook Simon, careful not to inadvertently strike Mattie in the process. His effort gained him nothing, as Simon merely shifted his position to be further out of Luthor's reach.

Aggravated, Luthor pushed Simon firmly in the back, knocking him from the basket-like root system. He splayed across the ground, his arms not moving quickly enough to keep his face from smearing into the mud on the river's bank.

Mattie awoke with a start, temporarily disoriented as she looked around. As her gaze fell to Luthor, he gestured toward the cramped quarter's exit, to where Simon was only just prying himself free of the tacky mud.

They all exited and stood by the river, each stretching in their own way to release the tension of combat and awkward sleeping positions.

"The sun has risen," Luthor stated matter-of-factly. "We survived the vampire scourge for another day."

Simon nodded as he stifled a yawn. "Indeed we did, though I have no doubt they'll double their efforts tomorrow night. I wouldn't be at all surprised if their human cohorts were combing these woods even now, searching for us."

Mattie knelt by the river and dipped her hands in the cool water. She splashed it on her face and attempted to run her wet hands through the mats of her hair, but her curly, red hair refused to release to something as paltry as river water.

"If they're hunting us, we should be ready for them when they arrive," Mattie said.

Simon shook his head. "Fighting the humans will accomplish nothing of value and will only tire us further. What we need to do is something they would never expect."

"Such as?" Luthor asked.

"We return to Whitten Hall."

Luthor nodded, but his expression showed a significant lack of acceptance. "Have you taken a leave of your senses? Did Tom Wriggleton's beating leave your brain slightly rattled? Returning to Whitten Hall is like walking into the snake's den, then somehow being surprised when you get bit."

Simon arched an eyebrow. "Was that a euphemism of some sort?"

"It was intended more as an allegory, at best. I thought the snakes having two fangs would be reminiscent of the vampires also having a pair of fangs. Was that not clear?"

"My apologies," Simon replied. "I'm absolute rubbish at metaphors and the like."

"Which brings us full circle back to the issue at hand," Mattie said as she stood again. Her attire was still rather subpar, without proper pants of which to speak. "Metaphors aside, returning to Whitten Hall is a dangerous proposition."

"It would be, Miss Hawke, if it were full of humans colluding with vampires."

Mattie turned to Luthor. "Is it not? Did I miss a part of the conversation?"

Luthor smiled. "It normally would be, except Simon already told us it won't. The humans will be out in the woods searching for us."

"Of course, they'll be looking for us exactly where we should be but aren't, and we'll instead be exactly where they should be but aren't, simply because they're busy looking for us. It makes for a very complicated discussion but a brilliantly simple solution. We'll return to Whitten Hall, retrieve our belongings, and make our way out of the outpost before anyone is the wiser."

They stood, nodding to one another, each slowly realizing that no one in their group would ever be mistaken for morning people.

"Shall we be off then?" Luthor finally asked, breaking the silence.

They nodded once more before turning in the direction of Whitten Hall.

CHAPTER Twenty-nine

THEY FORDED THE RIVER A LITTLE UPSTREAM FROM the covered bridge, but far enough away that passersby couldn't see them. The water was bitterly cold but refreshing; none of the trio complained as it washed away the grime that had accumulated from their previous day's misadventures. Simon paused midstream and lowered his face to the water, washing away the mud that was caked across the side of his face. He seemed oblivious to the water that soaked the front of his suit in the process.

They climbed the far bank and entered the woods once more. Simon led the way through the underbrush, though not a word was said between them as they walked. Luthor fell back in step beside Mattie, though he knew the redhead hardly needed his protection. From the corner of his eye, however, he could see her shivering. Her body was soaked from the river crossing, and her loss of clothing the previous night left her ill prepared for the harshness of the cold stream. His gaze fell over her body, and he noted ashamedly that the thin, white blouse now clung tightly to the curves of her lower body. The apothecary cleared his throat and removed his jacket, offering it to her. She smiled appreciatively and tied it around her waist, warming her damp legs and adding a modicum of modesty.

By Simon's guess, they were quickly coming parallel to the chancellor's manor house. Despite the fact that the chancellor and his ilk were firmly entrenched in the mines, protecting themselves from the blazing sun, there was a good chance that the human conspirators would be near the estate. The trio continued forward, moving as quietly as possible between the trees.

As Simon ducked beneath a low-hanging tangle of branches, leaves crunched nearby. Raising his hand abruptly, he brought the other two to a halt. They quickly crouched and hid amongst the brush as well as possible. Bushes blocked their view, though they could hear the labored breathing of a man pushing his way through the woods.

The sounds echoed in the woods, the exact direction of their hunter's approach seemed distorted. Simon closed his eyes as he strained to pinpoint a direction. The footfalls grew progressively louder, as did the man's labored breathing. A soft curse rolled through the woods as the man's clothing became entangled on a thorny vine.

Simon opened his eyes and shifted his gaze slightly to the right. The bushes shook softly as someone brushed against them. The Inquisitor could hear the tearing of fabric as the man, in his haste, tore free from the thorns, leaving shreds of his fabric behind.

Looking down, Simon's eyes alighted on a fallen branch. Part of it had begun to rot and insects crawled just beneath the bark. The rest of the branch, however, seemed solid. As he hefted it in his hand, he could feel its weight.

A broad-shouldered man broke through the underbrush, swearing again as he tried to untangle himself from the small, clinging branches. He spun slowly in a circle as his thick hands fidgeted with far-too-narrow twigs that pulled at his shirt and the waistband of his pants. His dark ponytail bounced with his frustration, and his deep voice rolled from his chest as he grunted excitedly until he finally pulled his clothes free.

The bartender sighed contently as he turned back in the direction he had been traveling. Gregory's eyes opened wide in surprise as he saw Simon standing before him, disheveled as he was but hoisting an impressively large log in his hands.

"Can we—?" Gregory began.

"No," Simon interrupted. "We cannot."

Simon silenced him in midsentence with a powerful swing of the log. It connected with the side of Gregory's head, splitting his cheek and jarring teeth loose in his mouth. The large man staggered to the side as he tried to maintain his balance. Simon responded by swinging again. Despite the bartender's hand already held protectively to the side of his head, the log still managed to connect solidly above Gregory's ear. The bartender's knees buckled, and he dropped to the ground. He caught himself on his hands and knees, not fully falling to the dense grass and moss of the forest floor. The Inquisitor raised the club, preparing to strike again, when Gregory's arms shook one final time before the large man dropped unconscious into the plush flora.

Simon smiled as he tossed the log aside. He crouched beside Gregory and checked the man's pulse, nodding as he felt the fluttering heartbeat.

Luthor crouched beside him and examined the damage, gingerly touching the flayed skin just beneath the bartender's left eye. "That was quite a strike, sir. He'll carry that scar with him for the rest of his life."

"As well he should," Simon retorted as he withdrew his hand from the man's neck. He brushed his hands on his damp pants and stood.

The apothecary glanced at the unconscious man once more before standing as well. "I see that you are holding a grudge for your earlier treatment?"

Simon glanced toward the distance, ensuring no one else stumbled upon their ambush. "You'd be amazed how many times during our investigations I've found myself punched in the face. I'm growing quite tired of it, to be honest."

"Technically," Mattie said as she walked past the two men, "it wasn't the bartender who hit you in the face. He only clubbed you across the head. It was more Tom who kicked you in the face a few times after you were unconscious. It seems that he isn't fond of being punched in the face either."

Simon followed Mattie as she led them toward Whitten Hall. "Believe you me, I have something special planned for Mister Wriggleton."

Luthor sneered at the unconscious bartender. "The whole town deserves similar treatment for colluding with vampires. Gregory got off easy with just a scar, if you ask my opinion."

Simon shook his head. "While I may not agree with their decision, harboring such ill will against the entire town is hardly healthy behavior. I'm not concerned about revenge; it's not what I want."

"Sometimes, it's not about what you want, sir, but what's right; right for yourself, right for your friends, and right for the crown. Whether you harbor ill will against them or not, they may not leave you any other options."

Simon stroked his chin thoughtfully but offered no response.

Luthor stepped over the bartender, glancing back briefly toward Gregory. "Should we at least hide the body?"

"Leave it," Simon replied. "Leave them confused about which direction we are traveling. The bartender's body could either mean we were hiding near the outpost and are now heading toward the mines or vice versa. That discovery will keep them confused and separated."

They set off again, moving with a greater sense of urgency. It was still early morning, the sun barely breaking through the canopy of leaves to the east, but there was much they needed to accomplish before the sun set. The quicker they retrieved their belongings from Whitten Hall, the quicker they could be on their way back toward Callifax.

"Please do be kind and move your foot out of my face," Simon growled from his position below the window.

Luthor shifted his position slightly, though it only further forced the toe of his shoe into Simon's cheek. The apothecary clung to the windowsill as he tried to lift himself into the second story window.

"When we return to Callifax," Simon continued as he pushed on Luthor's heel, lifting the apothecary higher, "I'm placing you on a strict weight training regimen until you improve your upper body strength."

Luthor pulled heartily until he slipped through the upstairs window and fell onto the hardwood floor of the bedroom. On the ground below, Simon and Mattie glanced around cautiously, hoping no one heard the clutter from upstairs. When the tavern remained silent, Simon turned toward the redhead.

"You're next, Matilda."

Mattie shook her head. "If you lift me, how will you climb to the window?"

Simon careened his neck backward until he had a view of the window high above. He arched an eyebrow as he glanced back at his female companion. "I'm sure I'll find a way."

"Or, hear me out, I can lift you and then climb of my own accord," she offered. "You forget that I have other skills at my disposal."

"I have never forgotten, nor do I believe it possible to forget your myriad of capabilities, Miss Hawke. Very well, lift me, if you please."

Mattie cupped her hands, and Simon pressed his heel into her grip. She lifted with little strain, forcing Simon quickly toward the window's ledge above. Reaching out, he grasped the wooden sill and pulled until his upper body was cresting the edge. Luthor appeared on the far side, cupping him under the armpits and pulling him handily into the room.

A scraping against the building's wooden exterior alerted them to Mattie's climb moments before she appeared in the window. Both Simon and Luthor turned to assist, but she needed none, pulling herself easily over the ledge and rolling gracefully to her feet as she entered the room.

Luthor glanced around the room and frowned. They had entered his previous room first, only to find that his belongings had been thoroughly rifled through. Articles of clothing were strewn across the bed. The few reagents that he had left behind during their mine expedition had been poured onto the table or smashed. Even his suitcase had been gouged by a knife, as though someone had searched for a secret compartment within the innocuous luggage.

"Simply fantastic," Luthor said dourly.

"Ignore it," Simon remarked. "Gather whatever you will need to travel quickly and leave everything else behind. We can always purchase new clothing once we return to Callifax."

Simon gestured toward the closed door. "Matilda, I believe we have rooms to examine as well, though I encourage you to be quick. I doubt we're alone in the inn. There is most assuredly at least one other person downstairs that I would hate to disturb unless absolutely necessary."

They opened the door quietly, cringing at the soft creak that sounded as the dry metal hinges grinded against one another. They moved quickly to their respective rooms.

Simon opened the door to a similar scene as was found in Luthor's bedroom. Clothes were strewn haphazardly about. His toiletry kit had been torn nearly in two, his straight razor and scissors for trimming his moustache both taken. Simon frowned as he picked up his discarded toothbrush from the floor, but upon glancing around the dingy room, he decided instead to drop it into the wastebasket.

The Inquisitor walked to the partially opened closet, though he retained little hope that it would have remained unscathed during the frantic search. He pushed the door fully open to find his suits in disarray, badly wrinkled after being tossed aimlessly upon the floor. The color rose quickly to his cheeks as he glanced toward the top shelf. He had left his top hat behind during their investigation of the mine. To his dismay and growing rage, it was missing.

He knew his revolver had been taken upon his capture, though that was to be expected. Stealing his hat, however, was an unforgivable and frankly bewildering turn of events.

His heart sank as he realized that everything in his room had been inspected. Before they had gone downstairs to catch the train, he had packed all his belongings, to include his beloved Inquisitor kit. Simon walked quickly around the bed, hoping beyond hope that it would still be present, though he already knew in the back of his mind it was gone.

"Damn them all," he growled, slamming his fist onto the mantle above the fireplace.

His eyes fell upon a square of unburned wood resting in the fireplace. Though its edges had been charred, it still appeared solid and relatively heavy. Simon knelt and retrieved the piece of wood, savoring its weight in his hand. With a smile that bordered an unhappy sneer, he walked out of his room.

Mattie was emerging from her room as he passed. Amongst her belongings, she had found another change of clothes and looked much like her old self once more. She glanced at the man inquisitively, her expression turning to concern as Simon walked past Luthor's room as well and approached the top of the stairs.

"Simon?" she asked in a hoarse whisper. "I thought you said we only wanted to confront the man downstairs if it was an emergency."

Simon didn't look back as he replied. "It just became an emergency."

He walked down the steps, not bothering to conceal his footfalls on the wooden stairs. He turned the corner as the tavern below came into view. A man sat at a table near the foot of the stairs, enjoying a drink. Another gentleman had taken Gregory's place behind the bar, though he seemed far more interested in helping himself to a pint of beer than tending to the needs of the tavern.

The man at the foot of the stairs turned at the footsteps, his eyes widening with surprise at the sight of the Royal Inquisitor. He spun in his chair and tried to stand as Simon reached the last step. As the man climbed to his feet, Simon slammed the chunk of wood into the man's forehead. He collapsed back into his chair, his arm catching on the table and nearly tumbling it as well in the process.

The replacement bartender reached quickly behind the bar as Simon dropped the wood to the floor. The Inquisitor's long strides carried him to the bar as the bartender reemerged, a dagger held firmly in his grasp. The man lunged across the platform, the point of the dagger aiming true for Simon's chest.

The Inquisitor grasped the man's wrist with one hand while grabbing a handful of his hair with the other. With the man stretched across the bar, he was overbalanced and in a poor position to stop Simon from slamming his face into the wooden counter. With a twist of the man's wrist, Simon took the knife from his grasp. Spinning the blade with practiced grace, the Inquisitor slammed the blade down into the wooden bar top, less than an inch from the bartender's nose.

The bartender whimpered and his eyes crossed as he tried to focus on the dagger's sharp edge dangling so close to his flesh.

"You have taken from me my pistol, which was a priceless gift and something I adore; my top hat, which is closer to me than my immediate family; and my Inquisitor kit, a square, wooden box which contains of number of items I'll need in the foreseeable future. Where are they?"

"I'm... I don't really—" the bartender began, his words faltering with every attempt.

Simon yanked backward on the man's hair, lifting his face a couple inches from the table before slamming it back down onto the bar. The man spat blood across the wooden counter as he groaned in pain.

"I lost patience with this town nearly twenty-four hours ago," Simon continued. "Do not be the man on whom I express my displeasure. My belongings, if you please."

The bartender's shaking hand pointed toward a door behind him.

"I am much obliged," Simon said with a soft smile.

The bartender tried to return a nervous smile from his awkward position, but Simon slammed his head back down into the bar. The bartender slumped limply as the Inquisitor released his hair, and he slid out of view as he collapsed.

Simon pulled free the knife and walked around the bar.

"So much for discretion, I assume, sir?" Luthor asked as he and Mattie descended the stairs.

The man near the foot of the stairs stirred and groaned, grasping toward the large welt on his forehead. A swift kick from Mattie laid him out once more.

"There is a time and place for discretion, Luthor."

233

"A time and a place that you will change at your whim, I notice."

Simon glanced over his shoulder toward his traveling companion, his face devoid of amusement. He turned the handle to the tavern's rear office and entered the dimly lit room.

The room was cramped, with an office desk and coat rack pressed against one wall and a bookshelf against the other, with little room between. Stacks of papers covered the desk, seemingly without rhyme or reason to their placement. Simon's gaze shifted instead to the bookshelf and the coat rack, and his eyes lit with excitement.

His top hat hung from the coat rack, dusty but seemingly unscathed. His Inquisitor's kit and pistol had been placed upon one of the empty shelves like trophies. Simon retrieved them all and, as he slid the revolver into its holster and the top hat on his head, felt again like himself.

"Sir?" Luthor asked from the doorway. "We should be going soon. Surely people will be returning to the town before long. Plus, it's growing close to noon already and we have miles to go before nightfall."

Simon opened the Inquisitor's kit and began retrieving items that he thought would help against the vampire horde. "Were you able to salvage anything from your room?"

The apothecary shrugged as he retrieved a handful of glass vials from his coat pocket. "There was little unbroken, but these will have to do until we can return to Callifax and resupply."

Wooden stakes, vials of holy water, and the remaining silver bullets filled his pockets as he finished with the Inquisitor's kit. He closed it, handing the wooden box to Luthor. Simon's gaze fell once more to the papers on the desk, many of which were blank. A quill and inkwell were pressed against the back of the narrow desk.

Simon sat in the office's chair and pulled a fresh piece of paper in front of him. He flipped the inkwell open as he picked up the quill.

"We don't have time for memoirs, sir," Luthor insisted.

Simon shook his head as he began scribbling quickly on the paper, his words barely legible even to his own trained eyes. "This is important. You'll have to bear with me a moment longer."

His note took no time to complete. When he was finished, Simon read his words and frowned deeply, an ache reverberating in his chest. He pushed back the chair and stood. Folding the letter in half, he handed it to Luthor.

"Take this with you when you go," Simon ordered. "When you get back to Callifax, make sure this gets in the right hands."

"When *we* get back to Callifax, you mean, sir."

Simon shook his head. "If I don't stay, the vampires will catch you within the first night. Someone needs to delay their pursuit, and no one is better suited for that than me. Moreover, if we did by some miracle escape, the vampires would merely scatter long before a sufficient force could be mustered to return to Whitten Hall."

Luthor unfolded the note as Mattie stepped beside him.

"This was your plan all along, wasn't it?" Mattie asked. "You never intended to come back."

Simon scoffed at the idea. "Don't be preposterous, Matilda. Of course I intend to come back. I wouldn't dream of doing something this foolish if I thought I might die."

Luthor looked up from the letter and blanched. "Sir, you can't be serious."

"About not dying? I most certainly am."

"About the letter, you damned fool!"

Simon's expression lost its humor, and he nodded seriously. "I'm most serious about that as well, Luthor. You said it yourself. Sometimes, it's not about doing what we want; sometimes, we just have to do what's right."

The Inquisitor exited the back office, leading the other two toward the tavern's front door. He glanced out the window and nodded, as he saw no one else on the outpost's solitary road. He turned back toward his two companions.

"The train just departed yesterday and usually takes four days to return to Callifax. That makes seven days remaining total before it makes a return to Whitten Hall. Therefore, I will keep the vampires occupied for exactly seven days. If you're late, I can't uphold my promise of not dying. Am I understood?"

"Sir—" Luthor began before Simon silenced him.

"We hardly have time for sentimental goodbyes, my good man. Keep focused on the task at hand."

The Inquisitor glanced to Mattie, sensing that she would be the more sensible of the two at the moment. "Sunset is in approximately…" He pulled his pocket watch from his vest and glanced at the time, which read just past noon. "Six hours from now. That won't be much of a head start. Stay away from the train tracks, since I'm certain the humans will be watching that avenue. Your best bet is to move through the crags and ravines we saw from the train as we approached."

Luthor shook his head as he slowly absorbed everything his mentor was saying. "Those rocky canyons are a maze of trails. We'd be lost in no time at all."

"I can find our way through," Mattie replied. "If people have passed that way, they've left a scent that I can follow."

"Good," Simon said, nodding to his friends. "The train will reach Callifax in three days' time and then immediately prepare for a return trip. Luckily, the train moves slowly. If you can find another means of conveyance, you can beat the train to Callifax and have everything ready before its return departure."

Luthor stepped forward and embraced the Inquisitor. "I know you're not one for sentimental farewells, sir, but do be safe."

Simon returned the man's embrace before inviting Mattie to join them. "I would prefer to be alive upon your return. Do try not to be late."

They released one another, and Luthor cleared his throat hoarsely.

"We should be going," Mattie said sorrowfully, glancing at the Inquisitor.

"Take care of him," Simon told her. He turned his attention to the apothecary. "Take care of yourself. Now go, both of you, before we waste any more daylight."

They stopped at the door and glanced once more down the road. Seeing no one still, they pulled open the door. Mattie stepped through cautiously as Luthor held the door. Simon handed the apothecary the knife he had taken from the bartender. The two men nodded to one another.

"I'll come back, sir, I promise."

Simon smiled as he gestured toward the street. "If you don't and they turn me into a vampire, I promise you'll be the first one I feed upon."

Luthor smiled wistfully as he stepped through the door and into the glaring sunlight.

Simon stood by the door for a moment longer, watching his two companions hurry toward the far side of the town before stepping through the doorway himself and disappearing into the woods.

CHAPTER Thirty

LUTHOR CLAMPED HIS HAND TIGHTLY OVER MATTIE'S mouth as they pressed themselves into the shadow of the boulder. The scuffle of footsteps could be heard all around them as the search party grew ever closer.

"Where the bloody hell are they?" one of the hunters asked.

Someone else scoffed derisively nearby. "We spotted them from the last ridge. They couldn't have gotten far. Spread out and find them."

Dust fell onto them from above as one of the men stepped atop the boulder underneath which they hid. The toe of his boot pushed dirt onto them, and Luthor had to fight to stifle a sneeze. He furiously blinked away the dirt from his eyelashes. Sure that if he moved his arms, they'd both be spotted.

For a painful few minutes, the man merely stood atop his perch, scanning the labyrinth of crags and canyons that marred the wooded countryside. A rockslide from times long past had left boulders strewn across the valley, forming a maze of interconnected passages that, to the unskilled and untrained, were nothing more than a veritable death sentence for those that got lost.

As the man began to step away, Luthor inhaled deeply and dust flew into his nose. It tickled his throat and despite his best efforts, he struggled to suppress the cough in his throat. Placing his free hand over his own mouth, he muffled the inevitable cough as much as possible.

The man turned at the sound and raised a hand to his brow, blocking out the light of the setting sun. He scanned amidst the boulders once more, looking for their long shadows cast upon the ground. Seeing none, he turned away begrudgingly and stepped back onto the path.

Luthor sighed quietly, thankful that his misstep hadn't revealed them to their pursuers. Mattie had been masterfully traversing the maze of stone, but she was working in unfamiliar territory. Their pursuers clearly knew the lay of the land far better and had little trouble catching up to the pair.

"I don't see them," their lookout called, his voice echoing over the boulders.

"They're here somewhere," the group's de facto leader replied. "The chancellor will have our hide if we don't find them."

"We'll find them."

Someone else called from across the stones. "The sun's setting. We won't be much good out here once it does."

Luthor glanced at the last rays of sunlight filtering through the trees on the far edge of the valley. The sun was setting quickly, and it wouldn't be long before the last of the sunlight was stolen from them. Though Mattie had exceptional nighttime vision, Luthor wasn't so blessed. The night would be dark and would most certainly favor the vampires.

The leader huffed loudly enough that Luthor heard it from their place of concealment. "Fine. Leave them; let the vampires hunt them tonight. It doesn't matter; they won't escape the chancellor's men alive."

The search party gathered together on the tall stones behind Luthor and Mattie and scanned the valley once more, hoping for some sign of life. When they saw none, they turned as a group and marched back toward Whitten Hall.

Luthor and Mattie remained silent until long after the sound of footfalls had fallen silent. Eventually, Mattie reached up and pulled Luthor's hand away from her mouth.

"They're right, you know," the redhead said, pointing toward the setting sun. "We haven't put nearly enough ground between us and the outpost. The vampires are going to catch us once the sun sets."

"Then we had best hurry before we lose the light completely," Luthor replied.

As he took her by the hand, they burst from the dark shadows of the boulders and hurried back into the labyrinth. Luthor slowed, letting Mattie take the lead. She ran quickly but paused often to sniff the air or stare intently at the ground before her.

Luthor followed close behind, but his gaze often fell instead to the rapidly setting sun. Simon had told them to put as much distance as possible between themselves and Whitten Hall before dusk, but none of the three had anticipated how long it would take to pass through the crevices, nor how quickly the human colluders would pursue. No sooner had Luthor and Mattie entered the valley than the group from Whitten Hall had been in pursuit.

The apothecary thought briefly of Simon and hoped his mentor was safe. Despite the Inquisitor's constant bluster, Simon was putting himself in great harm's way by remaining behind. The vampires would have to give chase if they wanted to catch Luthor and Mattie, but they'd have to spend no time at all pursuing Simon, assuming he didn't manage to find another exceptional hiding spot amongst the woods and underbrush.

The thought of Simon remaining alone and knowing they only had seven days in which to return drove Luthor on. With Mattie in the lead, they quickly emerged from the valley. They scrambled up the incline on the far side, their hands searching for purchase amongst the roots and thin grasses.

With a heaving chest and burning lungs, Luthor finally crested the hill. They paused, and he placed his hands on his knees as he struggled to catch his breath. Mattie stood beside him, her chest heaving as well but seemingly in much better control of her faculties. For a moment, Luthor envied her wolf-like stamina.

Luthor's gaze fell across the valley, and the burning in his legs was quickly forgotten. The sun had set during their ascent and now dark shadows settled over the valley below. The shade between the boulders that had served so well as concealment during their daytime pursuit now became black voids, pits in which inhuman monsters could pass unseen. The apothecary strained to hear the sound of a chase but heard nothing. He glanced toward Mattie, who was likewise listening, but she merely shook her head.

"I never thought I would say this, but I truly wish we were being chased again by a pack of werewolves," Luthor remarked. "At least then they would be howling as they caught our scent. This deathly silence is unnerving."

Mattie narrowed her gaze as she stared across the chasm of the valley. Her mouth fell into a frown as her eyes widened in surprise.

"That won't be necessary," she said, pointing toward gaps in the maze below. "They're coming."

Luthor followed her directions and saw human shapes flittering amidst the stones. They were moving quickly enough that his mind swore they were merely hallucinations, blurs in the shapes of men that were there one moment and gone the next. His rational mind refused to fully see the vampires that chased them through the boulders.

They weren't attempting to conceal their movements, instead running freely between the stones. Luthor struggled to identify specific figures. He counted at least a half dozen giving chase, though the number was most certainly higher.

"We need to run, now," he said, grabbing her hand once more and rushing into the woods.

"Where could we possibly go that they won't catch us?" Mattie asked, her breathing labored as much from fear as from exertion.

Luthor didn't reply, knowing he couldn't offer a decent answer. He didn't intend to run forever, just long enough to find a more neutral battleground.

"This is insanity," Mattie cried, pulling her hand free of his. Luthor turned toward her as she began to strip away her clothing. "If I'm going to fight, I'm going to do it on my terms."

She was pulling her shirt over her head as the first dark-robed figure crashed into her from behind. They both tumbled to the ground even as they separated. Mattie tossed her shirt aside as she began to stand.

The vampire was already on his feet. A dark cloak was tied at the neck and billowed out behind him. A hood had once covered his face but had since fallen aside, revealing his drawn and stretched skin. The vampire moved toward Mattie, even as she struggled to slip free of her pants and boots.

Luthor rushed forward and kicked the vampire in the back, sending it sprawling into the dirt. It quickly regained its feet and spun on the apothecary, who had few options but to hold up the dagger in his hands. The vampire looked at the meager weapon mockingly before hissing, spittle flying from its fangs. Before it could move, Mattie clamped her maw over its shoulder and bit down.

The vampire howled in pain and rage as Mattie shook it from side to side. Luthor could hear the wrenching of skin and bone as Mattie tore the vampire's arm from its body. The creature fell to the ground and writhed in pain as Mattie tossed the arm aside.

They had no time to celebrate as a second vampire pounced on Mattie's exposed back. It tried to sink its teeth into her neck but instead received a mouthful of white fur for its troubles. Mattie rolled to the side, but the vampire clutched to her fur, refusing to let go.

More dark-robed figures emerged from the woods, their attention alternating between the werewolf and the poorly armed apothecary. Luthor reached into his inside jacket pocket and pulled free one of the few remaining glass vials. It was filled with water, its original contents having been spilled during the tossing of their rooms.

"Keep them occupied for a moment longer," Luthor called out to Mattie, even as she struggled to dislodge the tenacious vampire locked tightly to her back.

She rolled over, crushing the vampire beneath her weight. For added measure, she rubbed her back against the dirt in a decidedly canine fashion. As she rolled aside, the vampire released its grip and lay unmoving on the ground.

A vampire charged her while another rushed in a blur toward Luthor. Mattie threw herself in the vampire's way as it charged toward the apothecary. It crashed into her bulk, unable to maneuver aside before the collision. Her own pursuer, however, caught her in the ribs with a firm kick. Mattie yelped in pain and rolled aside. She climbed back to her feet, albeit far slower than Luthor would have liked.

He scrambled to draw a rune on the cork of the vial. His fingers shook far too much for the necessary accuracy as his attention was split between the rune, Mattie's safety, and the remaining vampires who seemed intent on their immediate destruction.

Mattie rushed her vampire once more, but the monster stepped handily out of the way and sent her sprawling with nothing more than a firm shove. As Luthor looked up, a dark shape appeared before him. When the hood fell away, Luthor could see the sneer of his vampire adversary.

The vampire struck Luthor in the chest, and he spun end over end through the air before striking a tree. The vial in his hand shattered in his grip, piercing his palm. His shoulder was alive with pain and his hip ached. He tried standing, but the hip wouldn't support his weight and he fell back to the mossy ground.

Behind his attacker, Luthor could see another pair of vampires descending on Mattie. While the bite to her neck had been unsuccessful, he knew it wouldn't take them long to find somewhere less protected, like her belly or a leg.

His hand shaking, he reached up and pulled the long shard of glass from his palm. Blood oozed from the wound. Even in the darkness, he could see the vampires pause as the scent of his blood filled the air. Their eyes burned red with lust and hunger and even those that were focused moments before on Mattie were now staring intently at the apothecary.

Luthor looked at his palm as blood dripped onto the ground. He raised his palm in the air, turning it so that it was clearly visible to all the monsters filling the woods around them. His other hand slipped into his jacket pocket and closed around a second vial.

The vampires stalked slowly toward him, their frenzy barely restrained as they stared at the blood now running down his arm.

"Is this what you want?" Luthor cried out, stretching his hand over his head. "Is this what you've come for? I may not be much of a meal, hardly more than an appetizer, truthfully, but I can satisfy at least one of your hungers. Come and get me."

His hand moved furiously in his jacket as he sketched a rune atop of the vial. The vampires moved closer, jostling one another for position as they sought to be the first to reach the bleeding human. They licked their lips as their glowing red eyes bounced in the darkness.

"There you are," Luthor said. His gaze fell to Mattie, who was forcing herself up on all fours. His eyes pleaded for her to stay back as he hurried to finish the rune. "Come closer. You won't be able to get any blood standing all the way back there. You'd hate to be the last person to the dinner table, wouldn't you?"

They were nearly on top of him, their dark robes only deepening the shadows around him until it felt like an endless abyss was swallowing him. He could barely see their features any longer; the darkness was virtually impenetrable.

As the first vampire leaned toward him, Luthor smiled and closed his eyes. He pulled his hand from his pocket and shook the vial once, letting the water within slosh against the sealing cork.

The water exploded with brilliant light, a glow so bright that it mimicked the sun itself. The vampire closest to him hissed in anguish as cracks appeared across his exposed flesh. He raised his hands defensively, even as the fissures on his face and hands burned red with an inner fire. His already pale skin grew ashy as it slowly darkened toward black.

The vampire stepped backward as chunks of flesh fell away, crumbling to ash even as it struck the ground. With a final howl of horror, the vampire tilted its head backward and crumbled to dust.

The vampires to either side of him burned in place as well, smoldering before disintegrating under the glow of the false sun.

On the periphery, vampires threw their cloaks over their faces as tendrils of smoke rose from their clothing. They crashed into the woods, no longer moving stealthily, instead hurrying as quickly as possible away from the horrifying brilliance contained within the vial in Luthor's hand

Luthor cupped his hand over the glow and slowly opened his eyes. The woods around them were deserted. Piles of clothing were strewn about at his feet, smoke still rising in wisps as the ash settled into the spongy grass.

Mattie padded toward him, her look of astonishment evident even in her werewolf form.

"What did you do?" she asked, her voice revealing the evident pain wracking her body.

"In the words of Simon, I merely tested a theory," Luthor replied. "I'm pleased to report that the mythology about vampires is true."

Mattie smiled, a most unnatural look on a wolf's mouth. "You did very well, Luthor. Now hurry. I'm assuming your light won't last indefinitely, and we need to be clear before the vampires decide to return."

Luthor laughed, though each shake of his shoulders caused excruciating pain through his hip. "Funny you should say that, my love. I'm not sure I'm capable of either hurrying or getting away in my current state. Perhaps you should just leave me where I am and go for help yourself."

The fur fell away from Mattie as she transformed back into the redhead. Luthor admired the view even as she collected her clothes and dressed once more. "Don't be absurd, Luthor. I won't be leaving you behind."

Luthor smiled. "Even if you think me a coward?"

Mattie buttoned her tunic as she knelt before him. She cupped his cheeks with her hands and pulled his face to her, kissing him softly on the lips. He winced at the sudden movement but didn't dare refuse her.

"You're not a coward, Mister Strong. What you are is an invalid and even if I have to carry you myself, we're escaping this accursed forest."

She scooped Luthor in her arms and lifted him from the ground. Despite her own injuries, she didn't seem overly burdened by the extra weight.

"Do me a favor," Luthor said as she rushed into the woods, further and further away from Whitten Hall and the vampires. "Promise me that you'll let me walk of my own accord once we reach civilization. Forgive my perceived misogyny, but I don't think I could survive the embarrassment of being carried to safety in the arms of a woman."

CHAPTER Thirty-one

SIMON PUSHED THE LARGE ROCK ASIDE, LETTING IT crush the soggy leaves as it fell. He moved slowly as he emerged from the cave in which he had hidden the night before. Craning his neck upward, he closed his eyes and enjoyed the warmth of the sun on his face. Despite the previous night's pursuit, the vampires had been unable to locate him within the small cavern and he had slept fitfully until daybreak.

He shook his jacket, dislodging the moss and grass that clung to its sleeves and coattails. Likewise, he dusted his knees, though both actions were likely futile gestures. He was alone in the wilderness, hunted during the day by humans and at night by vampires. Moreover, he couldn't expect reinforcements for six more days, which lent itself to a lot more crawling through mud and grass, a lot more sleeping in uncomfortable but safe holes in the ground, and a lot more running with little option for bathing. Dusting his clothing made Simon feel better in the interim, but would hardly matter as the days progressed.

Simon slipped his jacket over his shoulders, pausing to check the silver revolver in its shoulder holster before fully pulling his coat into place. Begrudgingly, he set his top hat back within the narrow crack between the rocks, along with a small collection of wooden stakes. Kneeling, he pushed the large stone back into place in the front of the cave, concealing its entrance from view once again.

Glancing around the nearby forest, Simon paused as he listened for the sound of movement. When he heard none, he turned toward a steep hill nearby. The hill was covered with exposed stones, rising steeply toward a shallow plateau above. A few sparse trees clung to the side of the rock face, their roots finding purchase in the unlikeliest of nooks and crannies between the boulders.

Simon grasped the closest tree trunk and hauled himself partway up the knell. His hands and feet sought grooves in the weathered stones. Slowly, the Inquisitor lifted himself higher until his hand fell upon the smooth surface of the summit.

He slid, belly first, onto the flattened hilltop. Pushing himself upward, he stood upon the hill and scanned the surrounding forest. Simon knew that he was silhouetted against the sky as he stood, no longer concealed by the dense forest and its underbrush.

Ignoring the danger, he glanced toward the west, where the railroad tracks wound lazily through the countryside. The train was no longer visible. Not even a smear of smoke emerged from the horizon. Reaching down, Simon retrieved a rock from the ground and dragged it once across the hilltop, leaving behind a long line.

"One down, six to go," Simon muttered to himself.

He turned away from the train tracks and looked down on Whitten Hall, its single row of buildings stretching just a short way along the tracks. Its own dirt road disappeared quickly into the canopy of trees.

He sat upon the hilltop and looked down on the town. A few people moved between the buildings, eager to get indoors and avoid the warmth of the rising sun. They were oblivious to their observer high on the hilltop nearby.

Simon watched them for a few minutes as conflicting thoughts raced through his mind. He pitied them, of that he was sure. Humanity always sought the path of least resistance to power. It was an inalienable truth that defined mankind. The citizens of Whitten Hall had been no different. They had stumbled upon the shortest route from their mundane laborious existence to absolute power and had leapt at the opportunity. They didn't see the monsters when they looked in the mirror, if they could see themselves at all in a mirror. It was one myth Simon had yet to explore.

He wanted to hate them, but it wasn't anger that he felt. He felt sorrow. They moved between the buildings, oblivious to their unavoidable demise. They assumed themselves untouchable under the protection of their vampiric overlords. They never could believe that the crown would use everything at its disposal to destroy them, once the truth was revealed. The vampires would surely be destroyed, and woe unto those who stood between the crown and the abominations hiding even now in the iron mine.

"What a world this has become," Simon muttered quietly to himself, "when I have become the sympathetic soul while Luthor is the logical mind, calling for their destruction."

Thinking of Luthor made Simon's mind wander, hoping that he and Mattie had, indeed, escaped pursuit. He hadn't heard one way or another and the behaviors of those in town gave little information. He had to presume that they'd survived thus far, which meant Simon had to give both the humans and vampires a reason to search the very woods around their outpost, rather than chase the apothecary and werewolf all the way to Callifax. The vampires might be limited on how far they could pursue, but men like Tom Wriggleton would never rest so long as they were alive.

"Very well, Simon. How do you convince a town full of men that there are three of you running around these woods, rather than just the one of you?"

He stared at the outpost, his eyes drifting over the buildings. Near the end of the line, the inn sat unassumingly, its slanted rooftop bathed in sunlight. The Inquisitor smiled to himself as the first inklings of a plan formed in his mind.

He slipped over the edge of the hilltop, using the trees for support as he lowered himself back down to the ground. Casting a cursory glance toward the stone covering the entrance to his cavern, he ensured it was still properly concealed. Satisfied, he walked briskly into the tree line and toward the edge of the town.

The rear of the buildings formed nearly an impenetrable wall of poorly carved exposed wood beams. A few narrow alleyways cut between the buildings, leading to the town's main thoroughfare and the train tracks that ran parallel to the road. Simon ignored the alleys, other than to glance down them cautiously, ensuring no prying eyes caught his movement.

A few doors broke the otherwise interconnected wooden wall of buildings. No windows had been placed at the back of the businesses, though Simon understood why. The view from the back of the town would have been mundane, since the woods crept to the businesses' back doorstep.

He moved brazenly toward the furthest building, skirting through the shadows draped over the back of the structures. Reaching the inn, he peered cautiously around the corner marking the end of the town proper, but saw no guards pacing along the dirt road. Sliding around the side of the inn, he paused behind a capped rain barrel. He counted the seconds away in his head, ensuring no roaming patrol would wander by as he worked. When the town remained overtly quiet, he glanced upward, noting the window high overhead. With a weary sigh, he grasped the barrel and dragged it underneath the window. This ordeal had seemed far easier when there was a werewolf to handily toss him to the window above.

He climbed atop the barrel and reached for the windowsill, his fingers only barely brushing its bottom lip. Simon frowned as he stood upon his tiptoes, reaching again but with only slightly better results. Begrudgingly, he balanced upon the barrel and leapt upward, grasping the lip of the window with far better results. He pulled himself upward until he could brace his upper arms upon the ledge. Simon immediately scowled. Someone had lowered the window nearly to closing. Only a sliver remained open along the sill, just enough to allow a cool breeze to seep into the closed bedroom.

With a tenacious balance, he held on with his arms while he forced his fingertips underneath the partially opened window. Bending his fingers upward, he forced the window open further. He dangled as he slowly pried it open wide enough for him to slip through. He realized the precariousness of his position, with his body on full display and his legs hanging uselessly from the underside of a window.

When the window was open far enough, Simon climbed through. The blood rushed back into his arms and they ached, even as he stood.

Luthor's former room had been cleaned from its previous state of disarray. For a moment, Simon's heart sank at the thought that his plan, which was admittedly mediocre to begin with, was now in jeopardy. A quick review of the room, however, revealed that the apothecary's belongings had merely been pushed to a corner. Simon knelt before the pile and sorted through the clothes until he found an extra pair of Luthor's boots. Tucking them under his arm, he walked to the bedroom's door.

He opened it slowly, cringing again as the door creaked. No one responded to the noise if, indeed, it had been heard at all. He quickly crossed the hall and hurried toward its end, where Mattie's room had been. As he had found in Luthor's room, someone had sorted hastily through the belongings, leaving them in a disjointed pile on the floor. A pair of her dainty shoes was far easier to find, and he took them with him as he returned to the open window.

A quick glance ensured the way below was still devoid of patrols. Not for the first time, Simon was glad that the vampires had devoured so many of Whitten Hall's former residents. The remaining humans were far too few to watch all potential entrances into town, much less guard their former rooms in the inn.

He dropped the shoes unceremoniously from the window, ensuring he threw them out far enough to avoid the barrel. Rolling onto his belly, Simon lowered himself out the window, dropping gingerly onto the lid of the barrel before leaping to the ground. He gathered up the shoes before crouching behind the barrel once again.

The Inquisitor bit his lip as he made a mental list of everything else he would need to survive the next week. When he was confident he knew everything he would require, he walked around to the back of the buildings once more.

Glancing down the line, the Inquisitor counted to the fourth door before approaching the unremarkable back entryway. He took the handle firmly in his hand and turned it slowly, frowning slightly as his attempt was met with stern resistance. The door was locked. He patted his pockets, searching for anything that might be used as a makeshift lock pick, but found nothing of value.

Sighing, Simon turned on his heel and scanned the ground nearby. A few feet from the back door, a fist-sized stone jutted slightly from the packed earth. He walked over and dug the stone from the ground, feeling its weight in his hand. He shifted his grip until the edge of the stone protruded beyond his fingertips before walking back to the door. Standing before it, he dropped the shoes beside the rear entrance and tightened his grip on the rock.

Raising the stone over his head, he drove it down onto the door handle, knocking the metal knob free, albeit with more noise than he had intended. Simon hastily pushed the door open and entered the storage room quickly before someone could investigate the noise. There was no reason to close the door behind him, since the broken handle would be more than enough evidence of where he had gone.

Light entering from the open back door was the only illumination in the cramped pantry. Boxes of dry goods were stacked along the shelves lining each wall. Fruits and vegetables were packaged near the center of the room. A steady swarm of fruit flies buzzed above the fresh apples and pears.

Simon stepped around the fruit and approached the far wall. A door to his left led into the interior of the general store, but everything Simon needed could be found amidst the shelves. Coils of rope were bound on a shelf at eye level. Whetstones and shards of flint were stacked in small, wooden boxes near his waist.

He found a partially filled burlap satchel on the ground and dumped its contents onto the floor. Potatoes rolled away from the Inquisitor as he turned back to the shelf. Grabbing nearly a hundred feet of rope, he shoved the coils into the bag, along with some other survival equipment he'd need for the days ahead.

Stepping back, he glanced at the shelf in its entirety. There was still one object he was missing—a knife. He had given the bartender's knife to Luthor for his protection and while he didn't regret that decision, it bothered the Inquisitor immensely to be without one. He normally relied entirely on his revolver, but knew that the noise would draw far too much attention were it to be fired.

As he perused the storage room, he suddenly heard the handle to the door opening. Light from the front of the general store flooded the pantry, falling over Simon before he had a chance to find a place to hide.

"I swear I heard something," a man said, stepping into the doorway. "I'm not crazy."

The man in the doorway paused at the sight of the Inquisitor. His head was bandaged from a previous injury, and a small spot of red blood had soaked through a bulge on the man's forehead. Despite the bandage hanging nearly to the man's eyes, Simon had no trouble recognizing the bar's patron from the previous day.

Simon shifted the weight of the stone in his hand. The bandaged man's eyes widened for a brief moment before his gaze fell to the gray rock. The man's eyebrows fell pleadingly at the corners as he looked back toward Simon.

With a practiced throw, Simon sent the rock sailing across the storage room, catching the man on the eyebrow as he turned to run. The weight of the stone knocked him from his feet, and he crashed to the floor.

Simon turned toward the rear entrance to the building, but a glint of light off the knife on the man's waistband caught his attention. He lifted his satchel of pilfered goods before leaping over the few items between him and the unconscious man.

The knife was clearly not of high quality, but that mattered little for Simon's needs. He knelt beside the man and slipped it free from his belt loop.

The Inquisitor glanced up just in time to see a bag of flour sailing toward him. It landed at his feet, engulfing him in a cloud of white powder. Simon coughed as the flour settled over every exposed inch of his body. Wiping the powder angrily from his face, he looked up to see the general store manager perched high upon a ladder, reaching for a second bag of flour to continue his assault.

A small part of Simon wanted to rush over and kick the ladder out from underneath the man. He wanted to throttle the disrespectful storeowner, as much for his affiliation with the vampires as his attack on the Inquisitor. Simon knew Luthor would agree with that assessment, that all the humans still residing in Whitten Hall deserved their comeuppance.

As Simon stared at the storeowner, it wasn't rage or resentment splashed across his face, but rather fear. The general store manager wasn't attacking Simon out of spite, but because he knew the threat Simon posed to their very way of life.

The urge to harm the man bled away. Grabbing his stolen belongings, The Inquisitor glared once at the storeowner before hurrying back into the storeroom. The sound of an exploding bag of flour followed him as he leapt over the produce, grabbing a pair of apples as he passed.

Simon rushed out of the back door, grabbed the shoes he had left by the rear of the building, and disappeared into the woods before an alarm could be raised.

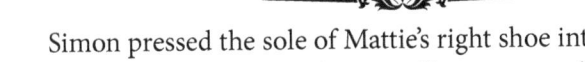

Simon pressed the sole of Mattie's right shoe into the soft mud near the riverbank, holding it in place until he was sure the shoe had sank far enough into the ground for what Simon estimated to be a hundred-and-twenty-pound woman. As he pulled the shoe away, it left the perfect imprint of a narrow heel followed by pointed toe. Leaning out over the bank from his place in the shallow water, Simon sank the left shoe a few paces away, matching Mattie's shorter stride. He continued the pattern until the tracks led into the river's edge, as though it had disappeared amongst the eddied currents in the shallow water.

These were the first solid footprints Simon had left behind of the other two. Despite his keen mind, he wasn't an outdoorsman and was only hoping that his tomfoolery would be enough to convince the townsfolk that he and his companions were still present in the forest around Whitten Hall.

He had left other marks throughout the woods as he walked, pressing one shoe or the other into any patches of soft mud he passed or kicking water out of small puddles, as though one of their shoes had dragged through the water inadvertently. He still wasn't convinced it would be enough, but the tracks to the river were his endgame.

Mattie's tracks now paralleled both his and Luthor's, all of which led into the water. Turning away from the shore, Simon discarded the empty shoes in the middle of the stream, watching as they sank beneath the current and drifted to the river's bottom.

Walking upstream a few hundred feet, ensuring the burlap satchel remained out of the water as best he could, Simon found a solid, low-hanging branch that reached out over the river. Wrapping his fingers around its girth, he pulled his legs out of the water and pulled himself up until he was sitting on the branch. Delicately, he slid along its length until he was hidden amongst the leaves and upper branches of the old oak tree.

He shivered involuntarily as the cold soaked through his socks and shoes. The day was still warm, but the river remained abrasively cold. He wiggled his toes, trying to force blood flow back through his feet. Draping the bag across his legs for warmth, he leaned into the trunk of the tree.

The shadows were growing longer as the sun began to set. Simon could feel the fatigue after his tiring day. He knew he would have to leave soon if he expected to make it back to his concealed cavern before nightfall, but fatigue caressed his tired back and legs as he rested in the tree.

When Simon opened his eyes again, the sun had nearly set. Light still filtered through the trees and danced across the flowing water below, but it was clearly setting far quicker than Simon would have liked.

The Inquisitor performed mental calculations, tracing a mental map of the area and estimating how long it would take him to return to his cave. At a full run, he would make it before dusk, but he doubted he would have the chance to run without being heard and pursued. Using caution, however, might result in him being caught in the woods after sunset, which was not at all optimal.

Despite his mental debate, he knew staying in the tree overnight was hardly a viable answer. He had no way of knowing the vampires' ability to track or if he would be as concealed in the eyes of one of the monsters as he was to the humans. Moreover, sleeping in the tree didn't seem possible. Though he had enjoyed his long nap, he was as surprised as anyone that he hadn't fallen gracelessly from the branches and awoken only because he was facedown on the ground below. Forced to spend the night in the tree, he doubted sleep would come willingly.

With a sigh, he swung his legs over the branch and prepared to lower himself down to the ground. He froze, instead, as he heard something sloshing through the river, heading in his direction. He quickly pulled his legs back into the concealment of the tree as he pulled his revolver from its holster.

A group of men emerged from upstream, wading through the knee-deep water. They shouldered rifles as they searched the banks for signs of tracks. Simon frowned at the sight. Tom Wriggleton led the hunters, his former suit and tie having been replaced by a multi-pocketed vest and waders. He carried a shotgun draped across his arms, its tip wavering inches above the flowing water.

"Do any of you see anything?" Tom asked, calling over his shoulders even as his eyes continued to scan downstream.

"Nothing, boss. You sure they came downriver?"

Tom shook his head. "Their tracks led this way and they're still pretty fresh, only a couple hours old by my reckoning."

"But they could have gone upstream, too," the hunter offered.

"It's possible, but we can only choose one direction to search at a time. If we don't find anything downstream, we'll search upriver next."

Simon scowled at the man, despite the fact that the townsfolk couldn't see him in his concealment. The Inquisitor raised his pistol, sighting down the barrel at the forehead of the group's leader. Simon realized his previous sentiment had been incorrect. He felt great sympathy for the unfortunate position in which most of the townsfolk found themselves, but not everyone in town deserved sympathy. He very much wanted to see Mister Wriggleton killed for his betrayal. Despite his grasp of logic and reason, Simon had a tendency to hold a grudge for such an affront. Coupled with the knowledge that Tom led the daytime hunters only further drove the foul taste left in Simon's mouth at the mere thought of the man

His pistol remained trained on Tom's skull even though he knew he wouldn't pull the trigger unless absolutely necessary.

Tom paused on the edge of the stream and scanned the surrounding forest, as though sensing his unseen assailant. Simon tensed, his hand clenching the pistol grip tighter as he prepared to fire. Tom stood for a long moment, just staring at the mass of trees, his gaze unblinking and his mouth a thin, bloodless line.

"You see something?" one of his hunters asked.

Tom stared at the canopy of leaves, his gaze practically boring into Simon's position. The Inquisitor was sure he'd been seen, but after a long pause, Tom shook his head.

"Nothing," he said. "There's nothing here. Let's keep moving downstream."

The party moved on, sloshing through the water as the current pushed them further down the river. Simon followed them with the barrel of his revolver, his steely gaze never leaving the man leading the way. Eventually, they disappeared from sight, covered as he was by branches and leaves of other low-hanging trees.

With the hunters gone, Simon relaxed and lowered his pistol. The setting sun glinted off the silver-plating on the revolver and shone in Simon's eyes. The Inquisitor raised his gaze toward the sun and frowned as he realized how far it had sunk toward the horizon. He knew the delay caused by the hunters stole his only chance of making it back to the cave by nightfall. Even if he rushed, he would get caught in the woods after dusk, fully exposed to the supernatural monsters hunting him.

For a moment, he considered trying to find the slanted tree under which he, Luthor, and Mattie had sheltered during the night, but the tree lay further downstream. With the hunters actively searching for him in that direction, it would be impossible to hide without being discovered.

He cringed at the realization that his only option was to stay where he was. There was nothing appealing about spending the night in the tree branches. There was no way to know if the vampires could see him where he hid. He hoped not, for his own sake, but he knew so little about vampire physiology.

Simon pushed his way back onto the crook of the tree, where his thick branch met the trunk. As the sun descended, it took with it the warmth from the day. It wasn't cold, necessarily, but it left him chilled and nervous. He wanted to close his eyes once more and sleep until morning, but the thought of being discovered amidst the branches, caught unaware by a vampire while he dozed, frightened him terribly.

Simon checked the available bullets in his revolver, noting the six silver rounds still loaded. He sat back against the trunk and closed his eyes, but his imagination ran wild with the thought of sharp claws and sharper fangs reaching toward his legs.

His eyes shot open, and he cradled his pistol to his chest. His free hand sank to his pockets, where the wooden stakes were concealed. Pulling one free, he set it on top of the burlap bag and settled in for a long night ahead.

Whether or not the vampires discovered him, there would be no sleep for the Inquisitor that night.

Tom shifted nervously as he walked toward the open doorway leading into the chancellor's manor. The vampire guards stood stoically by either side of the door, barely casting an inquisitive glance toward the sweaty human.

The candles were lit throughout the foyer and in the chandelier dangling high overhead. Where Simon had once seen an inviting old home, Tom saw it for what it was—candles lit in remembrance of those who had long ago died. His heart pounded as he strode into the room. His pulse was a war drum pounding in his ear, carrying even more weight with each beat since he realized it was the only heart that still beat amongst the house full of people.

Tom felt foolish. He still wore the lambskin waders, which dripped water onto the hardwood floor in a most uncivilized manner. He had wisely left his shotgun behind with his fellow hunters, all of whom stayed on the road at the end of the manor's drive, far away from the wrath they anticipated at their repeated failure to capture the prisoners.

As Tom turned toward the study, he caught glimpse of a man astride the top step, watching him intently. He turned toward the staircase as Chancellor Whitten glided down, his feet seeming to hover an inch or more above the steps themselves.

He stopped gracefully at the base of the stairwell and adjusted his velvet smoking jacket. Martelus was dressed exquisitely, as he often was when not playing the role of chancellor to visiting dignitaries. He had so readily embraced his role as vampire, quickly becoming a character straight from the books of mythology where vampires were immortal nobles who used their immense wealth and beauty to lure young women to their death.

Martelus glanced disapprovingly at his human compatriot, his eyes drifting over his outdoorsman's attire. A frown flashed quickly across the chancellor's face before his warm smile returned.

"Tell me of your hunt, Tom," Martelus said, gesturing toward the study. "Have you found the Royal Inquisitor and his companions?"

Tom swallowed hard as he followed the chancellor into the study. Unlike the foyer, few candles were lit in the smoking room. Just enough illumination filtered into the wide room for Tom to see the two plush couches.

Before Tom could sit, Martelus placed a hand on his chest. The chancellor moved incredibly quickly to a small bar, retrieving a thin towel from beside the tumblers. He reappeared at Tom's side equally as fast and draped the towel over the couch.

Tom noted the slight even as he sat on the towel, ensuring his attire would not stain the plush sofa.

"Would you care for a drink?" Martelus offered.

Tom shook his head, his face drained of its color as he awaited both the inevitable question and the punishment that he would receive as a result.

Martelus shrugged and sat down across from the human. "Where were we? Ah, yes, of course, you were about to tell me about your day's successes."

"Well, sir… we… that is to mean, I…" Tom struggled to find the right words, but he needn't try so hard. It was evident from the chancellor's stern visage that he understood all too well what Tom was trying to say.

"You're to tell me that you've had no luck locating the three wayward prisoners," Martelus said matter-of-factly. "Is this what you're trying to tell me?"

Tom tried to swallow again, but his throat felt dry and swollen. He wished now, more than ever, that he had accepted Martelus' offer for a drink.

The human cleared his throat. "We found their tracks by the river, not even a day old. They're still here in the forest. We have them trapped. It's only a matter of time until we find them, sir."

Martelus leaned back into the cushioned couch and stroked his chin thoughtfully. "My vampires tell me they encountered the apothecary and woman fleeing west through the valley, but you're telling me they're still near Whitten Hall?"

"I saw the tracks with my own eyes, sir."

The chancellor's eyes narrowed dangerously. "Perhaps you were deceived, Tom."

"Sir, if the other two have escaped the valley, then they will most certainly send reinforcements. We must get you and the others away from Whitten Hall with all haste."

Martelus scowled at the human. "Prepare the wagons and be ready to depart in two days' time. This time, don't fail me as you've done so readily in the past."

Tom shook his head nervously. "I can't ask enough for your forgiveness for letting them escape."

"I'm not talking about their escape!" Martelus roared. "I'm referring to the fact that you had them in your captivity, under careful observation since their arrival, yet you clearly didn't know that one of our guests was a sorcerer!"

The vampire slammed his fist down on the armrest, splintering the wood from the strike. Tom jumped, his heart rising quickly in his chest.

"I didn't know," Tom stuttered. "How could I know?"

"You searched their rooms while they were out and yet found no evidence that this supposed apothecary was anything more than a simple pharmacist? My vampires have died as a result of your ignorance."

Tom slid from the couch and fell to his knees before the chancellor. Tears welled in his eyes, not from sorrow but from absolute fear. "Forgive me, sir, please."

Martelus pulled his hand away as Tom reached for it. "Get up. You're embarrassing yourself."

Tom slowly regained his seat, though his body shook uncontrollably.

The vampire glanced toward the manor's front door. He pointed a long finger toward the entryway. "You will find them, Tom, and you won't fail me again." Each use of the human's name carried with it a more sinister edge. "If we have this conversation again, I promise that I'll drain you myself and add your desiccated husk to the top of my pile. Am I understood?"

Tom nodded feverishly before rising hastily. "Thank you, sir. I won't fail you again."

Screams filled the air from outside the house. Tom rushed toward the door, completely oblivious to the fact that Martelus moved not at all from his place on the couch.

As Tom reached the door, he saw his hunters strewn across the ground in a growing pool of their own blood. Their throats were torn and mangled, not by the careful use of the vampires' fangs, but by the careless ripping of flesh by the vampires' claws.

Tom stood, mortified, at the sight before him. The chancellor materialized beside him and stared upon the wanton destruction.

"Let this be a warning to you, the only one you'll receive until we meet again," Martelus explained. "In two days, we had better be ready to leave this abysmal town."

Tom nodded again, the fear and hatred stewing in his gut and making him nauseated. The human hurried forward, stopping beside the pile of still-cooling corpses. With a shaking hand, he reached into the pile and retrieved his shotgun, which was stained red and tacky to the touch. He fought the urge to vomit as he stood again and ran from the manor, not bothering to look back at the vampires who watched him depart.

When Tom was no longer within view of the home, Martelus turned toward his guards.

"Find me the Royal Inquisitor. Unlike our human friend, I don't believe we'll find his other two companions here in the woods, but Inquisitor Whitlock is most assuredly still about. I want him brought to me."

The chancellor stepped through the front door and began strolling determinedly down the lane. He paused and glanced over his shoulder. "On second thought, let me correct myself. I want his head brought to me; the rest of him is rather inconsequential."

Martelus walked unerringly toward the mine, crossing the covered bridge hurriedly. Upon reaching the edge, he leapt from the edge of the pit rather than take the winding path that followed the curve of the circular quarry.

His body floated unnaturally toward the ground below, and he touched down softly. No sooner had his feet touched rock than he was already walking toward the mineshaft's broad entrance.

The chancellor passed quickly through the mine and entered the barracks. A few vampires left behind looked up expectantly, but the chancellor offered not a word to the monsters as he moved toward the narrow passage beyond the sleeping quarters.

Still moving supernaturally fast, Martelus slid quickly through the narrow tunnel and entered the debris-strewn cavern beyond. Even in the darkness, his glowing red eyes could see the outline of the limestone door on the far side of the room. In the length of a blink, he was standing before the door and pulling it open.

His pupils contracted hastily as the torchlight from the room beyond flooded his vision. The ancient vampire raised his head slowly and he offered a half-hearted smile to the chancellor.

"To what do I owe the pleasure of your company, Whitten?" the archaic creature asked, his voice as frail as paper.

Martelus stepped into the room, pushing the doors shut behind him. He paced before the door, walking from one end of the room to the other as he stroked his chin. A wicked smile spread across his face, though it carried a malicious undertone.

"Tell me again how it came to pass that the Royal Inquisitor, weakened as he was, slipped from your grasp?"

The wizened creature shrugged his bony shoulders. "I was so frail when you brought him before me that he was able to overpower me and escape. Why, my dear Martelus? He hasn't been causing trouble, has he?"

Martelus stopped before the dais and snarled at the vampire. "You know damn well he's causing trouble. I know what game you're playing at, old man."

"I'm sure I have no idea of what you speak, blood thief. Perhaps if you fed me better, I would have had the strength to keep the Inquisitor contained. However, my lack of blood has left my arms so frail and meager."

He held up his limbs until the chains on his wrists snapped taut, emphasizing his point.

"I know what game you're playing, and it won't work!" Martelus replied. "You think the Inquisitor will somehow be your savior, but all he'll be is my next meal. I promise you that I will bring his head to you as a reminder of the consequences of betrayal."

The ancient vampire seemed unimpressed as he suppressed a cough. "I look forward to that day as well."

Martelus grew angry at the vampire's obvious lack of concern. "If you think your arms are frail now, you have no idea the pain I will inflict before all this is said and done. You won't get another meal until I see less insolence from you. Let's see how you feel about returning to the impotent old abomination I found when we blasted into this chamber."

The chancellor turned away abruptly and walked to the door. As he pulled it open, he turned back toward the vampire. "Mark my words, you will rue the day you chose to cross me."

Martelus exited, letting the door slam shut behind him. The ancient vampire smiled at the memory of the irritated chancellor.

"I have smelled the determination in his blood, blood thief. He will end you, and I long to be there when he does."

CHAPTER Thirty-two

THE SHIVERS CAME LIKE A FEVER, WASHING OVER SImon as he crouched in the tree. His eyes burned from fatigue, blurring his vision. The Inquisitor wrapped his arms around his knees, squeezing the burlap bag tightly against his stomach.

The time before the dawn was far colder and darker than the night. He knew that once the sun crested the treetops, the temperature would warm and the aches in his muscles and bones would soothe. The wait, however, was driving him mad. He longed only to hurry back to his cavern and sleep through the day, but he dared not lower himself from his tree until the sun's rays protected him.

As he had assumed they would, the vampires had roamed the woods at night, clearly searching for him. They had passed along the water's edge, just feet below where he sat upon his tentative perch, but they never made any outward indication that they saw him. Even having his confidence bolstered that the vampires' vision couldn't penetrate his concealment, sleep wouldn't come to Simon. He continued to fear that he would fall from the branch as soon as his eyes drooped closed.

The sun's rays fell across his face, and he blinked furiously at the brilliant glare. Despite the weariness that had settled into his bones, he forced a smile to welcome the rising sun. The effort of smiling hurt the bruises across his cheeks.

The smile faded from his face as he slid his legs over the branch and dropped gracefully to the ground below. Slinging the satchel across his back, he set off hastily toward the far side of Whitten Hall and his cavern amidst the base of the hills.

He skirted far beyond the borders of the outpost, knowing that he was in no condition to face the human hunters. His path took him toward the boulder-ridden valley to the west of the town and, so he still hoped, the safe concealment of the cavern at the base of the largest hill in the region. The hill had served him well as an overlook, from the top of which he could see the train tracks for miles in either direction. He would hopefully see Luthor's return well in advance of the vampires and humans within Whitten Hall.

He came upon a narrow animal trail winding through the woods. Hoof marks were dried in the hardened earth, leading in both directions. The trees had overgrown the trail, their drooping branches forming a shallow tunnel through which Simon passed. Thinner, spindly trees sprouted from the soil nearby, their sturdy yet flexible trunks easily brushed aside as he moved between them.

After nearly an hour of walking, the animal trail disappeared into a pair of domineering bushes pushing over the trail from either side. Simon forced them apart and was surprised by the brilliance of the sun on the far side.

The thick forest gave way to barren ground, spotted with large rocks protruding from the brown soil. The trees had been left behind, save for a few scraggly examples clinging to the patches of dirt between the rocky terrain. Without the trees for shelter, the sun shone brilliantly, illuminating the valley below.

Simon hadn't passed this way before, and was surprised to find a ravine carving its way along the side of the animal trail. From his vantage point, he could look down the chasm to the shallow river gurgling nearly twenty feet below. Though the ravine wasn't wide, no more than ten feet across, it stretched a good distance in either direction, farther than Simon could ascertain from where he stood.

Across the ravine, the land dropped away into the heart of the valley. Though he was sure he could jump the chasm with a running start, he strongly doubted his footing upon his landing on the other side. More likely than not, he'd find himself tumbling across loose gravel before collapsing gracelessly into a boulder or two.

Glancing behind, his gaze fell to the nearly impenetrable wall of the woods. He could see only a few feet within its dense border. For a moment, nervousness clutched him before he forced himself to relax. He needn't worry about pursuit, he reminded himself. The townsfolk of Whitten Hall were stretched far throughout the forest, searching both for Simon and for his companions. Even had they had their full complement of people living within the town, they'd still barely have enough to cover the varied terrain surrounding the outpost. As it were, with so many of their people sacrificed to the growing hungers of the vampires, there were far too many gaps through which Simon could pass unobstructed.

Simon paused and smiled to himself. The fact that they searched not just for Simon but for Luthor and Mattie as well brought Simon great joy, knowing that they hadn't already been captured. There was still hope that they would reach Callifax and return with help.

The Inquisitor blinked and stifled a yawn as he peered across the sunlit valley below. The scenery was spectacular, and he wanted nothing more than to sit upon the rocks beneath him and watch the sun continue its steady climb to its zenith far above his head. Sadly, the reminder of his exhaustion and danger ahead stole the pleasure from the moment. He stretched his arms far overhead and arched his back as a yawn came on once more.

Begrudgingly, he turned away from the valley and walked toward the hilltop, easily visible above the scrub brush clinging to life in the harsh ground.

To Simon's trained eyes, the cavern's entrance was easy to find, despite the large rock that concealed the way inside. Pushing the rock aside, the cool air spilled from the cave's narrow maw. He slid the burlap satchel inside, setting it beside his other belongings, before turning toward the steep hill nearby.

A small voice in the back of his mind reminded him that he could take care of this task at a later date, but Simon knew it was important. He walked to the base of the hill and sought out the familiar hand and foot holds that he could use to climb to the crest of the hill.

With weary hands, Simon pulled himself onto the flattened top of the hill and lay upon the cool stones, refusing even to sit properly. His sharpened stone was still resting on the rocks nearby. Forcing himself to a seated position, he took the rock with one hand while he traced the white vertical line he scratched into the gray stone the day before. With the rock in hand, he gouged a second line beside the first.

Replacing the rock, he raised his hand over his eyes and peered across the valley toward the railroad tracks beyond. Everything was painfully quiet; there was no indication that a train had ever passed along those tracks, save for the good working order of the rails themselves.

Simon touched the two parallel lines in the stone and mentally counted another day from his tally. Five to go, he reminded himself.

Simon climbed back down the hill using the trees and rocks for support, and sauntered back to the cavern. Slipping inside legs first, the Inquisitor slid far enough into the cool interior that he could roll the rock back into place. He was eternally glad for the rounded edges of the stone, allowing it to be rolled into place rather than lifted. Within the close confines of the cave, he had little leverage with which to lift the heavy rock.

As the capstone slid into place, the cave was bathed in cool darkness. Simon closed his eyes and soon thereafter fell asleep.

The sun was still in the sky when Simon awoke, though it had clearly begun its downward swing to the west. His body ached, but he felt significantly more refreshed than he had been earlier in the morning. Kneeling, Simon retrieved his coat from within the cave before reaching back inside and withdrawing the burlap satchel. Unbinding the top, he pulled out one of the apples, enjoying the meager meal. He knew he'd have to find food again, sooner rather than later, but his outdoors skills were severely lacking. He was far better suited as a scavenger than a hunter, though he knew exactly where he could go to steal more food, should the need arise.

Shouldering his bag, he set off back toward the valley and ravine, pausing only as he searched for the elusive animal trail he had followed before. He eventually found similar hoof markings on the thin earth between the jutting rocks and was able to follow the trail back to the edge of the woods. Though barely visible from this side of the foliage, Simon could faintly make out the start of the trampled ground leading deeper into the forest.

Pushing through the brush, he found himself once again amidst the narrow, reedy trees. He wrapped his hand around the trunk of one and pulled it toward him. The root system clung firmly to the soil while the tip of the tree bent nearly to Simon's waist. Satisfied, he released the tree and let it spring violently back into place.

Dropping the bag to the ground, Simon untied its top and dumped the contents haphazardly onto the ground. Adding to the pile of rope and the knife, Simon pulled some of the wooden stakes from his pockets and tossed them onto the ground.

Simon whistled softly as he began his work. Using the knife, he cut a few shorter lengths from the long coil of rope on the ground. He measured them at cubit lengths before adding the newly cut strands to a growing pile at his feet. When he had enough, he put his knife away.

He worked quickly, bending a nearby sapling until it was bent nearly parallel to the ground. He tied the longer length of rope to its tip before tying the other end firmly in place around a broader, older tree nearby. The reedy tree pulled tightly against the rope but it held in place, bent low and away from the bushes concealing the entrance to the animal trail.

Simon stepped back onto the trail, passing beyond the thick underbrush. From his vantage point, the bent sapling was invisible to the naked eye. He hoped the foliage similarly hindered the vampires' view.

Stepping back through the narrow opening of the animal trail, he noted how the sapling was set to spring across the trail. Even with the slight upward arc, it would strike a normal man at approximately chest level.

Retrieving his smaller lengths of rope and the stakes, Simon began tying them along the length of the sapling. The wooden stakes jutted like teeth from the sapling, pointing dangerously toward the edge of the dense woods.

He turned slowly and watched the sun sink behind the tips of the nearby pine trees. It wouldn't be long until sunset, sooner still until the trees blocked the sun's rays. Properly motivated by their hatred, the vampires could be awake and giving chase within the hour.

Simon hurriedly took the other coil of rope and formed a set of practiced knots. A series of loops ran its length by the time he was finished. He tossed the knotted end of the rope over a nearby hanging tree branch before tying off the other end of the rope to the tree's wider trunk. Satisfied, Simon collected the knife and sliver of flint before stepping back through the brush.

Jogging quickly toward his cavern, he realized that time was of the essence. He was losing the light and doubted the vampires would give him the benefit of the doubt by waiting until he was properly prepared. Reaching the bottom of the hill, Simon took some of the dry scrub brush from the ground nearby and formed a small pile. Holding out his knife, he struck its back edge with the flint. Sparks flickered but failed to fall on the brush below. Leaning forward, he tried again and again, each time sending a shower of sparks into the darkening night's air but igniting nothing.

Simon grumbled to himself and glanced cautiously over his shoulder. The sparks alone might be enough to attract one of the vampires, but he needed to be sure.

Insistently, Simon struck the flint again. This time, as sparks fell over the kindling, a small flame caught on the end of a pile of grass. Simon cupped his hands and blew gently, oxidizing the ember and helping it grow to a full-fledged flame. For a painful moment, he feared he had blown too hard and the ember had been extinguished, but a second gentle blow of air brought it roaring back to life. The small flame ignited more grass around it and within seconds, a small campfire was burning.

He didn't bother adding any wood to the pile, despite the fact that the grass would burn itself out fairly quickly. He didn't need or want a permanent flame. In fact, he wanted it to burn just long enough to catch a vampire's attention before it extinguished.

Simon took his knife and stood, turning away from the already dwindling flame. He started as he saw a dark-robed figure watching him from across the rocky ground.

The Inquisitor clutched the knife before him, more reflexively than as a true threat to the vampire. His eyes darted from side to side, an action that he was sure looked like nervousness to the vampire. Rather, Simon was ensuring there was but one vampire. More than one would have been difficult to handle, though not impossible.

Seeing no one else, Simon nodded toward the vampire. "Shall we dance, you and I?"

The vampire stepped toward him as the glow from the small fire faded into obscurity. Rather than advancing on the monster, Simon turned and ran in the opposite direction as quickly as his legs could handle. He knew the vampire was far quicker, but they didn't have far to go.

The vampire struck him across the back as it quickly closed the distance between them. Simon tumbled forward, barely avoiding a jutting stone that most certainly would have fractured bones. He rolled gracefully to his feet and continued running, ignoring the vampire behind him as best as possible.

The tree line rapidly approached, but the vampire was once again quicker. It ran beside Simon before throwing its weight into his shoulder. He careened to the side, tripping over a stone and skidding to his hands and knees. He could feel the uneven ground biting into his knees and palms, and he winced at the sharp pain. Where he had clutched the knife, it had been his knuckles that had dragged across the ground and acute agony rolled up his arm.

The vampire paused at the smell of blood. Simon glanced over his shoulder. Even in the darkness, he could see the conflicting emotions on the creature's face. It clearly intended to kill him, but seemed hesitant to simply drain him of his blood. There was no doubt in the Inquisitor's mind that the vampire had received specific orders about his treatment and eventual disposition.

With the vampire temporarily distracted, Simon crawled into the underbrush. When he was clear of the bushes, he stood and stumbled forward, even as the vampire crashed unceremoniously through the foliage.

It paused as it realized that Simon had stopped his retreat. He stood facing the vampire, the knife held aloft in his hand. The vampire barely had a moment to register the rope beside him before Simon brought down his arm.

The rope severed as he cut through it with the blade. With the released tension, the sapling sprung blindingly forward, the sharpened stakes leading its arc. The vampire hissed and tried to step aside, but he moved too late. The stakes pierced his right chest and down into his stomach. The vampire tilted its head backward and howled in pain.

Simon smiled, glad that the abominations could properly feel pain. Though everything he was doing held a clinical detachment for him, there was a gleeful side to his experimentation, one in which he willingly caused the anguish of the monsters trying to kill him.

The vampire clutched the branch and tried to remove the wooden stakes, though it clearly moved with great hesitation. It realized its own mortality against the wooden spears puncturing its body and refused to be too hasty. Simon counted on its hesitation as he grabbed the looped and knotted end of the second rope and ran behind the vampire.

He slipped the longest loop around the vampire's throat, pulling the noose tight. As it pulled its arms away from the branch in surprise, Simon placed slipknots over each arm. He placed his foot in the creature's back and pulled with all his weight. As the knots cinched tightly, it jerked the monster's arms backward and together. The last two loops went around the vampire's ankles and were similarly tightened.

The vampire alternated struggling against its bonds and staring down at the stakes, which moved closer to its heart with every jerk of its body. Simon knew the creature would break free quickly, so he rushed to the tree trunk and grasped the far end of the knotted rope. Throwing his weight against it, the rope pulled taut, lifting the vampire from the ground. Its ankles were pulled awkwardly toward its wrists, stealing any hope of leverage and, hopefully, any chance of it breaking its bonds.

With the vampire incapacitated, Simon approached it cautiously. It glowered at him and hissed, revealing its fangs.

"I'll kill you for this, human!" it howled. "I'll drink your blood. The chancellor be damned, I'll crush your bloodless skull between my bare hands."

Simon's hand shot out and he slit the vampire's throat with the knife. The creature gurgled, despite the lack of blood that seeped from the wound. It stared at him in disbelief and then tried to rail against him once more, only to find that the slit to his throat stole his voice as well.

"Thank God," Simon muttered. "I was starting to think you'd perform a full monologue before I got you quiet."

Ignoring the vampire's rage, Simon pulled the stakes free of the creature's body. Without the wooden spears and the reedy tree holding him in place, the vampire spun lazily in the air at the end of the rope. The noose tightened further just above the gash to the creature's neck, yet neither was enough to kill the undead monster.

Simon returned to the rope and pulled the vampire higher until its feet hovered just above the Inquisitor's head. Satisfied, Simon sat down on the ground and stared up at the hate-filled visage.

"I'm sure you're wondering why you're here at all," Simon began. "Why I didn't just kill you to start with. The simple answer is that I need answers from you, answers that only you possess. The more complex answer is that you are, for all intents and purposes, a science experiment."

Simon reached into the burlap bag and pulled free the second apple. The exertion had left him bone weary and starving. He bit into the crisp apple and chewed noisily.

"I have a friend, as you're well aware, who would bemoan my need to perform science experiments. He's a much more straightforward man than you would ever believe, hardly ever making time for the finer pursuits in life."

Carving free another slice with his knife, he raised it to his lips before pausing. He glanced down at the knife as though realizing for the first time that the blade that just cut his fruit had, moments before, cut the throat of a vampire. Disgusted, he dropped the apple to the ground and wiped his hands on his pants.

"I'm sure what you want to know is what sort of experiment I intend to conduct and how you play a role. The first part of my experiment is how quickly you can heal from a wound like the one on your neck. My hypothesis is that you'll be fully healed before sunrise, but we shall see, won't we?"

The vampire gurgled angrily, but Simon ignored him.

"The second part is a confirmation of modern mythology. You see, it's said that vampires are destroyed by the first rays of morning."

The anger in the vampire's eyes quickly changed to fear, and he jerked futilely against his ropes.

"Since none of you have bothered to show yourself during the day, the truth would lend itself toward mythology. However, what good scientist would I be if I merely took the word of third-party observations and conjecture?"

Simon stood and dusted off his pants. He glanced through the woods, despite how dark it had grown underneath the canopy of leaves. Turning back toward the vampire, he knelt and collected his bag.

"I'm going to leave you for a bit," Simon said as he passed underneath the vampire. "Do keep in mind that I will be very put out should you not be here upon my return."

Simon stepped through the underbrush, ignoring the groaning of the rope as the vampire struggled to free itself.

The Inquisitor walked cautiously back to the cave, ensuring no other monsters had made their way to the edge of the valley in his absence. Seeing nothing, he rolled aside the rock and slipped into the cave. He wasn't overly tired, since he had only recently awoken from his day-long rest, but he could think of no better place to pass the vampire-infested night.

When the moon was starting to set and the cool night's breeze still crept around the edges of his capstone, Simon emerged from the cavern. The night was still and quiet, not necessarily something he appreciated.

In many ways, he'd much prefer the traipsing of booted feet on dried leaves or the quiet cursing of someone tangled in the briar patches.

He set off at once toward his vampire captive, knowing that he was racing against the rising sun. The sky above the forest had begun to lighten, with shades of purples and deep blues permeating the otherwise black, starry night.

No other vampires interrupted him as he approached the forest, nor did he expect to encounter any. The sun was rising quickly, and the monsters would be scurrying back to their sunless mines to sleep away the day. He would have a slight reprieve from now until shortly after dawn, when the vampires were returning to bed and the human hunters weren't yet out on the prowl. It was Simon's time to appreciate the finer things in life, such as a captive vampire.

He pushed through the underbrush. The woods themselves were still dark, an inky blackness against which Simon's eyes had to adjust. As he peered upward, he could see the vampire's legs still dangling slightly above his head. The monster rotated slowly at the end of the noose and as he turned toward Simon, the Inquisitor could see the hatred burning behind the creature's red eyes.

"Forgive this dreadful pun, but thank you for hanging around until I returned," Simon chided as he stepped past the creature.

"Release me," the vampire whispered, its voice a hoarse croak.

Simon turned toward the vampire inquisitively and squinted to see the wound on the creature's neck. The previously wide gash had mostly closed, leaving a puckered scar that, in time, would also disappear.

"You're healing quite nicely and at a rate slightly quicker than I would have anticipated. Scientifically, you're a fascinating specimen. I can't say that any of my Inquisitor brethren have ever had such a close encounter with a creature such as you."

The vampire jerked against his ropes, causing him to sway uncontrollably. "Release me, damn you!" the vampire said, though the harsh whisper lacked the conviction of his words.

Simon sat upon the ground and emptied his pockets onto the grass beside him. He set a pair of wooden stakes beside his stolen knife, arranging them neatly for future use. Pulling his pocket watch from his vest, he checked the time. If his estimation of sunrise were correct, they would have to speed their conversation along.

"I will free you but first, there are a few things we must discuss."

"Feck you!" the vampire spat.

Simon shook his head, his eyes still watching the second hand tick away on his pocket watch. "Your demise will only be hastened by your rudeness. By my estimation, you have but a few more minutes before the sun rises through the trees behind me. It won't be quick, mind you. The sunlight will filter through the dense leaves, sending small beams of light through the forest. You might—"

The vampire tossed himself about, bouncing wildly on the noose, but still to no avail. It remained a prisoner, despite its superhuman strength.

Simon glanced up, perturbed at the interruption. "You might get lucky and the first few rays will miss striking you, but your luck will eventually run out. Given enough time, your survivability is reduced to zero and, believe me, time is not on your side. It rather behooves you to answer my questions."

The vampire stopped moving and merely swung like a pendulum until his momentum was spent. "What do you want to know?"

"What is the chancellor planning?"

The vampire glared at the Inquisitor, who sat nonchalantly upon the dew-covered moss and grass. "He wants you dead."

Simon frowned and picked up one of the stakes, pointing its sharpened end toward the creature. "You'll have to do far better than that. You're painting your answers with a very broad brush, while I'd like to see a bit more minutia. Of course the chancellor wants me dead; it practically goes without saying. What I want to know is what he has planned for you and your kind. He knows I'm still alive in these woods and, by now, knows that I'm alone. Therefore, it's only a matter of time before my companions return with reinforcements. So I will ask again—what is the chancellor planning?"

The vampire remained silent, merely glowering at the Inquisitor. Simon shrugged and tilted his head backward, staring at the dark sky through the shifting leaves. The black of the night sky had mostly receded, replaced by shades of blue.

"Answer or don't answer," Simon remarked. "It makes little difference. I would prefer an answer, but I can just as easily sit here with abject curiosity and watch you destroyed by the morning sun."

The vampire tilted his head upward as well and looked at the lightening sky. His sheer hatred was tempered by a sudden fear.

"Release me," it said.

Simon shook his head and clicked his tongue disapprovingly. "That sounded an awful lot like a demand, and you're hardly in a position to make those."

Panic crept into the vampire's voice as it continued. "Release me and I'll tell you all that you want to know."

Simon feigned interest in the stake in his hand, as though something in the texture of the smooth wood interested him. "You'd be amazed how often I've heard that very offer." He looked up and arched an eyebrow. "You'd probably not be as surprised to know how many times I've refused that request."

The vampire glanced toward the sky. A morning breeze shifted the leaves and he could see faint shades of pink on the horizon. "He's planning on moving," it said hastily.

"Moving where and how?"

"I... I don't know where, but he has covered wagons and crates in which they can stay shielded from the sun."

Simon smiled faintly. "Where is he keeping these wagons?"

The vampire glanced down at Simon before his gaze returned to the ever-closer sunrise. "At his manor house. They are being staged at his manor house. Now please, damn you, I fulfilled my end of the bargain, now live up to yours."

Simon picked up the knife in his other hand and stood, shaking his head slightly. "I never made a bargain with you, vampire."

The vampire's eyes widened in surprise. "I promised to tell you in exchange for my freedom."

"To which I never gave an answer for or against," Simon said as he walked toward the rope holding the noose aloft. Before the vampire could protest, Simon raised his hand to silence it. "However, I'm a man of integrity. You gave me something I desired, so I shall set you free."

He slashed the rope, and the vampire dropped heavily to the ground. With its hands and feet still bound, it had no chance to brace against its rapid decent and it collapsed heavily onto the hard surface. Groaning, it rolled to its side.

"Cut me free, please," the vampire pleaded.

"Your manners have made an even more remarkable recovery than the cut to your throat," Simon remarked as he walked to the vampire's side.

He knelt before the creature, staring in its fearful red eyes. He drew back the hand with the wooden stake and slammed it into the vampire's chest. Its eyes widened in surprise even as its unnatural life drained from its body. Its mouth fell open, revealing the fangs within, but they were no longer a threat. The vampire's eyes no longer saw the forest around it.

"Now you're free," Simon whispered as he stood.

The Inquisitor returned to where he had left the other wooden stake and sat down in the grass, oblivious to the moisture that soaked into the backside of his pants.

The first ray of sunlight danced through the shifting leaves and settled on the ground beside him. Simon reached out his hand and let his fingers sift through the single ray of morning light. The beam was soon joined by others as the sun crested over the treetops.

Simon watched excitedly as the sunlight reached the vampire's corpse. As the light struck its skin, the flesh cracked and peeled, smoldering as it fell away from the creature's skull. Fissures that seemed to burn in their depths spread across the monster's skin, and smoke billowed from beneath its clothes. The once pale skin grew gray as it burned from within until the entire corpse collapsed into itself, turning to ash as it settled onto the forest floor.

"Fascinating," Simon whispered as he collected the second stake and stood. Emboldened with his newfound knowledge, Simon realized he had a very full day ahead of him.

CHAPTER
Thirty-three

THE ROAD OUT OF WHITTEN HALL WAS BUSIER THAN Simon had seen it in days. People, often in small groups of three or four, passed from the town, carrying armloads of supplies. Simon could see bags of meal and assorted canned goods burdening the arms of the townsfolk. They talked fairly merrily amongst themselves as they went, as though the horror of what was occurring within their township held no bearing on their current predicament.

Others carried personal belongings, strapped across their backs or laden in their arms. The whole town was preparing to leave; their homes and businesses were being abandoned. If their enthusiasm were any indication, they would be leaving with all haste, which didn't leave Simon much time at all.

He remained hidden as he watched more and more townsfolk pass. He perused their personal affects as well as the satchels of foodstuffs laden in their arms. With a sigh, Simon adjusted his position. Thus far, he had seen little more than grain bags and assorted foods, but nothing of what he actually wanted to see.

After some time, a man walked by with two large glass jars. Thick corks stopped the brownish fluid from sloshing through the mouth of the carafes. Despite the man's thick muscles, he was clearly huffing with exertion as he carried the two jars down the road.

Simon immediately rose to a crouch and proceeded through the woods, paralleling the road and ensuring he kept the laden man in constant view. Though he glanced occasionally toward the man himself, his eyes rarely left the brown fluid and the greasy residue it left on the inside of the glass as it sloshed back and forth like a pendulum.

At the entrance to the manor house's long lane, the man with the jars turned and hurried toward the throng of other townsfolk. The front was a beehive of activity. The manor itself was barely visible through the caravan of covered wagons that were parked in the lane. The wagons were long and covered with a cloth tarp that hung low on both ends. The ends of the carts were currently opened as men excitedly loaded supplies into their interiors.

Only half of the carts were being loaded with supplies. The other half was the focus of most of the townsfolk's attention. In teams, they loaded large, wooden crates that closely resembled makeshift coffins into the backs of the wagons. Simon didn't need to guess to know what they'd be for. Moreover, he frowned at the sight of so many of the coffins. He had never truly understood just how many vampires had already been created until he saw the need for dozens of boxes, pulled in a long row of horse-drawn wagons.

Standing in the center of the workers directing their actions was Tom Wriggleton. Tom barked orders to the laborers, directing which coffins were loaded onto which wagons. Simon scowled at the sight of the man. Of everyone in the town, Tom had caused Simon the most trouble thus far, nearly as much as the vampires themselves. If his plan were to succeed, Simon would have to find a way to remove Tom from the picture.

The man with the jars temporarily disappeared behind a set of tall wagons, and Simon felt a moment of panic. So much of his haphazard plan relied on following the movements of that single man. Without knowing the man's destination, he doubted he would succeed.

Simon scoffed at the idea. He doubted his current plan would succeed either. There was a good chance he'd shortly be shot dead.

As he muddled through his dismal options, he caught sight of the man emerging near the right side of the manor house. A few wagons, nearly loaded to capacity, rested against the building, mostly abandoned as the workers moved on to other priorities.

The man whom Simon was intently watching loaded his two jugs into the back of one of these wagons, placing the glass carafes beside similarly filled jars. Simon smiled to himself before observing the rest of the work being conducted.

None of the horses were yet hitched to the wagons, since it would be hours before the vampires awoke and were ready to depart. He scanned the estate until he saw the horses hitched to the far side of the house. Their bridles were tied to hitching posts that looked recently constructed solely for this purpose.

Satisfied, Simon slipped back into the woods, disappearing from view of the road. Amidst the trees and bushes, he found a small clearing in which he could work. Sitting upon the ground, he pulled out his burlap satchel and knife and began cutting away small squares of the fabric.

From his waistcoat, he retrieved the remainder of his bullets, save the six that were still loaded in his revolver. Without proper tools, it was difficult to remove the lead tip to the rounds. He used his blade as best he could, but the first set of bullets spilled most of their contents onto the ground as soon as the bullet gave way. Through some trial and error, he managed to separate the rest of the bullets with a greater degree of success. With the bullets removed, he tipped the casings over, pouring the powder charge into the small squares of fabric. Simon frowned as some of the grains of gunpowder slipped through the loosely woven fabric and disappeared into thick grass. He was working with subpar supplies and had to expect that some of his explosives would be lost. Still, when waging a one-man guerilla war against an army of vampires, a bit of positive karma would have been greatly appreciated.

Simon glanced down at his handiwork without much satisfaction. "I could certainly use your expertise right about now, Luthor," he muttered. "Something tells me your apothecary skills would be far better suited for this task. I'm just fumbling around like a double-arm amputee attempting surgery."

With a sigh, he accepted that he was alone on this task. Luthor, God willing, was well on his way to Callifax and would soon be returning with all haste. Simon would just have to make do until his return.

With the bullets emptied of their powder, he discarded the shell casings. He pulled up the edges of his powder-filled bags and tied the top with strands unwoven from the remains of his rope. His raid on the storeroom had garnered quite a few supplies, nearly all of which he had now exhausted.

Simon glanced down at the small pile of explosives and sighed. It wasn't much to look at, but he hoped it was enough for the task at hand.

Near the clearing, Simon found a thick fallen branch that would serve well as a torch. Begrudgingly, he removed his jacket and laid it on the ground before him. He needed something that would burn well once lit, and the only thing he had on hand was his own clothing. He nearly felt a pang of heartache as he tore the lining from his suit coat. The finely woven fabric and inner padding wound itself well around the tip of the log.

He glanced down at his supplies. As he reached out to retrieve the small pouches, he caught sight of his hands and the stained dress shirt he still wore. He hadn't bothered looking in a mirror in days now and dreaded his appearance. If his clothes were any indication, he was sure he looked absolutely appalling. His pants were caked with mud and dust, staining the once rich black fabric nearly tan. His well-manicured hands were filthy, the nails nearly black.

Brushing aside concerns of his appearance, he shoved the explosive pouches into the pockets of his waistcoat. Replacing his knife in his belt on the side opposite from his holstered revolver, Simon rolled up the sleeves of his once white dress shirt and turned back toward the manor house. Reaching down, he picked up the torch before setting off.

Simon slipped back into the woods and hurried further down the road, away from the manor. There were too many people milling about the front of the house and it would do him no good to exit amidst the workers. Instead, he hurried until he reached the river, past a bend in the road around which he wouldn't be seen.

The covered bridge that spanned the river was unguarded, though he could be certain that there would be guards closer to the mines. He had no intention of disrupting those guards or, truth be told, even alerting them to his presence.

Simon hurried across the road and back into the woods on the far side. Admittedly, all the woods looked the same to Simon, but he hadn't spent the past few days traversing the forest on the far side of the road. It felt foreign, as though it knew he was an unfamiliar invader to their private sanctum. He moved with far more practiced steps as he turned back toward the estate.

He approached the house from its rear, ensuring he avoided the majority of activity around the front of the plantation. The line of wagons wrapped fully around to the side of the house nearest where Simon emerged from the woods, though these carts had long ago been loaded with supplies. He slipped toward the closest wagon, using it for cover so as not to be seen.

Simon paused beside the wagon's wheel and forced his raging heartbeat to slow to a more normal pace. Everything he had done to this point had been in preparation for this moment, but his entire plan would be for naught if he were caught now.

Peering around the corner of the wagon, he saw a guard walking around the perimeter of the house. Simon quickly slid back into the cover of the wagon, all the while cursing himself for trying to hide behind the wheels of a wagon, which had narrow spokes and giant visible gaps. To his relief, the guard never looked beneath the tall wagon to see the dirt-stained pants concealed on the far side.

When the guard had reached the far corner of the home and turned around the back of the house, Simon stepped around the wagon and lifted its flap. Inside, a mound of bags filled with assorted fresh fruit was stacked nearly to overflowing. Shrugging, Simon pulled one of the bags from the back and hoisted it onto his shoulder. Even if he were successful, his mission would be for naught if he starved to death before Luthor and Mattie's return.

Glancing once more around the wagon to ensure no one was actively watching him, he set off in pursuit of the roaming guard.

The guard hadn't made it far around the back of the house when Simon turned the rear corner. He jogged to catch up, the nearly thirty-pound bag of fruit flopping heavily on his shoulder as he moved. Despite his pistol being strapped tightly into place on his hip, all his belongings seemed to jostle unnecessarily as he moved, orchestrating a rattling cadence with every step.

Passing the servant's entrance to the home, the guard heard the noise behind him and turned, his hands tightening on the flintlock rifle in his hands. He narrowed his eyes at the man approaching, his appearance blocked by a heavy sack in his hands.

"Who are you?" the guard asked, not maliciously as much as curiously.

Simon didn't break stride as he hoisted the fruit bag and tossed it handily toward the guard. The man froze as he tried to raise his rifle but, instinctually, lifted his hands to catch the heavy bag soaring toward him. The rifle temporarily forgotten, the guard caught the bag in his midriff, nearly knocking the wind from his lungs in the process. The extra weight bent him forward at the waist, and he only partially recovered before Simon struck him handily across the face. The man tumbled to the ground, dragged down by the thirty pounds in his arms. He quickly recovered, shoving the bag off him and opening his mouth to yell a warning when Simon's shoe caught him below the chin. The guard's head snapped backward and his mouth immediately shut. Blood flowed freely and rapidly from the man's mouth, and Simon wondered if he had bitten off part of his tongue in the process.

The guard was still partially conscious, but a second kick to the head left him asleep and bleeding on the house's back porch.

Simon glanced around furtively, unsure if anyone heard the noise of the scuffle. There were a lot of distractions coming from the front of the house and Simon hoped it was enough to conceal their fight. When no one immediately appeared, Simon retrieved his fruit bag and rushed toward the opposite end of the house. He glanced over his shoulder at the unconscious guard but left him where he lay, knowing that the Inquisitor's presence would be discovered soon enough, regardless of the beaten guard prostrate on the ground.

A cautious glance around the building revealed the wagons for which he'd been searching. The man who had carried the glass jars had long since departed and no one else had approached the filled covered wagons. Hurrying across the grassy lawn, he rushed to the back of the nearest wagon and lifted its rearmost flap. A myriad of glass jars stared back at him, packed tightly across the bottom of the carriage.

Simon reached in and removed the closest cork. The pungent smell of lantern oil rolled over him, choking the air from the enclosed space. Simon coughed faintly but left the bottle uncorked. Reaching into his pocket, he pulled out a few of the explosive pouches.

"Explosive" might be a bit of a misnomer, Simon realized. Though packed with gunpowder, the pouches weren't compacted tightly enough to cause a real explosion, but rather would merely flare with sparks and heat. It would do for what Simon had planned, though, as he packed them tightly against the walls of the covered wagon.

Retrieving the remaining pouches, Simon tossed them haphazardly amidst the jars. Though they lacked the power to shatter the thick glass of the oil vessels, their added heat would serve well.

Simon dipped the torch into the oil, soaking the lining of his jacket.

He jammed the torch between a set of jars, ensuring it was wedged tightly into place. Pulling out the sliver of flint and his knife, he worked quickly, lighting the torch. He knew already that time was working against him and it wouldn't be long at all until he was discovered. After a few attempts, the torch lit. The fabric from his jacket burned brilliantly, soaked as it was in oil. The fine weave dissolved quickly in the flame, though, and fragments of smoldering cloth dropped into the wagon.

The Inquisitor stepped around the side of the wagon as the torch burned brightly within. A pair of logs blocked the back wheels, keeping the wagon from rolling away. He quickly kicked aside the one closest before moving toward the far side of the wagon.

A gunshot rang out, and the wood near his shoulder splintered from the impact. Simon jumped in surprise and glanced quickly around. A guard near the horses chambered a second round and took aim. Simon dove behind the wagon as the guard fired again, barely missing the Inquisitor.

"A repeater rifle," Simon bemoaned. He glanced skyward as he drew his revolver. "A bit of karma, even the slightest little bit, would go a long way right about now, you realize? Of course you couldn't just give him a single-shot flintlock rifle like the rest of the guards."

The wheel near his head reverberated as a bullet struck it from the opposite side. Armed townsfolk were coming around the far end of the building, alerted by the sound of gunfire. Simon took aim at the new guards, but the one nearest the horses fired again, forcing the Inquisitor to duck once more.

Growling in frustration, Simon rolled toward the corral of horses and took aim. The guard chambered another round as Simon pulled the trigger. Both weapons fired, but the guard's bullet went far wide as he collapsed into the grass. The horses behind him bucked in fear, their leather thongs nearly pulling the top beam of the hitch out of place.

From his prone position, Simon was able to push the other log out of place near the back wheel. He leapt to his feet despite the rain of gunfire that now filled the air. When he threw his shoulder into the back of the wagon, it started rolling forward of its own volition. Simon ensured it picked up enough speed, pushing it past the nearest wagon before stepping away and letting it careen toward the front of the manor. Raising his pistol, he fired into the back of the wagon. The bullet shattered some of the jars as it passed cleanly through the thick glass. Oil spilled into the back of the wagon. As the oil struck some of the burning pitch falling from the torch, it ignited brilliantly. The flames burned high, igniting the gunpowder pouches. The wagon threw sparks high into the air as its cloth cover was consumed in flames.

Sparks and burning tarp flittered through the air, settling onto other wagons nearby. Their covers, likewise, ignited, and the fire spread unbidden throughout the nearest wagons.

Simon had little time to appreciate his handiwork before a hail of gunfire forced him to turn and run. He could hear the panicked yells of the townsfolk loading the coffins into the wagons and hoped that his wanton destruction continued even as he fled.

He fired blindly behind him as he ran toward the horses. They pulled away at his approach, rocking the top of the hitch. Simon leapt into the air and struck the hitch with his feet. His extra force, coupled with the panicked horses, knocked the top log free from the post. The horses' harnesses unwound from the beam as it rolled away and they stampeded away from the manor house, disappearing into the woods.

Simon used the fleeing horses for cover as he also ran into the woods.

Simon raced through the forest, chased at every step by the pursuing gunfire. Leaves rained down around him as the whizzing bullets destroyed them. Trunks of trees splintered and shattered under the barrage. Simon wanted to return fire but was more than acutely aware that only three bullets remained in his revolver.

They had raced past Whitten Hall proper with all haste; Simon kept his pursuers at bay by remaining in the now familiar woods rather than chancing entry into the outpost. His shoulders and neck ached from carrying the heavy bag of food, but it was a necessary evil. The adrenaline coursing through his system gave him the strength to run on, despite its weight.

Glancing quickly over his shoulder, he looked past the onslaught of muzzle flashes and stared, instead, toward the black pillar of smoke that rose over the tree line. There was no doubt that a good number of wagons had been consumed by the flames and, judging solely from the thickness of the choking smoke, the manor house itself might have been ignited as well.

Ahead, the trees began to thin, something that would be dangerous for Simon. The only reason he remained uninjured was the dense woods through which he ran. Thinning trees would give the hunters a much better chance of putting a bullet somewhere vital.

The ground began sloping gently downward as he reached the top of the valley on the west side of town. The slew of boulders filled the valley, leaving behind a maze of interconnecting pathways. None of which Simon actually knew, he realized morosely, though he doubted the same could be said for Tom and his men.

"I'll kill you when I catch you!" Tom yelled, reaffirming the man's dogged pursuit.

Reaching the crest of the bowl-shaped depression, the Inquisitor glanced quickly left and right. The right continued its graceful downward slope before being intersected by a set of large stones. To his left, a gash appeared in the terrain. Simon remembered walking along the edge of the ravine earlier. At its widest, it was ten feet across. While not an impossible jump, he assumed he was better suited for the leap than those chasing him. It might be the best way to lose his pursuers, at least temporarily.

He turned and raced along the ravine. Behind him, hunters emerged from the woods and continued firing. He felt fire in his arm as a bullet grazed his shoulder. The satchel of fruit tumbled from his wounded shoulder and disappeared into the bushes nearby. Blood seeped into the white dress shirt even as Simon tried to stem the flow with pressure on the wound. Realizing he had no more time, he turned and leapt for the far side of the ravine.

For a glorious moment, it seemed like everything would play out in Simon's favor. That moment passed in a brief, sad moment as the arc of his leap carried him far short of the opposite side of the gully. His eyes widening in surprise, Simon reached out and grasped the lip of the cliff. The exposed stone of the ridge struck him in the chest, knocking the wind out of him even as he sought purchase with his hands. He dug the butt of the pistol into the dirt, refusing to relinquish the weapon. His other hand found only grass, which gave way at the roots as he struggled to maintain his precarious position.

Simon glanced down and saw the fast moving but shallow stream nearly twenty feet below. Dropping wasn't an option he readily considered, until sparks flew from beside him as a bullet barely missed. Dangling as he was, he was exposed and an easy target for the trained hunters.

As the pain grew in his injured shoulder, Simon whimpered and let go with his arms. He dropped heavily into the gloomy ravine. The walls narrowed slightly around him during his quick drop, though he refused to use his hands to retard his descent. He was as likely to break his wrist as he was to effectively slow his fall.

He crashed into the water with a thunderous splash. The stream, if it were even to be called that, was barely two feet deep. His feet struck the rocky bottom of the water first, and he felt something give painfully in his ankle. A scream escaped his lips as he collapsed into the cold water.

Simon grasped his ankle as it immediately began to swell. He didn't know if it was broken or merely sprained, but neither answer appealed to him. Grasping the stones nearby, he clawed his way out of the water and dragged himself under an overhang of rock that would protect him from view from above.

As he pushed himself tightly against the stone wall, Simon shivered from the combination of cold and shock settling over his system. Glancing down at his ankle, he willed it to move. Very slowly, and with great pain, he was able to move his foot slightly up and down. The Inquisitor winced but forced a smile. The ankle wasn't broken. Despite all the complications a badly sprained ankle would cause, a broken ankle would most certainly be a death sentence.

Simon raised his pistol and flipped open the drum. Three casings were spent, and he pulled these from the revolver and dropped them into the dirt. Rotating the drum, he lined up the next round before closing the pistol. He leaned his head back against the stone and sighed, discouraged by his current predicament.

Dirt and stone drifted down past the overhang of rock under which he hid. He pulled his limbs in tightly, ensuring he left nothing visible from above.

"I know you're down there, Inquisitor," Tom Wriggleton yelled from above. "You won't get away from me."

Simon bit back a series of biting retorts, knowing none of them would help in his current situation.

"You are by far the worst, and definitely the most irksome, Royal Inquisitor I've ever met."

Simon shrugged. One stinging retort might not cause too much trouble. "Technically, I'm the only Royal Inquisitor you've met, which makes me, by default, also the best you've ever met."

A bullet crashed harmlessly into the water in front of him, splashing the rocks nearby.

"Tell me, Tom, how are your travel plans progressing?"

More than one gunshot rang out in response. Sparks flew from the rocks nearby, though none came close to striking the concealed Inquisitor.

"I'm going to kill you," Tom yelled back. "I hope you realize that. I'm going to personally find you and your friends and kill you with my bare hands."

Simon smirked at the obvious irritation in the man's voice. "Nonsense. You're merely a pawn, answering to a devilish master. Do you really think your vampire masters will allow you to—?"

"The vampires be damned!" Tom interrupted. "I'll take my punishment after I've killed you all. Better to ask for forgiveness and all that."

Simon frowned deeply. Tom was quickly becoming a liability, one that could greatly hinder his ability to escape with his life. Simon knew he'd only survive if the vampires wanted to personally kill him. With Tom's personal vendetta, Simon's plans were quickly becoming jeopardized.

"If you want me, you know where I am," Simon said. "Why don't you come down and kill me with your bare hands?"

The Inquisitor heard nothing for a long moment before a scuffle broke out above him. Moments later, a yell broke the air and a body crashed into the water. The man groaned from his prone position, even as he tried to retrieve the rifle he had dropped into the stream.

The man caught sight of Simon huddled beneath the overhang. He raised the rifle from the water and pulled the trigger. His efforts were met with only a dry click as the hammer fell forward.

"Your powder got wet," Simon remarked as he raised his pistol.

He fired once, striking the man in the chest. He fell backward with a soft groan before lying still. The water downstream from the body began running red with his seeping blood.

"I do apologize, Tom. Your man appears to have suffered a rather lethal allergic reaction to lead," Simon said. "Perhaps you could come down personally next time?"

Predictably, Tom and his men fired into the gulch. Simon was forced to pull his legs closer to his chest to avoid dangerously close ricochets.

The Inquisitor glanced upstream and noted that the overhang extended for some distance to his left. Stifling a whimper of pain, he forced himself to his feet. The ankle screamed in protest, but it supported his weight well enough for him to walk, albeit slowly.

The drone of gunfire continued unabated for a few minutes, giving him time to slide further away from the hunters. Even as he retreated, the echo of Tom's impetuous curses dogged him.

The ravine splintered into offshoot tributaries a short ways past where Tom and his minions searched for Simon. He chose a branch that led further away from the human hunters. He could hear their movements along the ridges above but caught no sight as he fled.

Simon was forced to pause often to catch his breath, as the pain in his ankle sapped his energy. It radiated through his knee and rested in his hip. His other leg was growing equally as exhausted as he overcompensated for the injury.

His narrow tributary ended abruptly at a sloped incline. Water poured from between a fissure in the rock face, feeding the narrow creek at his feet. The slope was rocky but not impossible to climb, even in his hobbled state. Clenching his jaw against the strain to his ankle, Simon braced himself against an outcropping of rock and began climbing.

His pace was slow, pausing as he did every so often both to rest and strain to hear any sound of pursuit. The ravine had divided so many times that it certainly looked like a river delta when viewed from above. It would be hard to search every branch of the crevice, which boded well for Simon's escape.

The incline crested and quickly fell away on the far side, leading into the boulder-strewn valley. The sun was beginning to set, so much of the day having been spent in either observation or fleeing. Though he didn't envy the thought of being caught outdoors at night with a sprained ankle, the gloom of the impending dusk offered some concealment.

With a heavy sigh, Simon turned away from the valley and scanned the horizon, eventually smiling as he noted his steep hill, at the base of which was his concealed cavern. He could see no signs of Tom or his men, though he was sure they'd be nearby. With awkward steps, he began his slow march back to his cave with the plan to sleep away the next few days.

Martellus examined the burnt husks that had once been his wagons. Nearly half were destroyed, but amongst those remaining were nearly a dozen coffins. They no longer had the supplies necessary for the vampires to evacuate Whitten Hall, something he was sure the Royal Inquisitor had intended.

The chancellor glanced to his left, where a pile of human bodies were stacked. Those foolish enough to be present upon his awakening had paid the ultimate price, satiating his eternal bloodlust. He had heard their pleas, begging for their lives even as they brought word that the Inquisitor had been injured and that it was only a matter of time before he was found. Yet Martellus believed nothing they said. He believed Simon had been injured, of that there was little doubt in his mind. What he doubted was that he would be found unless he absolutely wanted to be.

It wasn't that the humans providing the report were untrustworthy; it was simply that a specific human was curiously absent from the update. Tom Wriggleton, his most trusted human advisor, had managed to avoid briefing the infuriated vampire, offering excuses through the humans present about being called away at the last minute. Tom's absence told Martellus everything he needed to know—the outlook for catching the Inquisitor was poor indeed.

He scowled at the ruins of the wagons as his gaze drifted to the manor house beyond. The right side of the home was charred, its windows shattered and exterior blackened. The fire had been contained before it spread into the house's interior, though the plantation home reeked of smoke, the smell having permeated every inch of fabric within the home.

Martellus clenched his hands into fists, his long nails digging into the flesh of his palm until he felt the bone beneath. Had blood pumped through his veins, it would have poured from his fists and pooled at his feet.

"Sir?" one of the vampires asked as he approached the chancellor. "We can start working on new coffins at once, if that's your order."

The chancellor shook his head. "Begin construction, but I fear it won't matter. The Inquisitor's friends have escaped. They'll bring reinforcements."

"I'll make the humans work through the days and nights until coffins are repaired," the vampire hissed.

Martellus shifted his gaze to the pile of corpses beside the wagon, recalling the similarities to the other humans his men had killed a few nights before. "I don't know if there are enough humans left to make a difference. The Inquisitor has put us at odds with ourselves." The chancellor sighed as he looked back at his family's ruined home. "Push them as hard as you can. We can only hope we'll be quick enough."

The vampire nodded before stepping in close, whispering so that only Chancellor Whitten could hear. "What of the Royal Inquisitor, sir? Let me and my kin hunt him down. We'll bring him to you in pieces."

Martellus shook his head. "No, you've been as useless at finding the Inquisitor as Wriggleton. If you find him, you'll bring him directly to me. He's caused enough trouble that I won't trust his death to anyone else."

The vampire nodded begrudgingly before walking away. Martellus waited for him to go before walking toward an undamaged covered wagon near the head of the convoy. He pulled aside the tarp, exposing a series of innocuous bags. Their loosely tied strings allowed the occasional garment to protrude, only adding to the innocence of the cargo.

Martellus tossed them handily aside until he exposed the white top of the container concealed underneath. He pressed his hand against its lid, feeling the soothing cool seeping through the painted metal. Pulling a key from beneath his tunic, Martellus unlocked the heavy metal lock and pulled it aside. As he opened the metal container, a blast of frigid air poured over him. Ice crystals clung to the edges of the cooler, but his eyes were focused solely on the prize within. Jars of vibrant red blood were carefully placed within, each drop of which was enough to start a new army of vampires, wherever his forces should settle after Whitten Hall.

He had the blood, which meant the elder vampire's usefulness was quickly coming to an end. He would be glad to be rid of the incessant mewling of the ancient creature and his repeated insults of "blood thief".

Martellus quickly closed the lid and replaced the lock. Gesturing toward vampires nearby, they carefully placed the clothing bags back atop the cooler, once again disguising the prized treasures from prying eyes.

CHAPTER Thirty-four

THE PAIN IN SIMON'S ANKLE EBBED AND FLOWED, RIS-
ing acutely in waves that settled into his lower abdomen before
receding to a mere ache. He longed to cradle the ankle or, at the
very least, to massage it whenever the pain flared. In the confines of his
small cave, however, he barely had the space to prop himself up, much
less to care for his injuries.

Despite the anguish in his leg, it was his shoulder that concerned
him far more. He could feel the heat radiating from the cut where the
bullet had grazed his arm. Upon escaping Tom and his hunters, Simon
had tried his best to treat the wound but had been able to do little to stave
off the burgeoning infection.

The heat now radiated up his neck and rested in his temples, where
he could feel each pulse of his heartbeat roaring past his ears. Every inch
of his body ached as it struggled against the rapidly spreading infection.
His brow was drenched in sweat and his shirt, already filthy from evading
his pursuers, was now matted to his body.

Within the narrow width of the cave, Simon alternated bringing his
knees to his chest before extending his legs. Nothing felt comfortable. He
had left the cave a few times, once to collect his discarded fruit and another to collect as much drinking water as possible from the small stream

at the base of the ravine, but standing upright was exhausting. Even slipping cautiously outside to relieve himself felt like a chore. Though he knew the movement would be good rehabilitation for his sprained ankle, it did little other than sap his strength.

The Inquisitor had only the faintest of ideas as to the day. He had marked the inside of his cavern with a sharp stone each time he saw the sun rise, though he couldn't be certain he saw every sunrise. Most of his day was spent sleeping, a necessary and involuntary bodily reaction as he tried to heal. By his count, it had been four days since Luthor and Mattie departed and two full days since his injury, but those were merely guesses.

Discouraged, Simon rolled to his side and retrieved an apple. Brown spots had already appeared along the tough exterior. The interior was still juicy and satisfying, despite a much softer texture than he remembered. He laid his head back as he chewed, savoring the moisture on his lips.

The heat of his body had left him feeling perpetually dehydrated. His tongue often stuck to the roof of his mouth every time he tried to swallow. Running his tongue across his lips felt as futile as dragging a broom over a sand dune. The water seemed to do little to satisfy the unending thirst. It gave him slight reprieves from the burning in his gut, but every drink seemed to sit on his stomach, only increasing his hunger.

Sighing wearily, Simon laid his head back onto the cool, hard stone ground of the cavern. The faint streams of light seeping from around the edges of the capstone were enough to illuminate the small cave, though it only offered a glimpse of weather-worn stones pressed closely overhead. The Inquisitor was eternally grateful that he was petrified of water and not enclosed spaces. Claustrophobia would have made his current predicament a living hell.

"You look terrible, sir," Luthor said from the end of the cave.

Simon glanced toward his feet. The apothecary sat cross-legged just beyond the tips of Simon's shoes, his face obscured by the darker shadows.

"Thank you for your vote of confidence," Simon muttered through a parched throat.

"It wasn't meant to boost your confidence, merely to state a glaringly obvious fact."

Logically, Simon knew that the cave ceiling was far too shallow for someone to sit upright, nor was the cave deep enough for someone to position themselves past Simon's shoes. The logical realization of his situation only further upset the Inquisitor.

"You're not real, of course," Simon said, returning his gaze to the rocks overhead.

"Of course," Luthor replied, "but aren't you far happier talking to a familiar face than spending another day alone in this dark cave? Speaking of which, I seem to remember you preferring a far better caliber establishment in the past."

Simon laughed drily. "You seem to have forgotten the quality of the inn in Whitten Hall, or the fur-lined huts amongst the tribesmen outside Haversham."

"I can't very well forget them, sir, since I'm in your head."

Simon frowned, the mirth suddenly drained from the situation. Imaginary Luthor was correct that he was glad to have a familiar face with which he could talk, but the implications of seeing a friend who wasn't there wasn't lost on him.

"I'm dying, aren't I?" Simon asked.

Luthor shrugged in the dark. "How am I supposed to know, sir? I'm just a painful hallucination caused by an unmitigated fever burning through your body. Though, when put that way, yes, sir, there's a good chance you're dying."

"You're rather insolent today."

Luthor shook his head. "Actually, sir, *you're* rather insolent. I'm merely a figment of your imagination."

Simon rolled away from Luthor, turning his face toward the wall. "All those times I wished you were here, keeping me company? I've suddenly changed my mind."

He could hear the scuffling in the cave, as Luthor shifted positions. Though, he realized, he actually heard nothing at all. There was no Luthor, which meant there was no one who could shift positions.

"It's getting a bit confusing, isn't it, sir?" Luthor asked, his voice nearby.

"More than you could possibly realize," Simon muttered. "There's no escaping you, is there?"

Luthor shrugged. "Possibly, though somehow, I believe that's entirely up to you. Maybe your fevered subconscious needs something familiar to which it can cling as your body tries to heal. Maybe you're just lonely, sir. Maybe you've always longed to be accepted and part of a family and, though you'd never admit as much to me in person, Matilda and I have become the closest thing you have to a real family. Maybe you just miss us."

Simon stared unwaveringly toward the wall in front of him. He wasn't sure if imaginary Luthor was vocalizing Simon's own buried thoughts or if, like he was prone to do with so many others, Simon was merely belittling himself.

A scuffling came from beyond the cave entrance. Simon fell silent, holding his breath as he always did when he feared the hunters had returned. No one had discovered his secret spot, though that was hardly surprising. The ground around the cave was rock, allowing for no footprints that the human townsfolk could follow. The capstone itself was one amongst dozens in the rocky terrain, nondescript from the others nearby. Aside from literally leaving no stone unturned, they were unlikely to find him, concealed as he was.

"They're persistent," Luthor said.

"Hush!" Simon whispered harshly.

Luthor laughed, though his voice failed to echo in the enclosed space. "They can't hear me, sir. I don't have to be quiet."

Simon frowned and stretched his arm. It burned as he moved it, the thin gash oozing as he strained against the haggard scab forming over the wound. The pain radiated through his neck, temporarily seizing the muscles and stiffening his shoulders.

The sound of booted feet continued outside for a short while. For a moment, Simon could hear them climbing the steep hillside on which he'd perched more than once, searching for Luthor's—the real Luthor's—return. A short time later, the sound of scraping arose as someone slid down the hill. As quickly as they had come, the sound of footsteps receded until once again everything fell silent.

"As I was saying, sir," Luthor said, "Tom Wriggleton is a very persistent man. He intends to kill you rather than turn you over to his vampiric overlords."

"I know," Simon replied.

"He's a bishop."

Simon arched an eyebrow and rolled toward Luthor, though in hindsight, he assumed the action was unnecessary. His imaginary friend could hear him no matter how he lay. He winced as his injured arm pressed against the stone and Simon, instead, resolved himself to lying on his back while continuing his one-person conversation.

Simon knew Luthor wasn't referring to the religious figure when he mentioned a bishop. The Inquisitor's mind immediately fell to the domed marble figure on the chessboard in his study.

Luthor rested his hands on his knees as he continued. "On a chessboard, there are pawns, rooks, and kings. They're easy to figure out. They move, mostly, in straight lines. To me—well, to you—the bishop was always a perplexing piece. No matter how much you stared at a chessboard, the movements of the bishop were always hard to see until they struck. Tom is a bishop. You even know his movement, but his diagonal moves will perplex you until you remove him from the board."

Simon remained silent as he stared at the ceiling. He knew what Luthor was insinuating. The same thought had crossed his mind earlier. Simon frowned… of course the same thought had crossed his mind.

"Not now," Luthor said. "Rest now, sir, since you're awfully tired."

Simon stifled a yawn. He turned his head toward his friend, despite the stiffness in his neck. The area of the cave where Luthor had been sitting was empty and Simon was alone. The heat in the cave was intense as it radiated from his body, but the warmth was also soothing and within moments, Simon was asleep.

Simon awoke to the gloom of the cavern. A cool breeze blew from between the crevices between the capstone and the rock walls, a cool wind that soothed his sweat-soaked skin. He breathed deeply, sucking in lungs full of the cooling air and sighing blissfully.

The Inquisitor's skin no longer burned with an inner fire. Though his clothing was matted to his body and his once well-coifed hair dripped sweat, the fever had broken at some point during the night. He turned merrily toward the far end of the narrow cavern, but his illusionary companion wasn't there. For a pained moment, Simon felt conflicting emotions. He was glad that his feverish hallucination was gone but it only strengthened his sadness at being alone, without his erstwhile friend.

He brought his legs up toward his chest and noted the pain in his ankle was still present, though it waned from the acute pangs that had previously existed. The nausea in his stomach was also gone but had been replaced by a yearning, hollow sensation. It was a hunger that he had never felt before that left him feeling ill for an entirely different reason. He sought the satchel of fruit within the cave and retrieved yet another soiled apple. The bruising on the fruit was far more advanced than he remembered and the taste of its flesh was slightly bitter. Despite the early stages of decay, he devoured the apple and quickly retrieved a second.

With food in his belly, he forced aside the capstone. Brilliant sunlight flooded into the cave, blinding Simon. Pain lanced behind his eyeballs as his vision tried to absorb the outpouring of white light. He blinked furiously until his vision cleared, leaving behind dancing blue spots that colored his sight.

The sun was shining, though Simon's small stretch of rocky terrain was empty. He had the land to himself for the moment. He turned toward the hilltop behind him as he took a step forward. His ankle angrily protested, but it was healed enough to support his weight. He grasped the lowest protruding tree branch and pulled himself up to the first level of the sloped hillside.

Though the climb caused minor pain both in his ankle and arm, Simon climbed to the top of the hill. The view was still unfettered, though there was still nothing on the horizon that offered a reprieve from the cat-and-mouse game he'd been playing with both the humans and the vampires. Sitting on the hilltop, Simon smiled wistfully. It had been some time since he'd encountered a vampire, choosing instead to remain hidden in his cave whenever the sun set. He had no idea the damage or infuriation he had caused when he destroyed the wagons, but he certainly hoped it was enough to delay, if not completely stop, the vampires' retreat from Whitten Hall.

Retrieving a sharp rock from the hill's apex, he carved three more lines beside the other two already present. If Luthor and Mattie stuck to the train's timeline, he was just past halfway through his time at the outpost. It would be at least another two or three days until their return.

Simon felt a weight in his chest at the thought. He had only barely survived a dangerous infection caused by a gunshot and nearly broken his ankle jumping into a ravine. Though healthier now, his body was drained and exhausted. His heart was still racing from the short climb up the hill. If this small exertion was any indication, it would be nearly impossible to once again outrun the human pursuers, much less a vampire during the night.

Still, there was something he could do to lessen the pursuit. He frowned at the thought, knowing it went against his best moral standings, yet there was no real love lost. Slowly, careful not to reinjure his ankle, Simon slid down the hill and crept back into his cave, awaiting the setting of the sun.

Simon leaned back in the chair, savoring the room's cool interior. He glanced out the dirt-smeared window. In the distance, barely visible through the myriad of trees, torches and lanterns burned in Whitten Hall. The faint sound of sawing and hammering crept into the room, even from this great a distance.

The humans were busy reconstructing all the coffins destroyed by Simon's escapade. It would take them a while to complete their work, no doubt, but their vampire lords were driving them day and night. The chancellor and his ilk were more than acutely aware what would happen if they were still present when Luthor and Mattie returned.

Despite their best efforts, Simon doubted they'd finish in time. Certainly, they'd do their best, but a mere three more days was hardly enough time to complete not just the coffins but the major repairs on the damaged wagons. Even foregoing food and supplies for the mortals amongst them, there weren't enough wagons remaining for the coffins.

Simon shrugged in the dark. He presumed the vampires could leave some of their own behind, just taking those closest to Martellus when they departed town. Honestly, Simon hoped they would. Let those being informed that they'd be left behind revolt against those leaving Whitten Hall. Let the vampires eat their own for once.

He turned his gaze away from the window and let his eyes readjust to the thick darkness within the bedroom. A small table was pushed underneath the window, on which a tin print photograph of a woman was painted. Her features were hard to discern in the low light, but she looked pretty. There was no telling what had happened to the pretty girl in the photo. She might have left Whitten Hall some time ago or never came in the first place. More likely than not, she was rotting on a pile of other husks in the mines, her once pretty features emaciated and ruined.

A faint snore caught Simon's attention, and he turned toward the room's single narrow bed. A man was asleep beneath the thin blanket, his head resting comfortably on a down-filled pillow. Simon frowned, more aware than ever of the aches and pains throughout his own body from sleeping and convalescing on cold rock.

He didn't need to see the man's features to feel the bile in the back of his throat. Simon considered himself a relatively levelheaded man, his emotions usually kept fairly well in check. Yet the man beneath the covers upset him greatly.

The Inquisitor drew the knife from his belt, deftly spinning the blade in his hand. Tom Wriggleton was asleep and oblivious to the night's intruder. A part of Simon wanted to wake Tom, to let him understand the errors of his ways before the Inquisitor did… what needed to be done.

Instead, Simon stood and stepped to the bedside without a sound. Tom snorted as he rolled onto his back. Simon paused, waiting for the man's steady circadian sleep to return.

In his sleep, Tom licked his lips before sighing. Almost immediately, the steady snore of a man deep in sleep returned.

Simon clamped his hand over Tom's mouth to stifle any chance at screams as he plunged the knife into the sleeping man's chest. The blade easily split Tom's nightshirt and slid into the flesh between his ribs. Tom's eyes shot open in surprise, but almost immediately lost their focus. The knife continued unabated until it passed cleanly through Tom's heart and struck a rib near his shoulder blades.

Simon kept his hand over Tom's mouth for a second longer, even as the man's eyes fluttered and fell closed once more. A warm breath caressed the inside of Simon's hand as Tom breathed his last, slumping into bed once more as though merely falling back into sleep.

After a moment longer, Simon removed his hand, though he left the knife in place. Turning away from the body, he walked calmly back to the chair. He took his seat, staring at the mound of blankets and the man beneath, the silhouette broken only by the protruding hilt of the dagger.

"You won't hear this admonition," Simon began, his voice filling the room, "since you're long past caring about the goings on of the living. Then again, perhaps that's not true. I suppose I should reconsider the notion of ghosts, since I've been embroiled now with both werewolves and vampires, but I hardly believe you're sitting on the other side eavesdropping on your killer's diatribe."

Simon leaned forward, resting his elbows on his knees. "I'm truthfully saying all this for my own edification, more than a cry of grief or an attempt at forgiveness from you."

Simon looked down at his hands, noting the droplets of blood near the tips of his fingers. He took a handkerchief from the table beside him and absently wiped his hands as he continued.

"You may not believe this, but I didn't kill you out of malice. I didn't care for you, of that you can be certain, but it wasn't hatred that drove that knife into your chest. You became too personally involved in my demise and your feverish pursuit would have ruined my carefully devised plans. For that alone, you had to die."

Simon leaned back in the chair, listening to it creak under his weight. "I would ask your forgiveness for one thing. Forgive me for slaying you the cowardly way, stabbing you through your heart in your sleep. It wasn't the brave actions of a Royal Inquisitor and for that, I do apologize. Some things, however, just need to be done with a bit more discretion than pistols at dawn."

Standing abruptly, Simon replaced the now-bloodstained handkerchief on the table. He winced as he put pressure on his ankle but it was now only tender, rather than damaged. Limping to the bedside, he pulled the blade free with some effort.

"Forgive my abrupt departure, but there is still much to be done in the next few days."

Simon began to turn toward the bedroom door but paused. Turning back toward Tom, the Inquisitor leaned over and gently cradled Tom's head in his hand. As he lifted it upward, he slid the down pillow off the bed before dropping Tom unceremoniously back onto the mattress.

"It's nothing personal, but I'm sure I'll get much better use out of this than you will."

Simon glanced backward once more as he exited the room, the pillow tucked under his arm. Tom's death would cause an uproar, but it would also grant a slight reprieve on the perpetual hunt. Cut off the head of the snake and… Simon paused as he realized the analogy didn't truly work in this instance. The body wouldn't die, but at least it would be a touch longer before a new head emerged.

With a shrug of his shoulders, Simon left the room.

CHAPTER Thirty-Five

A FAINT WHISTLE INVADED SIMON'S SLUMBER. FOR A moment, he refused to acknowledge the offending noise, instead pulling his newly acquired pillow closer to him and burying his face in its fluffiness.

There was an eerie familiarity to the whistle. It pulled at recent memories and yearned for Simon's conscious attention, which the Inquisitor quite readily denied. The noise came with a warning or, more precisely, a casual reminder of something important.

A reminder of something important for which Simon was impatiently waiting.

It was a reminder of something that would save Simon's life.

By the time the second whistle blew, Simon was fully awake. The train whistle was distant still, barely piercing the cocoon in which he had slept and lived intermittently for the past six days. Despite its faintness, Simon scrambled within the close confines to collect whatever belongings he still had. He slipped his pistol into its holster, despite the ridiculously few bullets still at his disposal. The knife, cleaned after the previous night's unfortunate business, slipped into his belt.

He glanced around expectantly, but he realized that there was only one more possession of his that he had not yet claimed. Reaching toward his feet, he collected his top hat and pulled it toward his chest.

Thusly prepared, Simon pushed aside the protective capstone and slid out into the morning sunlight.

The whistle sounded again, a high, chilling noise that gave him goose bumps that had nothing to do with the cool morning's air. Limping slightly, Simon quickly scaled the side of the hill behind him and took his place on its apex. He raised a hand to his forehead, blocking out the glare of the rising sun. The sun was behind him, but it painted the forest and valley in brilliant shades of yellow and orange.

The gash of railroad tracks cut through the woods, a barren, winding strip amidst the densely packed trees. His eyes traced the tracks as they approached the horizon. There, at the extreme end of what he could see from his perch, a greasy, gray pillar of smoke rose into the air.

Glancing down, Simon noted the five scratches in the stone beside him. He picked up a loose shard of rock and carved a sixth line. For a moment, he merely stared at the marks. The train was early by two days. It wasn't random happenstance, Simon realized. This train was meant for him. Luthor and Mattie had not only survived but had delivered his note.

The realization of what was on the train left a solemn dichotomy of emotions within him. He was elated, to be sure, that his saviors had arrived. His weakened state surely wouldn't have survived another two days or, if it had, he wasn't sure he would have kept the vampires contained within Whitten Hall. Conversely, the train was death—a black vileness contained within the winding rail cars, a grim reaper seated within each of its passenger compartments. The world of Whitten Hall would soon be irrevocably changed by his actions.

Another blast of the train's whistle broke Simon from his musings. He slid quickly back down the hill, the path before him predetermined by the events of the past week. There was still much to do, to ensure everyone was in their proper place for the train's arrival.

He staggered off into the woods, intentionally crashing through the underbrush. His movements reverberated between the trees, sending small creatures hurtling through the brush to escape the noise. Birds took flight from the high branches of the canopy overhead.

Simon paused briefly and frowned. Every other day of his self-imposed guerrilla war, Tom Wriggleton's human cohorts would have flocked to the sound of Simon charging like a bull through the trees. They would have been patrolling the area, searching for him day after day.

Tom wouldn't have let them rest until he was sure the Inquisitor would be found. Yet, Simon quickly realized, there was no Tom any longer. He had eliminated the man from the board for that very reason. Now, when he needed to find some of the townsfolk, they were curiously absent, an unfortunate side effect of his actions. Despite the minor setback, Simon knew where to find people if he really needed them.

His path was unerring as he pushed on through the woods. Within minutes, the outskirts of Whitten Hall were visible through the trees. The sound of his own movements was quickly masked by the sounds of sawing and hammering, of yells of warning and encouragement.

Simon stepped into the street that ran between the railroad tracks and the town's storefronts. The street was a busy affair as the final touches were being put on the repaired wagons and piles of refurbished and newly crafted coffins were gathered in preparation for a near-future move from the outpost.

The Inquisitor ran a hand over his moustache, despite the fact that his telltale facial hair had long since disappeared into a new black beard that coated his face. Foregoing smoothing the moustache, he instead removed his top hat and ran a hand through his hair, smoothing down the unruly mop upon his head. His hands came away oily, and he scowled at the feeling. He would kill for a proper bath and a shave, both of which he hoped to soon have.

A worker nearby happened to glance over and see the Inquisitor standing defiantly in the middle of the road, his feet spread and his hands braced against his hips. He let out a cry of alarm that drew the attention of others nearby.

An angry mob rushed toward him, but Simon offered no resistance. As they grew close, he carefully withdrew both his revolver and knife and dropped them into the dirt at his feet before raising his hands above his head.

"I surrender," he said, having to raise his voice to be heard over the din of excitement and anger.

Rough hands grabbed him and forced him to his knees. Someone called for ropes, which quickly appeared. His hands were bound, and he was dragged toward the center of town.

"Someone find Gregory," one of the townsfolk ordered. "He'll want to see this bastard!"

Simon swallowed hard and tried his best to look solemn and defeated, despite the excitement and dread that was bubbling within him.

He was dropped unceremoniously into the dirt, his hands bound and unable to break his fall. A cloud of dust raised around him, forcing him to cough hoarsely. He tried to roll so that his face was no longer buried in the dirt but booted feet pressed down on his back, forcing him further into the packed earth of the road. Simon closed his mouth, save for a small opening at the corner through which he could draw air.

Aside from those holding him in place, the rest of the townsfolk formed a circle around him but kept their distance. He had earned a healthy respect from the people of Whitten Hall, rightly deserved after all the destruction and death he had caused.

From his prone perspective, Simon saw the crowd part and large, powerful legs approach. This was a moment that Simon feared, since revenge was a strong emotion that often overrode common sense.

The bartender reached down and grasped Simon's hair. Gregory jerked his arm upward, dragging Simon from the ground. The Inquisitor winced at the burly man's firm grip but didn't shrink away, even as he was turned to meet the man's gaze.

Gregory's eyes burned with hatred, but his anger was tempered by the knowledge that Chancellor Whitten had demanded Simon be brought to him alive.

A jagged and curved scar ran the length of Gregory's cheek, a puckered mess that was still red and inflamed. It gave the already large man a monstrous appearance.

Pulling Simon close, Gregory sneered at the Inquisitor. "I would… I want nothing more…"

He started his sentence a number of times; in all instances his words failed him as he was overcome with anger. Gregory reached up with his free hand and wiped away spittle that had accumulated on his lips.

"Were it not for the chancellor's personal request to keep you alive, I would flay the skin from your bones right here in front of everyone."

Simon nodded, relieved that common sense would, indeed, prevail. "Then it's lucky for me that he made such a request."

Gregory reared back and struck Simon across the cheek with the back of his hand. The Inquisitor tumbled back into the dirt, groaning at the burst of heat he felt rising on his skin. He felt the first trickle of blood seeping from a split beneath his eye.

The bartender reached down and forced Simon back to his knees, clenching the collar of his shirt tightly between his massive hands.

"You'll be alive," Gregory explained, "but I'll be damned if you'll be coherent by the time you see the chancellor."

Releasing his shirt with one hand, the bartender drew back his fist and slammed it down onto Simon's nose. The Inquisitor heard the cartilage crack from the strike, and his head rocked backward until he stared at the sky. His top hat rolled from his head into the dirt. The blue, cloudless sky grew suddenly blurry as tears filled his vision.

Blood dripped down his throat, and he choked momentarily before he was able to force his head upright again. He coughed and blood flew from his mouth unintentionally, splattering Gregory's tunic. The bartender glanced down at the mess, growing even more infuriated.

He struck Simon once more in the face, this time between his eyes. Colors exploded in the Inquisitor's vision and his thoughts grew blurred. A single thought slid through the haze that had overcome his mind:

Despite Gregory's realization that the chancellor wanted Simon alive, there was a good chance the burly man would kill him here in the dirt.

Simon didn't want to die in the dirt. He just had to hold on for a little while longer.

He barely registered the next punch that landed, this one further opening the gash under his eye. Blood poured from the wound, soaking into his beard and dripping from his chin. Simon could taste copper in his mouth but he daren't spit out the blood again, else he only encouraged Gregory to strike him again.

"Gregory, I think he's had enough," someone said from the surrounding townsfolk.

"He's had enough when I fecking say he's had enough," the bartender yelled.

As Gregory drew back his fist again, the air was split by a train's whistle. The blast was joined by the sound of brakes being applied. Metal screeched against metal, and sparks filled the air as the engine of a train rolled into view.

Simon tried his best to suppress a smile, but it rose unbidden on his lips.

Gregory released Simon's shirt and the Inquisitor fell into the dirt, lacking the strength to hold himself up. The townsfolk turned as one and watched the train slide into the station. It wasn't a long train, consisting of only the engine and a couple of cargo cars, their sides concealed by taut tarps rather than sliding doors. The last two cars were passenger cars, though the interiors were dimly lit and it was hard to see how many people were onboard.

"The train's not due yet," someone offered.

"It's early," replied someone else. Simon couldn't see who spoke, though it mattered little.

"Are we expecting the train?" someone nearby asked.

The bartender shook his head. "No, we're not."

Simon coughed and spit a mouth full of blood onto the dry dirt road. "You may not be, but I am."

Before anyone could reply, the door to one of the passenger cars opened and a man stepped off. He wore a brown tweed suit and seemed terribly uncomfortable in Whitten Hall's heat and humidity. The barrel of a long rifle protruded from over his shoulder, held in place by a leather strap drawn across the man's chest. Reaching up, the man removed his hat and wiped the sweat from his bald head.

"Ladies and gentlemen of Whitten Hall," the man said as he replaced his hat. His voice carried clearly as the townsfolk fell into a hush. "My name is Royal Inquisitor Creary, a member in good standing of the Order of Kinder Pel."

The hush became a low, worried murmur at the mention of the Pellites. Even somewhere as distal as Whitten Hall knew the ruthless reputation of the Order of Kinder Pel. Simon lay back on the dirt road and stared up at the blue sky overhead as Inquisitor Creary continued.

"It has come to our attention that you have been colluding with mystical creatures, in direct violation of the edicts put forth by the King of Ocker. You will immediately surrender to the Order and face judgment. You have five seconds to respond."

The townsfolk glanced nervously toward Gregory, who stood defiantly amongst his brethren.

"Four," Creary counted.

Gregory tilted his chin upward defiantly. "You're mistaken, Inquisitor. There are no monsters here."

"Three," the Pellite said, unfazed by the bartender's feeble lies.

"There's nothing devious happening here," the bartender said, his stoic visage cracking as his gaze shifted to the seated figures within the passenger cars. "There are no monsters in Whitten Hall."

"Two."

"Is it your fellow Inquisitor?" Gregory asked, motioning toward the battered Simon. "Take him. Take whatever you want. We're not here to cause trouble."

"One."

Gregory blanched before gesturing wildly toward those around him. "Shoot him! Someone shoot him!"

Simon closed his eyes as he felt a pang of guilt pierce his chest. He knew what was to come and didn't want to see it unfold.

"Judgment has been passed," Creary replied calmly, seemingly oblivious to the weapons being drawn and pointed in his direction.

The snapping of ropes preceded the tarps falling away from the sides of the train's cargo cars. As they fell to the ground, it revealed Pellites standing within, manning a series of Gatling guns pointed dangerously toward the townsfolk of Whitten Hall.

Gregory dropped to the ground as the Pellites spun the cranks on the sides of the machine guns. The weapons roared to life, spitting fire in a steady stream as bullet after bullet flew from their barrels.

The bullets tore into the startled townsfolk, tearing them apart even as they tried to shift their aim to the new threats. Screams of anguish filled the air as blood splattered onto the dry, thirsty earth. Simon could only imagine the absolute horror of what was occurring around him. In his mind's eye, the massacre was far worse than what he had witnessed by the werewolves, demons, or vampires thus far.

Shell casings dropped noisily to the steel floor of the train car as the Pellites fed belts of ammunition into the Gatling guns. The barrels turned red from the heat yet the gunners didn't slow their steady assault, swinging the barrels left to right as they strafed the townsfolk.

The sound of gunfire and of bullets whizzing dangerously close overhead continued for what seemed like an eternity as Simon lay bleeding on the ground. His face was ablaze from the damage dealt and his ears now rang steadily from the battle. Nausea rose unabated from his gut, and he wanted to vomit as he heard bodies fall lifelessly to the ground all around him. Screams of anguish filled the air from those who were merely injured, though Simon doubted their screams would last much longer. Pellites didn't take prisoners. They came for one purpose only—a mission of cleansing within Whitten Hall. Worst of all, Simon had intentionally brought them here.

As the belts ran dry, the Gatling guns stopped firing one after another. The last few pops of gunfire dwindled to nothing, leaving the air filled with an eerie quiet. Even the screams of pain seemed distant without the harmony of bullets flying overhead.

Simon opened his eyes, staring once again toward the blue sky above him. He sighed heavily, despite the pain it caused in his broken nose and split cheek, before pushing himself up to his elbows. He faced the storefronts as he slowly rose and, to his dismay, the sea of bodies that had once been the inhabitants of Whitten Hall. Simon cringed as the sand grew ever more red with blood, the liquid no longer being absorbed by the thirsty sand and, instead, sitting atop it like a lake.

Glancing over his shoulder, Simon saw the train and the Pellites still mounted in the compartments. Creary stood before the door, as he had been upon his arrival, his face still a steely mask of disinterest. He didn't seem bothered by how close he had come to death or the slaughter that had been initiated on his command.

To Simon's surprise, someone leapt from the pile of bodies beside the Inquisitor and ran toward the far end of town. The burly bartender, who had avoided the hail of gunfire in a selfish act of self-preservation, sprinted toward the chancellor's manor house and the mine beyond.

Simon tried to call out a warning to the Pellites, knowing that a single warning to the vampires would be disastrous to their assault on the mines, but his warning was unnecessary. Inquisitor Creary slid his rifle free from his back. On top of the long rifle was mounted a complex scope of brass and bronze. A series of glass lenses jutted from the side of the scope like jeweler's lenses, each magnifying the image to a greater degree.

Creary glanced toward the fleeing bartender and bit his inner lip. Simon turned toward Gregory as well, noting with surprise how far the large man had run in such a short time. He was easily outside the range of Simon's pistol, and the Inquisitor even doubted he would have been able to shoot the man with a rifle either. Creary, however, looked unbothered by the distance. He flipped a pair of lenses into place before pulling the stock of the rifle into his shoulder. For a moment, he didn't move, just merely aimed at the burly man quickly receding into the distance. With a smooth trigger pull, the rifle fired. Gregory staggered for a second before dropping facedown onto the ground. With a faint smile, Creary lowered the rifle before turning his attention back to the injured Simon.

"Simon!" Mattie yelled as she stepped from the train.

Simon's previous misery was washed away at the sight of his friend.

It was increased exponentially as Luthor climbed down the stairs beside her, each step labored as he used his cane far more for support than merely aesthetics.

The apothecary smiled broadly at the sight of the Inquisitor, though even from the distance, Simon could see the man's obvious concern at Simon's appearance.

Simon pushed himself to his knees as he tried to stand, though his ankle, shoulder, and face all ached at the attempt. The two companions rushed to Simon's side and, bracing him under the arms, helped him to his feet.

"Sir, you look dreadful," Luthor said.

"It's good to see you too, Luthor."

Simon pulled the surprised apothecary into a tight embrace. Slowly, Luthor's arms slipped around his mentor and they hugged, glad to be in one another's presence once more.

"You came back for me," Simon said wearily.

Luthor slipped from Simon's embrace and smiled at his friend. "Was there ever any doubt?"

As Luthor released the Inquisitor, Simon almost fell to the ground once more. Mattie and Luthor caught him and supported him as best as possible.

"We need to get you some help," Mattie replied, quickly breaking the awkwardness of the situation. "Come, Simon, let's get you to the train where you can sit and rest."

As they walked away from the bloodshed, the gunners climbed down from the train and drew pistols before moving amongst the dying and dead townsfolk. Simon kept his head stoically forward, despite the lurch he felt as the first gunshot rang out behind him, forever silencing one person's pleading cry of anguish.

They helped Simon toward the open doors of the cargo cars, where he sat heavily on the steel edge of the train. Though he had been tired and in pain before, the weight of his ordeal seemed to settle on his shoulder even heavier as the stress of his very survival lifted. His chin lowered to his chest, and he merely stared at the ground below. Mattie and Luthor glanced at one another nervously, though they granted Simon the peace and quiet he so clearly desired.

Inquisitor Creary walked toward Simon as the rest of the Pellites, a veritable army of men, dismounted from the passenger cars. They wielded a myriad of weapons as though armed for war.

"It's good to see you still alive, Inquisitor Whitlock," the bald Pellite said.

Simon glanced up at the man with tired eyes, but he didn't offer a response.

Creary merely nodded, as though expecting the response. "You did the right thing in calling us, though admittedly, I was surprised to receive your letter."

Simon glanced toward the bodies sitting under the blazing sun. "I'm not entirely convinced that I did do the right thing."

"Regardless, what's done is done. Now we have a mission to complete."

"Better the devil you know, right Creary?" Simon asked.

Creary sneered at the insult, one that was especially painful to a Pellite, who fought against magic and demons in all their forms. "Where are the vampires, Simon?"

Simon glanced at the man, staring at him intently for a long moment before gesturing toward the road out of town. "You'll find a mine only a few miles down that road. The vampires have made their home within."

Inquisitor Creary smiled, though it lacked the charisma it did with most men. "We have a physician with us who will tend to your wounds. Whether you accept it or not, you've done a great service to your kingdom and the crown."

Simon looked away from the Pellite and stared, instead, at the dead men strewn across the ground. He felt disgusted with himself, far more than he was with Creary.

"We're not your enemy, Simon," Creary said as he leaned forward "They are. Not just the vampires but the townsfolk who would rather side with abominations like vampires than the crown. You may not always agree with the Order's methods, and your facial expression tells me all that your mouth refuses to say, but we yearn for the same thing—peace and tranquility within the kingdom."

When Simon didn't reply, Creary leaned back and glanced over his shoulder to where his fellow Pellites were lighting torches.

"You asked us to be here, and it was your mission to begin with. What will you have us do about the vampires?"

"What of those inside?" the Pellite asked.

Simon looked at the Pellites surrounding him, with their weapons drawn and torches held aloft despite the brightness of the midday sun.

They came to serve justice against the abominations within the mine, but Simon didn't see justiciars standing before him.

They were a lynch mob. In another time not so long past, nooses would have replaced their swords.

Simon glanced morosely down the road, toward the entrance to the mine. He had condemned the townsfolk to death. Though there was only one response to Creary's question, he hesitated anyway. As the memories of his abuse at the hands of his captives, the saddened expression hardened into a steely resolve.

"They made their choice and now must bear its burden," he replied. "Kill them all."

CHAPTER Thirty-six

THE PHYSICIAN GINGERLY TOUCHED SIMON'S NOSE. The Inquisitor winced, feeling the cracked cartilage as the doctor probed the flattened bridge.

"Forgive me, but this will hurt," the older physician said. "I have to reset the broken nose or it will heal poorly."

Simon glanced pleadingly toward Luthor. The apothecary held up a flask in his hand with a sad smile.

"What's in it?" Simon asked, his voice sounding nasally to his ears.

"Do you really want to know?" Luthor asked. He shook the flask, letting the liquid within slosh against the metal container.

Simon shook his head and took the flask. "Not in the least."

The liquid burned like fire as it poured down his throat. It felt thick, like it was coating his esophagus as it passed. The fire in his belly felt far worse than even his sprained ankle, but it quickly converted to general warmth that spread through his limbs.

Simon coughed softly before taking a second draw. "Okay, doctor, I believe I'm ready now."

The physician worked quickly, with a practiced stroke. His thumbs pressed toward one another on either side of his nose, and everyone heard an audible crack. Simon jerked involuntarily, though he realized afterward that there was little pain. In retrospect, he didn't remember his shoulder or cheek aching as badly either.

The physician smiled a crooked but wizened smile. He reached up and wiped away a bit of sweat from the gray hair above his ears. "We still need to suture your cheek and wrap your ankle, sir, before I can release you."

"Nothing for the shoulder?" Mattie asked as she touched the scabbed wound.

Simon flinched and pulled away, glancing incredulously toward the redhead.

"The wound is already healing and to suture it, I would have to completely reopen the injury. It will leave a remarkable scar if left untended, of that you can be certain."

Simon shook his head. "Leave it. This injury and I have had our words and have now come to a mutually beneficial understanding."

Luthor glanced at his mentor with a raised eyebrow, but Simon offered no explanation.

The doctor withdrew a curved needle and some thread and set to work closing the open gash underneath Simon's eye. Simon averted his gaze, glancing instead toward the apothecary.

"I'm glad to see you and Miss Hawke escaped the vampires."

"Please don't talk while I'm working, sir," the physician ordered.

Luthor sat down beside his mentor. "It was a tiresome chase for the first night, certainly, sir, but they quickly lost interest. It seems they had a much more bothersome adversary about which to worry a bit closer to home."

Simon started to smile but quickly stopped, lest he upset the physician once more.

"We're just glad to see you alive and well, Simon," Mattie said, resting her hand on his shoulder. "We feared the whole trip that we would find you captured or worse."

Simon waited patiently for the doctor to finish his work and tie off the last stitch before speaking again. As he opened his mouth, he could feel the stiffness in his cheek.

"Despite their intimate knowledge of these woods, there weren't many of their kind to search. I found a good place in which to hide and remained there for as long as I dared."

He thought of his misadventures with Tom Wriggleton and the

man's eventual assassination, but he decided against sharing those more bothersome details with his friends.

"Help me up, if you please," he said, extending his arms toward Luthor and Mattie.

"I haven't yet wrapped your sprained ankle," the physician protested.

Simon waved the man away so he could stand. "My ankle has survived far worse than a walk down a dirt road. I'm assuming you will still be here upon our return?"

The physician nodded. "Of course, sir."

"Then my ankle will, everything willing, still be attached to my body upon my return. You may treat it then."

Mattie and Luthor took him under the arms and helped him to his feet. Simon felt rejuvenated, though he wasn't sure if it was from the rescue or the draught that Luthor had him drink.

"I'm feeling better," the Inquisitor offered. "I think I would like to walk on my own, if it's all the same."

They withdrew their hands, and Simon took a step forward before his leg began to buckle. Mattie hurried to his side and held him up with her exceptional strength.

"Perhaps I misjudged my abilities."

Luthor stepped beside him and offered his cane. "I can move well enough on my own right now, sir. Please, take it."

Simon nodded and took the cane, leaning heavily on it as he stepped into the street. Though he longed to return to the mines and see the Pellite's progress in routing the vampire horde, he instead walked through the collection of bodies littering the street. He kept his eyes downcast to watch where he stepped, but he tried his best not to personify the corpses around him. There was a familiarity to most of their faces, either having been seen during their first entrance into the town or subsequently during Simon's guerrilla war, but the Inquisitor didn't want to recognize those around him. They were the enemy, he reminded himself, and they deserved their punishment.

Reaching a small clearing in the middle of the bodies, Simon bent forward and picked up his top hat from the ground. Resting the cane against his hip, he used his hands to dust it off, though the hat still retained more of a brown color than its usual stark black. Unperturbed, Simon placed it canted upon his head.

He quickly exited the center of the bullet-ridden corpses and rejoined his friends. Wordlessly, they turned as one and made their way out of town.

Simon offered Gregory little more than a second glance as they passed his body near the tavern. A blossom of blood stained the back of his shirt from Creary's single shot. Simon admired the man's accuracy once more before they moved along.

Their pace was painfully slow, with Luthor's broken gait from his as-of-yet unhealed hip and Simon's twisted ankle. Mattie showed eternal patience walking slowly beside the two, though they both knew she longed only to run freely through the woods in her wolf form.

"You've both cleaned up nicely," Simon remarked, hoping to break the chilling spell that had settled over them, as though none of their group could find the words to explain their latest ordeal.

"Luthor genuinely considered not bathing before our return, just so you wouldn't feel so put out," Mattie replied.

Simon smirked, acutely aware of his own stench as compared to his clean companions. "I appreciate the thought, Luthor."

"I considered it, sir."

"Yet in the end, you did bathe."

Luthor shrugged. "If your current fragrance is any indication of how we smelled upon our return, then you should thank God that we did."

"Are you insinuating I smell?" Simon asked in mock indignation.

"Like garbage left to rot in the sun," Luthor replied. "If you don't believe me, you should see Mattie's face every time you turn away from her. I can only imagine that to her astute senses, you smell like a veritable sewer."

Simon paused for a second, glancing at both his companions before starting once more at his slow gait. "I don't think I like either of you anymore."

Luthor shrugged even as Mattie laughed. The apothecary withdrew a large muffin from his doctor's bag as they walked, holding it in the palm of his hand. "That's unfortunate, sir, because I happened to have taken a muffin from the train. It's blueberry, I believe, your favorite. I figured you might have grown—"

Simon didn't let Luthor finish before taking it from his hand and stuffing a good portion of the muffin into his mouth.

"I think he was hungry," Mattie said.

"The only way you could have made me happier is if this muffin had been made out of steak instead," Simon replied through a mouthful of moist crumbs.

All three paused as they passed the chancellor's manor. The house was abuzz with activity as the Pellites ransacked the home. Men in suits crawled amongst the repaired wagons, tossing aside bags of food and other supplies as they searched the grounds.

Simon frowned, feeling violated as these latecomers completed a mission he began nearly a week before. He should have felt closure at the event but instead, he felt disappointment.

Turning away, he led them onward toward the mine.

The sun was still high in the sky when the trio reached the edge of the quarry. They paused at the lip before descending the winding perimeter road that led to the mine floor. Far below them, the Pellites were already hard at work.

From the mouth of the mine, a group of suited men emerged. They held the ends of taut ropes in their hands and strained to pull something from the shadowed entrance. From the distance, it was hard to discern details, but Simon needed none. His imagination filled in the details that his eyes failed to see.

The Pellites pulled as a group, making headway against the vampire within. The creature hissed and yelled, pulling with superhuman strength against the ropes tied around its arms and neck. Its booted feet dug into the ground, seeking purchase in the rocky floor of the cavern, but it lost ground with each stern pull on the far end of the ropes.

It looked over its shoulder, its eyes widening in fear as the line of embarkation grew closer. The sunlight was a sheet, dangling across the mouth of the mine. As it was dragged closer to the first beams of brilliant light, it could feel its skin heating in response.

From their perch on the top of the quarry, Simon watched as the Pellites pulled again and the vampire came tumbling from the protective gloom of the mine. It fell to the ground, its head downturned as sunlight poured onto its back. Smoke rose from its body as it lifted an arm protectively, trying to block the glaring sun. Fissures appeared on its skin, and it screamed in horror as its body ignited from within before tumbling to ash. Its mound of gray ash joined a dozen others on the stones below.

Simon gestured toward the trail, and the trio made their way to the cavern floor. As they reached the edge of the poisoned water pool, Inquisitor Creary met them.

"I didn't expect you to be here, Inquisitor Whitlock," Creary said.

"I had to see this done," Simon replied, watching even as they pulled another vampire into the sun. "I had to make sure it was finished."

"It will be soon enough."

Luthor pointed toward the mine's mouth. "Did you meet much resistance?"

Creary shrugged. "No more than we expected. We caught the bastards while they were sleeping in their bunks."

"How fared your men?" Simon asked.

"We lost some but, again, no more than we expected."

Simon frowned at the man's blasé response. To the Order of Kinder Pel, the ends always justified the means. He doubted Creary even acknowledged the loss of life as anything more than necessary collateral damage.

They walked toward the mine, Creary keeping pace as they did. From out of the mine, a larger group of Pellites emerged. They strained against the ropes as a vampire clearly pulled with incredible might against them. One of the group broke away and hurried to Inquisitor Creary's side.

"We've found their leader, sir," the Pellite said. "He's putting up quite a fight, but we'll have him finished soon enough."

"You have the chancellor?" Simon asked.

The Pellite nodded as he turned his attention toward Simon. "He fought like a fiend, but we were finally able to bind him."

Simon turned toward Creary. "Forgive me, but I'd like to watch this."

He, Luthor, and Mattie left the Pellites where they were and walked toward the mine's entrance. They walked past the Pellites tugging firmly on the taut rope until they were standing beside the wooden supports at the entryway.

"Sir, would you like to watch this alone?" Luthor asked.

Simon set his jaw, eager to see this completed. "No, please stay. I want us all to witness this moment."

The Pellites pulled again, and the chancellor was dragged into the sunlight. He howled in rage, his anger overwhelming even the pain he must have been feeling. The once manicured Martellus Whitten looked animalistic as he stood defiantly in the sunlight. He tossed his head from side to side and strained savagely against the ropes holding him, oblivious to the noose tightening around his neck.

His skin began to crack and smolder, red flames rolling from an internal furnace licking his flesh. Charred skin peeled away like old wallpaper as he dropped to his knees. Despite his pending demise, his head was raised defiantly to the end.

As his body began to crumble, Simon yelled out for him. Chancellor Whitten glanced toward the Inquisitor, his red eyes filled with bile and hate. They locked eyes, and continued watching one another even as Martellus' body turned gray and crumbled. The ropes went slack as they severed first the vampire's wrists and finally pulled off his head. As the chancellor's head struck the stone ground, it shattered to dust.

The Pellites within the quarry relaxed visibly at the chancellor's death. A few other Pellites emerged and approached Creary. They talked excitedly amongst themselves, pointing fervently toward the mine. Curious, Simon approached the group.

"What have you found?" he asked.

Creary silenced the Pellite before him. "My men have found a sealed doorway in the back of the mine. They're preparing to breech it."

"Tell them to hold," Simon replied hastily.

Creary furrowed his brow. "Why should they?"

Simon frowned at the Pellite's skepticism. "This began as my mission, and it should end as such. Through that doorway is something that I must deal with myself."

Creary looked very mistrusting, but he slowly nodded his approval. Simon nodded as well without offering any further explanation and turned toward the mine. With Luthor and Mattie in tow, they moved as quickly as possible inside.

They followed familiar twists and turns through the mine on their way to the barracks. The doorway to the living quarters was thrown open, the wooden door nearly torn from its hinges. Simon stepped past the debris and entered the barracks.

A few Pellite milled about, searching the individual rooms for personal affects. They paused at the sight of Simon and his entourage, but they quickly returned to their work.

Simon frowned at the sight of both Pellite's and vampires strewn across the floor. The vampires stared blindingly at the ceiling, their red eyes no longer seeing as wooden stakes protruded from their chest. The Pellites looked far more brutalized. Limbs had been torn from bodies. Some looked emaciated, as though all their blood had been drained very rapidly. He averted his eyes, tired of seeing the multitude of death.

The narrow tunnel led them to the large chamber. There were Pellites here as well, examining the slew of corpses piled upon one another. A larger group stood before the limestone door, chiseling at a new seal that had been placed across the entryway.

Simon didn't recognize the seal, clearly it having been placed since his last visit with the ancient vampire. The Pellites worked diligently, severing shards of what appeared to be concrete from the center and bottom of the doorway.

One of the Pellites noticed Simon waiting. "We're almost there now, sir."

Simon nodded, but his eyes remained fixed on the door. He had made a promise to the creature within, and he now had returned to fulfill his end of the bargain. Martellus Whitten was already dead. His ordeal was nearly done.

With a powerful stroke, the remaining concrete fell away. The Pellites quickly carried away the pieces, clearing the doorway. Simon didn't wait for them to finish before he approached and pushed firmly on the portal. Slowly, the doors gave way, swinging inward into the archaic monster's prison.

The room was dark, the torches having burned out from a lack of maintenance. Light from the Pellites' torches fell into the room, casting deep shadows. Simon paused at the entrance, allowing his eyes to adjust to the gloom beyond.

His gaze fell upon the dais across the room. The vampire sat upon his throne, the manacles still binding his limbs. The creature looked thinner than before, emaciated almost to the point of appearing like the corpses in the room beyond.

Simon took one of the torches from a Pellite and entered the room. For a moment, he thought the vampire was dead. Its head listed to the side and its eyes were closed as though in sleep. A rubber hose dangled from the vampire's arm, its end no longer in one of the glass jars but instead left to spill upon the dais. Blood stained the platform beside the throne in a pool far larger than what should have been possible from a single person.

Foolishly, Simon looked for the rise and fall of the creature's chest before remembering the creature's state of un-death. It no longer had any need to breathe and sat as still as the dead.

Simon stepped closer until he reached the base of the stairs leading up to the throne. He leaned forward cautiously, glancing into the vampire's dangerously thin face. It remained unmoving, instead resting limply on the throne.

Simon was prepared to turn away when the vampire's eyes opened and it lurched forward, mouth open. Simon withdrew hastily, but he needn't worry. The chain around the ancient vampire's neck caught, and its head snapped backward.

It bit the air ineffectually a few times before the cloud of hunger lifted from its eyes. Simon stared at the creature in horror. With each opening of its mouth, he saw the bloody stumps in its gums where its fangs had been torn from their places.

It stared at Simon unblinking for a moment before it seemed to finally recognize him.

"Inquisitor," it whispered, its voice far more hoarse than Simon remembered.

"I thought you already dead," Simon replied. He could feel the probing eyes of the Pellites behind him, but he ignored their curiosity.

"He took my fangs," it whimpered. "The blood thief stole them from my very mouth, even as he drained me of the last drops of my blood."

Simon felt genuine sympathy for the imprisoned vampire. He was glad to deliver the happy news. "Chancellor Whitten is dead, killed by my kind."

The ancient vampire looked genuinely happy, offering a smile that seemed disjointed without its telltale fangs. "Good riddance to the blood thief."

The vampire lifted its head, though it was clearly a great effort to do so. He looked at the nervous Pellites huddling in the doorway. He could taste their fear in the air, intermixed with their glaring hatred of the abomination.

"Have you come to drive a stake through my heart, as they had threatened to do so many times before?" the vampire asked weakly. "I can feel their desire to do so."

His eyes returned to Simon, and they looked at him with soft understanding. "I would be okay if they did. It would be an end to my misery."

Simon glanced over his shoulder toward the Pellites and shook his head. Without its fangs and its strength leached as its blood was drained away, the vampire posed him no threat.

"On the contrary," Simon replied softly, "I'm here to finally set you free."

The vampire nodded, its eyes sad but relieved. Simon bit the inside of his lip before approaching the pale monster. The hoses still dangled from the needles driven into its arms, legs, and chest. He pulled them from the vampire's skin with reckless abandon, knowing that the creature would hardly feel the sting of the needles' withdrawal. Droplets of blood from within the hoses seeped from the puncture wounds, but the open sores clotted almost immediately, stemming the flow of blood.

Simon gestured for the Pellites to approach. They moved forward hesitantly, unsure of the purpose behind the ancient creature.

"Unlock his shackles," Simon ordered.

The Pellites hesitated, glancing back and forth between one another.

"Unlock him," Simon repeated. "He's no longer a threat to us."

After a further moment of hesitation, they moved forward cautiously and cut away the iron locks on its ankles, wrists, and neck. As soon as their work was done, they quickly stepped away.

Simon slid his arms under the vampire's legs and back, lifting it from its stone chair. Though Simon doubted its ability to feel pain in the way a man would, the vampire still winced when its back was straightened as it was cradled in the Inquisitor's arms.

The creature was frail, like an old man in the last vestiges of his life. His skin felt like paper, and he weighed almost nothing.

As the vampire was lifted from the throne, a worn book dropped into the chair. The vampire reached back feebly, straining toward the book that had been concealed behind him for so many centuries.

"Please, I must have my book."

Simon glanced toward the chair and saw the black, leather-bound journal, on the cover of which was a once brightly painted red hand, its five fingers extended toward the corners of the book.

"Luthor, if you please," Simon said.

The apothecary approached and retrieved the book. The vampire showed great interest in the book as soon as it was offered. It cradled the journal to its chest as it sank into Simon's arms.

Simon felt no strain carrying the creature through the tunnels and suffered barely any inconvenience, even when stepping over the slain remains of the converted townsfolk.

Pellites watched them pass with interest and disdain, but no one tried to stop Simon. The vampire lifted up to watch where they were headed, his head bobbing under its own weight with each step.

"It's been so long," it whispered. "So very long, since I've felt the night's air upon my face. Trapped first by the rock and then by the vindictive humans. I'm so very tired and just want to look upon the stars once more."

Simon blinked away the tear that formed in the corner of his eye. He carried the feeble creature past the barracks and into the mine proper.

As Simon rounded a corner, bright light flooded the tunnel and the mouth of the mine appeared. The vampire hissed and tightened its grip on Simon's arm, but it lacked the strength to resist. It strained feebly against Simon's hold on its body but to no avail.

The Inquisitor didn't look down at the vampire as he walked boldly into the light. The sun struck the vampire's exposed skin, and the beast let out an awful scream that nearly stopped Simon in his tracks.

Simon looked down at the ill-fated creature as the vampire's skin split and cracked like drying clay. Red liquid, like blood, oozed from the wounds that covered its face, arms, and chest like latticework. Simon could feel the heat radiating from the vampire's core, as though a furnace had been ignited just below its skin.

From the fissures along its flayed skin, a glow emanated from within the vampire. It grew in intensity as the air above the wounds wavered from the intense heat. Simon nearly dropped the vampire as his own skin felt like it was smoldering. Sweat beaded along the Inquisitor's brow and ran down his face, dripping from his nose. Where the water struck the vampire's inflamed skin, it sizzled and evaporated.

The vampire's cry of anguish continued, even as it turned its head toward the Inquisitor. It locked its red eyes with Simon's, a sense of betrayal painted across his face, before suddenly falling silent. The fragile frame of the vampire crumbled in Simon's arms, collapsing to the ground in a cloud of gray ash.

Simon stood with his arms outstretched for a moment longer before slowly lowering them and brushing the clinging gray soot from his suit.

CHAPTER Thirty-seven

SIMON WASHED HIS FACE IN THE SINK FOR THE THIRD time, though it had come clean after the first. The bowl was stained dark, an artifact from his previous washings. It seemed that no matter the amount of scrubbing he did, he still felt filthy. It was a stain on his soul, he knew, rather than one on his skin.

Glancing up, he looked at himself in the mirror. He was clean shaven again, save his telltale moustache. His hair had been washed and was once again well coifed. Luthor had the foresight to provide him a clean shirt and suit from his armoire. By all accounts, he looked like himself once more. Only the dark bruises under his eyes, the red inflammation around his broken nose, and the sutured cut on his cheek remained of his days' long escapades in the woods around Whitten Hall.

He draped the blood-and dirt-stained washcloth on a towel rack beside the train's sink and rubbed his eyes wearily. He longed to sleep for the rest of the four days back to Callifax. His desire to talk to even his friends had waned shortly after seeing them again. It didn't help that the rocking of the train was lulling him to sleep even as he stood in the bathroom.

Standing upright, he walked to the door and unlocked it, stepping through and into the narrow hallway that opened into the passenger car.

The Pellites talked excitedly amongst themselves, celebrating their victory over the vampire horde. They seemed oblivious to the fact that quite a number of their own kind had been slaughtered during their short battle. To them, it was another victory and further justification for the existence of the Order of Kinder Pel. The Pellites had been called when no one else could defeat a threat to the crown. Simon, in his desire to end the vampiric threat, had only further validated their cause.

He walked quickly through the car, eager to reach the vestibule between their passenger car and the more private car at the end of the train. A few Pellites marked his passing with polite nods; even the Pellites appreciated the work he had done containing the threat before their arrival.

Ignoring the looks he received from them, he walked to the door that led to the narrow vestibule between the train cars and opened it. The blast of warm air struck him as the train rolled slowly but mechanically down the tracks.

He took hold of the metal railing as he walked between the cars. It was far noisier outside, with the steady clacking and squealing of the metal wheels rolling along the tracks. It was loud enough that Simon had trouble thinking, which made it blissful. He closed his eyes and braced his feet, so that he wouldn't fall over as he enjoyed the noise and warm sunlight.

The door to the rear car opened, and Luthor coughed politely.

"I was just coming to look for you, sir," the apothecary said. "We were worried about you; it's been some time since you left to clean up."

Simon slowly opened his eyes, the magic of the moment broken. "There was a lot of me to clean, Luthor."

Luthor nodded. "Well, you did a remarkable job. You practically look like your old self once more."

Simon didn't respond but continued to watch the trees slide by as the train rolled onward.

"Shall we return to the cabin, sir? I've had some food brought in, since you look absolutely famished."

"Food would be good." Simon sighed. "Please do lead the way."

They walked to their private cabin, passing a few others along the way. Inquisitor Creary looked up from his reading as they passed, his cabin seemingly far too large for a man traveling alone. Upon reaching their cabin, Luthor slid open the door and stepped aside, allowing Simon to enter.

The smell of cooked meat struck Simon immediately upon entering. His mouth watered involuntarily, and his stomach grumbled a stern reminder of how long it had been since he had eaten a proper meal. Despite his morose disposition, he couldn't deny the feast lay out before him.

Mattie stood from the table, hastily closing the clasp on Luthor's doctor's bag. Simon caught a glimpse of a soot-stained book before she stepped to him and hugged him tightly. Simon groaned under the pressure but welcomed her embrace.

"It's good to see you well again," she said as she finally released him.

"'Well' is a relative term, my dear," he replied, "but I'm feeling significantly more human."

Simon motioned toward the table and Mattie took a seat, pushing the doctor's bag against the wall. He sat at the table as well, taking a seat across from Mattie. Luthor quickly joined the pair, taking his place beside the redhead.

His gentlemanly visage dissipated along with his proper dining manners. He stuffed food into his mouth with gluttonous abandon. After some time of eating, Simon leaned back in the chair and sighed contently. He couldn't remember food ever tasting so satisfying. He glanced toward his friends but was surprised to see them looking away, thoughtfully staring out the window.

"You have questions, of course," he said.

"Of course," Luthor replied, bringing his attention back to his mentor, "though I haven't the foggiest of what to say."

"They killed them all," Mattie said, her bluntness sometimes needed when civilized decorum failed. "The townsfolk, I mean, of course."

"I know very well what you mean," Simon said, finding a reason to stare intently at his hands resting upon the table.

Luthor swallowed hard, his throat bouncing from the effort. "I didn't know the Pellites would be so savage upon their arrival, sir, you must believe me. I knew they would destroy the vampires but not the humans of Whitten Hall."

Simon shook his head as he glanced toward his friend. "I don't blame you, Luthor. You may not have known, but I did when I wrote the note."

Luthor appeared crestfallen. "You knew, and yet you sent for the Pellites all the same?"

"What choice did I have? You don't send for the Order of Kinder Pel with the instructions to preserve life. They're assassins, one and all.

They're under the guise of Inquisitors like myself, but we're nothing alike."

Luthor shook his head. "Some of them were evil, sir, like Tom and Gregory, but I can't believe the entire town was vile. Misguided, perhaps, but there existed a chance for redemption, didn't there?"

"You're a good man, Luthor, but a foolish one. You see the good in people and harbor hope that they can change. Not every man can change. Not every man was meant to."

"And those men that cannot, sir? What of them?"

Simon glanced out the window, his reply halfhearted. "Those men are evil, Luthor. We do not abide evil men."

A silence fell between the men. Luthor stared at Simon for some time, even as his mentor's gaze remained affixed on the glass window beside him. Eventually, the apothecary shook his head.

"I've known you for some time, sir, and I don't think that you truly believe what you're saying. This decision wasn't as black and white as you are trying to portray it."

Mattie reached across the table and squeezed his hands. "We're your friends, Simon. You can talk to us freely."

Simon sighed heavily and took back his hands from her grip.

"Whitten Hall just feels like one gigantic mistake," Simon said.

Mattie shook her head. "Right or wrong, you made the only decision available."

"You made the right choice, sir," Luthor corrected.

Simon looked out the window and imagined the ruined town drifting past, bullet holes marring the storefronts, bodies twisted and baking in the street under the hot sun, and lakes of blood soaking into the dry sand. "Did I? Then why do I feel that it was so wrong? Why do I feel like I made a foolish, hasty decision?"

"Sir, it wasn't foolish; you're not foolish. You're the smartest man I know."

Simon took a deep breath. "Luthor, if ever I've given you a piece of advice to which you should closely adhere, this is it. Intelligence without conscience is as great an evil as any that plagues our land. Intelligence isn't a gift; it's a burden, one that should be tempered with experience and wisdom. Today, I made the intelligent choice in spite of its morality. Today, I wasn't the better man. Today, I was merely the lesser of two evils."

Simon didn't actively avoid his friends through the rest of the trip, but he kept well enough to himself as they finished their journey back to the capital city. He slept, mostly, resting for nearly an entire day as his body tried to heal from his ordeal. He ate quietly in the cabin, often with Luthor and Mattie, but offered little conversation. Just as often as not, he found himself perched in the vestibule between the cars, feeling the day's air turn slightly cooler the further they rode away from Whitten Hall.

With rest, food, and proper hygiene, his wounds healed nicely. His nose was still tender to the touch, but the bruising under his eyes was nearly gone by the time Callifax came into view.

The capital city towered over the nearby landscape. Suburbs beyond the city walls sprawled in tightly formed neighborhoods as the train rolled past, but they paled in comparison to the sloping summit on top of which the king's castle rose like a spear from the earth. Even from the distance, Simon could see the other landmarks: the rising spires of the Callifax Abbey, the unsurprisingly multi-storied debtor's prison rising over the northern part of town, and the stark white dome of the Grand Hall. It was home and just the sight of the great city was more reassuring than any of his friends' words during their return journey.

Simon entered the rear car and returned to their cabin. Luthor and Mattie were packing their belongings into small pieces of luggage. They had rightfully packed light for their rescue trip, and it was easy to gather what few objects they had removed during the train ride.

The Inquisitor paused at the doorway as he realized that he had no personal effects to pack. The few sets of clothing that Luthor had brought with him had been packed in the apothecary's bags. Simon didn't even have a suitcase to call his own. The extent of his belongings from this trip now consisted solely of the clothes on his body, his revolver, pocket watch, and top hat.

Realizing there was no preparation that needed to be done, he instead made his way toward the rear of the train, where a narrow catwalk clung to the back of the train car. He opened the door and stepped onto the caboose's back deck.

The sun was setting over the horizon, its last rays clinging to the sky, casting the air in shades of red and orange. For a moment, Simon cringed. Memories of being caught outside during the night flooded his mind, and he fought the urge to rush indoors where he would be protected from the pursuing vampires. As logic and sense reasserted itself, he breathed deeply until he forced his heart rate to slow to a healthy pace once more.

The sun disappeared from view as the train passed beneath the towering arch that marked the beginning of the city proper. The train's whistle blasted loudly, and a few pedestrians nearby looked up at its passing. The train jostled as it rolled over tracks set across one of the roads. Cars waited patiently on either side, their drivers staring at Simon as the train rolled by.

The train blew its whistle once more, a long, drawn-out blast that split the evening air, as it slid into the Callifax station. It slipped into its berth. The station was alive with people either loading or unloading similar trains, all parked alongside one another. Wide walkways ran between them, a communal ground through which people bustled and pushed as they made their way on and off the platforms.

Constables kept the other pedestrians at bay as the Pellites began disembarking. Curious onlookers watched, though there was little of interest to see. There were no corpses that could be brought home for examination, unlike Gideon's body. Instead, the Pellites climbed down from the passenger cars and simply walked away from the train, heading back to the Grand Hall where they would return their firearms before they returned to their homes.

Simon climbed down from the rear deck, feeling a surge of comfort as his feet touched down on Callifax concrete. He walked down the platform as the tarps were removed from the cargo cars. The heavy Gatling guns were removed and placed onto awaiting carts. A pair of the gunners climbed back onboard before reemerging, this time carrying a large, white box between them.

It looked like a cooler or freezer, from where Simon stood, though not one he recognized. Even from a distance, he could see the shattered lock dangling from its hinges on the front. The Pellites loaded the cooler nonchalantly beside the Gatling guns before pushing away the cart.

Luthor and Mattie climbed down from the train and joined Simon on the platform.

"Can we interest you in dinner, sir?" Luthor asked.

"Yes, Simon," Mattie agreed. "Do come with us."

Simon glanced back and forth between his friends but shook his head. "Forgive me, but there's something else I need to do instead."

He stepped away from his companions, leaving them bewildered as he left the station.

There was a gentle knock on Veronica's door. She glanced at the clock on the mantle, noting the late hour. The sun had set some time before and, having the night off, she had already changed into her nightgown.

She looked about until she located a robe draped over one of the chairs nearby. As she slipped it over her shoulders and tied it in the front, the knock came again.

"I'm coming," Veronica said, just loudly enough to be heard by whoever waited on the far side of the door.

She started walking toward the door before she paused. It wouldn't do at all to open the door to a stranger, especially at this late hour. Who knew the type of person who could be waiting? Her line of work seemed to invite the lowest common denominator of mankind. Glancing toward the mantle, she noted an empty glass vase. She took it in her hands, feeling its considerable weight. Satisfied that she was thusly armed, she walked to the door.

Leaning forward, she peered through the narrow peephole. At first, the man on the other side looked like a stranger. He was haggard in appearance, despite being well dressed. As he turned toward her, she immediately recognized him, despite the obvious injuries.

Throwing the locks aside, she opened the door and threw herself into Simon's arms. Before he could speak, she kissed him passionately, wrapping her arms around his neck and sliding her fingers into his hair. She eventually pulled away, breathless.

Simon smiled broadly, but he winced at the effort. His cheek ached from the effort of smiling, and he was forced to return his expression to a more serious demeanor.

Veronica's expression softened considerably as she reached up and gingerly touched the sutures under his eye. "My God, Simon, are you okay?"

Simon caught her wrist before she pressed too firmly. He looked at her lovingly, glad to be with her once more.

She smiled but looked worried simultaneously. "Is anything the matter?"

"Of course," he said, trying to set her mind at ease. "I just made it back and could think of no other place I'd rather go."

She smiled and reached up, caressing his uninjured cheek. "You're always welcome. You can stay as long as you'd like."

"I'd like to stay the night, if it's all the same."

Veronica smiled broadly and stepped aside, allowing Simon to enter her apartment.

Epilogue

LUTHOR APPROACHED THE BOOKCASE IN HIS STUDY and ran his fingers along the spines of the leather-bound novels. He paused as he reached an innocuous book, one that looked unremarkable amongst the multitude of other similarly bound books. Placing his finger atop the tome, he pulled it toward him. The book tilted, and Luthor heard the telltale clicking of gears behind the wall. The clicking continued until it stopped with a sudden rattle of chains, as though a heavy weight had been released behind the bookcase.

With a bit of effort, Luthor placed his hands against the edge of the wooden shelves and pulled them toward him. The entire bookcase swung aside on well-oiled hinges, revealing a spiral staircase leading into the basement.

As Luthor stepped into the stairwell, torches lit of their own volition along the stairs, illuminating the path before him. Tucking the small, black journal under his arm, Luthor descended the stairwell.

The stairs ended abruptly at a door with no handle. No windows marred the front of the perfectly crafted wooden portal and the edges of the door fit snuggly against its frame, allowing no light to seep around it. Luthor reached out and felt the cool wood, lacquered so heavily that it nearly reflected his image. Near the top of the door, he drew a circle. He made similar circles on the left and right before bisecting all three with lines that met in the center. As the lines connected, they glowed a soft blue. On the far side of the door, tumblers fell into place and locks slid aside. With a hiss of escaping air, the door opened.

Luthor's second study, for that was what this room was, looked nothing like the book-laden room upstairs. Flasks and beakers lined tables against the walls, though their concoctions were anything but science. Within one, black fluid swirled of its own volition as twinkling lights like stars drifted through its miasma.

The walls held artifacts that he had collected from his journeys, both with Simon and alone. Maps of the three continents were pinned to the wall with red wax pencil markings across their surfaces. Arcane runes were drawn above the marked locations, though only Luthor could read his annotations.

In the center of the room was a large design similar to the one used to unlock the door. Each circle was large enough for a man to stand within, but Luthor stepped instead to where the lines intersected one another.

Pulling a piece of chalk from his pocket, he knelt down and drew a pentagram around his feet, so that he stood in the center of its inverted five-pointed star. As he stood, a gentle breeze blew through the room, fluttering maps affixed to the wall.

Luthor closed his eyes as he slipped a hand into his pocket, feeling the thin journal concealed within. He could feel his body shift slightly, as though the ground beneath him was made of sliding sand. As his body settled back into place, he opened his eyes.

He no longer saw the mystical study in which he'd been standing. He was now in a garden. The leaves rustled overhead as the same gentle breeze blew through the trees. A stream gurgled nearby, and the scent of freshly cut grass reached his nose. The garden was peaceful, though Luthor still felt very much on edge.

Six people sat amongst the trees, in varying stages of relaxation. A man in polished armor paced anxiously through the grove. A man and woman in similar silk robes sat cross-legged in the grass. A dark-skinned woman sat on a bench by the stream, her back to the apothecary. The last two men wore such heavy robes that their faces were concealed in deep shadows.

As they recognized Luthor's presence amongst them, the six turned toward the apothecary.

"Agent Strong," the dark-skinned woman said. "We have been waiting for you. How goes your mission?"

"Brothers and Sisters of the Cabal, I have much to report," Luthor replied. He pulled the ancient vampire's journal from his pocket, holding it aloft so that the bloody palm print on its cover was visible.

"The symbol of the Five," the armored man said, frowning, though Luthor knew a deep frown was his general disposition. "One finger for each of the demon lords. Where did you find that?"

"On one of their servants here in the northern continent, an archaic vampire who had been trapped in our realm for hundreds of years."

"Impossible," the silk-covered man said. "The Five have not had access to our lands—"

"—but until recently," the silk-covered woman finished.

"Yet this book is most certainly one of theirs, and it was trapped with this vampire deep under the ground. This is proof that there were servants of the Five in our lands in advance of their arrival, very possibly paving the way for their conquest."

"Conjecture," a dark robed man replied.

"Assumption without fact," the other said.

"It's neither conjecture nor assumption and this… this is the proof." Luthor opened the book, revealing arcane markings across the pages. "These are incantations and summoning rituals, the types that would be necessary to open a gateway between our worlds. This vampire is the proof that incursions into our world have happened before. Quite likely, there are dozens more monsters just like him scattered throughout our kingdoms."

"What are you insinuating, Agent Strong?" the dark-skinned woman asked.

Luthor sighed as he forced himself to calm down. "I believe these rituals could be used to open a rift."

Before the Cabal could respond, and they looked quite ready to respond angrily to his allegations, Luthor interjected. "Nothing to the degree of *the* Rift, but minor breaks in the barriers that divide our realms, a test of sorts that would pave the way for the invasion by the Five. With all your combined wisdom and intellect, you have to see this as a viable possibility. Even with our combined magic, we've never been able to satisfactorily explain how the Rift was formed. This could very possibly be our answer."

"Similar magic?" a dark-robed man asked.

"Could be tracked?"

Luthor shrugged. "I can't be certain. I couldn't discern any residual magic on the creature, but it could have very well dissipated during the vampire's imprisonment. If the vampire was sent here as a vanguard to the demons' forces, then others could be here as well, monsters with a more potent magical signature."

"It's an interesting dilemma. If their magic is similar to that of the Rift, then we might be able to scry their locations. I would assume the beasts would be shielded—"

"—but our magic is strong. We will see what we can do," the second silken twin concluded.

"How do you suppose the vampire became trapped deep beneath the earth?" the dark-skinned magician asked.

"He's been here for ages," Luthor said. "It's possible his spell casting went awry, sending him far from his predetermined location. The teleportation magic could have created the pocket in the rock in which he was found, but it wouldn't have provided him a means to escape."

The Cabal nodded but said nothing.

"Thank you all," Luthor said. "Is there any other word on the other four demon lords?"

"None, though we will continue to search," the dark-skinned mage replied. "We would ask that you continue your search as well, under the guise of assisting the Inquisitor."

"Of course."

The armored man stomped across the grass, his metal boots crushing the delicate garden grounds. "Speaking of the Inquisitor, does he suspect your true identity?"

Luthor shook his head. "He's had no reason to assume I'm anything other than an apothecary."

The armored man huffed. "If he determines the truth, you know what'll have to be done. He won't allow you to live."

Luthor frowned at the insinuation. "I think Inquisitor Whitlock might surprise you. We knowingly travel in the company of a werewolf already. He might be accepting—"

"A werewolf is a far cry different from a wizard," the armored sorcerer interrupted. "If he discovers the truth, he will burn you at the stake. You must be ready to do what needs to be done."

Luthor stared defiantly at the Brother, though the armored man seemed unfazed by Luthor's resistance.

"We will search for these other incursions and let you know what we discover," the dark-skinned woman said, interjecting between the two men. "You've served us well, Agent Strong."

The apothecary turned his attention back to the leader of the Cabal. "I live to serve the Cabal."

"Go in peace," she said as the illusion began to fade.

Stone walls replaced the trees in the distance. The stream dissipated into flagstones on the floor. The bench near the stream revealed itself as one of his worktables. The six members of the Cabal faded into the ether, leaving Luthor alone once more.

He frowned as he crossed the room. He set the book on the table beside the broken piece of Gideon Dosett's horn. His hand lingered on the book, its bloody palm staring upward, before he turned and walked away. As he left the room, the electric lanterns turned dark and the handle-less door swung closed behind him.

END OF BOOK 2

About the Author

Jon Messenger, born 1979 in London, England, serves as a United States Army Major in the Medical Service Corps. Since graduating from the University of Southern California in 2002, writing Science Fiction has remained his passion, a passion that has continued through two deployments to Iraq and a humanitarian relief mission to Haiti. Jon wrote the "Brink of Distinction" trilogy, of which "Burden of Sisyphus" is the first book, while serving a 16-month deployment in Baghdad, Iraq. Visit Jon on his website at www.JonMessengerAuthor.com.

www.ingramcontent.com/pod-product-compliance
Ingram Content Group UK Ltd.
Pitfield, Milton Keynes, MK11 3LW, UK
UKHW041304180426
11947UKWH00009B/685